Hiding
Haelo

First published by Naniloa Books, 2016.

Second edition print with cover by James T. Egan and new editing published in 2022.

Copyright © 2022 by T.M. Holladay

All rights reserved. No part of this publication may be reproduced, stored, or transmitted in any form or by any means, electronic, mechanical, photocopying, recording, scanning, or otherwise without written permission from the publisher. It is illegal to copy this book, post it to a website, or distribute it by any other means without permission.

Second Print.

ISBN: 978-0-9973759-6-1

Edited by Tamara Hart Heiner

Cover design by James T. Egan

Typeset by Naniloa Books

To my kids.
Be brave. Be kind. Be smart. Be awesome.

HIDING HAELO

Book One in the Candeon Heirs Series
Second Edition

T.M. HOLLADAY

naniloa
BOOKS

CHAPTERS

To Fudge or Not to Fudge	1
Did Not See That Coming	9
Fish Out of Water	29
Break Up, Catch Up	47
Secrets, Secrets Are No Fun	67
Turning and Turning in the Widening Gyre	85
Checked	105
A Walk in the Park	117
Happy Birthday to Me	133
Gettin' Out of Dodge	159
Outstanding Citizens	187
Miriam	205
Aurora Borealis	217
The Sixth Man	241
Relocation	255
Blind Date	265
Dinner Party	283
Blurred	311
Pronunciations	320
Thank You	322
About the Author	324

I
TO FUDGE OR NOT TO FUDGE

I usually didn't mind Neo's whining. I'd learned to filter it into a homey sort of background noise. True, I'd rather be alone, but if I had to have a partner, my brother Neo was the only one still alive that I ever wanted to dive with.

We should get home, Haelo. It's been nine hours. Aren't you hungry? Now that he was an "adult," Neo's body no longer craved the dive as much as mine.

You head home, I thought back to him. *I'll be twenty minutes behind you.*

Hurry, Grandpa Aaram will be worried. If Neo knew twenty minutes was a sham estimate, he kept his skepticism to himself.

I watched the warped traces of his current trail behind him as he took off toward the shore—his red and orange swim shorts were easy to follow. He'd probably walk home once he got to the beach, proving my car wasn't any better at getting from point A to point B than a pair of flip flops.

I looked up toward the surface, knowing that a hundred meters above me, the moon had abandoned its post and Mother Nature brewed a nasty storm, suffocating the starlight in thick clouds. My sight was as lucid as ever; it just took a little more concentration. Underneath the whipping, dancing winds, below the tossing waves and churning Pacific foam, my world was completely peaceful.

We'd been in the water since lunch; I had told Aaram I needed to regain my strength and clear my head so I'd be ready for tomorrow, the first day of my very last semester of high school. Really, I just wanted to fly, to feel the rush of the ocean currents propel me forward through the water. The ocean was my real home, no matter how much Aaram insisted we live on land like normal people.

People.

I smiled. The human idea of a mermaid was ridiculous: legendary fin, seductive glances from behind swaying kelp forests, luxurious long hair lying perfectly over the risqué parts of a modelesque nudie torso. I am a lot of things, but one thing I am not is a mermaid.

I am a candeon.

I can sense the buzz of life around me, feel individual human and candeon auras—no fishtail required. I can manipulate deep currents to launch me forward underwater. I can even *think* with other candeons in our own private underwater communication; it doesn't work on land, and I dive alone half the time anyway, but it is still a perk. And yet, I can blend in with every other human at Loma Heights High School. To them, I'm just Haelo Marley: the tall, closet math whiz with a dated camera in her bag and a reluctant approach to friendship.

I coaxed the current faster, guiding me forward. My skin relished the saturation of salt, minerals, and oxygen. Breathing was over-rated.

I was free. I had no need to pretend. Masquerading as a semi-normal seventeen-year-old human took its toll. It's not that I was striving for moral perfection by any means, but starting every day as a liar would do a number to anyone's mood.

Admittedly, the human world has its advantages: the food is certainly better; "dry" technology started out as a convenience, then quickly moved its way up to an addiction; and despite the occasional faux pas, southern California culture is easy to get used to. Relax, smile, enjoy a taco or two. . . .

The water felt refreshing on my tough, shark-like skin, despite the frigid January temperatures. My body could taste the ocean. The cold, the wet, the organic. I soared through summoned currents, untied and unleashed. Though it didn't make a difference to me while I stayed below the surface, I knew the approaching storm was a big one. Distant white light strobed through the tossing waves above, followed by the faint echoes of thunder. I only hoped the rain wouldn't waterlog my rusted-out '86 hatchback Civic parked just south of Mission Beach.

Beneath me, the ocean floor was stunning. My candeon vision penetrated through the blackness and into the expanse of marinescape below. The next flash of lightning directly overhead illuminated the rocky bottom with eerie, fascinating shadows. The warbled crack of thunder sent an excited shiver down my spine. But my revelry was short-lived.

A subtle, rhythmic hum crept up on me, like the deep purr of an approaching motorcycle. I looked up, and my heart froze. Probing lights cut through the swells two hundred feet above. It was not the wind that made that drone; it was a helicopter.

The rules of my world dictated that I stay away from humans when in the water. Grandpa Aaram made it perfectly *un*clear what would happen if I were ever discovered. I still had disjointed, fractured memories of how the candeon world handled consequences; I'd seen it first-hand years ago as a child. Unfortunately, the human consequences were a gaping unknown, and that scared me more than anything.

It wasn't like humans would really *see* anything: I didn't have a fishtail; I didn't have fins, or gills, or even the seashell bra (which, by the way, is an awful idea), but there was no way to explain what I was doing out in the middle of the ocean or why I wasn't freezing.

Still, the chaos above sucked me in: I couldn't help but slow down and stare, looking for a cause, a reason, a victim. A large boat—half sunk—tipped to its side as the helicopter spotlights circled the water around it. Once on its side, it inverted upside down and released a flurry of debris which spiraled toward me. My curiosity turned into panic when a piece of broken metal railing swung at me on its way down to the distant bottom. My chest tightened and my pulse raced. I tried to calm myself so I could feel for human auras in the now submersed boat. *Nothing.* They were either free from the sinking ship, or they were dead. Just before I summoned a current to sweep me away toward the shore, something metallic twinkled above me.

In the distance, unconscious and at least twenty feet below the surface, a small boy slowly descended, a gold cross necklace intertwined in his hair. I stared in horror for a stand-still moment, then bolted up past the plummeting boat toward him, leaving my careful, rational mind behind. I pushed the currents faster than I ever had before. With a snowstorm of debris falling around me, I wrapped my arms around his still torso—even smaller than I had thought!

In seconds we broke through the deep currents and into the uncontrollable shallows, where I swam as fast as I could to the surface. Praying for the ability to manipulate shallow currents would do me no good. I didn't scan the scene for witnesses. I didn't care about the shouting and the lights or the violent rumble of the storm.

The child's face was so pale it was almost translucent next to my light olive skin. Too peaceful. I could sense life in his small body, though I was too frantic to tell if he was breathing. If he didn't get out of the water soon, he'd freeze to death. In desperation, I looked around for help.

Thirty yards away was a man in a wetsuit, tied to a line dangling from a U.S. Coast Guard helicopter. I waved, but he couldn't see us through the torrential rain.

With the boy over my shoulder, I swam frantically toward the rescue diver. Thirty yards that had just seconds ago seemed so minuscule now felt like an impossible distance. The boy slipped as a deep swell pummeled us. I hung onto him with every bit of strength I had left. Each wave slammed us into the next, challenging me to keep the boy's head above the water.

The Coast Guard diver finally turned in our direction. He swam faster than I expected, and by the time we met he had covered twice the distance I had. I released the boy and pushed him toward his rescuer. The man wrapped a harness around the child and pulled on a secondary line to signal retrieval to the men in the chopper.

I should have dived. I should have hidden myself beneath the dark waves—but I didn't.

He faced me, and I froze. He wasn't a burly man as I had assumed. He was a little older than me, twenty, twenty-one at most. His dark eyes were alive with adrenaline. We looked at each other in complete silence as if an invisible shield held back the fiery sounds of chaos. He reached for me, trying to tell me something, but I heard only muted vowels as he yelled the same thing over and over again. I shook my head clear, focusing on his words.

"I'm here to help you! You've got to grab onto me!" His eyes urged me forward. My eyes dilated as my breathing raced faster and faster, panic once again setting in.

"Come on! Let's get you out of here!" he yelled.

As if on cue, the wind, the waves, the chopper . . . everything screamed. Throbbed. With violent noise. Without thought, I ducked under a wave as it barreled at us, swimming deeper and deeper, fleeing the surface currents.

Once safely below, I turned and looked up. There, in the thick darkness of the midnight ocean, I watched the rescue diver search, unable to find me. Eventually the storm escalated and his line retreated back toward the helicopter. He fought it. His arms plowed through the waves, pointlessly fighting the hydraulic pulley reeling him into safety. Suddenly, he was ripped from the water, and I was left alone, stunned.

The old Civic sputtered into the driveway just as the exhaust blew. She was falling apart, but she was all I could afford after years of stashing birthday money. For a second, I reconsidered my stance to not use my penchant for sports statistics to pocket some extra cash. Mr. Huckleberry and Ms. Trex—teachers of mine last semester—both mumbled hypothetical requests for "advice" about twice a semester, usually as I was leaving class a few days before "the big game." I shook my head and reminded myself not to enable others' vices, even if it would contribute toward a transportation upgrade.

When I walked in the door, Grandpa Aaram didn't ask any questions; he just gave me the *nice to have you back* smile he always gave when I returned from a dive. Neo ran into me in the hallway. Though I was a little taller, he had two years and at least fifty solid, stocky pounds on me, yet thanks to his childish freckles and long-overdue haircut, he didn't look nearly as intimidating as he should have.

"You didn't expect me in the parking lot, did you?" he asked. "I would have waited, but I swear I could smell Aaram's sweet pork from the beach. Want me to dish you up some? Hey, where you going?"

"To bed. I'm not hungry."

"You okay, Lo? You're pretty dazed."

His sincere question made me stop and turn around. "I'm fine," I lied with a smile. Then, with eyes half shut, I sighed, "School starts tomorrow. I'm thrilled."

His brow furrowed. "I'm here if you need me."

"Thanks, Neo."

I turned the knob to my bedroom door just as another voice bellowed into the cramped hallway.

"Neo buggin' you? Just say the word and I'll take him." It was Neo's loud best friend, Kingston, a fellow candeon. He stood in a confident bravado, yet all three of us knew that King's obnoxious bark was much worse than his bite.

King practically lived in our home. For the past few weeks, it seemed like he was here when I woke up in the morning, and he and Neo were still watching SportsCenter in the basement after I went to bed. It should not have bothered me that he was standing there in our hallway with that smirk on his face.

Go home. "Not tonight, King." I slumped into my room.

I shut the door behind me, cutting off his, "What's with her?"

As expected, my room looked the same as I had left it: the same quilt and overstuffed, tufted peach armchair; the same scattering of books, retro film canisters, empty cups, a granola bar wrapper, and picture frames. Dirty clothes cascaded over the hamper and flooded the far corner, merging with my overflowing swimsuit drawer.

I set my camera on the dresser and tried not to look at it, shaking off an uneasy feeling that someone was watching me. *It's just the camera.* The end of the roll had shots of the eerily abandoned stormy beach. I don't usually get goosebumps, but standing alone on the ledge between the wet parking lot and the cold sand to get those shots had given me the willies. I remembered looking around—*sensing*—making sure no one had seen me emerge alone from the dark, frigid ocean, and yet I still felt unsatisfied. The experience with the rescue diver had made me paranoid.

I changed, threw my wet swimsuit into the mess of dirty clothes, grabbed a stray towel to rub dry my wavy black hair, and crashed onto my bed. *What in the world was I thinking?* The diver had seen me! He would have noticed my swimsuit, that I wasn't exactly dressed for a January boat ride. He would find out that I wasn't originally on that yacht and wonder how I ended up miles from the closest shoreline. Anxiety curled in my throat as I hoped he would shake me off as a hallucination.

But that beautiful little boy. I *was* nervous, though if time rewound itself and I once again witnessed his pale body descending into the black, I would do the same thing.

This is why we don't fudge the rules, I tried to convince myself. *If I hadn't gotten close, I wouldn't have been seen by the rescue diver.* That logic did not help much—if I had not seen the boy, I knew what would have happened, and it made my stomach sick.

Beyond my window, I heard the neighborhood stray cat settling into the bush for the night; its usual spot. I couldn't complain; in some small way, the orange cat was welcome company.

Fleeting memories of my last day with my parents suddenly haunted me. *That was years ago. Let it go, they're gone.* I needed sleep. I sighed and let the distant, drifting sounds of ESPN lull me into unconsciousness.

2
DID NOT SEE THAT COMING

Unsettling dreams—the kind you can't quite remember—came and went all night. Surprisingly, however, I felt much better when I woke. I avoided any lingering thoughts of the evening before, aided by the heavenly smells wafting in from the kitchen where Grandpa Aaram had made my favorite breakfast.

"Welcome to another beautiful Monday morning!" he said with entirely too much enthusiasm. I winced. He wouldn't ask me about my swim last night—he never did. He liked to think that our way of life as candeons was a fantasy, like an imaginary friend, but even he had to dive every once in a while.

Aaram Gevgenis was a retired world history professor from the University of California, San Diego, and knew more about humans than most humans did. He radiated mysterious wisdom with his silver and white peppered hair, perfect yet seasoned posture, and subtle, knowing squint.

I was gorging myself on crunchy waffles when it clicked: today was the first day back to school.

"I see dawning recollection painted upon thy face." He nearly sang the words.

My opinion of his bad Shakespeare accent vacillated with my mood, but luckily it was a smile-and-scoff kind of morning.

Aaram dropped the accent. "Classes start in an hour."

I hung my head. *At least I'll see my friends.* I ignored the buzz-kill in the back of my mind reminding me that my "friends" were more the acquaintance-type. I had one friend, and then she had friends, and they all let me hang around even though I wasn't the chatty counterpart they usually expected in a friend.

Neo's morning shuffle made its way down the hallway.

"Good morning, Neo. Glad to see you're awake," Aaram mumbled, pretending not to enjoy too much the victory of getting Neo out of bed.

"Your voice carries, Grandpa. I had no choice."

"Son, 'tis a beautiful day. Waff—?"

"Somethin' smells good in here!" boomed Kingston, emerging from the kitchen side door. "You ready for school, Haelo? Your Gramps asked me to take you." Aaram hated *Gramps*. "He said your car is too pathetic to make it the fourteen blocks to Loma Heights."

Aaram was right. The rusted hole in the middle of the hood made the car temperamental after rainstorms.

"I haven't showered," I said as I popped up from the table, tossing my sticky plate of leftover syrup piled high with orange rinds into the sink.

When I emerged from the bathroom half an hour later, Neo and Kingston were waiting in the driveway.

"Thanks for breakfast, Grandpa. Wish me luck."

"Good luck. Don't forget a sweater; it's supposed to be cold." I was used to wearing warm clothes in public, even though as a candeon I didn't need them. I grabbed a jacket without any hesitation. Grandpa gave me a kiss on the forehead as I headed out the side door to the driveway.

Kingston hung his arm outside the driver's side window of his purring black BMW, admiring his own hair through dark Gucci sunglasses in the rear-view mirror. I reached for my camera, but he heard me and smiled. It ruined the shot.

"King got us jobs at Torrey Pines," Neo said, putting on his seatbelt.

"We'll drop you off at Loma Heights on our way to work every day," King added.

"You're joking." I laughed, and then sobered at their lack of response. "King, you got a job? By choice?" I rummaged through my backpack, hoping I hadn't forgotten my new class schedule at home.

Faster than I expected, Kingston pulled the car up at the side entrance to the high school. The buzz of life around us hit me like a tidal wave. The influx of teenaged, hormonal auras made the air vibrate and my senses spark like a tangle of live wires. I hadn't been that close to so many people in a-while. Over winter break, I spent most of my dry time analyzing football playoffs and pre-season baseball prospects, or with my camera, capturing quiet moments at the beach and national parks. I felt safe and in control with my camera; crowds of humans were uncomfortable.

King turned around to face me when I opened the car door. "Have fun. I'll be here at three-thirty."

Something felt fishy in a very bad pun sort of way.

Kingston Michael Soli was one of a kind: a beacon of brazen confidence. He was *that guy*. People couldn't help but love him. Girls melted. Neo, Aaram and I knew the truth, however: that he was just as reckless and arrogant as he was confident. All things aside, he was a good person, and I usually enjoyed his friendship, despite the general tool-ishness.

He hadn't finished high school. He was a candeon orphan like Neo and me, but with a fat inheritance left to him by his parents. They died in the middle of his senior year, and he decided he didn't want to waste any more time at school—"a human institution"—so he dropped out. Grandpa tried to talk him into finishing but gave up after a few months.

He was a free spirit, one of those guys with a vibe that hinted at an adventure on the horizon—an adventure you wanted to be a part of. He looked the part, with a rugged, Hollywood haircut and dimpled smile.

Sometimes his shenanigans led to serious trouble, like the time he played a prank on what he thought were whale-watching tourists but were, in fact, U.S. Navy men in the middle of a torpedo exercise. That was one mistake he learned from. Other times, when his adventures *should* have gotten him in trouble, he somehow came out smelling like a friggin' rose, with authority figures thinking aloud about "how great a young man that Kingston is." Even Principal Hartford openly admired him. He was the only student in the history of the world who waltzed into the principal's office, circumvented an explanation for not finishing his diploma, and left with a handshake and a smile from said principal.

I turned to face the school as the black sedan pulled away. I looked just like them; no shark-like skin, at least while I was dry, anyway. I was just another student among hundreds, albeit a tall and gangly one; but that wasn't a candeon thing. I'm just that lucky.

The nerds were fidgeting under the scowls of the goths. The jocks were showing off to the unimpressed cheerleaders. The self-proclaimed band geeks were rehearsing without a care in the world; the hipsters were pretending not to eye each other's satchels; the surfer crowd hadn't arrived yet; and everyone else was doing their best to ignore them all. Stereotypes? Probably. Truth? For sure.

The only other candeon at Loma Heights was a senior named Dagger Stravins, a name I was sure he made up to add to his threatening wayfarer image. He showed up at school last fall and, despite the odds, had been in five of my seven classes last semester. Making me uneasy seemed to be a specialty of his. He always kept to himself, sitting in the back of the classroom like the unspoken ruler, watching over his domain. Teachers never questioned him, and students rarely risked talking about him. Rumors quietly circulated around campus about him being on parole for assault. But the worst thing about Dagger: he lived alone twelve houses down from us and practically stank of stalker—though any evidence to prove my theory had yet to be discovered.

Compared to the rest of the student body, he was huge: six feet four inches, two hundred and twenty pounds of toned muscle with dark hair, dark olive skin, and a chiseled face. He looked like a multiracial model. There was no way he was really eighteen. If it weren't for the reputational creep-factor, he'd score an *absolutely* on a ten-point scale.

Dagger wore a common charcoal-gray shirt and dark jeans every day, though I swear he had more shoes than the La Jolla girls did. Today looked like a new pair of Converse Chuck Taylors, a surprisingly light choice considering his rotating selection of work boots, dark suede skate shoes, and expensive athletic trainers. His ever-present gold ring—wide with an intricate design etched into the crest—always around the middle finger of his right hand.

I could tell he was candeon, even though I had never actually talked to him. He had a slight squint from trying to see clearly through the haze that clouds our dry vision, and he tucked in his shirt whenever he bent down to keep his lower back hidden. I'd even glimpsed the subtle flinch when his headaches would come.

All of this is just circumstantial evidence, of course. Really, I could *sense* him, and he was not human. He felt candeon, like Neo, Aaram, and Kingston. He could sense me too, but we didn't talk. Neo once said that Dagger was a monos: a candeon drifter who moved from place to place. I was beginning to wonder when he would decide to move on.

I felt Lauryn across the courtyard and made my way through the mess of students to her direction. Lauryn Locke was my best friend and the closest thing I had to a sister; a sister who did not know I wasn't human. She saw me and waved. Her long, natural blonde hair draped over an adorable tunic sweater that I recognized from her favorite shop. She had that mischievous look on her face; she was dying to tell me the hot new gossip sloshing around campus.

Before I could reach her, the minute bell rang and everyone (including the coffee-wielding, jaded veteran teachers) lurched like mules to a starter's pistol.

I made it through calculus without pointing out any of the teacher's mistakes, then government and Spanish before heading to the cafeteria to spend my lunch hour with Lauryn, Thalia, Ashlee, Dean, Shamsa, and Tito, hearing about all the hook-ups, break-ups, and guess-whats that I'd missed. Ashlee and Dean were now dating, which didn't surprise me. Though it was uncomfortable sitting in the cafeteria surrounded by hundreds of humans, it was nice to see my "friends" again. Lauryn was the only one I had seen over the break.

I lowered my gaze as Mr. Huckleberry rounded the corner, caught my eye, and raised his disappointed eyebrows. I hadn't given in to his request for "advice", and I suspected he was in a huff about losing money on Saturday's Chargers game.

Fourth hour Biology II was a breeding ground for teenage drama. There were four cheerleaders, two of whom hated each other, a handful of basketball players, a baseball player who got cuter every year, a pair of melodramatic thespians who were dating (nauseatingly), a gruff Swedish foreign-exchange student named Hans, and then William Martin and Trisha Goodman, the top two students in our grade and die-hard competitors for the title of Valedictorian. In the back of the room sat Dagger. *Of course.*

I shook off the notion that he was scrutinizing me and looked to Lauryn, who smiled in amused anticipation of the drama that was sure to come. We chatted about our Christmases, then she scolded me for not joining her at the "amazing" New Year's Eve party at Trevor Allen's house.

By the time Mrs. Samuels took roll, attempted a private but rather colorful debate with one of the aforementioned melodramatic thespians about her grade last semester, confiscated a foam football being tossed around, and then got everyone's attention, only twenty minutes remained of class.

"Welcome back to biology," Mrs. Samuels said with little fluster. "Things are going to be a bit different this term. You will be divided into groups to research a topic of *my* choice. You will give presentations throughout the semester on different aspects of that topic. Be forewarned: you'll need to put a lot of effort into these; they are worth one-third of your grade." Several moans reverberated off the white boards, laminated charts, and linoleum tile.

She continued, "We only have a few minutes left. Use that time to meet with your group and get to know each other a little better."

I groaned. That would mean that—

"Mrs. Samuels, are you going to be assigning us to groups or will we be choosing our partners?" William asked the question we were all waiting for.

"I have already assigned them" she replied with a self-satisfied smile.

More moans.

I was assigned to work with Olivia Ortiz (head cheerleader extraordinaire), Hans Eriksson (the Swede), and (thankfully) Lauryn Locke. The class shuffled desks to situate into their groups.

Hans was the first to speak in ours, though it was more of a heavily accented grumble. "We better not get hard topic. I have much more things to do than hang in the library with the pep-leader."

Mine and Lauryn's smiles were accompanied with uncontrollable giggles. With all her usual grace, Olivia snapped that we should choose a topic from the list on the board. We settled on the human circulatory system and scheduled to meet at Lauryn's house to divvy up subtopics the following Monday.

Lauryn walked with me to the Fine Arts building where I had choir practice with *her* Trevor Allen. When she saw him, she backed away down the hall toward her English class, mumbling incoherently, while I smoothly headed into class behind Trevor. It was plain as day to the rest of the civilized world, but for some baffling reason he was still unaware of Lauryn's crush.

Mrs. Snyder, the British expatriate with a strange half-accent, started class with the announcement we all expected. "As I'm sure you are fully aware, second semester honor choir is devoted to the spring musical. This year, we will be doing *West Side Story,* a re-telling of Shakespeare's epic *Romeo and Juliet,* set in New York City in the 1950s."

My mild enthusiasm redirected when I felt a familiar candeon coming toward our classroom. It didn't make sense. What could have brought him to this side of campus? Choir was the one class I knew I did not have to share with him.

Seconds later, Dagger Stravins walked through the door. Even Mrs. Snyder looked bewildered.

His low, resonating voice permeated the silence. "I heard that you were doing a spring musical." The room warmed, or maybe it was just me. "I'd like to try out." His voice echoed off of the acoustic panels behind us.

Mrs. Snyder was the first to speak. "Of course, Dagger. It is *Dagger,* right?" He was infamous. "Why don't you take a seat in the men's section? Did you register for this class?"

"Just did."

"Oh . . . great. Class, this is Dagger." Like he needed an introduction. "As I was saying, *West Side Story.* . . ."

When I walked out to the curb after seventh hour, King was waiting for me, posed against a polished, silver Mercedes convertible—the show-off car.

"Hey kid, how was the first day back?" he joked.

"Pretty good." I smiled as I remembered the twenty dollar bill I found at the bottom of my neglected locker. I glanced at the empty car. "Where's Neo?"

"He had a monster headache, so I dropped him off at Ocean Beach. He said he'd be home late tonight. Should we get going?"

"Sure." I didn't believe it for a second. Neo and I had spent half of the day before in the ocean. If he had a headache, it wasn't because he needed to dive.

My enthusiasm sank when I felt Principal Hartford coming our direction. Ron Hartford loved Kingston, and Kingston loved hearing praises from Ron Hartford.

"Hurry, get in the car!" King's instructions jolted me out of my slump; I was inside in record time. King pulled away from the curb and was on the main road without a backward glance.

"Wow. King, I'm impressed."

"At what?"

"You passed on a chance to hear Hartford tell you you're wonderful."

He shrugged.

I scoffed.

"What's that supposed to mean?" He looked at me with an amused, wrinkled brow.

"First, you get a job at a golf course to which you are already a paying member. Second, you offer to take your best friend's little sister to school every day for the rest of the semester. Third, you were on time to pick me up—we both know that's a first. And fourth, *you*, Mr. Aren't-I-Your-Favorite, ran from the flattery of an influential member of the human community." I awaited his comeback with a smile. He didn't disappoint.

"First of all, the job is for fun. I'm an event consultant, which means I get to help plan rich booze parties. The wealthy, when drunk, prove to be fine entertainment. Number two: I didn't offer, Aaram asked, and you're only irritating some of the time—"

"Hey! I said nothing about being irritating."

Pretty soon that smirk of his would have a name for itself. "Number three: don't be mean. I believe there was a fourth, though I can't remember what it was."

"Ditching Mr. Hartford."

"I'm done with high school."

I didn't respond. I didn't like it when King got ornery. We drove another block or two. "How is Mrs. James?" I asked. "I haven't seen her in a while."

Mrs. James had been the housekeeper at the Soli residence for over twenty years. Candeons had a hard time having close relationships with humans while keeping their true selves hidden, what with the constant need to dive and all, but Mrs. James was a unique exception. King said that she never asked any probing questions about the family secret. Sometimes I wondered what she thought was going on, if she thought that the Solis had been drug lords or government assassins, anything to find a reason why they would leave so often for a day or two with no explanation. I'm sure her imagination had mused all kinds of possibilities.

Still, despite being out of the loop, she was loyal to the family. She was Kingston's surrogate guardian now; she loved him and treated him like a son.

"Mrs. James is the same as always. She's been begging me to finish school and go to college. Hey, you hungry?" He looked at me with a hopeful eye.

"I'm starving. Aaram has a bunch of stuff in the fridge at home." As I thought about the leftovers I'd throw in the microwave, King turned away from the street to my house and instead headed toward the city.

"Let's go somewhere," he said.

"But we're almost there! I don't want to pay for food when I can get it for free."

He rolled his eyes. "I can't think of enough ways to spend my money. Please let me buy you some lunch . . . or early dinner."

I was about to say that I was fine eating at home, but something told me he had already decided. "Should we go get Neo? I'm sure he'd like some free lun—"

"He's in the water, remember?"

Hanging out with Kingston sans Neo was a new thing. Jury was out on whether or not it would be a comfortable thing.

"Where are we going?"

"How does Mexican sound?" It was a courtesy question, almost rhetorical.

"My *favorite*," I cooed.

"Last week you said barbeque was your favorite."

"I'm easy to please."

Kingston looked just as pleased. I quickly pulled my camera from my bag and snapped a shot of him, one arm stretched out straight on the steering wheel, dark sunglasses looking ahead. He didn't protest.

We set off toward what I thought would be a casual run to a roadside roach-coach, but after a longer than expected drive, Kingston turned into the ritzy Gaslamp Quarter: a place that both my wallet and I avoided like the plague.

I scowled. *Is this a date?*

"Here we are," King said as we pulled into a reserved parking space for one of the more glamorous Mexican restaurants in the district.

Really, is this a date? "King? Are you sure this is where you want to go? I'd be very happy with a Filiberto's burrito."

"Come on. Their ceviche is legit."

I left my backpack and camera in the car and fidgeted with my tee shirt. I was way underdressed. *At least it's a good hair day,* I thought to myself as I perked up the roots.

Inside, a model/hostess posed with a smile in her little black dress. She sat us in a corner table, away from the few other four o'clock diners. The low ceilings glowed as busboys lit candles on every surface and wall, despite the afternoon sunlight pouring in from behind shuttered windows. Either the room was getting smaller, or I was getting claustrophobic.

Shouldn't I be doing homework? Do I have homework? I debated whether I felt awkward because I was at a romantic restaurant so early on a Monday evening, or because I was alone with Kingston. Maybe it was both.

We sat down just before a leggy, tan, voluptuous waitress asked what we'd like to drink. King smiled and ordered a lemonade; I mumbled something about cold water.

"Marcela," he said, then paused, *appreciating* her more closely, "I am going to have the shrimp ceviche tonight, and Haelo here mentioned something earlier about a burrito. Do you have a really, really great burrito?" Kingston Soli had turned on his charm, and Marcela the waitress was wrapped around his fingers.

"Yes," she replied in her Latin accent, staring under long eyelashes into King's flattering gaze. "We have a new chile verde burrito with a mango salsa that is just heavenly. I bet I can even get the chef to make you something special for dessert, on the house."

She put a little too much flair on the words "heavenly" and "special." I had to cough back a giggle.

"That sounds amazing, Marcela. Thanks."

She continued to stare at King; I could tell he was enjoying himself. As soon as she walked away with our orders, we caught each other's eyes and laughed.

"Do you always do that to waitresses?"

"Do what?"

I cocked a brow. "Turn them into embarrassing displays of seduction."

"Females in the service industry are easy to seduce, yes. For lack of a better word."

"Oh, gross. Stop talking."

He put up a hand. "No, not like that. You know what I mean. You just have to know how to approach people in order to get them on your side. It's good to be personable, Haelo."

"Right. Personable." We grinned at each other and I remembered my earlier question about whether or not this was a date. "Have you ever met someone you couldn't *seduce*?"

He smiled his standard, charming grin, but this time his eyes winced.

The food was fantastic, our waitress *very* accommodating. After a brief conversation about my first day back at Loma Heights, I asked him how his first day as an event consultant was.

He dipped his head while he searched for an answer. "To be honest, I'm not an event consultant, never was. Neo was looking for a job and couldn't find anything, so I told him that I got both of us jobs at Torrey Pines. I'll go hang out at the clubhouse every day—look like I'm busy—then by the end of the week I'll 'quit' and let him do his own thing. I didn't want him to think I got him the job out of pity."

"Oh." I was a little taken aback, almost offended on behalf of my brother. It took a few moments for me to realize that I wasn't wholly surprised. King was trying to be helpful. It was—sweet?—in his own way. Sort of.

I quickly redirected the conversation to the football play-offs. I knew the stats, and I could hold a decent conversation about field strategy. King pretended like he knew football, and I let him think I was impressed by his comments. You know, out of *pity*.

It didn't take long for the conversation to ease into a pleasant, mutually entertaining banter. At one point, he had me laughing like I hadn't in months. It felt so good. As the evening went on and King settled into his natural self, his arrogant façade fell away. At his core, King was a good guy, when he wasn't trying so hard.

The restaurant filled and then dwindled, giving us enough time to eat through dinner and two desserts. (Don't judge.) It was easy to forget the constant weight in my head that came with living dry. We talked about our favorite memories of our parents—his entitled childhood very different than mine spent mostly in the sunny reefs of Polynesia. I wished I hadn't left my camera in the car; King was so photogenic.

He asked about the day my parents had been killed, but I wasn't ready to talk about that. Almost nine years had passed since Neo and I were orphaned. We had to leave the water, abandon our given names, and live on land with a man we had never met before: Grandpa Aaram. *Nine years* and I still couldn't talk about it. King understood my silence and changed the subject.

I found myself thinking of King as though he were a dear friend, not just my older brother's bro. It wasn't until we got up to leave that I realized we had been talking and laughing for over four hours and hadn't talked about Neo much at all.

"Thanks for dinner, King. I had a great time."

"You say that like you're surprised?" He raised his tone to sound like a question.

"We've never hung out before, just us, and I guess I didn't know what to expect."

"I had a good time, too. Let's get out of here, though. If we stay, they'll bring us another round of chocolate empanadas."

He took my hand and led me out the front entrance and into the bustling street. We found the car—it was easy to spot the small crowd of admirers positioned around it—and slid into the seats.

Did he just hold my hand? Something in the back of my mind scolded me that I should feel awkward. I didn't.

Kingston pulled out of the parking lot and headed for the highway. With the wind in our hair, we meandered our way home, listening to King's favorite radio station.

Besides the rusty heap that was my car, the first thing I noticed when we pulled into the dimly lit driveway of Grandpa Aaram's house was the light coming from Neo's bedroom. Kingston cut the engine but didn't reach for the door handle.

I looked from Neo's window back to King. "I thought Neo was diving tonight?"

He didn't answer me right away. Instead, he shifted in his seat, flashing a weak attempt at his persuasive smile. "I might have lied about that."

A cricket actually chirped.

"Haelo, remember your earlier question? You asked me if I'd ever come across someone who I wanted to like me and couldn't quite convince."

"Yes. . . ."

"I have," he said. "You."

I leaned back into the door. "That's absurd. Of course I like you. You're my brother's best friend. You're almost family."

"That's just it. I don't want to be just your brother's friend to you, Haelo. I'm tired of being your brother's friend."

My stomach slammed into my ankles.

"Neo didn't go diving. I asked him to give me some space so I could take you on a date."

"And he was okay with that? You've been trying to . . . woo me?" The word made me feel like I needed a shower. I wasn't sure I wanted to know the answer.

"I guess I have," he replied with a stubborn stare, making it hard to look away.

We sat in silence while I collected my thoughts. "King, I had a lot of fun with you tonight. But so far, the only reason I've heard for you wanting to *woo* me—" again the word just sounded stupid, "—is all for your ego. You don't really like me. You just want to add me to your list of swooning waitresses and co-eds."

His stunned face told me that I had said enough. The seats of the Mercedes didn't feel so luxurious anymore.

What was wrong with me? A great guy, who happened to be a close friend and fellow candeon, just took me out for one of the best nights I'd had in a long time with good food and great conversation, and I was questioning his intentions? I dropped my head into my hands to keep him from seeing my doubt.

"Wow." His voice cracked. "That was unexpected." He took in a deep breath and held it. Out of the corner of my eye, I saw him look up into the night above.

"Haelo, I'm going to tell you something that you probably don't want to hear, but if I don't, I'll always regret it. I don't just like you. For months now, well, I've been crazy about you."

I looked at him, and he looked at me—like a bad chick-flick. It didn't feel romantic; it felt cheesy.

He continued. "Neo is an awesome friend, but you're the reason I come over every day. You have been for a long time now. You don't care about my money. Or charisma. You smile at me for me, not because I charmed you into doing so. We're friends, real friends, and there's never before been a girl on this planet to see me as just a friend." He paused.

"But I want more than that. I don't want you to be my best friend's sister, I want you to be my girl."

The air between us thinned. I stared at his mouth, silently urging it to take back everything it had just said. Blue and white flashes came through the curtains of the front room—it was just another normal evening for Aaram, watching the local news before bed. I tried to find comfort in the idea that I could leap out of the Mercedes and lock myself in my bedroom.

"Kingston, what are you saying?"

"I'm saying, give me a chance. Let me prove to you how much you mean to me."

I remembered how comfortable I had felt with him earlier tonight, just the two of us. "What does Neo think about this?"

"It doesn't matter what Neo thinks, it only matters what you and I think. But he did mention that if I ever hurt you he'd beat my face in." His eyes lit up at my smile. He again took my hand in his and looked at it. "Haelo, you're so beautiful." The words were barely out when he started coming closer. I closed my eyes.

At first, it was like kissing a cousin: cringe-worthy. My stomach flexed and knotted. Then, unrushed, his lips caressed mine softly, carefully. He reached his hand to my arm. At some point, the kiss became tender, not creepy. He pulled away, looking at me intently. I couldn't tell if he was searching for words to say or waiting for me to speak first.

He's crazy about me? Thinks I'm beautiful? Were these just lines from a well-versed playbook?

A twig snapped in the dark yard across the street. The idea that my neighbors might be watching made ending this conversation a priority.

He released his amused smile, and I gave a hesitant one in return.

"Is that a yes?"

I need more time! What the heck just happened? "Yes," I shot back faster than intended. *I'm going to regret this.*

He sighed in relief and kissed me again, this time not quite as tenderly. "Haelo, you're not going to regret this."

I looked in my lap and blinked. *I am* definitely *going to regret this.*

He leapt over the door of the car and came around to get mine. Holding his hand up the front walkway was an unnerving sort of surreal; when I left home this morning, King was just King: he was Neo's bro and my ride to school. Now, as we made our way toward the front door, Kingston Michael Soli had become much more than that. He paused on the porch and kissed me goodnight, placing a hand on my lower back. Then he returned to his car and sped away.

Neo was waiting for me in my room, sitting in my squishy orange pink chair. A living oxymoron. For a split-second, I thought about getting another shot on my camera. *Not the time.* His raised his eyebrows like he was trying to look happy and supportive—the rest of his face just looked pained.

He waited until I shut the door and sat on the bed. "How was your night?" he asked.

When I didn't answer, he came over and sat next to me. I glued my eyes to the wallpaper.

With a loud sigh meant to ease the tension and in a voice like Grandpa Aaram's, he jibed, "You really should pick up this place every once in a while. How can you find anything?"

I couldn't look at him as I said it. "King kissed me. And I think I'm his girlfriend."

"You don't look too thrilled about it."

"I am." My eyes shot up to his. As soon as I saw his brotherly countenance, I reverted back to the wallpaper. "I don't know."

He sighed. "He gave me a big speech today about how much he liked you and how you were going to be different from any other girl he's . . . dated." Neo's knuckles popped in his tightened fists. "It was a great speech; the things he said about you, he's never said about any other girl. But he's still King."

"I had a really great time with him, up until he dropped the dating bomb."

He put his hand on my shoulder, and I leaned into his side. Neo and I had been through the worst together. We watched our parents fight. We watched our parents die. Aaram said we were the only two survivors of that black day that took our mother, father and little sister—the day that I'd spent nine years trying to forget. We depended on each other during the transition from the way of life that we had always known to the dry lifestyle of the grandfather that we came to live with. Neo was my best friend. If it weren't for him, I would not have made it; I wouldn't be the girl that I was today.

I stared at the top of my hands. "What should I do, Neo?"

"What do you want to do?"

"King is a good guy, right?"

His jaw clenched.

"He was really sweet tonight. We talked for hours. I didn't feel like his best friend's little sister."

"At work, he sounded so whipped. He definitely likes you, Lo."

I wanted to change the subject, because one: their "work" wasn't something I wanted to discuss, and two: what could I say to that, especially to my brother? The silence grew as I searched for a new conversation. My mind went to the night of the storm and the little boy. My breath quickened as I debated whether or not it was right to tell Neo. I finally gave up and the story sputtered out like a broken fire hose.

"Neo, a human saw me. In the water. I was diving and minding my own business, distracted, and then next thing I knew there was a sinking yacht and helicopters and a rescue diver and shouting and lights, and then there was this little boy and he looked so small—I couldn't just leave him there—so I raced to him and pulled him to the surface. I couldn't tell if he was breathing, so I swam and swam and then I pushed him to the Coast Guard diver. After he got the little boy into the helicopter, well, he looked at me. He *talked* to me. He thought I was another victim and he tried to get me to go with him. I didn't know what to do, so I dived. I got away, but he kept searching."

Neo didn't even blink. "That was brave, Haelo."

"What about the rescue diver?"

"He didn't touch you, right? So he wouldn't have noticed your skin. I think you're probably overreacting."

I felt relieved. Neo always made things better.

"I bet he thinks he was seeing things. Or that you drowned."

Neo stayed with me until I was too tired to talk anymore.

"Don't worry, Lo," he said. I couldn't help feeling that it sounded like a warning.

"About King or the storm?"

His answer was quick. "The storm."

3

FISH OUT OF WATER

Every morning when I awoke, I found King waiting for me in the kitchen. Neo's protective brotherly instincts made it difficult to be supportive, but he tried anyway. Aaram was hesitant to embrace King as his only granddaughter's boyfriend, but he had not yet lectured me about it. I didn't have high hopes of avoiding that lecture—it hadn't even been a week since our first date.

On Thursday, King asked for a rain check on our planned dive, saying something about business with Mrs. James that needed his attention. Instead, I worked on homework and tried to figure out what was sabotaging the engine of my Civic. Aaram and Neo were too busy discussing Neo's much-delayed future plans for college to help me, and my own mechanic skills ranked at novice level, so I surrendered to being just as rideless as I was before I bought the stupid thing.

On Friday evening, I pulled out a swimsuit only to hear King give me the same story—he had business with Mrs. James. He pouted when I mentioned I'd go alone. I was losing my patience, but I agreed to wait for him and tossed the swimsuit back in my drawer. *I need a girls' night anyway.*

A short phone call and twenty minutes later, Lauryn waltzed through the front door. "Hello, Mr. Gevgenis!"

"Lauryn, once again I need to remind you to call me Aaram. How are you, my dear? It is good to see you."

"It's good to be seen," she tossed back, then winked and added some genuine pleasantries. Aaram gave her a quick side-hug and then left us to our own cunning devices. In a gesture much more rewarding than romanticized Friday night antics, we plopped lazily on the couch.

"What's on the menu for tonight? Movie? Cookie dough? Eyebrow waxing?" Lauryn hinted as she fluffed one of the pillows.

I scrunched my face.

"Haelo. You've got this Frida Kahlo thing going on."

"What?" I sat up a little to look in the mirror hanging above the couch. *Maybe a little.* "Well, whatever we decide to do, we have the whole night."

"I'm not going to get kicked out when His Majesty the King of all Crap gets here? I can't stand seeing him so romantic with you. It gives me the willies."

"No. King won't come by, promise. His Majesty the King of all Crap?" The banter exhausted me. I was so tired. *I need to dive.*

"Oh, come on, like you don't think it's funny. The guy is the world's biggest schmoozer." Lauryn's filter was selective—tonight it seemed to be MIA. But I had learned a long time ago to appreciate her commentary.

"Yeah, yeah. Were you still thinking about asking Trevor to Sweethearts?"

"Trevor Allen?" She always said his full name. "Yeah. How did you know?"

I rolled my eyes. "You'd better hurry. I heard Holly Gardner say something earlier today about asking him."

She sat up straighter. "What? Dagnammit! I'll ask him tomorrow. You think he'll say yes?"

"Of course he'll say yes; only jerks say no. Besides, he likes you."

"Really?" Her smile was contagious.

We talked about dances, Thai food, high school drama, and old Carey Grant movies until midnight.

"I'd better go. My mom is going to freak. We have family pictures at some ungodly hour in the morning." Lauryn got up from the couch to set a bowl of leftover popcorn kernels by the kitchen sink.

"Tell her I said hi." I waved from the couch.

"Will do. Goodnight!" She shut the door. Seconds later, it reopened and she popped her head back inside. "And don't forget to pluck your eyebrows." The door shut before the couch pillow could whack her in the face.

I contemplated a fleeting thought about brushing my teeth, but before I could gather the energy to get up, I fell asleep.

I awoke, reluctantly, because of a quick kiss on the top of my head. "Grandpa?" I moaned. My eyes squinted against the morning sunlight.

"No. It's me."

Through the haze, I made out the carefree shape of Kingston's hair.

"Oh, hi King." I was *so* not ready to wake up.

"Did you miss me yesterday?" he asked. When I didn't respond, he asked again.

"All right, all right. I'm up."

I had that gross feeling of messy hair, unbrushed teeth, and sleeping on a couch in yesterday's clothes. I was disgusted with myself and too groggy to do anything about it. Grandpa called us for breakfast.

All morning King acted like he had something on his mind. He'd fidget. He'd hold his breath like he was about to say something. He'd even stare off into space for long moments. Eventually he must have shaken it off, because by lunch he was back to his normal self. We drove to

Los Angeles and went shopping in pricey boutiques where King bought three pairs of sunglasses and a fedora. A *fedora*.

I didn't buy anything. He tried to get me a pair of designer jeans, but I vehemently insisted I'd never wear them; they did unfamiliar things to my butt. He paraded me in and out of shops like I was his personal princess. My head throbbed, and I was super tired, but I was functioning. Another day or two without a dive wouldn't hurt me.

On Sunday, King joined us at church, then spent the afternoon with us at home playing card games with Grandpa and Neo. With wise concern, Aaram asked me when I had been in the water last.

"You look pasty and weak, Haelo," he warned.

Before I could respond, King shouted, "See that? I win—you lose!" He tossed his winning hand onto the coffee table, then picked me up off the floor and twirled me around the room and out the back door. We sat talking on the back porch swing until I was ready to sleep.

"It's only nine-thirty," he whined.

"Sorry, King. I'm really tired." I left him outside and headed for the bathroom. I could hear Neo and King arguing about something while I washed my face, but I was too tired to care. I didn't even dream.

The whole school knew I was dating Kingston Soli. Every morning he would drop me off and kiss me passionately, like he had something to prove. Neo would look away, grunt from the backseat of the car, and tap furiously on his knee, but that never stopped King. I was beginning to feel more comfortable with the idea of being his girlfriend.

"Hey, baby?" he asked in a whine probably meant to sound endearing. "Let's dive later today. My headache hit me pretty hard last night."

My own skin was dangerously dry, and the dull weight in my head throbbed. I could feel myself getting weaker by the hour. "It will have to be after six. I have a group project meeting after school. You won't need to pick me up today; I have a ride there."

He looked a little disappointed, then smiled and kissed me goodbye again.

I got out of the car and looked around for Lauryn. I could sense her behind the tall pack of basketball players on the far side of the courtyard. In my weakened state, the mass of humans buzzed even more uncomfortably than usual. When I reached her, she was finishing up a quiet conversation with the team point guard.

Lauryn had a hard time with me dating King. Every time we talked about him, I would end up defending his intentions. She had always been suspicious of him, though, so this was nothing new. Thankfully, the minute bell rang before I had to pleasantly acknowledge our difference of opinion on one Kingston Soli.

During biology, Hans reminded our group that our meeting after school "had better be short" because he had "place to go and people to look." Lauryn fought to not look so giddy when Trevor walked in and told Mrs. Samuels that he had been transferred into that hour. Mrs. Samuels assigned him to our group, which made Lauryn noticeably perk up.

The sun was much too bright on my walk to English; I had to slow down a little to avoid feeling lightheaded. I was about to rest on a bench when I felt Dagger come up behind me.

Suddenly but carefully, he grabbed my arm and turned me toward him, his gold ring unnaturally warm against my deteriorating skin. "Haelo, you need to dive. Now." Everything about his expression scared me. "Do you understand?"

I was too stunned to respond immediately. He waited until I nodded shakily, then asked with deathly serious eyes, "Would you like me to go with you? We can go right now."

"No, n-no. I'll go. Promise. I'll be fine." He held me while he studied my response, waiting for more. "I'm going tonight. Mind your own business."

Finally—gently—he released my arm, and he was gone.

I stood in shock. Was it that obvious? And where was the, "Hello, my name is Dagger and by the way, we are both of the same species"? I tried to process his strange behavior, to think through why, but it only hurt my head more. My skin, vision, and strength were deteriorating. The day was flying by in an exhausting whirlwind, and I was starting to lose it. I reasoned with myself that a couple of hours more wouldn't kill me. But my group might if I no-showed our meeting.

We headed for Lauryn's home as soon as I caught up to her after seventh hour. When we arrived, Mrs. Locke had homemade peanut butter chocolate chip oatmeal cookies in the oven.

My mouth salivated. "Gwen, you're the best."

"I know, aren't I?" she drawled in a slow, hip tone. "When Lauryn told me you were coming, I *had* to make your favorite cookie."

I knew I always liked her.

The doorbell rang. I could see the disappointment in Lauryn's face when she opened the door and Hans walked in; she had hoped Trevor would arrive first. Hans sank himself into an armchair and shut his eyes, looking as annoyed as ever. I fought back a giggle.

Trevor arrived next, giving a warm "hello" to a suspicious Mrs. Locke. He twitched slightly under her stare and slowly lowered himself into the couch across from our favorite Swede.

I could feel Olivia coming closer before I heard the rumble of the engine pull up to the house. She wasn't alone; I could sense another human with her. A human who felt oddly familiar, despite an agitated (or maybe angry) aura. The emotion distorted their aura enough so that I couldn't quite recognize them. The engine cut, and two doors opened.

You didn't have to be a candeon to tell it was Olivia—we could hear her shouting. We all gaped at each other with knowing eyes. I casually looked out the bay window to sneak a glimpse: a perfect view of Olivia runwaying up the walkway with eyes of fury. I couldn't see the face of the boy behind her; her big head (both literally and figuratively) was in the way.

Lauryn opened the door and Olivia stormed in, leaving me with a clear view of the boy.

My heart stopped. It was him! It was the Coast Guard rescue diver from the storm! The human that had seen me! I blinked a half dozen times in a futile attempt to focus my eyes, hoping that I was seeing things.

"Olivia." Same voice. It really was him. "Can we talk more about this later?"

"No. I'll find my own ride home."

He looked at her with an uncertain expression. There was no question; he was the rescue diver. Still, there was something else about him that had me searching through memories. Olivia turned dramatically to sit on the couch, where Trevor was seated upright and alert. The young man at the door gave Lauryn an apologetic look and lowered his eyes in respect. "I'm really sorry about this. You didn't need to hear that."

His eyes, deep blue like the sky on that stormy night, turned to Olivia and winced. "I'd better get going."

As he turned to leave, he looked at me for the first time and paused, a slight hesitation in his gait. I looked down and fiddled with the pencil in my hand, praying for the beads of sweat saturating my forehead to go away. I felt his eyes dig into me just as he resumed his exit.

I almost yelled out to him. I wanted to know what happened to the little boy! Did he make it? Was he okay? But the engine of his yellow, late-eighties Ford pick-up whirled to life and took him away, leaving me with a teasing sort of déjà vu. I had met him before the storm. I was sure of it.

Olivia didn't say anything about what had happened except that he was an idiot and she could do better, though I could tell by her somber, thoughtful look that she was heartbroken.

I couldn't concentrate during our meeting and ate more than half of the cookies. I always eat too much when I'm nervous. At one point Hans remarked that I might as well eat the plate since I devoured everything else.

Shut it, Hans. My mind spun. *When is this meeting going to end?*

Finally, Olivia and Hans stood up and collected their things. I hurriedly swept my backpack over my shoulders, then remembered that I didn't have a ride. Lauryn and Trevor were deep in a flirt-fest, so it would be a wasted effort to ask her to take me home. I shot off a text to Kingston, which he answered surprisingly quickly.

"Um, Haelo? Do you mind if I get a ride with you?" Olivia asked, fidgeting.

"Sure. That shouldn't be a problem." I hoped that King wasn't coming in the two-seater Mercedes. I once again thanked Mrs. Locke for the treats while Olivia politely responded to everyone's goodbyes as we made our way outside to wait.

She sat down on the front porch step, folded her arms around herself in a hug, and curled forward into her knees. I was definitely unprepared for this. I sat down beside her, trying to find consoling words. Nothing helpful came to mind.

"You know what? It was my fault," she mumbled, staring straight ahead into the dry asphalt in front of us. "I messed up. He saw right through my lies." She lowered her head into her folded arms to hide her eyes. "I'm not good enough for him."

"That's definitely not true." I tried to sound convincing.

She smeared tears and mascara along her arm as she turned to face me. "He knew I was a spoiled brat. Maybe . . . maybe he thought I had potential underneath it all. I don't know why he gave me the chance. I treated him like he was disposable." She sniffled and wiped her streaking make-up on the inside of her sweater. "He deserves better than me. Sam Legend is the best person I know."

Sam Legend? I suddenly knew why old memories flickered in the background of my mind when I saw him at Lauryn's door: Sam had been my neighbor. He was the first human I'd ever met. In those first few years that Neo and I came to live with Aaram, he was the only friend I had. At just over three years older than me, Sam should have been Neo's friend, but Neo had a harder time with humans.

He had changed a lot; he was much taller, had muscles that he never had before, his shaggy blonde hair was now cropped neatly, and he looked so much more like a man than the boy from my childhood. Thinking about the hundreds of memories and moments I had shared with him in my past, I matched up the unrecognizable new Sam with the familiar old one. He still had his super long eyelashes and a single cheek dimple, though his jawline had definitely manned-out. I even remembered the old yellow truck. His dad had promised it to him on his sixteenth birthday.

I shook my head in disbelief that I had not recognized his blue eyes during the storm. I had dozens of questions. I wanted to know about him, about the last four and a half years of his life.

Olivia sighed, slumping lower into her shoulders. I quickly ran over the last few things she had said. Try as I might, I didn't know what to say in return. I put my arm around her, hoping it was enough.

The sun hung just above the horizon, and the sidewalk glowed in a warm, orange hue. It was a surprisingly warm January day. Every few seconds, rays of light danced through the rustling fronds of the palm trees and freckled us in the sun's last moments of heat. I shut my eyes and let the whisper of a breeze curve its way around me. My fingers toasted on the warm cement step. We sat together in silence, listening to the birds, the gentle wind, and distant cars bring the day to an end.

When King pulled around the corner, Olivia stiffened. "Who's coming to pick us up?" she asked.

"Kingston Soli."

She froze. "Not your mom, or dad, or . . . someone?"

"My grandpa is in San Francisco for a conference. King won't mind, I promise."

She looked back through the screen door into Lauryn's front room. "I think I'll ask Trevor for a ride home. Or I can call a friend. I don't want to be a third wheel." She tried frantically to erase all evidence of crying from her eyes and face. She even shimmied a little and sat up straight, as if her posture might give her away.

"Don't be ridiculous; there's plenty of room. King won't mind. Come on." I lead the way to the car. She hesitated before opening the back passenger door, then looked up into the sky and got in.

The ride to Olivia's house stretched in uncomfortable silence, despite my efforts to make conversation. Even King was silent. When we pulled into her driveway, she mumbled a "thanks" and bolted.

"What's with her?" King asked. He hadn't looked at me once the entire drive.

"What's with *her*? What's with you! You completely ignored her!"

"I did not. She looked like she didn't want to be bothered. I gave her some space."

"Her boyfriend just broke up with her." As I said the word "boyfriend," an unfamiliar twinge tightened in my stomach. Sam had been her boyfriend. "Our whole bio group saw it happen."

King didn't say anything for two blocks. When he finally spoke, his voice lacked its usual luster. "She had a boyfriend?" His chin turned toward me, though his eyes stayed transfixed on the intersection's red light.

"Why so surprised?"

"No reason."

"No, really. You look confused. Why does it surprise you that Olivia Ortiz had a boyfriend? She seems to be what every guy wants."

"No, she's what *some* guys want, and what a lot of guys *had*."

"What are you trying to say?"

"Take it any way you like. Let's just say she's . . . friendly." King shrugged.

"Friendly?"

He got right to the point. "She's been around. *That* kind of friendly."

"Oh." My gender defensiveness melted into a strange sort of shame.

"Looks like her boyfriend found out," King mumbled as he put on a new pair of sunglasses. "Do you mind if we drop in on Neo for a minute before we dive? He said it's a good game. You'll like it."

I rubbed my temples. "That's fine. I need to grab a suit anyway."

He turned up the audio system so the rest of the drive home swam in top-forty radio.

Back at home, the boys parked themselves in front of the TV. I watched for a few minutes, taking in the stats scrolling along the bottom of the screen and mentally noting who was injured. I readjusted my fantasy league roster (which was kicking serious butt), then got bored. I was good at it, but sports statistics were losing their charm. I threw a swimsuit on under my clothes and waited.

I must have drifted off, because when I awoke, there were three minutes left of the fourth quarter and the game was close. Neo blinked away from the screen during a time out and scrutinized me, then reached for the remote.

"Hey! Three more minutes!" King shouted before Neo could turn off the TV. Neo acquiesced with a furrowed brow.

A part of me wanted to just leave, but I was nearly broken down with exhaustion; I needed *help* getting to the beach. I made it thirty more seconds of game time before I passed out for good, sleep claiming me for the night.

My dreams surged with images of Sam Legend. I dreamed us both back in the stormy ocean, Sam once again reaching out to save me. I dreamed I was struggling in an angry river, boat wreckage bobbing past me, and there he was, swimming toward me again. I dreamed I was resting against a hot, dusty rock in the middle of a desert, ready to give up in defeat, and then, when all was surely lost and the scorching sun had won, there was Sam with cold salt water and a ride out. I dreamed I was lying underneath a harsh, white lamp on a glowing table, unable to move or speak, hushed whispers all around me, alone, restrained, and scared; then an arm extended from above, pulling me away from the paralyzing, fluorescent prison and into safety. But it wasn't Sam; it was Dagger Stravins.

I jolted awake. *What in the world?* I tried to shake off the last image of Dagger's serious stare, but I didn't have the energy. Despite a night's sleep, I was more exhausted than I had been the day before. Someone must have carried me to my bed.

The dead weight in my head pounded with my weak heartbeat. My straining muscles threatened to collapse under my body weight as I tried to stand up. It had been far too long since my last dive.

My room looked the same; I just wasn't so certain I was really standing in it. I felt detached from everything. My dry, pastry-like skin flaked dangerously thin. I heard a thundering knock at the front door, then bellows in a distant voice yelling at Grandpa Aaram. I couldn't feel anything. I reeled at the sight of the old stray cat perched outside my window sill, staring at me, meowing loudly.

My knees buckled on the way to the bedroom door, warning me to stop. I reached out to the wooden bedpost, but my fingers refused to close around it. For a moment, I was somewhere else, entirely removed from reality. I forced myself to blink and process my real surroundings, to focus my mind onto something concrete. The harder I tried to think, the harder thinking became.

Without any resistance or struggle, my knees gave out completely. My shoulder and head slammed into the cold hardwood floor with an odd sound, like an echo from far away, harmonized by cat clawings on my window screen.

I shut my eyes and let the color from fresh bruises puddle under my paper skin, probably the only color left in my drained, translucent body. A delusional respite on the cool surface, as if I could somehow absorb moisture from the cold. The pulsing deep in my head slowed with my blood pressure. Somewhere in my consciousness, I heard hollow footsteps in the hall. *Breathe. Breathe.*

My bedroom door swung open and crashed into my limp back.

"Haelo! Haelo, you need to wake up! Come on, honey!" Aaram's loving tone scolded me as he stroked my cheek and lifted my eyelids, which I fluttered in annoyance. "Neo! We need to get her to the water!"

Neo slid his arms underneath me, separating my purple bruises from the cold, clammy wood. He swung me around the door, throwing off any sense of equilibrium I had left. The white light of the sun seared my closed eyes.

Kingston's voice rang out from behind me. "Neo! Put her in my car, it's the fastest. I'll take her to the coast. You guys follow behind—"

"Dagger! Go home, we have this," Aaram barked. It sounded so far away that I was certain I was not hearing him correctly.

The familiar leather of Kingston's Mercedes did not feel so familiar anymore; only harsh and stiff. My eyes refused to open to the painful sunlight. I curled up in the bucket seat and drifted to sleep over the sounds of King's engine.

The mechanical sound of the car door opening startled me awake. The ocean breeze wrapped me in moist salt air and kick-started my energy. My eyes ripped open, and I took a deep breath of welcome wind.

Kingston drilled me with his eyes, watching my every movement. He spoke at me like I was a child. "Haelo, you need to get in the water. Here." His outstretched arms begged for my compliance.

I leaned forward, wrapping my arms around his neck. He swept me away from the car into the disorienting sunlight, where everything was so illuminated in white light that colors were almost completely indistinguishable from one another. I tried to seal my eyes against the pain.

My weak senses detected humans nearby, probably staring at the nearly unconscious girl being carried into the frigid January waves. A public relations nightmare. And I didn't care.

The moment the water hit my papery skin, I felt mortal relief. King held me in his arms and walked farther down the ocean incline. Though my skin had already started soaking in oxygen and minerals, I drew a deep breath anyway. My skin tightened in the nourishing water.

King pulled me under, and my vision cleared for the first time in over a week. He towed me alongside himself until we left the surface currents and were free to glide. Together we flew, hand in hand, above the ocean floor.

He looked at me with concern and protection. His anxious thoughts asked me over and over again if I was okay, but I was too absorbed in recovery to direct a thought back to him. He rubbed my arms, feeling for the return of my tough, shark-like skin. He promised that we would not go back until I felt strong and my headache had melted away. He guided me through the water for hours.

We both felt Grandpa Aaram and Neo approaching. King went rigid. Aaram must have told him something that he didn't want me to hear. I had never wished until that moment that candeons could hear all of the thoughts of other nearby diving candeons, not just the thoughts specifically directed at them. Aaram came up from behind and asked me if I was okay.

I'm fine, Grandpa, really.

Neo's relieved voice entered my head. *Lo, you had me pretty scared.*

I could tell that Aaram, Neo, and King were communicating without letting me in on the conversation. Aaram stared at Neo with fuming disappointment and at King with outright contempt. King's expression wasn't much different than Aaram's. My heartbeat raced as my mind rolodexed through all the possible reasons for their fury. Were they both angry with me? Was Aaram mad that King and I took off without him and Neo? Was he mad at King for not noticing my weakening state earlier? Was this the scale-tipper of reasons why Grandpa Aaram didn't want me dating Kingston? Was King firing back attitude? And what about Neo? What was going on?

When I finally got Aaram's attention, I gave him the most determined look I could muster. *Anything you have to say to Kingston, you can share with me.*

He ignored me and continued in his silent tirade, now apparently directed only at King.

When I couldn't take it any longer, I threw my hands up and let out a loud, bubbly scream through my locked jaw. All three sets of eyes flashed to my direction.

I'll see you at home. The current that pulled me away pushed against the three men, knocking them sideways and delaying their protesting voices until I was far enough away that their pleading thoughts sounded garbled and muted. I needed time alone. They'd catch up eventually.

Neo found me a half hour later and, surprisingly, I was grateful for his company. *You mind if I ride beside?* I could tell he was trying to keep things light.

No, I don't mind. Our two currents side-by-side kicked up our speed significantly. *Where are King and Grandpa Aaram?*

King got ticked and left; Aaram got angrier. He told me to come find you and tell you to ride as long as you need. Then he bailed, as well.

Did they let you hear their conversation?

No. I'm not so sure I wanted to hear it. Besides, I didn't stick around much longer after you bolted. Man, for being a young candeon, you've got some speed.

A weak smile crept across my face. As it often did, my heart once again filled with a rush of gratitude for Neo.

I love you, Neo.

Love you too, Lo.

Together we rode the current until the sunset breaking through the surface burned a deep red-orange.

Aaram, Neo, King, and I sat around the kitchen table, no one willing to be the first to speak. Aaram stayed calm despite being noticeably irate. Neo munched from a bowl of trail mix in the center of the table, hoping to escape the tension in the room. The crunching just magnified the silence.

Even though the words didn't really apply, I recited *innocent until proven guilty* in my lonely head. We couldn't hear each other's thoughts anymore; that power only worked in the ocean. I sat toga'd in a towel, my hair hanging wet and limp down the front of my shoulders. My soggy sweat pants squished at my knees.

I was on trial.

Grandpa Aaram's grave voice broke the silence. "Haelo, why did you go so long without diving?"

I stared into the maple wood grain and reached for a pretzel diversion. "I'm not sure. I was distracted, I guess. King and I *planned* on going last Thursday."

"And why didn't you?"

This time King spoke up. "Sir, as I told you before, that was my fault." Neo and I stared nervously at King. "When I stayed behind Thursday, I should have insisted that Haelo go diving without me."

Aaram's powerful gaze slowly made its way to the boy beside me. "Kingston Soli." His voice was eerily steady. "She is younger, she has yet to form her adult scales, and therefore she needs to dive more often than you. But *we* have already had this conversation; I'm here to talk to Haelo." He stopped his next comment, shaking his head in furious disappointment.

A minute went by in uncomfortable silence. Aaram eventually sighed in defeat. "Haelo, I should have been more on top of things. I'm sorry. I should have noticed earlier and insisted before I left for San Francisco. When I got home this morning and realized you hadn't—." He shook his head again.

It killed me to see him taking the blame for my lapse in judgment.

Neo joined in. "It's my fault, too. I should have taken her diving." He glared at Kingston. "On multiple occasions." He bowed his head to Aaram. "Last night when I couldn't get her to wake up, I should have taken her to the water instead of putting her in her bed. I reasoned that I'd take her in the morning before you got back, but that was obviously a bad call."

Fury simmered in my chest as I saw all three men try to take responsibility for my mistake. "No, Neo. It's not your job to *take* me diving! I can dive on my own. And Grandpa, you shouldn't be blaming yourself. I am almost a legal adult in this human world that you insist on living in; you don't need to babysit me! I can take care of myself."

"Clearly."

That one word hit me like a cinderblock, disintegrating my pride. I felt small. Irresponsible. Aaram looked weary, and deadly serious. My tail was so far between my legs it smacked me in the face. I was in trouble; I had nearly killed myself.

I thought I understood that my body could deteriorate—even fatally deteriorate—if I didn't take care of it and dive often. I had overestimated my own strength and subconsciously compared my stamina to the stamina of the full-grown candeons around me. I thought I could wait until King or Neo dove; I thought that I could distract myself from the symptoms. Aaram, Neo, and King didn't crave diving as much as I did. Stupidly, I thought I could keep up and show them that I was an adult candeon.

Neo's eyebrows cinched together in concern, but he wore a small, loving smile. Since Kingston had not yet looked at me, I had no clue what he was thinking.

Aaram continued. "Haelo, I am disappointed in myself, in King, in *Neo*—" his pitch went up slightly with the name, "—and in you. I came this close to having another funeral in my family." His eyes were pinched as tightly as his displayed fingers. "Do not do this again."

If I thought I had felt bad before, "bad" was a colossal understatement now. The three of us sat very still as Aaram got up to putter in the kitchen. He mumbled something about needing to be awake early in the morning and left for bed without stopping to watch news headlines.

King stood. He kept his eyes on the wall across from him as he apologized. "I'm sorry, Haelo." He put his hands in his pockets. "I'll see you both tomorrow. Mrs. James needs to talk to me about something before she goes to bed." He walked out without a glance back at me.

It was the final blow. A few hours earlier, I had been King's princess. *Now what?*

4
BREAK UP, CATCH UP

Wednesday morning felt unsettlingly subdued, like the entire world was on pause and I was the only one aware of it. Neo slept, the house was silent, and Kingston had not arrived.

The pings of my cereal hitting the glass bowl echoed in the kitchen. *Sigh*. Cap'n Crunch was not going to cut it. I threw some bread in the toaster, grabbed an orange, bacon and eggs from the fridge, and then pulled out the bag of frozen hash browns. I half expected to hear Neo chime in and say something hypocritical about my petite appetite this morning. I cooked and ate in the eerie quiet.

Halfway through my potatoes, I realized I'd have to walk to school. And I would be late. "Crap," I groaned out loud to the empty kitchen.

Neo's morning mumbling broke the silence, winding its way down the hallway. "What? Smells pretty good to me. If you won't eat it, I will."

I hesitated before asking, "Have you heard from King?"

"No." He scratched the back of his head. "I wouldn't blame you if you decide to blow him off." He looked hopeful.

I noticed he wasn't dressed for work. "You're not coming with us?"

"No."

I sensed King ebbing closer to our house. I put my dishes in the sink, grabbed my bag from the back of a chair, and made my way toward the side door in the kitchen where King always came in.

A knock at the front door stopped me short.

I looked to Neo, hoping for an explanation, but he wouldn't look at me.

The door creaked when I opened it.

There was Kingston Soli, standing in a butler-worthy façade, completely void of emotion or judgment.

"Ready?" he said, voice formal and numb, eyes forced in my direction.

For the second time—though for drastically different reasons—he made my stomach hit my ankles. Yesterday morning I had felt like the most important person in his life; now I was a stranger, at most an acquaintance.

"Yes," I whispered, hurt. He turned down the front walk to the black car parked in the street, not the driveway. My feet stuck to the floor. Before I could process what had happened, the *ca-click* of his driver's side door opening startled me into motion.

For a split-second, I debated whether to get in the front seat, or the back. I finally sank down into my usual spot up front next to what felt like an imaginary wall separating me from King.

He spoke up before we left the curb, his careful, monotone manner piercing our relationship with each statement. "I'm sorry for the way I acted. You deserve much better than that." He cut off my intended protest I even started. "I should have noticed how weak you were days ago. And yesterday in the water, I should have kept you closer to shore so your grandfather could be near you. It won't happen again." He stared at the road as if the dirty white lines offered the only distraction from the unwanted girl sitting next to him.

"King...."

"It won't happen again."

My mouth fell open. The rest of the trip to school was silent. When he pulled up to the side entrance of Loma Heights High, he faced me for the first time since my front door.

"If it's what you want, I'll be there every morning to take you to school, just like I promised Aaram, and I'll be here at three-thirty to take you home. But that's all I can offer you." He had dark circles under his eyes. For the first time, I noticed that one of his eyebrows was swollen, a little sliver of dark, dried blood slicing through it.

"King, wha—?" I questioned as I raised my hand to his head.

"Don't worry about it," he almost spat as he pushed my hand down. "None of your business."

"But—"

"Haelo! Leave it alone!" He sucked in an impatient breath. "Please."

Fine, Your Majesty. So much for trying to help. Without a word, I got myself out of the car and turned to face the incoming rush of hormonal auras. I stood there like a zombie waiting for King to pull away.

He didn't. The purr of his car idled behind me as a stinging reminder that King and I were no longer "King and I."

I forced my head up high and walked away.

Don't look back....

Do not look back....

Keep walking.

Lauryn spotted me through a ring of band geeks and waved, her smile morphing into a concerned twist as she mouthed the words, "What's up?" Her eyes strained to see past me through the shadowed windows of the shiny, black car at the curb, and then her mouth fell. When I finally reached her, she pulled me aside, demanding in a hushed voice, "Why does Kingston look so pathetic?"

"Pathetic?" My head shot in his direction, glaring into the windows. Even with the haze, I could still see what Lauryn could.

It was true. King lay over the steering wheel; shoulders slumped, staring blankly into the dashboard. Through the buzz of human life, through the shuffling crowd of bodies in between us, and through the tinted glass, I thought I saw a tear fall down his cheek.

At lunch, Ashlee, Dean, Tito, Shamsa, and Thalia all questioned me about what had happened with King. Apparently the whole school wondered. I tried to avoid the conversation, but they were relentless. It wasn't until Lauryn told them all to shut up about it that I got away from the third degree.

"Haelo, I have some bad news," she whispered.

It can't get much worse, I thought to myself.

"It's about King. I need to talk to you in private, right now."

Okay. It could get worse.

Outside, Lauryn didn't bother putting on her jacket before she started explaining.

"Haelo, I just ran into Isabelle and Olivia out in the parking lot. Isabelle told me how *sorry* she felt for you."

"Ignore her, Lauryn. She and the rest of the varsity cheerleaders can just—"

"I confronted her and asked her what her problem was. After a profane tirade from the both of them, they blurted out that King, well, he cheated on you, Haelo."

I waited.

"Did you hear me? His Majesty, the King of all Crap, the Lord of the Playboys—he cheated on you."

For the briefest of moments, I genuinely hurt. Then came a round of hellfire fury. And then, with a slight shake of the head, I suddenly didn't care. I should have been surprised by King's exploits, but I wasn't. "What did they say?"

"King wasn't with you on Friday night, was he?" It was a statement. "You were with me, remember?"

I nodded. "He said he had some business to take care of."

"That business was with Olivia. He went over to break up with her. Apparently they were secretly seeing each other before you and King started dating, and the turd never really let it go."

I didn't breathe any faster, I didn't clench my teeth, I didn't even scowl. Nothing happened. I was the same Haelo Marley that I had been five minutes before. I nodded for her to continue.

"He went over to end it, and they ended up, well...." She moved her hands around for the added dramatics of body language—a last ditch effort to incite my emotions. I reached out and hugged her instead.

"Thanks, Lauryn. For telling me." I let go and turned toward the cafeteria.

"Wait! Do you understand what I just told you?" she yelped as she caught up to me.

"Yeah, and I'm mad that he didn't tell me. I'm mad that he used me." I stopped and looked her in the eyes for emphasis. "I'm mad that he thought he could treat me like a queen this weekend and it would make up for his hook up with Olivia. I'm mad, trust me. But it doesn't make a difference. I've been thinking about it all day, and I now realize that he was all wrong for me, from the first date."

Lauryn looked back and forth from me to the empty space between us.

"Seriously, I'm okay, Lauryn. King is a tool. I deserve better." I let her gape for a good three seconds before adding, "Don't worry—I'll let you help me egg his house or something."

This time, she hugged me, mumbling something about her mom's new taser.

"What?" I asked.

"Don't worry about it. What you don't know, you can't testify about." She smiled ear to ear. "So where were you yesterday?" she asked as we continued our way through the campus courtyard.

Fighting for my life against the weaknesses of being a freaky non-human. "Headache, no biggie. Did you ask Trevor to Sweetheart's?"

"Yes." She frowned. "But Holly asked him first. You know, I could really hurt that girl."

"No, you couldn't."

"You sure about that?"

We both laughed. It felt great.

I stopped short of the main building's steps. "Lord of the Playboys?"

Lauryn raised her eyebrows in an *Mmm-hmm*.

"Girl, preach."

Lauryn took me home after seventh hour—I didn't bother letting King know that I wouldn't need his chauffeur services. She stayed for a few minutes and let Aaram ask her the standard questions about her classes and favorite subjects. After she left, Aaram sat down on the couch with me.

"You look like you've had a long day." He put his arm around me and coyly snuck a bowl of ice cream into my lap.

"Shameless," I murmured.

"Bribes are an essential part of parenting."

I sighed and succumbed to the mint chip. "I have had a long day. Thankfully, it's over now."

"I have a feeling so are you and King."

I wasn't surprised he knew; he knew everything. He smiled a loving smile, far from gloating, and waited for more, but I didn't really know what to say. A long, comfortable silence later, he turned on the History Channel and we watched an episode of their latest reality documentary.

When Neo got home, he and I went downstairs, where I proceeded to tell him everything about the break up (minus King's mysterious brow cut). It was easier to talk to Neo than Aaram.

"I'll kill him," he said matter-of-factly. His muscles rippled in place.

I almost nodded my blessing. Instead, I leaned over to his side of the basement couch and playfully punched him in the arm, hoping to release some tension in the room. "He's still your friend, Neo."

"My friend? He's a. . . ." he sighed after struggling to find a word deserving enough that could be said in front of his little sister.

I laughed lightly. "Really, and oddly enough, I'm fine. I always knew he was a royal crap-face. It's nice to have it all done with and out in the open."

"I'm still gonna kill him, Lo."

"Let's dive," I suggested. "You look like you need to cool off."

Neo and I got back from our short dive just as Aaram pulled a late dinner from the oven.

"Smells good, Grandpa," I said as I dropped my bag on the counter. "Do I have time for a shower?"

"Sure, sure. This casserole needs to cool a little, anyway."

The hot water felt good. Not the same as the overwhelming, life-saving relief of salt water, but it was relaxing in its own way. I rested my head against the tiled walls and let the water rinse shampoo out of my hair.

I remembered the first day that Sam Legend asked me if I wanted to go swimming with him at his grandmother's house. Swimming in a pool would have been fine—it was salt water that changed my skin texture—however, if he knew I could swim in a pool, then the beach could be the next invitation. Against my pride, I had to tell him I didn't know how to swim. He begged all summer to teach me how. I tried telling him that I was scared of the water—it just made him beg more. I tried distracting him with other activities, but it was a hot summer and all he wanted to do was cool off in the water. I faked a lot of sickness and family outings to get out of his constant invitations to swim.

I smiled when I remembered the night we lay in the bed of his dad's yellow truck and watched the meteor shower. We were like that: comfortable; never romantic. We stared at the sky for hours. Every once in a while he would crack a lame astronomy joke. *What do you call a crazy moon?* He chuckled to himself before giving up the answer. *A lunar-tic.* He made me laugh; he always made me laugh, even when I didn't actually get the joke.

He was the only human that I ever wished I could tell our secret to. I wanted him to know what I was, and achingly, I also knew that wish was impossible.

When the water ran cold, I shut off the valve and wrapped myself in a towel. By the time I made it out to the kitchen, Aaram and Neo were finished eating. I microwaved a cold portion of the casserole and ate while they did the dishes.

Later, after the men had gone to bed, I pulled out an old shoebox from the top of my closet and sat on the floor, sifting through the first year's collection of my photography obsession. There were more pictures of Sam and me than I remembered.

When I got to the small section of my first trip to Belmont Park, the memories came flooding back. He gave me my first camera, one of the really old yellow and black disposable ones his mom found online. I was nine, and his mom invited me to go with his family to Belmont Park and ride the roller coaster. The two of us rode it over and over and over again. We took pictures of ourselves making funny faces in front of each of the eclectic booths and carnival-esque attractions. The last two shots were of the sunset around the back corner of the park. One of them had a silhouette of Sam's hand making a peace sign in the foreground. After months of grief over the deaths of my parents and sister, that was a very perfect day.

It was still dark outside when I woke up from the hard floor. I glanced at my alarm clock: five-thirty in the morning. Moaning, I flopped onto my bed, but try as I might, I couldn't fall back asleep. A leisurely change, teeth brush, and hair comb later, I headed out the door, ready to shoot a roll or two of film before school. *Might even have time for an hour or so in the school's ancient photography studio and dark room.* It had been at least a month since I had the chance to develop some film.

I tried the old Civic first, then huffed when the ignition turned like a sick camel.

The walk to the bus stop was peaceful except for the light on in Dagger's house. For a short minute, my curiosity interrupted the quiet, sleepy world resting around me.

I got on the bus with no idea where I was going. When it fatefully stopped at Belmont Park, I got out with a content sigh. Early morning joggers made their way up and down the boardwalk. After getting some great shots of the pier and the morning calm of the ocean, I turned the camera to the nearly desolate park grounds. It would be alive with people soon, but in the early morning hours, it looked calm and content, as if it were contemplating old memories just as I was. The welcoming, rickety wood of the vintage roller coaster was comfortable and familiar, like the wrinkled skin of a dear grandparent.

I took one last shot of the park grounds in the morning glow and then ducked into the only open shop—a coffee house. I took a chair by the window to watch the day begin. The joggers had multiplied, and business owners were setting up shop. The bell above the door tinkled as another customer came in for a morning cup of coffee.

A man's warm voice ordered a simple orange juice. I didn't turn from my window—the morning was too beautiful. I heard the storeowner finish the transaction with a "Here you go."

Right as I registered the familiar aura of Mr. Orange Juice, I heard the chair on the other side of my small table slide back. I turned, startled, and looked up as a tall, sweaty, smiling young man took his seat. It wasn't even surprising that he was here. It fit perfectly into this dreamlike morning.

Sam Legend.

At first, neither of us said anything, just sat and took in the moment.

"Hello, Haelo Marley," he said with a slight grin.

I didn't know whether to melt into the feelings of friendship that we had shared years ago, or to re-introduce myself to this *man* that I no longer knew.

"Hi, Sam." My voice was clear as a bell, though I expected it to crack.

He laughed quietly and looked into his juice. "It's been a long time."

"It has. How are you?" I asked calmly.

"I'm doing really well. Just finishing up my morning run," he said with confidence. His smile grew bigger. "And how have you been?"

"Can't complain."

"You look great," he said, sighing comfortably. He propped one of his ankles up on his other knee and leaned back into his chair.

Something about his relaxed demeanor flooded me with eager ease.

He cocked his head and said, "I think I saw you the other day when I dropped off a friend at her group project. You didn't look at me, so I wasn't sure if it was really you."

"Yeah, that was me. I didn't recognize you at first, not until later that day." I paused a moment, then added just as easily, "You look good, too."

He laughed a little and leaned in closer. His knowing, mischievous face looked for the real story. "So really, how have you been?"

Nothing new, still as candeon as ever. Did I not mention that before? Huh, must have slipped my mind. Oh, cheating boyfriend and I just broke up, so there's that. "Just school and... life, I guess. Neo graduated. He's working at the golf course. Aaram's mostly retired except for the lecture trips he likes to take."

"You're still taking pictures. I will forever remember you with a camera in your hand." He looked out the window, smiling, a distant look in his eye.

"What about you, Sam?"

He sighed. "Life is good. I went into the Coast Guard like my dad. My little sister Norah—I don't know if you remember her or not—is growing up fast."

He spoke like a parent. "How old is she now?" I did remember her. She was always twirling and doing somersaults in the Legends' front lawn.

"She's ten and really into dancing. I'm trying to keep up with all of her lessons and recitals." He laughed again. I liked it; there was something warm and inviting about the subdued sound. He continued, "I've failed miserably at being her practice dance partner."

He was a good brother.

"How's your mom?" I asked.

He dropped his eyes. My heart stuttered. Sam's mother, Ginger, was the sweetest person I had ever known. His expression made me nervous.

"My dad passed away last year. She's struggling. The chemo doesn't help."

Cancer? Widowed? I couldn't believe it. Everything I had read and seen about the perfect human family could be summed up by the Legends: a caring mom and dad who were very much still in love with each other, four happy kids, long family vacations, smiling faces. The only thing missing was a golden retriever. My eyes pricked with tears.

"But she's strong, she'll pull through. For now, she takes comfort knowing that my dad is waiting for her in heaven, whether she can join him soon or have a long life with her kids before being with him again."

He sounded almost at peace with such a devastating situation. He took a sip of his orange juice.

I tried to hide the sympathy that I knew he didn't need, but a tear peaked on the edge of my lower lid and fell to the table anyway.

"Hey, don't feel bad, Haelo. I didn't tell you all this to make you sad."

I tried to smile. He chuckled at my attempt and continued before I could come up with something to say. "My brother, B.C., is away at grad school on the East Coast. Amy got married a year after we moved from the old neighborhood and now lives in Boise with her husband and two kids."

I swallowed, testing whether my voice had recovered. "It's just you and Norah and Ginger?"

"Pretty much. My mom spends most of the week at the hospital; I try to take care of Norah. She's a handful, but pretty fun most of the time. I've reached my limit on bedazzling dance leotards, however." No wonder he sounded like a parent. He basically was. "I work a Coast Guard shift during the day and take online classes toward my degree at night."

"You sound like a busy guy . . . but happy. You really do sound happy, Sam."

"I try to be. Some days are easier than others." He looked toward the shop counter and then back to me. "Would you like anything?"

"Oh, no. I'm fine, thanks, though."

We sat in silence for a moment. More people scattered the pier now, the shops busier. He was the first to speak.

"You know, I've actually been thinking about you a lot the past few days. I saw someone on a rescue mission during a nasty storm a couple of weekends ago that looked like you. Scared me half to death." His voice trailed a little. "I'm glad to see you sitting safely here in front of me."

His tone was far too serious, like an eerie warning. Or was it a scolding? Or a reminder, maybe? I rummaged for something to say, trying to hide a blush. "Don't worry about me being anywhere near the ocean. I don't swim, remember?"

He laughed a little louder this time. "Still? I would have thought you got over your fear of the water by now."

I playfully shook my head over the distant sound of a bus horn. *School!* I jumped up from my stool. "Do you know what time it is?"

"Yeah, it is a little after seven thirty," he said with a glance at his watch.

I was going to be late. The city bus made a wide circle around to the school with multiple stops along the way, taking at least forty-five minutes.

"You look like you're in a hurry. I'd better let you go."

"It's just that the bus takes forever, and I have to be at school by eight."

He smirked and shook his head. "Can I give you a ride? Loma Heights is on my way."

I looked at him skeptically. My school was inland, not anywhere near a Coast Guard station.

He caught my look and amended, "Okay, not on my way. I definitely have time, though. I'd love to offer you a ride." He extended his arm, beckoning me toward the door.

I put away my camera and followed him out to where he'd parked his truck a little ways down the cracked sidewalk. We walked through the morning buzz in easy silence, like two old friends. I wasn't cold—I never was—but the sun felt good on my cheeks against the chill of the ocean breeze.

Like a gentleman, he opened the passenger door for me. The long bench seat was homey and familiar. I remembered the earthy, metallic smell of worms from the day that Sam's dad took us fishing on Lake Cuyamaca. The current air freshener looked like the same dark-green tree cutout that had been hanging on the rearview mirror that day at the lake.

Sam got in and started the engine.

"Thank you, Sam. You really don't have to do this."

"My pleasure, Lo."

A wonderful rush of nostalgia flooded over me. He and Neo were the only ones who called me "Lo," though Kingston had said it once, uncomfortably. Coming from Sam, it felt expected.

He pulled into the school parking lot before I was ready to leave. I wanted to stay and talk with him.

"Looks like I got you here early. No one's running for their classes."

I looked around the packed but groggy-looking student body congregating in the courtyard. "I found some old pictures of us the other day. It brought back a lot of memories."

"I'm not surprised. You were always taking pictures," Sam whined playfully. "You probably have hundreds of us. I remember coming home from spending the day with you and my cheeks would hurt from hours of making faces at your camera."

"It's your own fault. You were the one who gave me that first one."

He chuckled and then sighed. "That's right. I forgot about that. That was the day at Belmont." We both stared out the windows for a moment.

"I better go." I rested my hand on the door handle and paused. "Thanks for the ride, Sam. It's been nice catching up. Maybe we could catch up some more later?"

"Sure. I'd like that."

I didn't know what to do then. Ask for his phone number?

He interrupted my thought with a question. "Were you planning on walking home?"

I had forgotten that I no longer had nor wanted the chauffeur services of Kingston Soli. "Um, I think so." I tried to remember how long the city bus would take to get me home and whether or not walking would be faster.

"What if I pick you up? My shift today ends at three, and I don't pick up Norah from her after-school student council activity until five-thirty."

I smiled and picked up my bag. "That sounds great. Thanks again for the ride."

"You're welcome, Haelo Marley."

My classes dragged on and on all morning, each class moving slower than the one before it. The only thoughts that kept time moving were mysteries about Sam. It dawned on me in second hour that up until a few days ago, Sam had been dating Olivia Ortiz. *Wasn't that taboo?* A graduated, working man dating a high school girl?

I had to chuckle when I realized that the same question could have been applied to Kingston and me. At least I was only a year younger than King.

At lunch, Lauryn tried very hard to keep the conversation among our friends away from Kingston Soli. I reminded her that it didn't bother me at all; I felt so free and happy. Still, she continued steering the conversation and changing subjects that had anything to do with dating. I noticed Ashlee and Dean holding hands. They were good together. They fit. Dean absentmindedly stroked the back of her hand with his thumb while he talked to Tito about their government homework. When Dean caught me staring, I pulled out my camera to replace the film. My friends had already stopped bugging me about using my phone, or even a digital camera. They knew I preferred the surprises of real film. Or maybe I was just being stubborn. Or *vintage;* that sounded better.

Lauryn looked a little frazzled in biology when Mrs. Samuels announced a pop quiz. Throughout class, I kept snatching quick glances at Olivia, wondering what things Sam had liked about her.

I jumped from my trance when the bell rang. Lauryn asked me how I did on the quiz, but I honestly couldn't remember much about it.

I settled into my usual spot in the back row of choir and listened to a couple of juniors giggle about a new transfer student they met at lunch. Mrs. Snyder opened the class with some warm up scales and then pulled out a green folder from behind her podium.

"I have chosen the parts for the musical based on your solo warm ups from last week. I think we will have some great performances by many of you!"

My stomach tightened. I suddenly wished that I had tanked those warm ups. I should have suspected that she would use these as "auditions." I wanted nothing more than to melt into the background chorus.

"Michelle, you will be playing Anita. Trevor, you will be Bernardo. Van, you will be Officer Krupke. . . ."

I saw Van grimace; he had wanted the part of Tony. Mrs. Snyder continued down the list.

"Our male lead will be played by the newest member of our choir, Dagger." A few people clapped pathetically out of obligation; a few whispered to their friends. Some of the boys looked at him, surprised.

I couldn't see it. *Dagger?* Singing and acting on stage in front of hundreds of humans?

The girl next to me clapped and patted me on the back. I scowled at her. Looking around, I realized the rest of the class was also turned to face me, most of them clapping.

"Haelo, did you hear me? I said that you will be playing Maria, our leading damsel."

The girls in front of me nodded in encouragement. The junior girls in the front row stared me down. I could easily deduce what swear words they were thinking. When I finally realized that I had indeed been assigned to the part, I took a sheepish head-bow. *What was with this day?*

Mrs. Snyder handed out lines and music. She called Dagger over to come stand next to me, explaining that we would have to practice our lines and duets on our own, at least until dress rehearsals. This was going to be a long semester. Dagger scared me. The only time he'd ever spoken directly to me was when he yelled at me to go diving the other day.

He looked politely at Mrs. Snyder and assured her that we would get more than enough practice in before the big opening night. I glanced up at him, hoping he wasn't looking in my direction. When his eyes met mine, I shivered.

We didn't say a word to each other the rest of the hour. When the bell rang, I collected my things and made for the door.

"Haelo, may I have a word?"

Dagger's low, overly proper voice made the muscles in my neck twitch. I turned back to him and tried to smile. "Sure."

"I should have introduced myself earlier. I'm Dagger." He extended his hand forward in an invitation to shake.

I complied and suppressed another shiver.

"You're looking better. You looked, uh, nearly dead on Monday."

I chuckled nervously.

"I don't think it's very funny. You shouldn't have waited so long to dive."

I glanced around the room, checking for witnesses. "That's not really any of your business," I whispered sternly. I could not look him straight in the eyes.

He picked up his bag and gestured for me to follow him. Once outside, he held my elbow. "We don't need to talk about that here. We do, however, have an appointment with our scripts. I'll see you tonight? Your house. Seven o'clock." And he was gone.

I stood there, dumfounded, until Lauryn, Ashlee, and Dean caught up to me.

"What was that? Was Dagger Stravins talking to you?"

"It was nothing, Ashlee. Mrs. Snyder decided to cast us as counterparts in *West Side Story*."

"Dagger's in choir?" they all gasped in unison.

The three of them analyzed the new musical mystery of the school's bad-boy until the late bell rang for sixth hour.

He didn't show up in English or seventh hour study hall. I doodled on my notebook, thinking about how I would tell Aaram and Neo about Dagger coming over tonight. Surely they wouldn't mind a fellow candeon stopping by.

I walked toward the parking lot, trying to figure out why we had never really talked of him before, or even tried to get to know him. *Odd.*

I was deep in thought when my eyes flashed up to see an old, familiar Ford F150 idling in front of me. Every thought of Dagger was swept away by the anticipation of hanging out with Sam. I threw my hair back into a ponytail and headed to the truck. From his seat inside, Sam opened the door for me before I could get there.

"You've turned into quite the gentleman, Sam Legend."

"You can thank my mother for that." There was no sadness behind the mentioning of his sick mother.

"What are we going to do?"

"You have the final say, of course, but I was thinking we'd take on another round of that old roller coaster up at Belmont Park."

"Sounds perfect."

He pulled out of the parking lot just as Olivia Ortiz drove by from around the front of the school. Something told me that she wasn't as oblivious to his truck as she appeared to be. Sam sighed and shifted his weight.

The smell of the ocean breeze when I stepped out of the car at the Belmont parking lot made me hungry for another dive, but I ignored my headache and put on a very genuine smile. As we approached the old coaster, I couldn't help but think . . .

"So what happened with you and Olivia?" It slipped out before I could censor myself.

Sam wrinkled his brow and cast his eyes to the ground. He then looked to his left and put his hands in his pockets, avoiding my gaze.

"I'm sorry. I had no right to ask you about it. I don't know what I was thinking, it just sort of popped out."

"No, it's okay. I'm just not sure how I feel about it yet. I met her at the beach awhile back, and we hit it off pretty fast."

Really? There must have been a bikini involved.

"We started dating under very false pretenses—she told me she was a student at UCSD. I had no reason not to believe her. She's great with Norah; she made her a Halloween costume. And she's been to every one of her dance recitals. She once took Norah out on a girls' date to one of those tea party places—it was pretty cute to see my little sister all dressed up and excited. And my mom *loves* her. I had fallen for her—even thought about marrying her—by the time I figured out she lied to me about how young she was."

He was talking to himself like he was trying to replay an old dream. He sighed. "That was the beginning of the end. She's an amazing woma—uh, girl . . . no offense—but it was hard to get over the fact that she was still in high school. *And* she lied to me about it. Like *really* lied; fake major, fake classes, everything.

"I told myself to just step back, you know, wait until she graduated. So I did. I stepped back. A week later I went over to her house to make sure she was okay. We had never been apart for more than a few days at most; I wanted to make sure she was holding it together. It was selfish, I know, but I had to come up with an excuse to see her." His eyes narrowed. "I caught her with another guy. They were . . . well, passionate, to say the least." He attempted to mask his discomfort. "When you saw us fighting on Monday before your meeting, it was because she tried to apologize and start over." He kicked a stray pebble from the sidewalk back into the landscaping. "I don't think that is a relationship I can try again, even when she grows up."

My heart clenched in anger, and my chest swelled with an overwhelming need to protect Sam from any future betrayers. I wanted to punch Olivia in the face.

"I bet you've had much better luck than me in the dating department," he teased with a playful elbow to my arm.

"Not really." I grinned, though I had no idea why.

He squinted at me. "Now that my pity story is out in the open, do you want to talk about yours?" He smiled at the jab, facing me as he walked backwards.

My grin turned into a rather amused sigh. We could probably commiserate about being cheated on, but still, I couldn't tell him my story: not only did King cheat on me *with* Olivia, but I was also an underage high school girl who dated an older guy. I didn't want him comparing me to her. I wasn't ashamed or anything, I just wanted to avoid the comparison.

Sam could tell I was stalling. He stopped in the shade of a tall palm tree. "Never mind." He shifted his weight, looking around for a distraction. When nothing seemed to fit, he turned back to me and asked, "Well, hey, the roller coaster hasn't run the whole time we've been here. I bet it's closed. You want to go see my mom? I told her I ran into you earlier today, and she was excited to see how you've been doing."

It was almost as if we had never parted. "Sure, Sam. I'd love to see your mom."

5
SECRETS, SECRETS ARE NO FUN

It was nearly seven by the time I walked through the door into Aaram's kitchen, frustrated and confused as ever.

Sam and I had gone to the hospital, where we all talked and chatted and crunched on the pellet ice from the machine down the hall. It was hard to see Ginger so frail, her wispy hair dull against her gray complexion. Sam introduced me to the nurses as an old family friend—a blast from the cherished past. *A sister*, he had said. For that short time in room 302, I was a part of the family, and it felt so good. I teased Sam, he teased me, and we both teased his brother B.C. while he wasn't there to defend himself.

Then things got weird. Maybe it was one of those rebound things, but I found myself staring at his lips a little too much. Every time he'd nudge me with another joke, a part of me wanted his arm to stay there, maybe even wrap around my waist. *Stop it*, I'd tell myself, over and over. I definitely wasn't having sisterly thoughts. I tried to shake it off, but he'd give me these looks that made it entirely too hard.

He caught me staring and shifted uncomfortably, then mumbled something about a phone call and left the room. I looked to Ginger, who just smiled at me with her eyes and patted my hand.

"It's been so good to see you, Haelo," she murmured before closing her eyes. I kissed her forehead and walked into the hallway, searching for Sam.

I heard his voice from around a corner and stopped to shamelessly listen to his call. "I understand that but—. Yeah, yeah, I know.... Of course I like her, I wouldn't be doing this if I didn't. It's just.... What if I steer her elsewh—?"

I heard a *thud*. I carefully peeked around the corner and saw him leaning his forehead against the wall, staring at the floor and holding the phone to his ear. "Are you sure this is fair to her?" Another pause. "Then I'll do my best."

It sounded like the conversation was over, so I booked it back toward Ginger's room, in my rush almost knocking over a rolling cart near her door. I took the seat at her side and waited for Sam to enter.

When he did, it took him a good ten seconds to look at me. "Sorry about that. Didn't mean to leave you for so long." He glanced at his mom and sighed. "Looks like she's down for a nap. You ready to go?"

I stood and met him at the door. He hesitated, and then put his hand on the small of my back to lead me out.

The awkward vibe between us was nearly tangible. I had no idea what to think. I tried to tell myself his phone conversation wasn't about me, but paranoia crept into my thoughts. It was as if a switch flipped on our relationship, and I didn't miss that the phone call was right in time with that switch.

We drove in silence to the elementary school. Norah didn't seem interested in asking me questions, but instead recited to me all of the exciting things she was doing. Every proud moment in her monologue was accentuated with her admiring eyes looking to her brother for cheerful validation. Sam dropped her off at the hospital before taking me home where we clumsily chatted some more in his truck.

He was trying too hard. He even patted my hand like his mother had. *What is happening? This is supposed to be easy. It's Sam, for crying out loud!*

He got out of the truck when I did and hugged me at the curb. At least the hug felt real, until he kissed me on the cheek with pursed lips. "I'll see you later?" he asked with a smile. An ever-so-slightly strained smile.

I was super confused. Was this my fault? Did I freak him out when he caught me staring? "Later," I echoed.

Aaram stood over a frying pan with tongs, humming an old Billie Holiday tune; Neo sat at the counter perusing his phone. He raised his head discreetly to give me a piercing look. He mouthed the word *King* before I cut him off with a raised hand.

I'm fine, I mouthed back, *really.* I stretched out my shirt collar and fanned it back and forth. The kitchen was stifling. Images of Sam, King, and even Dagger rolled through my mind while I tried to cool down.

I put my hand on Aaram's shoulder. "Grandpa, I'll just grab a granola bar. Save me a plate? I have a meeting. . . ." I trailed off, trying to figure out the best way to say that my duet partner in the school musical was the mysterious monos candeon that lived down the street. The one who we had never tried to meet before. *And* that he was coming over in just a few minutes.

"With whom, Haelo?" Aaram could tell I was fishing around for something to say.

"Um, Dagger Stravins. From down the street. You know, the quiet candeon that—"

The tongs splashed into the pan with a simultaneous curse from under Aaram's breath. I watched the vein in his neck pulse as he ran his blistering fingers under the cold tap water. "Have you met with Dagger before?" he said pseudo-casually.

"No. We were just assigned this today. We're supposed to practice our duets for the choir spring musical on our own time. It's okay that he's coming, right?"

Aaram stared into the sink for a few seconds. "Of course it's okay."

An awkward, breathless pause held me captive until we were saved by the doorbell. I focused back to my senses, realizing that the boy behind the door was not Dagger. It was someone much more familiar than that. From the window, I could see the black BMW parked out by the curb. *Hell's bells.*

Neo's thunderous steps marched in my direction; he too must have sensed who was here. I swung the door open to a nervous Kingston.

"King." Seeing him brought me back to a comment Sam had made earlier. I knew who Sam had caught Olivia with—I was staring right at him.

Shoving me to the side, Neo forced the door open wider. "You've got to be kidding me. Turn around and get back in your car before I put you in it myself."

"I'm not here to talk to you, Neo. I'm here to ask Haelo why she wasn't around for our rides."

"You think she's going to want a ride from you now? Go away. You know, between douche-former-friend and *sister*, sister wins, every time."

King's hands went up defensively. "I don't know what you heard, but it's probably a stupid rumor. I've done a lot of thinking, and I just want to talk to Lo."

Oh, no. I couldn't tell if I was more shocked about his use of my nickname or more scared for what Neo might do next. Neo released a deep breath, dropped his chin back, and stared King down. He stood there—a solid wall of brotherly protection—as he slowly shut the front door.

"Sorry, Neo. I should have known better." I was about to say more, but we both felt Dagger making his way up the street. Neo backed away, clearly not over his anger with King and in no mood to deal with another situation.

I didn't wait for him to ring the doorbell; I opened the door while he was still walking up the stone path. "Come on in, Dagger."

Instead of coming into the front room like a normal person, he stopped just inside the doorway, inches from me. I was used to being taller than everyone around me, so it was a little disorienting looking up at him.

He looked down, studying my expression. I was suddenly hyperaware of the beads of sweat in my hairline. Before he could assume any more than just exasperation on my part, I turned away and headed into the family room. He came in behind me and took a seat on the couch.

"Welcome," I said, throwing my hands up and slapping them back onto my legs. "Sorry about being such lame neighbors. We should have reached out earlier. I don't know why Aaram didn't mention it before."

"You call your grandfather by his name?"

"Um, not to his face. It's complicated. We haven't always lived here, and we didn't know him before we came. We just—"

"Haelo, are you going to introduce me to your friend?" Aaram said with a firm hand on my shoulder.

I blushed. "Yes, Grandpa, this is Dagger Stravins. He's playing Tony in the school musical. I'm Maria."

"West Side Story?"

"Yes."

He paused and stood up straighter than usual, eyes on Dagger. Neither of them broke the stare as Grandpa Aaram continued to talk to me. "Where do you plan on practicing?"

"We don't want to bug you. We'll practice in the basement if you want." The basement was just a few old couches, a computer desk, and the usual musty basement smell.

"No. Up here is perfect. I'd love to hear you practice."

Something told me it wasn't the music he was interested in hearing. He held both of my arms in his hands, kissed me on the forehead, and then walked back into the kitchen.

Dagger watched me with a weird expression. I quickly realized that my own brow was furrowed in confusion, and he was simply trying to figure out why. *Something is up with Aaram.* Between Sam, King, Aaram, and now having to spend time with Dagger, my brain wanted to explode. I shut everything off except the task at hand.

"Your grandpa seems very...."

"He is. Sorry about that. He's probably just worried about me because of something else."

"Someone else, you mean."

"Oh." I hesitated. "You heard the conversation at my front door?" *So much for shutting off.*

"Yes. I didn't mean to eavesdrop. If you ask me, you are much better off without him—he's kind of a neddy." He smiled at me and, for the first time, he appeared likeable. I had never noticed that his irises were a cool gray, which looked striking against the dark, midnight blue pupils that all candeons have. I was trying to pinpoint where I had seen similar eyes when he asked where a CD player was.

"Yikes, I don't think we have one. As you can see," I said, pointing to a wall covered in shelves of old vinyl records, "Aaram, I mean *Grandpa*, is even more vintage than CDs, and Neo and I just use our phones. We'll have to go downstairs to the desktop."

I had already started for the stairs when he asked, "Are you sure your grandpa will be okay with that?" He thumbed back toward the kitchen.

"Grandpa! We've got to go downstairs to the computer in order to play the accompaniment CD!"

I waited for his alternative solution to the problem. After a long pause, he called back, "Fine."

Dagger's eyebrows lifted. "Easy enough."

We headed downstairs. *Maybe Creepo's not so creepy,* I thought. He was being much friendlier than I'd ever given him credit for. With each step, I grew more and more hopeful about finally getting real answers to the hundreds of itching questions that I thought would never be satisfied. Was he a monos? What was it like? Where did he come from? Why had he pretty much ignored us up until this point? How old was he, really?

"Should we just get started?" I asked, leaving the opportunity open for conversation.

"Sure. I should probably let you know that I don't like singing."

I stopped. "Wait, what?"

"I *can* sing. I just hate singing in front of people."

"Why would you sign up for choir if you hate to sing?"

"Long story."

He didn't offer any other explanation. I raised my eyebrows and moved to the computer desk. Dagger handed me the CD and then stood in the middle of the room holding his sheet music. I took my place in front of him as the music started. He fidgeted with the page, missing his cue.

I stopped the disc. Sam, Aaram and King had already dazed and confused me—I didn't want a fourth downer.

"Dagger, if you're not ready, we can do this another time."

His chiseled posture twitched.

"Sorry, I didn't mean to be so blunt." A half-truth.

"No, it's okay. I'm actually more worried about you." His voice was nothing if not sincere.

"About me?"

"I know what happened the other day when you hadn't been in the ocean for what looked like weeks. I even came by that morning."

I sighed and collapsed into the couch. I remembered the knock at the door and the bellowing voices. So that *was* Dagger. "It wasn't weeks. I'm just . . . young." I was getting sick of all of the reminders about my age. "And I got distracted."

"The headaches, your eyes, muscle weakness.... You had every symptom, clear reminders to dive. You didn't get distracted." Though he remained calm and was graciously avoiding the well-deserved *I told you to dive*, he was definitely overstepping his bounds. I could feel myself getting defensive.

"Excuse me? What gives you the right to lecture?"

He sat down opposite me and clasped his hands in front of himself, leaning forward over his knees. He looked up, staring at me like I was the child, he the parent. I didn't move. I had no idea why, but I felt completely subordinate to him, and though his stare was uncomfortable, I could not look away. I was a kid waiting for my punishment. Waiting. Waiting.

He stood.

Flabbergasted, I watched him march back upstairs, two steps at a time. I jerked into motion when I heard him arguing with Aaram.

By the time I reached the top of the stairs and was within earshot, all I caught was Dagger saying, as if in a stern reminder, "How am I supposed to do that if—"

"Haelo?" Aaram called. "Please come in here."

I stepped slowly into the kitchen. Something about Dagger's last words sounded all too similar to Sam's phone call. Dagger looked at me; Aaram looked at Dagger. Dagger exhaled, folded his arms, and shifted his eyes back to Aaram just as Neo came in.

"What's going on?" Neo asked. No one answered.

"Grandpa? What's going on?" I reiterated.

He fluttered his eyes. "Haelo, there is some history here. You will be tempted to ask questions, to get to the bottom of it. I promise that eventually you will know everything. Now is not that time. Dagger will give up the part of Tony, and you are not to be around him for the time being. Now, Dagger, please leave."

I glanced back and forth between the two of them, painfully aware that I was missing something.

Dagger unfolded his arms, still staring at Aaram. When it was clear that Aaram was not going to change his mind, Dagger stepped out, brushing my arm on his way to the front door.

The door shut with a thud. It took me a few breaths before I could face Aaram. "What is going on? What are you not telling me?"

Without flinching, Aaram reached out, held me by the shoulders and repeated, "Now is not the time." Then he walked out.

I went to bed early that night, though I didn't sleep. Neo had confessed that he didn't know anything either, but tried to be supportive. I had never been so furious with Aaram. Flustered, I lay in bed trying to distract myself with some bluesy New Orleans music. When that didn't make me feel any better, I tried indie folk rock, then good old-fashioned Nirvana. Not even my girl T-Swift could clear the angry cloud from my head. Eventually, I threw my phone across the room. What I needed was a dive.

Crossing my fingers that Neo and Aaram were asleep (so they wouldn't sense that I was gone), I stuffed a swimsuit into an old tote. Sometimes candeon abilities were a nuisance. Since my bedroom door usually creaked, I snuck out the window above my bed, carefully dodging the thorns of the manicured bushes. The old stray cat meowed loudly. *Sorry to disturb your zzzs, little guy, but this is important.*

By the time I made it to the sidewalk, I had already changed my mind. Instead of heading west toward the beach, I turned east. Twelve houses later, I found myself standing on Dagger's porch, shaking. Whether from fear, excitement, or anger, I didn't really care—it didn't change the fact that Aaram and Dagger knew something that I did not. The only thing that mattered at that moment was getting the truth out of Dagger. The plan for how exactly I was going to do that was as of yet unformulated.

You could start with ringing the doorbell. I waited for my arm to reach through the dark, but it just hung hesitantly at my side. *What am I doing here?* The door opened before I could talk myself out of this crazy mission.

"Hi, Dagger?" I could only see his silhouette in the darkness of his home. "I'm really sorry to bother you. Could I . . . please can I—?"

"Come in, Haelo." He turned and walked away. I followed. He flipped a switch, flooding the large room with light.

The high walls were covered in original art. There were no chairs or couches, just bare wood floors. Some of the art were architectural watercolors and pen drawings, some bright minimalist paintings, some charcoal sketches; there was even a large, symmetrical pattern like something you'd see in a kaleidoscope made out of what appeared to be brass thumb tacks pegged into purple-stained wood.

I faced Dagger where he stood in a short archway. He wore a white t-shirt and gray jersey knit pants. For a guy who wore a lot of gray, his art gallery living room certainly pulsed with color.

He ahemed.

I shook off my stupor and smiled at him. "Aaram would probably kill us both if he found out I was here."

"You don't mean that."

"He'd definitely be irate." I giggled a nervous laugh, then continued more seriously. "I don't know where else to go for answers. There is obviously something going on that involves me, and I've been up all night trying to put pieces and clues together. I don't even know where to start." I'd lost the nervous shiver that started when I walked up his lawn. I felt strong.

"Come with me." He walked through the small archway into a sitting room that opened up to a large kitchen.

The room was immaculate. The light above the stainless steel gas stove was on, along with the lights underneath the upper cabinets. Copper and steel pans hung above the marble kitchen island. Herbs grew underneath a large window that stretched up to the high ceiling. The floors were the same warm wood from the front room and continued back into the sitting room, where a small white couch and stuffed chair sat around a large coffee table made from a smooth tree stump. On the table was a bowl of oranges. Sliding glass doors led out into a backyard. The moonlight cast dancing shadows from the greenery into the room. I was taken aback.

"I don't know what I imagined, but it definitely was not this," I muttered, then looked at the wall behind me. There was a chrome tiled fireplace that glimmered in the moonlight. The black whispers of old smoke curled up the back of the tile, remnants of previous fires. There were no photos on the mantle, just moss growing in planters and a large white canvas with the beginnings of a man's portrait sketched onto it. Weathered, with a dark, wrinkled face and a scruffy five o'clock shadow. The wisdom in his black eyes was humbling.

"There's not a whole lot I can tell you without your grandfather's permission." Dagger had folded his arms high across his chest. He released them to gesture me toward the couch; he sat in the chair across. "But if you word your questions carefully, there are some things I am allowed to say."

"Will you be honest?"

"Any answer that I am allowed to tell you, I will tell you truthfully. If I cannot answer your question, I will tell you that, too."

"Can we start with how far back this history goes?"

"That depends on where you start the story."

"How about wherever it starts to involve me."

He paused. "For tonight, I think your birth is a safe answer."

I took another deep breath and stared into the empty fireplace. Dagger got up and placed two logs on the grate, followed by a handful of kindling from a basket on the floor. Then he pulled out some matches from behind one of the potted moss plants. The match hissed when he struck the box. He lit the kindling and asked, "How much do you know about candeon history?"

"Not much." The more I thought about it, the more I realized just how little I knew. "All I really know is that my parents and little sister died during a rebel fight in the Pacific. Neo and I got separated, then somehow managed to escape and meet up again."

Dagger's eyes pinched somewhere between a grimace and a smile, making me even more unsure of my past.

I continued hesitantly, some of my statements sounding more like questions. "We were taken to our grandfather, Aaram. I was nine, Neo was eleven. I don't know what the rebellion was for and I don't know how it ended. I don't know how I escaped. I don't even know who or what the rebels fought against. It's all a blur. The few things I do remember... I've tried really hard to forget." I fought back the distant memory of my little sister Tilly being ripped away from my mother's grasp; other candeons surrounding us; everyone screaming in each other's thoughts.

I shook off the horrible image and came back to the present. "I don't know anything." I sounded terribly ignorant. I could not remember ever being told where we came from, either. I must have asked, but was never given a direct answer. "Where do candeons come from?"

"From the Mediterranean, originally; no one is sure exactly where. The legends say Greek witches cursed us. Whatever the case, sometimes it seems a curse, other times it seems a blessing—for me, anyway. *I* think we date back farther than the Greeks, but that is where the records begin. We've migrated and evolved to specific regions. There are some in the

Arctic, in the Caribbean, everywhere. There was once a clan living deep in the Marianas Trench." After seeing my quizzical look, he explained, "They evolved to be able to tolerate the pressure and darkness. They had huge eyes, no ears, and their skin was translucent. They only surfaced a few times during their lifetime, always at night. It was quite painful for them. But they've since died out."

I could tell this was going to be a long conversation, so I fell back into the cushions of the couch and pulled my knees up. "Where are you from?"

"The Indian Ocean. Off the east coast of South Africa."

"So you're not a monos?"

"No. Who told you about the monos?"

"My brother said something once . . . about you."

He laughed at that. Though my world was spinning, something about his manner made me feel safe.

"Technically, no, I am not a monos. Generally speaking, candeons live in ancestral clans—we are a very familial species. Monos, named after the Greek word for 'solo,' are candeons who choose to leave their families—their homes—and travel alone, not ever conforming or attaching to any group or tribe. They claim no purpose other than to travel and learn all that they can from anyone that they can, at least from a distance. Hermit hippies, really. Though you could call them lonely anthropologists."

Something about his casual, matter-of-fact tone made me acutely aware of the fact that Aaram, Neo, and I did not live in a clan. We didn't belong to any tribe. "And you're not a hermit hippie lonely anthropologist?"

Again, he laughed. "No, I am not. They are not very well known; I'm surprised your brother knew about them—even the most traditionally educated candeons usually don't."

"If you're not a monos, then where is your family?" As soon as I said it, I wanted to take it back.

Almost imperceptibly, his eyes flickered in pain. He breathed, "They have passed on."

I sat in silence with him. I had never thought about Dagger Stravins' personal life before. He was just the rogue mystery guy at school who everyone avoided. Hot guilt coursed through my veins as I thought about how lonely he must be. "I'm sorry, Dagger."

"It's okay. I have accepted it. It comes with the job."

"What job?"

"Southern African candeons are a big part of the military special forces behind the Candeon Empire. We're called the *Krypteia*—again, an ancient Greek word which loosely translated means an elite army. We've had to survive in dangerous, shark-infested waters for so long that we've become the biggest, strongest, most alert candeons in the oceans. We're the Spartans of the sea, I guess. My parents died, as humans say, in the line of duty."

I thought about that for a second. Guilt again rushed through me, this time accompanied by sorrow. I wondered how long ago they died, but I knew it was not the time to ask. I pictured a fierce army of shark hunters in Greek armor. When that mental image morphed into the glistening, bloody Spartans I'd seen in a movie, I shook it off and replayed what Dagger had just said. What duties was he talking about? "What are you doing in San Diego?"

"I cannot tell you that." His face was unwavering, like a marble statue.

"Who are you working for? Aaram? This Candeon Empire you mentioned? Does that mean there's an emperor?"

Again, he didn't move. I decided to go backwards to an easy question. "How old are you?"

"Isn't that impolite to ask?"

"You can't play that card."

He winced. "Twenty-three."

"No way. You're at least twenty-eight."

"I told you before: I will give you an honest answer to any question that I am allowed to. Remember, I said that candeons from my homelands east of South Africa are big."

"Big? You're a man-hunk."

He shifted uncomfortably, furrowing his brow, but kept his smile.

"Why don't you have an accent?"

"Also part of my job."

And back to the job thing. The more frustrating his answers were, the more curious I became. For a moment I got sidetracked thinking about how soothing the pellet ice from the hospital would be to chomp on, which lead to thoughts of Sam's mysterious phone call. The heat from the fire was starting to smother me. *Why on earth would someone tile a fireplace in chrome? It's exponentially radiating the heat!* I took another deep breath and exhaled into the hot, crackling room, acknowledging that heat radiation was probably the point.

Dagger must have noticed my discomfort. "My apologies. Would you like me to put out the fire?"

Yes, I want you to put out the blazing gates of Hades that currently reside in your furnace of a fireplace. "Whatever's good for you."

He scrutinized me before getting up to fill a pitcher with water from the sink. He poured a steady drizzle over the log, sending hissing steam into the already humid room. Most of the fire went out, though in a few places the log still glowed in warm, red flickers. The orange glow from the doused fire mingled with the blue moonlight and the soft under-cabinet light of the kitchen, lighting the room more than I expected. Still, Dagger turned on a lamp. The room cooled down quickly.

"Can you tell me whose house this is?"

"It's mine."

"It's nice."

"Thank you. Though I don't deserve any credit for its niceness; it came that way."

This line of conversation—out-of-place pleasantries—wasn't getting me anywhere. I moved on. "How did you get into high school if you are twenty-three?"

"My career comes with resources." It was a very carefully worded answer.

"How long have you been in San Diego?"

This question had him stumped. I could tell he was warring with himself to come up with an allowed response. Finally he admitted, "Two years, give or take."

"How come I didn't know about you until last semester? Where exactly do you come into the story?"

He stared into me, willing me to take back the question. "You are tweaking with the terms of my contract right now," he said playfully. "I can only partially answer your questions. There's more to it than I can say, so please . . . don't feel weird about it."

Well, now.

"I came into the story a long time ago when I was just a child, but not in the capacity I currently fill. I didn't come to San Diego until I was requested to replace another *kryptes*—a soldier in the Krypteia. I was told not to let you know about me until last semester."

The word 'kryptes' sounded familiar. "So you're here because of me?"

"I told you not to feel weird."

I didn't change my quizzical stare; instead, I waited for my mind to catch up. Finally, I blurted, "A shark-cohabitating, semi-monos, art-loving, chiseled South African Spartan has been ordered to stake out and secretly—what, watch me?—for the past two years? I'd say you lowballed it a little with 'feel weird.'" My words were harsh, but I didn't feel upset. In a strange way, I felt protected, not stalked. I softened. "I am an awkward orphan with no special abilities or qualities. I am weak and stubborn, a very frustrating combination, by the way, and have no money or powerful information. What could you possibly be doing here with me?"

"You are not weak. You are a strong young woman. Don't forget that." His eyes were fierce and unwavering. I didn't realize that I had stopped breathing until he relaxed his head to the side and added, "Though you are quite stubborn sometimes."

I exhaled. "I don't feel very strong. Stubborn is not strong."

"You are. You just have to find it."

He got up and walked to the back glass doors. The night sky grew violet in color; dawn would soon break. Without looking back to me, he said the last thing I wanted to hear. "You need to go. Your family will be up soon."

It was like leaving a movie right after the first plot twist. It was unfair. Still, I couldn't say no to Dagger. I may have gotten to know him a little better; however, knowing that he was a member of a powerful military force made me feel obligated to concede to him even more. I stood, smoothed out my wrinkled pajama pants, picked up my neglected dive bag, and headed toward the front room gallery. I was leaving with more questions than I had come with. My quiet world was crumbling, yet in Dagger's home, I felt safe. What would happen when I left?

"Thank you, Dagger," I muttered as I reached for the door handle.

He was right behind me. "Don't mention it. *Really*. Your grandfather would not be happy if he found out about this."

"Would you be in trouble," I hesitated, then continued, "with your boss?"

"Not really. Just Aaram." The last comment had an added emphasis, as if he was trying to tell me something. Aaram was not his boss. Yet, was Aaram the only one keeping me from the truth? "You are welcome in my home any time—though it is necessary that it stays on the down low."

I hesitated in the entrance, not wanting to leave, then gave in and stepped out into the dark, indigo world. The sky was lighter in the east. When I looked left, westward toward Aaram's house, the sky seemed darker than necessary. Not foreboding or scary. Just dark.

Before I left the porch, Dagger added, "Haelo?"

I turned to face him.

"Good morning."

"Good morning, Dagger."

6
TURNING AND TURNING IN THE WIDENING GYRE

I barely made it into my sheets when I heard Aaram's morning alarm blare from the far room. I lay in bed thinking about all that had transpired during the past few days. It was a menu of disasters: running into Sam and praying he didn't recognize me from the storm; dating my older brother's best friend; my body's breakdown and subsequent rush to the beach; the fight between Aaram, Neo, and King; our break-up; hearing of King's cheating exploits; learning that my own grandfather was keeping secrets from me; and then a covert mission in pajamas to stalker-Dagger's home to fish out the truth. I was a magnet for self-humiliating situations. Thinking about it made me sweat.

I kicked off the sheets, which didn't help. Even my hang-out with Sam had felt different than it should have. I still didn't quite have a handle on what happened at the hospital, nor with Sam's weird phone call. Frustrated, I headed for a cold drink.

I half-expected Aaram to pretend as if nothing had happened. When I walked into the kitchen, however, he was seated at the table staring blankly at a glass of orange juice with puffy, tired eyes, his hair sticking out in all directions. If I had not been so hurt by his secrets, I would have felt sorry for him.

"You don't have to go to school today if you'd rather stay home. I would understand." His words were raspy and quiet.

"If I stay, are you going to tell me my history?" I asked.

"No, Haelo, not now. Be grateful. You'll know soon enough."

His warning should have scared me off, but I'd had it. If he was going to play this game, I was going to play one of my own.

"Okay." I grabbed my backpack and headed for the door.

"Haelo, listen to me," he pleaded in defeat. I waited. "Please." He beckoned to a chair. I stood taller. His lips turned up in a pseudo-smile as he closed his eyes and nodded his head. He continued somberly, "Soon your world is going to irreversibly change, and when it does, you will want to be here. You need protection."

"What is that supposed to mean? If I'm in such danger, why do I dive alone, whenever I please? Why do I go to school? Please, be honest with me!"

He stood up so fast the chair slammed into the back wall. "I can't!"

In all the years I had known him, Aaram had never yelled like that. For the first time in nearly a decade, I was genuinely terrified. I lowered myself into the chair across from him.

I mustered a controlled voice. "You can't? Or you won't?"

Pinched, his eyes pleaded with me.

I swallowed. "Thank you for trying to keep me sheltered. Neo and I have been happy here, despite what happened to our family. I will forever be grateful to you. I love you . . . so much." My eyes pricked with tears. I dropped my head and heard him sit back down. I took a small breath—whether to stall or gather courage, I wasn't sure. With surprising certainty, I declared, "I need to know who I am and where I come from." I looked up. "And I need to know whatever it is that you are so determined to keep from me. After all that's happened, you can't hide it from me any longer. Are you even my real grandfather?"

Aaram furrowed his brow in offense. "Of course." He sighed and looked out the window at a bird sitting in a tree branch. It cocked its head and eyed him, as if it were listening to every word we said.

I waited. He was going to finish, not me.

"You are the daughter of Jade and Ana. Ana was the daughter of your grandmother Anhaela and me."

"I already know this, Grandpa."

"Then you shouldn't have questioned it."

I was not going to apologize—I had every right to question him! Something was going on! Again, I waited for him to continue.

"Jade was an orphan, originally from the Atlantic waters of Europe, I think. I don't know much about his childhood, other than that for a time he was raised by humans in Hawai'i. He was a fine young man, one of the best I have ever known. Ana was clever, and so beautiful. She had this glow about her. She was as sweet as your grandmother and had a contagious laugh. She could laugh about anything. Just being around her made your day feel lighter and your burdens seem . . . trivial."

I replayed the few memories from my childhood. I should have remembered more; most of them were gone. I remembered some carefree days in shallow Pacific reefs, exploring natural coral mazes and rock caves. Sure, we lived in the water most of the time, but our occasional family day trips inland were magical. I remembered a family hike up what seemed like the world's tallest mountain. Eating butter rolls and pie for the first time from a small bakery near the shore. Us kids asked for human food almost daily after that.

I remembered mom's laugh and the Eskimo kisses before bed. Our secret pinky handshake. I remembered Dad's slender, freckled arms and reassuring smile. I remembered sitting on the front of his orange and white surfboard; he'd smirk and call it "dry-diving." I remembered how we used to fall over and laugh at the end of every family hug. Mom pretended to hate that. She also pretended not to know that it was Neo who intentionally knocked us over every time.

Aaram handed me a napkin. I had just as many tears on my cheeks as he did. I stared into the wet makeshift tissue in my hands, stroking it with my thumb.

"Why didn't we know about you? I didn't even know I had a grandfather until after they were gone."

"I loved your mom, and she loved me. Things got complicated when you were born. It wasn't safe for you to be associated with me."

I was getting more confused. "I thought you said that I was the one in danger. It's because of you? You're in danger?"

"No. You were. You are. I mean, you will be." He got up and moved to the chair next to me. He sighed, then took my hand and held it between his stiff palms, not rough, but like dried, smooth jerky. "This is a lot for you to handle. We can resume this talk later. Would you like to go to school to get your mind—"

"Grandpa, I need to know. Please."

Neo crept out from behind the family room wall and shrugged, sheepishly admitting he had been listening. He sat with us.

Aaram took one of Neo's hands as well. "If I promise to tell you everything, first can we enjoy one last day of uncomplicated time together?" He pulled us both so we were all standing. With his arms flung around our shoulders, he walked us into the family room. We sat on the couch and waited while Aaram fished through a cupboard under the TV and pulled out a small box of old family videos.

Neo nudged me and tilted his head toward the TV. I sat back into the comfy cushions. I should have demanded the conversation. But honestly? I was scared. "All right, Grandpa. One day."

Aaram put the first disc in: a video of the morning of our first day of school, only weeks after coming to live with him. I had known he was filming that day, but I'd never seen the video. It was shaky. Aaram sounded a lot younger, and nervous. Neo and I were standing in front of the very same bookshelves still sitting in the family room. I had a messy ponytail (that had taken Grandpa four attempts) and a yellow and purple backpack, and Neo was wearing shoes he was obviously not used to wearing, fidgeting awkwardly. But he stayed close to me the whole time while Aaram talked us into not being too scared for school. The young me looked to the young, chubby Neo every few seconds, desperate for security.

We went through video after video, watching ourselves grow up. Some of the childhood moments I hadn't remembered at all. Some I very much remembered, but had no idea Aaram had filmed. I hadn't thought he was that kind of grandpa.

We watched for a few hours, snacking on fruit and bagels, until Aaram ran out of discs. There hadn't been a lot, but there was enough to remember the years.

Neo got up to stretch. "I say we go to the beach."

Aaram and I nodded simultaneously.

A few rounds of beach volleyball with a handful of local surfers, a late lunch of grilled hot dogs and potato salad, and a quiet bonfire a hundred yards away from a group with ukuleles later, the sun began to fall toward the horizon. The videos and spontaneous beach day had prepared me for what I knew I had to ask Grandpa Aaram. I still felt scared, but it was time.

I wasn't quite sure how to bring it up. I looked up from the fire into Aaram's awaiting gaze. He knew.

"Come here, Haelo, Neo."

We scooted our camping chairs closer. Toes digging into the sand, I rested my elbows on my knees and waited for Aaram to start.

"Haelo, you have a unique bloodline. As you already know, all candeons have a patch of scales on their lower back. This is called a *mosaiko*. Most English-speaking candeons call it a mosaic. You've noticed that Neo's, King's, and my scale patterns are all different?"

I reached back and rubbed the spot where my pattern—my mosaic—would soon be. Grandpa continued, explaining what I already knew, but I didn't stop him.

"Every candeon is born with their scale pattern; it fades away after a few months. It returns after the transition into adulthood. As you know, they are hard to see when dry, but if the light hits them right, you can just make out the pearlescent hues and patterns. They are much more obvious in the water."

I thought about his previous question. "And everyone's is different?"

"They are all unique but follow general patterns according to your bloodline. Neo inherited your father's. Both you and Tilly had Ana's. Ana inherited mine."

"So my pattern will look like yours?"

"Kind of. My mosaic is the noble pattern. You are part of the nobility."

My spine straightened, though not out of fear. "Is that why I will be in danger?"

"Yes."

Something was not right. "But you said you weren't."

"It's not because of your pattern—that will be like mine. Your coloring will not."

My coloring? My eyes shifted back and forth between Aaram and Neo.

"Haelo, most candeons' scales are a rainbow of pearlescent colors, like an oil slick. Yours will be iridescent blue."

"I take it this is more of a big deal than having red hair?"

He chuckled slightly, his features smoothing. "Yes, it is." The fire cackled and popped, sending an ember near Neo's bare feet.

"What does it mean?"

"It means that you are special. It also means that you do not get to control your life." He sighed, "It's already planned out for you. And there's nothing that you or I can do about it."

I could handle the danger and the anger and anything else that had worried me up until that point. But not controlling my own fate? For nine years I had lived in the United States of America. I was told over and over again in school and on TV that I could be anything I wanted to be. I had dreams. It hit me that Aaram had never spoken of that freedom; he had never given me the Land of Opportunity pep talk.

My voice caught. "And this plan for my life? Is that the danger you spoke of?"

He smiled a crooked, unreassuring smile, despite his hopeful eyes. "No. The plan is the best way to keep you from danger."

I couldn't tell whether or not he believed his own words.

I didn't know what to think. Maybe ignorance *was* bliss? No. Not bliss. Ignorance is ignorance. Knowledge is power. Wasn't it?

I no longer felt comfort from the warmth of the fire. I sat back, trying to distance myself from the heat. Or maybe from the conversation.

"Come with me." Aaram beckoned to a cluster of wave-worn rocks in the tide. Neo stayed at the fire just a few feet behind us.

I sat down on a rock with my feet in the water. The chill radiated up my legs as if my body were a sponge. It felt so good, and I hated it. For the first time in my life, I wished I were human. I wanted my biggest problem to be how much homework I had—I'd even take boy-drama with a smile. I laughed out loud when I remembered that I hadn't done homework in days. It startled Aaram. When he saw my *to heck with it* smile, his face changed to concern.

He sat down next to me and picked up a small, smooth stone out of the shallow water. The wrinkled skin of his hand tightened as it absorbed the salt water, toughening up like the thick, sandpaper skin of a shark. He played with the stone a little before tossing it into the mellow surf.

"I suppose we should start at the beginning."

I raised my head into the fading sun and shut my eyes.

"A lot of candeon history is not much more than legend. No one really knows our genesis, though it is generally accepted that we came from the Mediterranean. Most of us still look Mediterranean. We were once a powerful people, with clans, families, and tribes all over the world, our numbers matching those of the humans.

"Every era has its end, though. Ours was horrific. There was a civil war, and it finally ended just before our extinction. A few families survived in some remote places, but we never returned to our golden age." Aaram looked into the sunset before rallying the strength to continue. "There is a royal bloodline, and from that bloodline we have always had a *Basileus*, or ruler. An emperor of sorts."

My breath grew shallow as I anticipated where this was going. I heard Neo approach, taking a seat on the rock right behind me.

"Your scale pattern does not mean you are our next *Basilessa*."

The butterflies in my stomach bit me. I didn't want to rule a species, necessarily, but I did feel a strange disappointment.

"We'll come back to that. About two hundred years ago, the kind, beautiful Basilessa Kalas died, leaving two sons. This should not have been a problem, because the ruling line is passed down based on the royal mosaic: much like the noble pattern of many royal descendants, but larger, with metallic gold differences. It was the younger son, Prince Agothos, who had the royal, gilded pattern. The older son, Kryos, was just another noble. Kryos claimed, however, that their mother had wished on her deathbed for the eldest to be the new Basileus. It was an unheard of notion to have a noble—not the destined, marked royal—as the ruler. Very few sided with the eldest son, and it seemed to be a fleeting scandal that would die out quickly.

"Here's where it gets complicated. A ruler must marry and produce an heir with the royal mosaic for the royal bloodline to continue. A few years after Basileus Agothos' marriage, a daughter was born with the royal pattern. The court rejoiced; that is, until three years later, when the eldest son publicly announced a child of his own, also having the royal pattern. This had never happened before, two heirs at the same time—our world turned upside down. Bickering, fighting, even violence. The Council tried to keep order and support Agothos, but members began to turn on each other. Eventually, Basileus Agothos heeded terrible advice and enlisted the help of an elite warrior candeon from the southern waters, a *kryptes*, to murder Kryos' child."

My heart skipped. In my head, I imagined a massive soldier walking away toward a far cradle, stalking like the assassin he was. I forced my mind back to the present before my imagination showed Dagger as the soldier retreating from the silent crib.

"You can imagine the shock that rippled through our world. A respected ruler had ordered the death of an infant. Nobody knew whom to support. Basileus Agothos continued on in the confusion, ordering the *Krypteia* warrior clan to protect and enforce the authority of his monarchy. It wasn't hard to convince them; Agothos' father, Basilessa Kalas' husband Tomak, had been raised by the warrior clan.

"The war that ensued nearly wiped out our species. Our numbers were completely decimated. Agothos won—if you can call it winning—forcing Kryos and his supporters to flee into hiding. The few that survived lived in relative peace for decades, almost two centuries." He smiled longingly into the tranquil past. "And then you were born."

The only thing I could do to keep from shaking was squish my toes in the sand. Maybe I thought that if I kept at it, the next part of the story wouldn't be as crushing as I knew it would be. My toes curled over the watery sand so hard that they cramped, a welcoming, distracting pain. My part of the story had not even started, and yet . . . I held my knees, curled and bent.

Neo came closer, sitting so his leg rested against mine. Grandpa Aaram put his arm around me. He kissed the top of my head, speaking quietly into the breeze. "Remember when I said that a new ruler must marry and produce a royal heir? Well, that marriage must be to a noble. It needs to be a very specific noble, as only a specific combination of the royal bloodline and these certain nobles will produce a royal heir. That noble—the destined spouse of the ruler of the candeon world—has an iridescent... blue... noble mosaic. She, or he, is called the Galana."

I froze, hyperaware of my exposed lower back peeking out from the bottom of my shirt. *What?* It didn't make sense. Nothing about this story felt right. So I was the Galana? Meant to be the bride of an emperor? The bride of a stranger? My thoughts went wild with images of a ridiculous underwater pearl palace. I pictured that future, suffocating in the customs of an ancient people. *No. No-no-no-no.* And I still didn't know what this had to do with danger and secrets and civil war.

"Grandpa, you said that a Basileus has to have a royal heir. What if they don't?"

"Apparently, if a Galana has a child with a noble *descended* from royalty, that child could very likely be royal, as in the case of Kryos. That is why the monarchy works so hard to ensure that the Galana is protected. Haelo, you will be a monarch, and the mother of the future ruler."

I tried to let it sink in. I'd always wanted to be a mother. My mother was such a strong part of me; I wanted to share that connection with my own children. But I had never imagined I wouldn't be able to choose my own husband. "They can't make me."

"Haelo, you don't have much of an alternative."

I sat up straight. "I can think of a few!"

Aaram shook his head, his penetrating eyes showing the hard truth.

"Grandpa... I can't... I don't think I can—"

He held me tight. Neo took my hand. Though his grip was gentle, I could see the muscles and tendons in his forearm flex. I couldn't fight the shaking anymore. They sat by my side until the tide started to come up.

"Do you want to dive?" Aaram offered.

"No. I don't want to be a candeon." I sounded like a child.

"You can't run from it, Haelo. It will find you. Wherever you go, you will always be the Galana."

"What if I wasn't anymore?"

"You can't change who you are."

"What if I never dove again and let myself dry up? Then I'd never be forced into marrying a—"

"Haelo, you don't mean that."

That was the second time in the past twenty-four hours that someone had said that to me. He was right. I could not do that to myself; I had neither the courage nor the morbid stupidity to commit suicide.

I felt sick.

I flinched at my earlier disappointment when Aaram told me I was not a Basilessa. I wanted nothing to do with it.

"Who am I being protected from?"

"The rebels descended from Kryos; the same rebels who killed your parents all in an attempt to get to you, thinking you might be the next Galana. They've waited a long time for Kryos' bloodline to be the acknowledged rulers. The longer they wait, the less likely their descendant will produce a royal."

"Why me? Why not another Galana?" The word felt like poison on my tongue.

"There isn't another Galana. You were born the very same night that the future Basileus was born, as always. There won't be another Galana until you give birth to the next royal. Even when both Agothos and Kryos had royal heirs, there was only one baby Galana: she, born the same day as Agothos' child. Again, the rebels are tired of waiting. They know that there will never be a spare Galana. They want you before you are under the complete and total protection of the monarchy."

"You said that two hundred years ago there were two heirs. How can that be if there cannot be two Galanas?"

"There can't be. Think about it. It would not be the first time two brothers loved the same woman."

My world was spinning into a soap-opera.

"If she had another child, wouldn't Agothos think that the second child was his own?"

"The second child, a son, had the gilded royal mosaic with many markers inherited from Kryos. As I said before, mosaics are similar and link large groups of families together, but the intricate details are inherited directly from parents. It is very easy to tell one's parentage—no DNA test required. Agothos knew right away that his wife's son was also Kryos' son."

"He had his wife's son murdered? His own nephew, the half-brother to his daughter?"

"Yes. Tragically, Galana Vespa, (Agothos' wife), was shamed, disciplined, and locked away. Years later she escaped to Kryos, and they had another child, a daughter. The rebels no longer have a royal to support, yet they insist that the bloodline of Kryos and Vespa will and should be the rightful royal line. If you were to conceive with one of their noble descendants, there is a chance that your child could have a royal mosaic."

Sex ed. took on an entirely different meaning. Forget the birds and the bees talk; my grandfather was talking to me about conceiving with rebel fugitives. *Change of subject. Change of subject.*

"If I am so important, why didn't the Basileus throw me in a locked tower years ago?"

Aaram smiled at my candor. "The midwife who delivered you told only the monarchy that you were the Galana. Your father did not grow up with candeons; he felt no obligation to the candeon throne. He didn't understand. He could not hide you, so he pleaded on your behalf and came to an agreement with the Basileus. The Basileus would allow you to be brought up by your family, to be educated in human knowledge, to experience a life free from the complications of being a Galana. The monarchy would not interfere or let you know about your fate, and would offer their silence and protection at a distance, in exchange that you not fight or run when the time came for you to be brought to the royal courts. It is a binding promise. Your parents agreed to the best possible compromise they could hope to be offered."

Aaram reached out the arm that had held me and rested his hand on Neo's shoulder. "So they took you both to the reefs of the Hawai'ian Islands and continued on as a happy, normal family, until the day that shattered everything and you came to live with me. Haelo, the rest of the candeon world does not really know that you, in particular, exist. A few have inquired about you two—I just tell them you're adopted. Neo, your scale pattern takes after your father, Jade. Jade is dead, so they cannot compare yours to your father's. You'd have to look very closely to see any markers from my scale pattern on yours. There are no obvious indications that you two are blood related to me, at least for now. Adoption is an easy sell. And Haelo, if you're adopted, then you're probably not noble, and you couldn't possibly be the nine-year-old girl the rebels thought they killed those many years ago in Hawai'i."

It stung the way Aaram so casually mentioned our dead father. "The Basileus lets you just . . . hide me? I go to school; I dive all the time! I am not exactly hidden, let alone protected."

"Sometimes the best hiding spot is in the open. The monarchy has had a watchman nearby from the beginning."

"Dagger."

"It wasn't always Dagger. Before, it was someone named Etulo. Dagger came about two years ago. Though I am sure that is not his real name, at least it doesn't sound like a warrior clan name."

The way he said "warrior clan" clashed with the sophisticated Dagger I had spoken to the previous night. Apparently these Krypteia warriors were much more domesticated than their reputation suggested. I remembered the murderous monster of my imagination stalking toward an infant's crib and shuddered.

"Dagger is here to protect me?" I asked. I already knew the answer.

"Yes. He is here to make sure you are not discovered and taken. Or that you don't run away."

Running away had been building as a viable option for the past half hour. I pushed the thought down, knowing that I could not run from Dagger. Something told me he'd find me in hours, if not minutes.

Neo piped up for the first time. "What if she fell off a cliff or got hit by a car?"

"That is an interesting question. Both legend and history have shown that the royal bloodline and the Galanas are somehow mystically shielded from danger. All of them but two have died naturally, despite the many attempts on their lives."

"And those two?"

"First, Kryos and Vespa's pseudo-royal son. No one knows how Agothos' kryptes was able to kill the child. Perhaps because the boy was a second royal heir, the protection normally surrounding royals was weakened. Agothos was the second unnatural death. He died when he . . . dried up. As you so delicately put it."

"That's why you were so angry the other day. I can dry out. My only weakness almost killed me." For a split second, I toyed with the notion that I could do anything dangerous without fear of mortal harm—until Aaram interrupted with an addendum.

"I was angry, yes. But did Agothos die because his body could dry up? Or did he die because he committed suicide? No one really knows which of those is the exception to a royal's death. Agothos *did* commit suicide. He could not live with the pain and guilt that had consumed his life. But he picked a long, horrendous way to die, which makes me wonder if he had tried other ways unsuccessfully. That is why I believe, though I am unsure—so don't try anything stupid—that staying out of the oceans is your only mortal weakness."

I thought about the morning when I dropped to the floor, utterly deteriorated. I did not doubt that being away from the ocean for too long would kill me. I knew it could. It almost did.

This day had been a rally of emotions: I went from an empowered granddaughter, to a slave to my own fate, to a practically immortal being. Well, a practically immortal being that was also a slave to my own fate, at least.

The sun had set. I could see the misty exhaust of cars passing on the highway. We sat in silence, watching the surf come in and out. I thought back to Christmas break when I was just another normal (albeit non-human) teen going through the motions of everyday life. Bing Crosby's Christmas album played in my head as I wished, even prayed, that I could go back and enjoy that Christmas a little more. Christmas. Family. Nativity. Carols. Candy canes. Twinkling lights. *It's not such a bad little tree, Charlie Brown.* It *was* a wonderful life, and I had taken it for granted.

I couldn't go back to the way things were. Aaram was right to warn me about demanding the truth. Ignorance was a twisted bliss. Each day used to be another day forward; now each day was a countdown. I was a ticking clock. Neo was seventeen when he transitioned, and I would be eighteen in a week. My birthday was like a big red check on a small calendar. It was not a celebration, but a marker of impending imprisonment.

Aaram had once told me about transition. He said it was completely painless, physically not such a big deal. He said there would be night sweats and hot flashes for a few days, and then one night I would just keep sleeping. After hours, sometimes up to two days of sleeping, I would wake up with my mosaic on my back. I would be stronger and more capable of enduring extremes. I would be better attuned to sensing life forms at farther distances. I would not have to dive as often. And now I knew that I would be hauled away to another life.

"Who is he? The Basileus?" I whispered into the darkening night. The sky was a deep, royal purple.

"Basileus Alcaeus. He is a good, wise man. He is stubborn and stuck in his ways, but he is fair."

"How do you know?"

"That is a conversation for another day. I think you have enough to think about."

For the first time, I agreed with him. "He sounds... old." I double checked my memory of our conversation: *Aaram said we were born on the same day, right?*

"He is. Father-in-laws usually are."

I sat up straight. "I thought you said—"

"You are to be the wife of Griffin, Alcaeus' son," he said tenderly. Neo tensed.

"They sound like Greek gladiators."

"They are kind and compassionate. Griffin especially. He is a little spoiled, maybe too used to his life of luxury, but he has a good heart. If I thought that you were headed into a life of misery and pain, to be married to an evil man, I would risk running. But it will be a great life. Imagine the good you can do. This is an opportunity, Haelo." He cleared his throat. "Not only that, but frankly, you are too important to the monarchy and therefore the ultimate survival of our species. We've experienced civil war; another one would kill us off completely. Your marriage will ensure continued peace for our people. Hiding you away would only make things worse."

"You make it sound like we are on the brink of chaos. For the past nine years, I've come across a whopping grand total of six candeons besides you, Neo, and myself. How many of us could there possibly be to even participate in a civil war?"

"You'd be surprised. Not many, but enough. Isn't that the point? There aren't enough of us left to live through war. You've probably noticed that humans are a lot more fertile than candeons. We don't populate quickly. Your parents were able to have three children, but that is by no means commonplace."

Something made Aaram pause. "Did you say six? Who besides Kingston and Dagger?"

"There were Kingston's parents. And there was a guy in the park once, right after we moved here."

"What did he look like?"

"He was sitting down. He had a dark, curly mullet and a long tattoo down his arm. I told you about him at the time, and you told me it was nothing."

"Ah, yes, that was Etulo. His definition of 'distance' was infuriatingly flexible. And the other?"

"Two years ago. I ran into King when I was photographing the pier. He was there talking with a short, pudgy candeon at an outside café table. I said hi and King introduced the man as his parents' old friend here on business. He was the first outside candeon I had ever talked to, so it was definitely noteworthy, but you had left that morning for one of your lecture trips to Colombia or NYU or something. I forgot to mention it."

I could tell it was eating at him, but Aaram tried not to bother me with his concerns.

Neo shuffled. "I saw King with an older woman once. She was definitely candeon. And she looked super-sketch, now that I think about it."

I nudged his shoulder and grinned at his go-to phrase for all things suspicious.

The three of us watched as the last hint of purple gave way to a black night. Aaram rubbed my back and hummed a powerful tune. I'd heard it before. His simple voice was quiet and strong, making the melody even more beautiful and humbling. I waited until he finished before asking, "What is that song?"

"Your grandmother used to sing it to your mother and your Aunt Olesa when they were kids. It's a lullaby. Your mother probably sang it to you, too." He picked up where he left off, singing into the night.

Eventually a park ranger pulled into the lot and asked us to leave. The drive home went faster than I wanted. I wasn't ready for the quiet ride to end—there was something cathartic in the productive hum of an engine. We pulled into the garage, and Grandpa Aaram left Neo and me in the car. He said I could take all the time I needed.

I stared at the empty ignition, pondering what I could have done if he had left the keys. Did I have the courage to run? I didn't know what the Basileus and his elite Krypteia police force would do. Would Dagger harm my family? I looked at Neo in the back seat, pleading for answers to questions I was unable to ask.

Of all the people in the world, Neo was the only one that I truly trusted. No matter what happened, he would love me. Violent tears gushed from my eyes as sobs convulsed my chest. He got out of the back seat and opened my door, pulling me out into a hug. I held him as tightly as I could. Everything that I had experienced up to that point in my life I had gone through with Neo. Now he was consoling me over the first thing I would have to go through alone. I clung to him, willing his arms to stay tight. He let me cry on his shoulder for a few minutes before he leaned back to look at me.

"Lo, I wish I could take it all away."

I smiled through a sob. Most other brothers would say sorry—Neo didn't have to. Some might even try to say that it wouldn't be that bad—Neo was different. He hugged me again. I pulled back, wiping away the tears on my face. He didn't joke about the wet, slimy mess on his shirt.

We finally went into the dark house. The kitchen smelled of lemon cleanser. Neo sat down at the table and offered the chair next to him.

"What am I going to do, Neo?" I asked with my face in my hands.

Without any hesitation, he sputtered, "Let's run. Let's go somewhere no one can find you. We'll pack fast."

Again, my eyes pricked with hot tears, knowing that my brother was willing to sacrifice his life in order to free mine. "I can't do that to you. I can't do that to Aaram."

"We could punch 'em in the face. Then maybe he wouldn't want you for a wife."

I snorted a laugh through my tears.

It was an unsolvable problem. I remembered Dagger, the watchman down the street. He seemed sweet. How could such a person be okay with ripping a girl from her family? Aaram's words replayed over and over again: *You are too important to the monarchy and therefore the ultimate survival of our species.* Dagger was just doing what he was told, and what he was told was in the best interest of everyone . . . except me.

Except me.

7

CHECKED

Angry water crashed all around us. Mom and Dad told Neo to keep Tilly and me in the underwater cave with him. Neo protested. He wanted to help fight.

Dad held Neo's shoulders to look him in the eye. *Stay with your sisters. They need you.*

I knew that we couldn't hide in the dark cave—the bad people would sense us. I curled my arm around Tilly. Mom winked at me. *Be strong, Haelo, we'll be back before you have time to worry.*

And then the dream faded away.

The sun played shadows on my eyelids. I cracked them open. The bush outside my window danced in the wind; the sun watched from behind the leaves, peeking out with every gust to check on me.

Something didn't make sense—the sun didn't belong there. I looked at my clock and realized I had slept all the way into the next afternoon. I could feel the sun's heat through my blanket. My neck was sticky with sweat. I stretched and yawned, pulling my legs out from under the stifling covers. It had been years since I'd had that wretched dream, that hated memory. I had tried so hard to forget the last day with my parents. At least this time the dream didn't continue into the horrific ending that I never wanted to remember.

I jumped when my phone buzzed on the dresser, a rude jolt back to reality. It was a text from Lauryn wondering why I had skipped school the day before. I responded that I just needed a mental health day. I noticed a text from Sam as well: *You up for a show tomorrow night? The hospital is having a talent show and my sister is dancing.*

I didn't reply. One confusing hurdle at a time. And now that I knew my time in San Diego was very limited, I shouldn't be nurturing any sort of relationships, anyway.

Out in the family room, Aaram and Neo were eating cereal on the couch, streaming old Kardashians episodes. Aaram liked to pretend that he watched reality TV for the ethnographic study of it all. I knew the truth. He liked it.

"Saturday morning cartoons, Lo?" Neo never smiled at his own jokes.

"Come on in. We saved you a bowl," Aaram said, and handed me a bowl of Raisin Bran and a half-gallon of milk.

"Cereal for dinner, Grandpa?"

"For us, late lunch. For you, sleepyhead, this is breakfast." He didn't even look away from the screen to say it.

At first I was offended, and then overwhelming gratitude enveloped me like a warm blanket. Aaram and Neo were giving me a normal, lazy day.

For the next six hours, I did nothing but watch frivolous television and snack on processed food. Whenever my daunting future tried to rear its ugly, intimidating head, I pushed it away with a judgmental comment about whoever was on the screen. Eventually, Aaram got up and went to bed. Neo dozed next to me, the occasional fluttering snore sneaking out of his open mouth. He slept like an old man.

Around nine, my bubbled evening popped. I couldn't shake off thinking about Prince Griffin. Every girl has fantasized about becoming a princess. Some might even call me lucky. But I didn't feel like I'd won the lottery. I was a sacrificial mule. I hoped and prayed Griffin was kind. Was he understanding? Was he smart? Did he only know wet life, or had he ever lived on land? Would I be trapped, or would I be given certain liberties? Was he tall and handsome, or more on the Rumpelstiltskin end of things?

Neo bolted up from his slumber. "Haelo, go get Aaram," he ordered, looking east as if staring through the walls into a far off distance. He faced the front door, and held back a hand to prevent me from moving past him.

I hurried back down the hall to Aaram's bedroom. "Grandpa! Wake up! I think someone is coming." Before I could shake his shoulder, he shot out of bed and grabbed a robe, pausing at his bedroom door.

"What's going on? Who is it? Do you know them?" I sputtered. I was sweating with anxiety. My senses were not as perceptive as Aaram and Neo's adult senses.

"Shhh, Haelo. Nothing to worry about. Your brother sensed Dagger coming down the street and got defensive. Dagger will not touch you. He will not take you. Calm down." His tone was peaceful and warm.

I took deep breaths, willing myself toward bravery instead of terrified uncertainty. *One, two, three, four. . . .*

I startled when Aaram chuckled. "It's okay. Lauryn is here. She beat Dagger to the door." He smiled at me from across the room.

"And Dagger?" I asked.

Aaram's smile wavered as he started to explain, but I didn't really hear it; his voice sounded muffled in my ears. From the underbelly of my panic, I wrestled a strand of courage. I could hear Dagger making casual small talk with Lauryn in the family room. With an air of confidence, I joined them. The time for self-pity was gone. Besides, what would Dagger do in front of Lauryn? For the next few moments, I had the advantage, and I would not let Dagger see my fear.

"Lauryn! I am so glad you came!"

"You are?" She twitched her head at my exaggerated greeting.

I intended to ignore Dagger until Lauryn left. But seeing him standing in our family room, not a watchman warrior come to take me away, but a young man that had talked with me until the wee hours of the morning just a few nights previously... the anger that I had stoked during my walk down the hallway melted away. I wasn't scared of Dagger. I wasn't even mad at Dagger. I couldn't be. He was doing his job.

Dagger's eyes gently probed with curiosity, kindness. I glanced up to the ceiling in an attempt to prevent possible tears from falling.

"Am I missing something here?" Lauryn looked back and forth between Neo, Dagger, Aaram, and me. "Haelo, we had movie plans, remember?" When no one moved or said anything for an excruciatingly long moment, she muttered, "I'll come back later." Her retreat back to the door was beyond awkward.

I wanted to let her know everything was okay, but I was a terrible liar.

"Lauryn, I'm so sorry." I followed her to the entryway. "I completely forgot. Neo and I crashed on the couch today with a bag of Cheetos and some mint Milanos. It must have slipped my mind." She looked suspiciously at Dagger, so I added, "I asked Dagger to come by and practice for the musical."

He smiled at Lauryn from the family room.

I continued, "He's kind of embarrassed about practicing in front of people—don't ask."

She smirked, and I felt validated.

I took the opportunity to sneak in, "You'd think he would have thought about that before signing up for choir. Can we talk later?"

I knew it was rude to blow her off, but she reacted gracefully. At that moment, I could have told her everything. I could have shouted from the rooftops that I was a freaky water person who was about to be carted off as the princess bride to the heir of the underwater throne. I needed her to make some smart aleck comment. We could talk about my life like it was just another plot to just another movie; we could critique it and giggle out loud over the pros and cons of being a betrothed-mermaid-future-baby-momma; we could sit on the counter and make cookies, coming up with elaborate story twists while eating big pinches of raw dough. I could picture her pointed finger announcing, "The plot thickens! And we're gonna need more chocolate chips."

Back in reality, she smiled graciously, tipped me her understanding yet cheeky nod, and turned to leave, grumbling something about missing out on a Pepperidge Farm sin-fest. On her way out, she called back, "You could have at least saved me some Cheetos!" and slammed the door.

I turned back to Dagger. "What can we do for you?" It was a sincere question. My tone could have softened a little.

Neo quietly maneuvered between Dagger and me. It wasn't very subtle in a room as tense as this.

"Is it safe to assume that your grandfather has told you everything?" He gauged Aaram's reaction when he asked me.

"I believe so. He's told me enough, anyway." I glanced at Neo. His stare alone should have carved a slice from Dagger's concentration, though Dagger didn't seem too fazed. I stepped forward to get Dagger's attention, asking again, "What is it that we can do for you?"

His solid stance shifted a little. He was clearly uncomfortable. *Good.*

"You didn't go to school yesterday. I came by to—"

Aaram cut him off. "To check on you, Haelo. He wants to check on you. Show him your back, please."

I understood. Dagger was making sure I hadn't "matured" yet. I turned around slowly, lifting up the back of my shirt. I felt violated and sick to my stomach, humiliated. I was getting checked. I half expected a pat down and an "empty your pockets." My hands started shaking, and I spun back around. Neo looked away, trying to compose himself.

"See, she's still a youth." Aaram's calm exterior cracked.

I looked up enough to see Dagger. It was obvious that he did not enjoy this. I would even venture that he looked at my back for only the split second required. He looked almost ashamed. To my astonishment, I felt sorry for him.

He kept his head lowered. "My deepest apologies. I am only doing what I have been asked to do. In no way do I take this violation of your trust in me lightly." He turned to me and dropped his voice. "Haelo." He paused, as if not knowing what to say. Eventually, he sighed, his eyes dulled with what I could only guess was regret, and walked to the door.

"Wait!" I called. "Wait, Dagger." I caught up to him. Holding my head high, I asked, "What will happen when I do get my scales?"

"I hope that you will tell me as soon as it happens. We'll make preparations, and then I'll escort you to Pankyra."

"Where is that?"

"In the middle of the Aegean Sea. It's the seat of the Candeon Empire, where you will live."

Heat rose in my chest, though I wasn't angry. I calmed my breathing and asked, "Can they come with me?" I didn't have to point to Neo and Aaram.

"If you'd like. For a while." With that, he walked out into the night.

I stood in the doorway thinking about my choices. I didn't have a whole lot. It felt like they diminished by the day.

Time was ticking. I admitted to myself what my subconscious had been hiding for a week. I was almost there. Hot flashes, heat strokes. I was fighting one right then. It could happen anytime. I doubted that I would make it past my eighteenth birthday.

Funny how perspective changes with circumstance. I wanted to call Lauryn; I wanted to live up every last hour I had; I wanted to dive with Neo and laugh with my friends. I wanted to have a heart to heart with Aaram. He needed to know how much I loved and appreciated him. I wanted to take a thousand pictures and give each one special attention during the developing process, adding a handwritten caption and a sigh of approval. I wanted to feel the deep pulse of music, the warmth of the morning sun in the desert, and as much as I hated it before, I wanted to feel the sensational zip of live wires when I walked into a crowded mall or school or theater. Would I ever be around humans again? For the first time, I wanted to be one of them.

But I couldn't. It was time that I faced that.

"Neo? You want to dive?" I didn't even turn around to ask.

"Are you sure?"

"Yes, I'm sure." I still faced out the open doorway. It had been a few days since my last dive. More importantly, I would need my strength if I was going to transition.

"I'll grab my shorts."

We took Aaram's car out to the harbor where a few couples were making out along the docks. A knot in my stomach twisted up into my heart—love was a key part of the future I had intended to have. I allowed myself a moment to imagine it. My love and I could walk up a pier at sunset, holding hands. We could go on road trips just to see what was at the end of every highway. Maybe he would even propose on a remote island beach.

It was all perfectly cinematic. When the daydreaming got too painful, I shut it out, reminding myself that I already had a fiancé. The word was an anchor. I did not want to fear it, but that didn't mean I was excited.

All that was left of my emotions surrendered to defeat and a hope for the best.

We made our way out to the farthest marina slip where the yellow lights along the walkway washed my skin in a strange hue. Water sloshed lightly against the cables, buoys, and docks. At the end of the last, deserted slip, I pulled off my jacket, shirt, and pants, readjusted my swimsuit straps, and lunged off of the damp dock.

The cold water seeped into every pore. My body could taste the salt. Fuel, trash, and pollution poisoned the shore, but they would fade the farther out I went. All I cared about was the cold, metallic, salty rush. My headache melted, my eyes cleared, and my skin tightened like the strong, sandpaper flesh of a shark. The relief was overpowering. I stroked furiously through the surface currents to the controllable depths below.

Neo caught up soon after. We took off around a kelp forest and into the open ocean. I coaxed the current faster and faster, scaring away any sea life in our path.

Lo, you're kind of freaking me out right now. Can we stop a minute and talk?

I pushed harder. It felt like a dry run at escape. Only when I exhausted my energy did I stop, slumping to the sandy, rippled ocean floor.

Neo came up beside me, suspended a foot above the floor bed. At first he didn't say anything. Then he sputtered, *Lo, get it all out. Tell me what you're feeling. You've got to be near explosion. There's no way—*

I'm fine, Neo. The last thing I needed was to be told how I should feel. My blunt remark silenced him. He leaned back.

Why are you pushing me away?

Because. My throat throbbed. *It's happening no matter what. I don't get to cry and yell and be angry. I did that; it got me nowhere. Please let me deal with this with whatever dignity I have left.*

He lowered himself to the barren ocean floor beside me. *We're a team. We stick together. I promised Dad that I would always look out for you, and I intend to keep that promise.* His freckled, serious brow let up a little. *You sure you don't want to run?* He smiled, trying to hide the very real question in a playful joke.

I looked him straight in the eye. *No.*

It didn't satisfy him. *No, you don't want to run? Or no, you're not sure? You know what I mean.*

He still didn't look convinced.

Something piqued his interest before he could persuade me further. He looked westward, straining his eyes to see through the dark water. I looked as well, but my sensing abilities were not up to par with his adult skills. My watered vision could see farther than I could sense, so I looked instead of trying to feel for who was coming. I could see a half dozen sea lions, and farther out (though distant and vague), a family of grey whales. There were even a couple of leopard sharks schooling a few hundred yards behind us toward the shore.

We should go, Neo thought to me.

What is it? I can't tell.

Two candeons, and they're coming fast. Come on. Let's get home.

A few days ago this would have been a welcome occurrence. Now, the prospect of meeting new candeons did not sound very smart. It shouldn't have been a big deal— it's not like I had scales to hide—but Neo seemed so sure of himself that I didn't question him.

We turned back toward shore. I must not have been going fast enough because Neo kept insisting that I hurry. My senses sparked at the candeons behind us, though not enough to get a good reading. I stopped, waiting for them to get closer. One of them seemed familiar. Before I could place him (or her), the erratic sparks of their auras faded. The duo must have changed course.

I know one of them, Neo. Who was that?

He shook his head, so I whined a little more.

It was Kingston. I wanted to get out of there before you had to deal with that, too. You've got enough on your plate.

I didn't care about King, but I was rather curious about who was with him. He never mentioned other candeon friends before. Who could it have been? I was almost positive that I had never met the other person; the aura didn't feel familiar at all.

Back at the harbor, Neo climbed up the dock and reached back to pull me up. He pulled so hard I that I almost knocked him over.

"Dude, Lo, watch it!"

"*Dude*, Neo, I'm not the one built like a gorilla."

"Whatever," he said, grinning as he rubbed the top of my head.

"Hey, watch the hair!"

It felt good to be teased—it was proof that I wasn't getting special treatment just because he felt sorry for me. To top it off quite nicely, he nudged me into the guardrail. I smiled.

We collected our stuff and headed to the car. I caught Neo peeking at a black sedan pulling out of a distant parking lot. I squinted through the darkness. Inside were a handsome, tousled King and an older man.

"Just get in the car, Lo."

I got in and turned on the A/C. Neo gave me a nervous look; it wasn't very often that temperature change bothered candeons. It was even rarer that a cold January car would feel hot after a Pacific night dive. *Hot flashes*. I practically cursed the thought, then casually turned the A/C down and hoped Neo didn't notice. He didn't talk the rest of the drive, though his minute fidgeting gave away his anxiety.

At home, he went straight into Aaram's bedroom. They both came out before I even made it to the hallway.

"Haelo, are you feeling okay?" Aaram asked with folded arms.

"Yes, Grandpa, I'm fine. If Neo told you something about the air conditioner, I just thought it would help me dry off."

They both looked wary and unconvinced, but did not fight me on the subject further.

Back in my room, I couldn't settle down. I tried reading, listening to music, even cleaning my camera. In truth, I didn't want to sleep. I didn't want to transition. I figured it wouldn't happen if I never went to sleep. At three in the morning, exhausted, I crashed on the bed.

Stay with your sisters. They need you. Dad's voice was clearer this time, like the dream was getting more vivid.

Be strong, Haelo. We'll be back before you have time to worry, Mom said before she and Dad took off into the violent water.

Though the cave would not hide us from the bad, scary people, it did shield us from the chaos outside. A loud thud shook the cave ceiling, loosening rock and frightening eels from the crevices. The brutal thrashing of opposing currents outside our den created churning waters that would be hard to control. If the fight forced us out of the cave, we would be stuck in aerated suspension, unable to get away.

Another thud. This time Neo had to duck out of the path of a falling rock. The world shook. I held Tilly tighter and tighter and tighter. . . .

8

A Walk in the Park

"Haelo, wake up! You're having a bad dream."

With a gasp, I sat up straight, fighting to calm my heavy breathing. I released my pillow.

It was Tuesday. The past three nights were all the same. I'd tried for years to forget that cave, that fight. A whole lot of good it did me. Sweat dripped down my neck. Aaram sat on the edge of my bed, his hand on my forehead.

"You're burning up. Are you ready to stop trying to hide it and admit what's going on? Haelo, you are maturing. You'll be an adult any day now."

I took the orange juice from his hand and gulped until it was gone. I didn't answer him. Instead I got out of bed, muttering, "I'm late for school."

For two days I had tried to go through the motions. We went to church, we had family dinner, I went to school, had a movie and game night with Lauryn . . . I even did some homework. Useless, pointless, worthless, homework. Anything to escape my thoughts.

I had graciously backed out of the hospital talent show with a text to Sam about already having plans. His reply—*Some other time then?*—left me uncertain how I should respond. I couldn't say yes, then continually back out of his plans. I couldn't say no with no explanation, either. It was a predicament that required an honest conversation which I knew had no chance of ever happening. I ended up sending a lame, —*Yeah, sure.*

At school, Mrs. Samuels reminded us that the first phase of our group projects should be wrapping up. I tried to pretend that I cared; I knew I would not be around to present the project, anyway. Olivia and Hans were less than thrilled about my attitude—Lauryn had to talk them out of a mutiny. I didn't care that it bugged Olivia. In fact, all of the hate over my betrothed predicament now redirected onto Olivia. It felt good to be angry, even better to be angry at something that didn't matter.

Though Dagger was in most of my classes, we only interacted in choir, making it both the best and the worst part of the day. Singing was nigh impossible—I was relieved when Mrs. Snyder didn't ask us to sing the super lovey duet. Standing next to him made me detest who I was. Yet, at the same time, I was with someone who *knew*. Every time we parted ways, a rush of relief and anxiety clashed in my chest.

Now that I knew who he was—who *I* was—Dagger no longer felt obligated to Aaram's demand that he back out of the part. When I suggested we both back out since we might not be here for the performances in six weeks, Dagger said it would look suspicious and that I wasn't a very good liar when it came to explanations. So, I encouraged the understudies every chance I got.

The final bell rang, flooding the halls with students. I lingered a little to avoid the masses, then eventually made my way to the parking lot where Aaram would pick me up. His car wasn't there, so I sat on the curb, waiting.

"Haelo?"

I was so caught up in my thoughts that I didn't notice Dagger coming up behind me.

"Oh! Hi." There was not much more to say.

"I called your grandfather. May I take you home?" His voice was soft. I just nodded.

We walked down the length of the parking lot to a lifted, dark blue Tahoe in the back row. It was at least ten years old and showed a lot of wear and tear.

"Clementine has seen better days, but she's reliable. The guy who sold her to me was a park ranger in Bryce Canyon."

"Clementine?"

"The name came with her as a condition of sale." He smiled. When I didn't reciprocate, he stepped forward and opened my door.

I had to pull up on the courtesy handle above my head in order to lift myself into the seat. The interior was very clean. It even smelled like citrus. The floors were vacuumed, the dash dusted. Only a small bag of dried cherries cradled in a cup holder. Dagger put his book bag in the back, then stepped into the driver's seat. The truck thundered to life.

"Clementine is an awfully feminine name for such a loud diesel."

Dagger released a sigh. "I was nervous you wouldn't talk to me," he said. When I returned a stone cold face, his eyes dropped. *Momentary victory.* I grinned when he glanced at me a few seconds later. We both laughed, though his was a little hesitant.

"I don't hate you, Dagger. You're just doing your job." I wasn't scared to look him in the eyes anymore. He, however, seemed to be avoiding mine.

"I am sorry about the other day. It must have been humiliating to lift the back of your shirt to prove to me that you were still a youth."

Nice one.

He had found the one thing to say that forced my embarrassed eyes downward. I played with my own fingers, waiting for him to take the conversation elsewhere.

"I'm sorry," he muttered. "I'm just making things worse. Are you ready to go home?"

I said, "Please," before he had finished his question.

A hot flash started to radiate in my chest. I closed my eyes and took deep, careful breaths, willing the stifling heat to subside so Dagger wouldn't know that I was already in the beginning stages of transition.

A shot of cool air hit me in the face. When I opened my eyes, the air conditioning dial was pointed at full blast. Dagger tried to act like this was normal, but we both knew that candeons did not need A/C.

"You know?" I asked timidly.

"I've known for a while. That's why I went to your house Saturday. I was supposed to check on your status. But I really just wanted to check on *you*. I worried about you." It wasn't self-idolizing, as if he expected me to appreciate his concern; it was respectful. "I realized after I got there that I just inflamed your fears instead of eased them."

"Why would you care if I was scared?"

"I can see why you would wonder. Try to see things from my perspective: I've been looking out for you for two years now. My entire daily existence is to worry about you." He coughed a little, realizing how he sounded. "Paid, of course."

I scrunched my face. "Well, you're a pretty lame bodyguard, then."

"What?"

"I may not be an adult, but if I try, I can still sense a hundred, maybe a hundred and fifty feet or so around me. What kind of bodyguard never gets close enough to guard? I didn't even know you existed until last fall."

"Touché."

"Where were you when I broke my arm two Christmases ago?"

"Unfair question; you were in no danger. Who cracks their elbow on their own trash can, anyway?" He asked like it had been eating at him for months.

"I was mopping. It was slippery."

He laughed. My stomach flipped uncomfortably when I realized how much Dagger knew about my life.

"Where were you when I let a human see me in the water?" I held my breath, waiting for his answer.

He sighed and looked out his side window. "I was there." He seemed antsy.

"And you didn't stop me?"

"You did a very brave thing, Haelo. Why would I stop you from doing that?"

"I don't know much about candeons, but I do know that rule. What I did was illegal! Sam saw me! He could have recognized who I was."

"At the time, I did not know he was your former childhood friend. Yes, it was illegal to reveal yourself, but it was right. You saved that boy's life. Besides, what am I going to do? Throw the Galana in jail?" He smiled, not realizing how that word made me feel. *Galana* was not a title to me—it was a branding.

"You okay?" He had pulled over at the edge of a community park.

"Yes," I responded with a weak grimace. "How come I didn't see you or sense you?"

He searched deep into my eyes. He tapped the top of the steering wheel with two fingers for a long ten seconds before admitting, "Because I can hide it. I can make myself invisible to other candeons' sensory abilities."

I leaned back. *What a load of—*"Bull."

"No. It's not." He continued to look straight into my eyes. "Concentrate on me, feel me."

I decided to humor him, focusing only on Dagger, shutting out all of the humans I could sense driving by or walking the sidewalk. I waited.

Suddenly, his aura intensified, flaring up like a spill of liquor on a fire, making the hair on the back of my arms stand on end. Then, like a doused match . . . absolutely nothing. It was as if he wasn't there. I could see him; I even reached and touched his arm; he was there in front of me and I could feel him, but I couldn't *feel* him. It was like sitting front row at a concert watching the band rock out on stage, feeling the vibrations from the woofers, smelling the sweat and pyrotechnic smoke, yet not hearing a thing.

"I'm still here; you just can't sense me."

"How did you do that?"

"It's part of who I am. Well, no, that makes it sound like some gift dumped into my lap. I had to work hard at it, of course." He fidgeted with the gold ring on his finger. "I can also sense others from farther distances, miles and miles, even with my own aura hidden." His face tightened. "You must promise me something. Very few candeons know that I can do this: Basileus Alcaeus, Prince Griffin, and my commander, General Stratos. You are not to tell anyone about it."

His tone scared me. "Okay."

"Not even Aaram or Neo," he added.

"Not even Aaram or Neo," I agreed. His eye contact lingered uncomfortably. I didn't doubt the seriousness of what he was asking. The urban, modern image of Dagger Stravins cracked to unveil a trained soldier, a soldier that had been following me for years. "Why do I get to know?"

"You should be aware of it. It might come in handy in the future."

"That's how you have kept watch? You've been hiding from me?"

"Yes. Essentially." He tried to say it with confidence, though whispers of shame ruined it. "I do not take pleasure in stalking about like a peeping tom. I have *never* invaded your privacy. I have absolutely never watched you in your own home, but I have had to be nearby. In order to do that, I shut off my *avra*."

"I'm assuming that's the candeon word for aura?"

He nodded, still waiting for my reaction to his declarations.

I took a moment to come to terms with the thought of being watched so closely. "And Aaram never found out? How did you explain yourself?"

"Two years ago, Aaram asked for a new watchman. He said Etulo was too close. Basileus Alcaeus did not agree; he felt you needed constant watch. So he sent me, telling Aaram that I would be more distant. I wasn't, but Aaram believed it, at least until I moved down the street and registered for school. He complained to Alcaeus, but since you would be turning soon Alcaeus thought that you needed to be aware of me. He wanted to ease you into your future. He thought that getting to know me and then slowly learning your fate would be better for you. We tried to convince Aaram of this, but he was adamant that you live your life unaware of what was coming. Alcaeus agreed to let Aaram decide when and how you would be told, on the condition that I stay registered as a student. I was to be a constant in your daily life, at school, anyway."

"So you're nice to me because you have to be?"

"No. I'm a student at Loma Heights because I have to be. But I like our conversations, the few that we've had. I would without hesitation count you as my friend."

"Oh. Thanks." *I guess.* "We're friends, then?"

"If you'd like. I know it's a twisted sort of relationship right now." He took his hands from the steering wheel. "Hopefully in the future you won't see me as the bad guy."

"I don't see you as the bad guy—you're doing what you're told. It's all just a lot to process. Not exactly the future I planned for myself. Could be worse." I wouldn't admit that I didn't actually have any solid future plans. *College, maybe.*

The sidewalk outside my door called to me. I got out and beckoned Dagger to follow. He had to, right?

Dagger continued the conversation as we walked slowly through the park. "It really could be a lot worse, you know. I don't think you understand how privileged your life will be in Pankyra. You will be the wife and mother to royals, a monarch in your own right. It has its perks."

The words should have been exciting. I was not riding the wave.

"The perks don't sound perky enough to validate the cost. Dagger, I'm being rounded up! I'll be taken from my family and the world that

I know to be submersed—literally—into a culture I don't understand. I don't speak the language, know the food, or get the customs. I will have no friends. And I'll be married to a stranger! What could possibly be a pro worth all of those cons?"

I stopped to wait for an answer. Dagger just kept walking.

"Seriously, tell me something good about my future."

He turned around. Something in his longing expression startled me. "You will live in a stable home, you will have an excellent husband, you will have children and grandchildren, your grandfather and brother can come see you whenever you like, and you'll not want for anything. You'll be in a position to do amazing things. To uplift others, care for those in need. Bring joy and hope to our world. Compared to a lot of people out there—both candeon and human—that seems like a pretty great life."

He humbled me into silence. With piercing clarity, I remembered Aaram's words, *Just imagine the good you can do. This is an opportunity, Haelo.* We walked through the park and stopped at a bench.

He picked up a stick and drew figures in the dirt between his feet before apologizing. "I'm sorry, I didn't mean to sound preachy. I do understand the fear and anxiety you must be going through. It was not my place to talk to you that way."

I felt like a puddle of mud, stagnant, waiting to dry up. He was right. I was ungrateful. And yet, here he was the one apologizing. Though I couldn't get past the forced marriage, I had no right to think that my lot in life was nothing but awful.

"Haelo?"

The familiar voice made me jump. Dagger wasn't fazed; he probably sensed Sam coming closer a long time ago.

"Oh! Hi, Sam." I stood and put my hands in my pockets. I motioned to Dagger. "This is Dagger Stravins, a friend from school." It was a mammoth misrepresentation, but it was the best I could do. "Dagger, this is Sam Legend."

"It's nice to meet you, Sam." He stood to shake hands. I'd bet three months' allowance Sam didn't believe for a second that Dagger belonged in high school.

"Norah and I were just testing out her new kite. Are you okay, Haelo?" I must not have recovered from being the aforementioned puddle of mud. I tried to perk up. "Yeah, I'm okay. How's your mom today?"

"She's doing all right." He dropped his brow and admitted, "Not great. She always sees the best in things, though, so she keeps us hopeful." His words stung. I wasn't seeing the best in my situation at all, and I certainly wasn't facing death. "She says hello, or at least I'm sure she would if she knew I was talking to you."

"I'll meet you back at the car," Dagger said before turning back to Sam. "Again, nice to meet you."

"You too . . . Dagger?"

Dagger nodded back at Sam and walked away.

"You sure that guy is in high school? I mean, look at him. I bet he's bigger than Neo."

About six inches taller, thirty pounds heavier, and a different muscle/body fat ratio, but you get the idea. Clearly, Sam hadn't seen Neo in a while.

We both stared at Dagger as he retreated back toward his truck. "He's big for his age, I guess." I didn't know what else to say.

I turned back to Sam. Knowing this was likely the last time I'd ever see him made the nostalgia ten times worse. Despite our years of distance, I wanted him in my life! Neo and I were inseparable, and close, and fiercely protective of each other. But Neo carried the same baggage I did. Sam, however, was the boy that once made all my cares melt away. If I didn't already have a fiancé, I might even let myself fall for him.

Who was I kidding? Sam wasn't *the one*. And, he was a human, for heaven sakes.

Norah ran up and said hello, pointing out which of the bright kites hanging out in the sky was hers.

"Hello to you too, Norah." She was gone before I had to come up with something else to say.

"Sorry about that. I told her she'd never be able to fly it as well as I do, and she's been at it all afternoon trying to prove me wrong." Sam's smile was contagious. "You're welcome to join us," he offered before looking back at Dagger. "Or maybe next time."

"Maybe. It's good to see you, Sam. I, um, want you to know how much your friendship has meant to me. Please tell your mom I said hi and wish her the best. I have to get going." The longer I talked with him, the worse this would all feel the next time I was alone.

Sam reached over to gently rub my arm. "Why does this sound like a pretty heavy goodbye?"

"It's just been a long day. I'll see you later, Sam." I squeezed his arm in return and started to walk away.

"All right. Wait, Lo?" I turned around just in time to flinch as Sam laid a firm kiss on my tight lips. We both froze and opened our eyes, still lip-locked.

I stepped away and tried not to squirm my face. "Um. . . ."

"Dammit. Lo, I'm sorry. It's just, well you . . . ugh, I really messed this up." He ran his hand over his head. "I, uh, it's not what it looks like." He shot a quick glance at Dagger and sighed. His face softened. "Friends? I think I just, I don't know. I let someone convince me that—" A loud honk from a minivan in the parking lot cut off his thought. Three kids hustled from the basketball court into the van while Sam and I took a strained breather. My mind was blank. I was either in shock, or I was completely numbed to the unexpected.

Sam was the first to speak. "Never mind. Friends?" He held out his hand.

"Always," I assured him with a handshake.

We both scrunched our faces in mutual acknowledgement of the kiss's cringe factor, then laughed. It eased the embarrassment. His sigh oozed with relief. He once again glanced at Dagger. "Lo? I like him."

I scrambled to follow his train of thought. "Who? Dagger?"

"Yeah. You deserve someone who looks at you like that. It's pretty obvious he likes you." I looked over my shoulder at Dagger. He was sitting at a picnic table bench by his Tahoe, watching me protectively. "Good luck with that. I'll see you around."

I stared at his retreating back for no other reason than bewilderment. I was so far past confused that I almost didn't even want to try to figure out what had just happened. A few moments passed before I realized I was shaking my head. *Obvious he likes me? Dagger? Looks at me like what? He doesn't. Does he?* I nearly did the shake-out-the-wiggles dance in my attempt to get the thought out of my head. I couldn't afford to go down that road. Sam didn't know what he was talking about.

Back up by the car, Dagger sat patiently, leaning against the edge of the picnic table.

I straddled the other end of the bench, facing him, and blew out all the air I had been holding in. What would Dagger think of me now? I had a fiancé, and the bodyguard employed by that fiancé just witnessed a kiss between Sam and me. "So, that was not—"

"You don't have to explain anything to me, Haelo."

I could tell Dagger's comment was not meant to cause shame or guilt, but for some reason, I really needed him to know. "There's nothing romantic going on between Sam and me. Really. I have no clue where that ki—"

He interrupted me again. "I'm more perceptive than you're giving me credit for. I saw how you both reacted. I'm not all that concerned about romantic sparks between the two of you." He sat staring out at the park like he hadn't a care in the world.

I'd revisit whether or not I should feel offended by his matter-of-fact comment later. Right then, I had a bone to pick with Dagger. "Where were you when I had a huge messy crush on Matt Nicoll my junior year? Where were you when I got played by Kingston Soli? Where were you this past week when my rekindling with Sam *could* have turned romantic? You let me form attachments, knowing full well that you were about to rip me from any relationships I might have. Now what? You haul me off to the Mediterranean to marry someone I've never met? You let me taste freedom, and, and choice! You let me practice forming real relationships only to say, 'Sorry, but you don't get to choose who gets to be in your life—here's a husband!' That's not protection. If you knew I shouldn't get attached then you should have stopped me in the first place."

I pulled my leg out from between the bench and table. "What if I had actually fallen for Kingston? What were you going to tell Griffin about that, huh? What if I had real feelings for Sam?"

Dagger raised one eyebrow and pinched his eyes slightly, tilting his head. I could practically hear the *Really?* in his thoughts. It only furthered my anger. I tried to leave, but Dagger was up and standing in front of me before I could.

He sat down right next to me, relaxing his face to assure me that his skepticism was gone. "I'm sorry. I shouldn't have reacted that way." He was so close I could smell his laundry detergent. "It's just, I know you pretty well, and it was obvious that you weren't falling for Kingston Soli. I could tell by the way you *didn't* look at him."

I once again remembered Sam's comment about Dagger looking at me. *Stop it.*

He continued, oblivious to my mental tangent. "There were a few times when I wanted nothing more than to beat the kid, but I kept my distance." He thought through his next words, saying sensitively, "And I don't think you were falling for Sam, either."

I scooted a little farther down on the bench.

He shook his head once, then started over. "You are entitled to live as normal a life as your family and the royals can offer. I don't judge any relationships or feelings that happen in your life—they make you who you are. The whole point of you living out this normal life was so that you could learn and grow. You were offered a full youth, not a half youth. Even if you had fallen in love, I would not have stopped you, *nor* judged you for it." His voice had grown forceful, almost a scolding.

I slumped into my shoulders. "You sure know how to make a girl feel good about herself."

Dagger dropped his head and put his hands on knees. "Once again, I find myself needing to apologize. I'm sorry. I am quick to defend truth and well-intentioned people. Sometimes I overstep my bounds; please forgive me."

"I deserve it. Don't apologize."

"No, you don't."

I looked around the park. There were bundled children on the playground, a three-on-three game at the basketball court, and an overweight jogger plodding up a pathway. "I could really use a change of conversation."

"I could not agree more."

It was nice to see him smiling again, even if it was somewhat forced. We got back in Clementine and rolled down the windows.

"I know you want to spend any time you have left with your family, so if you would rather, don't feel the need to go to school. Tell your teachers and your friend Lauryn that you have pink eye, or . . . something. If you promise me now that you will come to me when you wake from transition, I will not come check on you every day. Not that it would make a difference—I'd find out anyway—but the trust would mean a lot to me."

Transition suddenly seemed more real than ever before.

"This is really happening, isn't it?" I looked up at him in subdued panic.

"Yes, Haelo, it's happening. Any day now. You've already had all of the warning signs for much longer than expected. That is partly why I wanted to take you home today; I have another favor to ask you. A few new candeons have come in from the Pacific over the past three days. It's probably nothing—it happens all the time—but because of your sensitive situation, if you do decide to leave the house, I would prefer to know ahead of time where you are going. I would like to make sure wherever you choose to go is free from unfamiliar candeons before you arrive. Then I will escort you to wherever it is. Also, I'm worried that your transition is stalling because you spend so little time in the water. Every passing day makes me fearful that eventually your body won't be able to take it anymore. You might just collapse into the transitory sleep. If you are not in your home when that happens, I want to be able to get you there as soon as possible without any other witnesses."

"Why not just ask me to stay home?"

"A full youth, Haelo, not a half youth. This is the best I can do. Just let me know if you're leaving the house. Please."

"I can do that." All this talk of witnesses and collapsing made me nervous. "Sounds like we won't be making opening night for West Side Story, huh? I was really looking forward to watching you sweat in front of hundreds." We both chuckled. The breeze picked up a little, blowing my hair out behind me. "Dagger?"

"Yes?"

"My birthday is on Saturday. If I change before that, can we at least stay until then?"

He tightened his grip on the steering wheel. "We'll see. I might be able to stall a little if it's close."

"Thank you. And Dagger?"

"Yes?"

"If we *are* here on Saturday, would you come to dinner?"

He paused. "I would love to." His smile was genuine this time. "Now, let's get you home."

The next few days were actually pretty fun, minus the hot flashes. Neo and I broke out the old gaming system and played nostalgic video games for hours on end; we sat on the back porch with Grandpa Aaram and reminisced about the past nine years in San Diego; we took a short, distantly chaperoned dive just outside of Mission Bay. (After what Dagger had said about my transition stalling, I did not want to spend any time longer than necessary in the water in the hopes that I could stall it further.) At night, we'd stay around the kitchen table after the food was gone and laugh until we were tired.

It wasn't until I was alone in my room every night that the anxiety really hit me. I mostly ignored a string of texts from Lauryn and Sam, not knowing what to say. Sam even called a few times, leaving messages that I didn't listen to. The handful of emails from my teachers went unopened. I tried so hard to stay up. I even set my alarm to go off every twenty minutes, hoping that it would keep me from a deep sleep. I didn't want to dream; I didn't want to transition.

By Friday evening, I was a zombie.

Even though we sat at dinner, I was only vaguely aware of what was on my plate and doing a poor job at keeping up with the conversation.

"Haelo, honey? You look beat. Why don't you go to bed?"

I could hear his words, but Aaram's mouth didn't match up quite right, like during a streaming movie when the sound and the video are off by a half second.

Neo spoke next. "Lo? Seriously, sis, you look half-dead. And you just put jam on your potato."

"What?" I looked at the sticky pink forkful of baked potato in my hand. My head dropped to the table with a thud.

Neo carried me to bed. I didn't protest; I wasn't even offended that he had to huff his way down the hall. The super soft pillow under my head felt quite nearly like a life-changing experience.

Aaram and Neo whispered in my doorway as I drifted off to sleep, but I was too content to care what they were saying.

9

Happy Birthday to Me

I woke up to the glorious smell of bacon. Without opening my eyes, I stretched and yawned under the covers. The sun was shining, my body felt rested, breakfast was on the stove, not even an inkling of a hot fla—

I shot out of bed, knocking the lamp off of my dresser. I practically convulsed out of my shirt trying to get a look at my back in the mirror. I didn't see any scales, but I had to check three times, scraping at my lower back, just to be sure.

Aaram knocked on the door. "What's going on? I heard a crash. Are you all right?"

I panted through my response. "Yes, Grandpa. I'm fine."

"Is everything okay? Are you okay? Are you feeling . . . different?"

I opened the door and threw myself into his arms. "Yeah, Grandpa, I'm okay. Really. Today is not my last day in San Diego."

Aaram's relieved exhale brought me more joy than I expected.

"Well, good. Because I made you breakfast. And for tonight, there's a cheesecake in the fridge with eighteen candles and your name on it. Happy Birthday, Haelo."

"Thanks. Hey, Gramps?" He twitched at the name. "Let's go do something today."

"Like what, Haels?" He tried to act coy. It ruined it.

"Like bungee jumping. Or sky diving. I don't know, I want a thrill."

"Not in your wildest dreams. Don't use what I told you last week as permission to do dangerous things. You may not die, but you could very well mangle yourself up pretty bad. You want to be a paraplegic?"

"People sky dive and bungee jump every day."

"You will not change my mind. Besides, Dagger might tie you to a chair if he found out you wanted to jump out of a plane."

He had a point. It's not like I could hide it from Dagger.

"Why not a hike, or a movie?" he suggested.

"Remember when we used to rent sandrails out at the dunes? It's been ages. Let's do that."

"*We* did not used to rent sandrails. You and Neo rented them unscrupulously behind my back. I don't much have a taste for gas-fume headaches and broken ribs."

I laid my best puppy dog eyes on him.

"How am I supposed to say no to that?" he whined.

"I'll call Dagger."

When he picked up the phone, a simple "Haelo," was greeting enough.

"Hi, Dagger. We were thinking about taking a day trip to the dunes. It's safe, I promise. Neo and I have done it a few times before."

"How are you feeling, Haelo?" His tone put a damper on my excitement.

"I feel great. Haven't felt this good in a long time."

He was slow to respond. "We need to talk. Is it all right if I come over?"

I had a sneaking suspicion he was going to try to lecture me out of the dunes—I didn't want Aaram hearing that. "How about I come to you? Neo is still sleeping, I don't want to wake him." It was a lame excuse, but he conceded. I scarfed down Aaram's omelet and headed out with a new-found skip in my step.

His front room was even more breathtaking in the daylight: the colors were brighter, even the walls somehow seemed taller. I followed him into the kitchen where a bowl of strawberries shined on the counter next to a big butcher block. A griddle steamed on the stovetop. The room smelled like a French pastry shop, or rather, it smelled like what I thought a French pastry shop might smell like. I sat on a bar stool, leaning over a bowl of cold, runny batter. It was too tempting to ignore; I dipped my finger in to snag a taste.

"Not so great, Dagger. To be honest, I sort of expected better."

He laughed out loud, then retorted, "You have to cook it first. Ever had crêpes?"

"Yes. Not with strawberries, though." It was a blatant hint. He slid a steaming crêpe onto a plate, spooned a dollop of thick whipped cream, and then piled it with sliced strawberries. I rolled up the crêpe, jumping a little when he stopped my hand.

"My secret weapon—reduced balsamic."

"Oh, heck no. Do not ruin a perfectly good breakfast with vinegar."

"Just trust me," he said as he drizzled the dark brown syrup thinly over the top, then pushed the plate toward me. I took a very hesitant bite. The strawberries were good, the crêpe sucked, the balsamic was even worse, but the cream . . . *oh, that cream.*

"What is this white stuff? I could marry it." It was funny in my head; out loud it sounded stupidly inappropriate. *Marry it?*

Dagger gave me a perfectly balanced smile-wince, which just made me feel worse. He cleared his throat. "Mascarpone and whipped heavy cream. But you have a little on your, um, lip. Right there."

I quickly wiped away the corner of my mouth and set the crêpe down.

Dagger turned back to the stove to pour out two more, giving me a short window to scrape all of the cream and strawberries to one side of the plate and quietly discard the nasty balsamic-soaked crêpe into a trashcan on the side of the counter.

"Just so you know," he chimed, still unaware of how bad I thought his cooking skills were, "this, omelets, and grilled meat are the only things on the planet that I know how to make. I'm the world's worst cook." He assembled his plate and walked around the counter to sit on the other stool, where he finally noticed my pile of creamed strawberries.

"That bad, huh?"

I nodded.

"I thought for sure these were okay. The lady who taught me this made hers straight out of heaven."

With squinted, apologetic eyes, I shook my head. "You should stick to art."

He chuckled and copied my cream-strawberry/vinegar-crêpe segregation.

My eyes wandered over the counter. "You said we needed to talk?" I asked, immediately stuffing my mouth with cream.

He swallowed, then answered a simple, "Yes."

I waited while he stared at his plate. Finally, he looked up at me and asked, "When was the last time you had a hot flash?"

His doctor-like tone made me feel a little interrogated. I thought about it, but could not be sure. "I don't know. I haven't had one today. That's good, right?"

"You started showing symptoms of transition five weeks ago. You may not have noticed, but I did. Normally, candeons transition within days of those first symptoms. Two weeks, at most. I was concerned and did a little research."

"Research?" I laughed; he didn't even crack a smile.

This day had started out so good, relatively speaking. It was going downhill fast.

I pushed my plate. "Dagger, I grew up with a lot of questions and not a lot of answers. I've tried research. There is nothing out there about candeons. There's a bunch of fantasy about *mermaids*. Forgive me if I don't trust your research." I was insulted. If there really was information out there, why couldn't I find it? My years of searching only came up empty.

Dagger waited with polite patience. He put his hand on my back, reassuring me through my wounded ego. An awareness sparked when he touched me, taking me back to Sam's assessment of Dagger's feelings for me. I was being an idiot. *Stop it. Seriously,* I scolded myself. Soon, a too-close feeling crept into the slight space between us, and Dagger quickly pulled his arm back. "Sorry. Here, come sit."

We walked over to the couches and sat opposite each other.

"There *is* information, it's just very hard to come by. There is a library—not public by any means—run by the same family of candeons that have overseen the Empirical Library for centuries. Technically, it is a royal library, but it cannot be censored by the monarchs. They can only give permission to enter, having no role in its upkeep and content. It contains thousands of manuscripts collected from all over the world, mostly about candeons, though there is mention of other kinds, as well.

"It's run down and largely ignored. Most of our history is well-known among us." His comment stung, even though I knew he wasn't trying to put me down. "So very few know, and even fewer care, about the library at all. It's sort of a hidden treasure. An extremely inaccessible hidden treasure."

"What do you mean?"

"I mean that getting permission to read the manuscripts is a very rare occurrence because the comprehensive genealogy of the royals, nobles, and Galanas is inside, and that information is heavily guarded, as you of all people should understand. It is a vault of protected information that no one ever cares to read. The people who want access are usually out to manipulate their position via family bloodline checks, or they want to guess to which noble the next Galana might be born. In the wrong hands, that is very dangerous information."

"Why do you get access?"

"For the same reason Alcaeus and Griffin asked me to be your watchman and bodyguard. They trust me."

"Then you are not here just because you can turn off your aura?"

"Not explicitly."

"Can anyone do it? Turn it off, I mean. Can you teach me?"

"I've never met another. And no, it is not something I can teach. I've tried."

"Who did you try to teach?"

"Alcaeus."

I nodded my head, though I did not know why. The more I talked to Dagger, the older he seemed. "What did you find?"

"Last week, I asked the library keeper for some information. It came yesterday."

"They just mailed it? I thought this was super-protected stuff."

"No, they didn't just mail it. You're getting sidetracked. Here." He picked up one of four leather-bound scrolls from the side table. I loosened the ties and unrolled it open. The characters looked sort of like the Latin alphabet, but not enough to be legible. At the bottom was a very different looking symbol, like a tribal seal with a diamond shape in the middle.

"I can't read Candeon. It might as well be Greek."

"It is Greek."

"Oh."

He chuckled to himself before adding, "There is no candeon language, just our own Greek dialect."

If ever a girl felt stupid, I was that girl.

"The scroll mentions a friend of Basileus Remus, a woman by the name of Keakahana," he continued. "She was not candeon; she was a Makole, one of the fire people of Hawai'i. It says that Keakahana helped Remus find the Galana when her parents hid her from the royal court."

"What does that have to do with me not transitioning?"

"It also says that the Makole magic Keakahana used took time. She searched for years trying to track the aura of the Galana, but did not find her until after the Galana's transition from youth into maturity. The Galana did not transition until her twenty-second year, which is unheard of. I think that her aura fought back against the magic of Keakahana, which stalled her transition."

"What are you saying?"

"I believe you are being tracked by Makole magic, and I believe the rebels have recruited one of Keakahana's descendants to do it."

I tried to digest this new information, but it sank into some bottomless abyss in the trenches of my mind. *Fire People? Magic? Trackers?* I refocused.

So it was. The bad people from my dreams—the ones from that last day with my parents—were hunting for me. "What happened? To the Galana?"

"After she finally transitioned, Keakahana located her and sent word to the Basileus. The Galana tried to run, but was eventually brought back to Pankyra."

"So I am not the first Galana to be less than thrilled at the prospect of an arranged marriage."

He shifted in his seat, unable to answer.

With half-genuine humility, I responded, "I'm sorry, I know you think I am being selfish. I shouldn't have said it."

"No, it's not that. To you, this whole ordeal is a terrifying unknown that contradicts the culture in which you've been raised. Haelo, you have every right to be scared. And yes, you and the Galana mentioned in the scroll are the only ones I know of to not want that privileged life. Other Galanas and their families have seen it as a blessing, one to be greatly excited about."

"Do you see it as a blessing?"

He looked into his folded hands and blew out a sigh before answering. "It is not my role to have an opinion on that. I am here to protect you. It is true that you will rise to the status of royalty, become an empress, live in wealth and comfort, and your family will be taken care of for the rest of their lives. Those seem like blessings, no?"

He had dodged the question.

I tried again. "It may not be your *role*, but you're still a free-thinking individual. Do you see it as a blessing?" I accented each word of the question. He just stared resolutely into my eyes.

I picked up the scroll. "This Galana, does she have a name?"

"It doesn't say. I could find out."

I nodded my head. *Of course.*

"Haelo, that doesn't mean that she's not important."

"Oh, I don't doubt that. She's real important, isn't she? Without her, the King or Emperor or whatever *Basileus* means would not be King, right? She's a crown; a child-bearing, nameless crown. And you can't have a kingdom without a crown."

"Don't say that. That's not how it works. Frankly, it's disrespectful to every Galana that has come before you. This is not about securing royal authority. Haelo, you will not only become the symbolic mother of the candeon race, but you will very literally be responsible for our survival."

"Aaram told me the story. That survival guilt trip is a stretch, don't you think? I've thought this over. Do you want to know what would happen if I did not marry Griffin? The Candeon Empire would just have to come up with different rules. This whole Galana/royal thing is nonsense. My mosaic is just a random mix of genetics. Griffin could marry anyone and have a slew of kids to which he could choose any one of them to pass down the throne—just change the rules."

"It's not that simple." His voice was stronger than it had ever been before. "You are talking about messing with thousands of years of tradition. The last time someone tried to shoot holes in our traditions, a civil war erupted, the likes of which no human in history can comprehend. In a few bloody years, we went from tens of millions to a few thousand. *A few thousand!* Men, women, and children. Dead. Millions brutally killed. And two hundred years later, our numbers haven't gotten much bigger!"

Tears pooled in my eyes. I shook so badly my teeth chattered. Dagger moved forward to sit next to me.

"I did not say that to belittle you," he said softly, leaning close to my downcast face. "I said it only so you can see the big picture. Tradition, especially tradition tied to the genesis and continued success of our entire species, means a great deal to the candeon world. A very great deal."

I curled up in a ball and fell deeper into the couch. "When you came last week to check my back, I told myself that I wouldn't be sad anymore. I didn't want you to ever see my fear. I wanted to be strong." I wiped my face and watched the tears glisten on the back of my hand. "A whole lot of good that did me."

He waited a moment, then got up and walked over to the mantel. "See this? This is a sketch of my father, Sideron. He was an incredible man, the strongest I've ever known. He could do anything. But even he cried when he needed to." He walked to the kitchen, adding, "Take as long as you need."

As the sketch of Dagger's father watched over me, I wondered what his story was. Dagger said he died in the line of duty. His duty was as a soldier; my duty was as a queen. I would live the life of royalty. I tried to see things through a different lens and be excited like the other Galanas before me might have been, but there was so much missing information. I had no idea what to expect. A palace? A castle on a beautiful Greek island? A secret underwater vault? Would there be amazing vacations and getaways to see the world, or would I be locked away, hidden and protected from the outside? Would I be married to a kind, patient man who wanted to make me happy? Or would he be a king that needed an heir, and I was just the vessel to deliver it? Every possible advantage seemed to have an equally possible tragic opposite. I wanted to be strong. I really did.

After cleaning up the kitchen, Dagger walked past me into the hallway at the other end of the house. I heard drawers open and shut, metal clanking, and a few swift, heavy zippers. He came out carrying a dark cargo duffel. I jumped when a powerful knock echoed through the house. I had been so caught up in my own emotions that I failed to sense the two candeons coming up the path.

"Come in, Hank, Zeta," Dagger called from the hallway.

The door opened, and in walked another tall-dark-and-handsome. I had thought Dagger was big, but Hank looked no smaller than a horse. He made Dagger look . . . athletic. Behind him stood a petite woman in tight jeans, black boots, and a small leather jacket. She had pale skin, sharp eyebrows, dark aviator sunglasses, and a jet-black pixie haircut. Though petite, she looked like she could hold her own. She stood just behind and to the side of Hank.

Dagger knelt down in front of me, making me feel like a scared toddler being consoled. Pointing to the Clydesdale of a man in the entryway, he said, "Haelo, this is Hank. He is the acting captain of *Alpha Agema*, the special missions unit of the Krypteia." Nodding to the woman, he added, "And this is Zeta, a member of that unit. They are here to protect you while I take a short trip west. How are you feeling?"

"You're leaving?" I floundered, wide-eyed.

"Yes. I need to take care of a few things that we talked about earlier. Don't worry—I won't be gone more than two days, maybe even just twenty-four hours. Hank is a good guy, so is Zeta. They'll watch out for you."

"Are you going to Hawai'i?"

Dagger looked over his shoulder at Hank, then turned back and whispered, "Yes. However, we should probably keep that between us. I trust them with my life, but this should be good practice keeping sensitive information quiet. I, I mean *we*, have silence orders from Basileus Alcaeus." He nodded reassuringly, then turned back to Hank. "No offense, Hank."

"None taken," Hank replied in the deepest bass I had ever heard. His arms were crossed over his chest in a menacing stack of muscle, but his smile was so welcoming and friendly that I thought for a crazy second that he might pick Dagger up in a bear hug. Zeta ignored Dagger and watched me intently.

"It is an honor to meet you, Miss Marley," Hank said in his powerful tone. He tipped his head forward.

Zeta did the same, adding, "Yes, an honor."

Dagger grabbed something from the kitchen. He zipped it into one of the outer pockets of the duffel bag and came back to the sitting room.

"Haelo, we have discussed a lot of things, most of which fall under that silence order. Hank and Zeta know who you are and how to protect you." Hank squinted in agreement, and Zeta nodded encouragingly. Dagger came closer and looked me in the eyes. "Your family has been promised that you will not be brought to the royal court until you have matured. That is the only reason we have not left already. However, remember when I promised you that I would not interfere with you living out a full youth? We have come to a point that requires some sacrifice. I am going to sort out what I can. Until I come back, you need to stay here, with them. This house is much more protected, and after our conversation earlier, you ought to know why you need more protection than ever. We can go get your things."

"What about Aaram and Neo?"

"They are more than welcome."

"What if I transition? Then what?"

"Based on the information I told you this morning about one of your fellow Galanas, I don't think that you will. If you do, Hank has orders to escort you to Pankyra. I will meet you there."

Wait, what? *Why would Dagger meet me there?* I had thought his job ended with my deliverance to the Basileus and the Prince.

"Zeta, take Miss Marley to her home, and bring her back after she has packed a bag. I have a few more things to do before I leave, so I should be here when you return."

I desperately wanted a better explanation, at least a better goodbye. Zeta already had the door open and stood waiting for me to lead the way. I turned back to Dagger, but he was in the back yard talking on his phone.

At home, Neo barraged me with questions. "Wait! You're going where? Why? Who is she?" he demanded, rudely pointing to Zeta. "Where's Dagger? I want to talk to him."

All I could do was shrug and answer as best I could. "Dagger is leaving Hank and *Zeta*," I nodded in her direction, "in charge while he goes away for a couple of days. In the meantime, I'm on house arrest or something in his house." Zeta had removed her sunglasses and stood rigidly in the entryway, listening to every word of our conversation. I continued, "Dagger vouches for them. Promise."

"Yeah, well, why should we trust Dagger?"

Zeta shifted her weight, offended.

My room looked strange, like it was someone else's. It was full of my things, but they did not add up the way I thought they should. It was the room of a teenage girl with no other cares than grades, friends, and an occasional dive in the ocean, which was no longer me. I packed a quick bag, grabbed my camera, and met Zeta at the front door. Aaram returned from the back bedroom, a sullen droop in posture.

"Grandpa, I've got to stay at Dagger's house for a day or two. He said it was—"

"I know. I just got off of the phone with him. He explained enough."

"Are you coming with me?"

"No, honey. Neo and I are going to stay here so we can warn you in case anyone comes looking. You and Prince Griffin are now eighteen. I imagine the candeon world is getting anxious to find the new Galana. It won't be long before some start snooping around the homes of nobles."

I gave him a tight hug. I knew it wasn't goodbye, but it felt close enough. He said he would bring over dinner tonight for a birthday celebration. On the way out, I took a picture of the door to my home of nine years.

Zeta carried my bag down the street. I thought about how we must look through the neighbors' windows. *There goes that Marley girl again. She's an oddball, isn't she? And who is that woman following her? She looks unpleasant. Should we call the police?*

Dagger was still in the backyard when we returned. The sliding glass door stood open, which I used as an invitation to join him.

"Anything I should know? Any trick for the toaster?"

He pocketed his phone and showed me to a corner of the yard where a large tree shaded a hammock. "This is the best seat in the house. If you are ever in trouble, there is an escape bunker behind this tree," he said, reaching through the leaves of a bush to show me a tree root in the ground. He lifted it slightly, revealing a hidden door beneath the thick sod.

I gasped. Or yelped. Or laughed. I'm not sure which, but it was out loud. These people were nuts. What had my life come to?

"Your aura will still be trackable, but if they can't find the entrance, you should be able to make it out to the ocean. There are two tunnels inside. The bigger one leads to Mission Bay; the smaller leads to the basement of your grandfather's house." When my eyes widened, he added, "That tunnel has never been used; it is for emergency use only. Here, let me show you to your room."

There were four doors in the hallway: a bathroom, Dagger's room, a guest room, and a study, though he did not show me the study.

"Zeta, you can bunk in the guest room; Haelo, you can stay in my room. There are clean sheets, towels, everything you should need."

Hank's deep voice murmured, "I never get clean sheets."

Without looking him in the eye, Dagger retorted, "The last time you crashed with me was in Beira. If you remember correctly, neither of us had beds, let alone clean sheets."

Hank chuckled. "I guess that means I get this itty bitty couch you've got over here?"

"It's a pull-out; you'll be fine. Much better than your last assignment, from what I hear." Dagger smirked; Hank just looked indignant. Dagger turned back to me. "Haelo, if you have any questions, text me, I'll get back to you as soon as I can. Make yourself at home. Hank? There's a run-bag under the aloe vera in the back yard. There's also an extra Glock beneath the counter in the kitchen and a silenced Browning on the top shelf in the guest closet."

"Still keep a knife in the toilet paper roll?"

"Always."

I had to sit down. This was not something I was prepared for. Guns? Escape tunnels? I had no idea what they were planning for, but it scared me to death. I could feel my heartbeat in my temples. My chest refused to open enough to take a decent breath.

"Haelo, everything is going to be okay. This is just part of staying prepared. The next few days will likely be pretty boring. But Hank is a dangerous poker player, so don't let him talk you into a game. He'll rob you blind."

He tried to laugh away my stress. It didn't work.

"If I thought you were in danger, I would not be leaving. We're just being thorough. I'll be back before you know it." He again knelt down in front of me. "I'm sorry I won't be here for your dinner tonight. Happy Birthday."

And in true Dagger fashion, he was gone.

It was a strange turn of events. Then it dawned on me: it was my birthday, which meant it was also Prince Griffin's birthday. *I bet his celebration is going better.*

Hank helped himself to the fridge; I didn't move from the couch. Zeta took a bag into the guest room and came out a few minutes later wearing more comfortable clothes, the kind that made her look like a yoga model. She took the seat next to me on the comfy couch, her posture envyingly perfect.

"Very nice to meet you, Miss Marley. My name is Zeta Andué. Is there anything that I can do for you?"

I didn't know what to say, so I started with, "Is that your real name?"

She nodded her head once at my cheeky question, approving of my intuition. "It is my name in the field. Our real names are kept private to protect our home life and families. You understand?"

I nodded as well. She didn't hide her accent as well as Dagger. Still, I could not place it. I should have shut up. Like an oblivious five-year-old, I asked, "Why are you so small? Dagger said that kryptes are from the clans in the eastern waters off of South Africa. He said they're all big."

Zeta giggled. "It's usually my pale skin that tips people off. But yes, I am one of the few kryptes not originally from those clans. Don't be fooled—I pack a mean punch." She winked at me.

Hank waltzed in from the kitchen with a plate of food, took a slight bow in my direction, and asked, "Miss Marley, can I get you a plate of crêpes?"

I shook my head with a slight grin. I'd let him find out for himself just how bad those crêpes were.

In a more casual tone, Hank turned to Zeta. "Zeta, you want some?" He dug in after she shook her head as well. "Suit yourselves." Two seconds into his first bite, his chewing slowed. "Not his best." He shrugged and dug in anyway.

Zeta smirked. "What did you expect? Remember his soup that night in Havana? It's a miracle we all didn't get food poisoning." With a shrug, she added, "Except for cooking, Dagger can do everything. And if he wasn't so humble about it, he'd be the cockiest little son of a—"

"You're ruining my breakfast." Hank didn't look up from his plate; his fork bounced over the top of it, anxiously selecting the next bite. Sunlight glinted off of a gold ring similar to Dagger's, and a bit of cream rested in the corner of his mouth. A glance at Zeta's hand revealed a ring there as well. *Hmm.* . . .

"I am sorry, Miss Marley. That was no way to speak in front of you," Zeta apologized.

Hank noticed his facial schmear and wiped it away, eyes glancing quickly in my direction as if he hoped I hadn't noticed. He resumed eating, this time with an air of elegance.

I walked to the back doors. Hank and Zeta treated me with an unfamiliar sort of reverence which made me uncomfortable. I ran my fingers along the glass door. Birds chirped merrily from the picturesque shade tree, and an orange cat rested on the top of the fence. It was the stray that usually slept beneath my window. I amused myself with a fleeting backstory: *His name is Mortimer. He's the neighborhood bookie, protected by a loyal posse of squirrels sired to do his bidding. He knows everyone's secrets. You can't hide anything from him.* As if on cue, the cat's eyes flashed to mine. I shook off the heebies just as Zeta joined me at the sliding door.

"Happy Birthday! I know this must be a crummy way to spend it. What do you want to do? I'm sure we could think of something fun."

"I think I'll go lie down."

Dagger's room was very white. White walls, white bedding, white furniture. Except for the large sunset painting on the wall above the bed, a book on the nightstand, and the wood floors, there wasn't much color anywhere.

I crashed face first on the bed—it smelled like Dagger's laundry detergent. An image of him doing laundry made me smile.

I popped up to see what book he was reading. The cover had soldiers plodding single file in the distance. I picked it up to read the synopsis and discovered another book sitting underneath it: a collection of Walt Whitman poetry. The more I learned about Dagger, the more mysterious he became.

The sunset painting above the bed was beautiful. Oranges, reds, and yellows swirled together behind a palm tree silhouette. It reminded me of my childhood. I closed my eyes to remember. When my thoughts approached that last horrible day in Hawai'i, I rose from the bed, looking around for a distraction.

I knew that if they were paying attention, Hank and Zeta could probably sense me leaving the bedroom, but I tiptoed anyway. From the hallway, I could see into the back sitting room where they were talking quietly on the couches, pretending to not notice me. I stopped in front of the door to the study. *Just a peek.* If I weren't allowed, they'd stop me.

I was expecting a dark room full of weapons, surveillance equipment, and body armor. Surprisingly, the room was flooded with sunlight. Empty canvases leaned against the paneled, white walls; pens, charcoals, brushes, paint, and dirty rags covered a long desk; a sophisticated easel posed empty in front of the window, waiting to be put to use; and a brown leather stool on rollers sat in the middle of the room atop old scuffs and scratches in the hardwood floors. Not a study. A *studio*.

In the near corner sat a smaller desk with a lamp. Atop were a locked safe and the four scrolls Dagger had shown me earlier. Resting on the safe was a simply framed photograph of a young boy and his parents, looking carefree and happy in the shadows of a pine forest. I picked it up to examine more closely, leaving clean prints in the dust. Wild red hair curled around the woman, tangling among her arms as she held her son. The man in the photo was the same darker-skinned man in the sketch above the fireplace. *Dagger's family.* I was drawn to the young, familiar-looking Dagger. I gently put the frame back and looked around further.

Hank's laugh thundered down the hallway, pulling me back into the present. I exited quietly, making sure the door handle didn't rattle.

Out in the sitting room, Hank was slapping his own knee, tears of laughter glistening in his eyes. Zeta sat smugly in the armchair, pleased with herself. They both stood when they saw me.

"What's so funny?" I asked.

Hank struggled to compose himself as Zeta explained. "Hank finds it hilarious that my last assignment was with both a clingy ex-boyfriend and an angry ex-girlfriend. It didn't end well."

I should have expected romantic relationships to be a part of Krypteia life; Dagger's parents must have dated before settling down together. Dagger probably had a girlfriend. *That must be one heck of a complicated relationship.* Again, I found myself feeling sorry for him, that he was stationed away from his real life to keep watch over a teenager. Without permission (or warning), Sam's voice echoed in my head. *It's pretty obvious he likes you.* I'd need hypnotherapy to get those stupid comments out of my memory.

There was nowhere else to wander in the house, so I stepped outside to the backyard. The hammock cradled my back like a glove. I lay in it and pondered the tree root handle in the bush. There was a tunnel to my house. *A tunnel to my house!* Thinking back to just a few weeks before when I was oblivious to such things, my life then seemed like a kiddie pool floating unaware in the deep end. I had thought my life to be inconsequential. Shallow. Now that I saw how extensive and connected my life had been all along, it was as if I had leaned over the edge of the kiddie pool and saw exactly how deep my reality really was. I had a feeling that pretty soon I was going to fall out of the kiddie pool and land in an expansive ocean filled with countless obstacles.

I dropped my foot to the grass, gently rocking the hammock. The Wailin' Jennys' *Storm Comin'* sang in my head as my heavy eyes shut.

Be strong, Haelo. We'll be back before you have time to worry.

I held Tilly tighter and tighter. The cave shook with the violence outside. Neo ducked from a falling boulder and curled up next to Tilly and me.

Lo, we need to get out of here, this cave is going to collapse! Give Tilly to me! Neo was already prying her fingers from around my neck.

No, Neo! Mom said they'd be back for us! Just wait a little longer.

We don't have time to wait, Haelo. Look around!

The last of the eel and fish scurried out of the crumbling cave. A loud crack broke behind us. I whipped around and saw part of the back wall of the cave fall away to reveal a small hole.

Neo held me by the shoulders, forcing me to look at him. *That's our way out. They won't be watching the back.*

It didn't feel right. *Neo, where are we going to go? We can't hide! They can sense us! Let's wait for Mom and Dad.*

Neo put his arm around Tilly's waist and grabbed my wrist. He pulled us halfway to the back by the time Dad's voice stopped us.

Neo, Haelo, grab Tilly and sit in the middle of the cave, close together. Cover your heads and don't move! Help has arrived. You must listen to me! Take cover and don't move!

We did as we were told. We put little Tilly between us and arched over her in a bear hug. The turbulent waters outside the cave entrance calmed; the crashing currents quieted. I pulled my head up to look outside, but Neo grabbed me and pushed me back down. Everything went eerily silent.

"Miss Marley?"

I jumped so suddenly I thought my heart had stopped.

"You need to wake up." Zeta spoke in a controlled, precise tone that scared me more than it should have. She knelt in front of the hammock, waiting for my eyes to focus on hers.

"What's going on?" I said, panting from the abrupt shock that had brought me out of my dream.

"Dagger is on his way back."

"Wait, what time is it?" The sun hadn't moved much.

"One-thirty. He said he would explain when he got here. With all respect, Miss, I need to move you into the house." She pulled me up by my arm and escorted me inside.

That's going to leave a bruise.

Inside, Hank stood in the archway between the front gallery and the sitting room, talking on his cell phone and looking toward the front door. There was a matte black handgun in his other hand.

Instead of protesting, fainting, hyperventilating, or even yelping, I said the one thing I never thought I'd ever say. "Where's my gun?"

Hank grinned so big I couldn't see his eyes. "That's my girl!"

Zeta did not think my comment as amusing as Hank did. She directed me to the couch. "Pardon me, Miss Marley, but you do not need a gun. The last thing we need is an eager novice with a loaded weapon. Stay here and don't move." She grimaced after calling me a novice, but (thankfully) didn't apologize. She probably hoped I didn't notice.

"Please tell me what is going on!" I started to stand to make the point that I was going to be a pain until I got answers.

She answered reluctantly, speeding through the words as her accent thickened. "Dagger sensed a group of candeons at the airport. One of them was Karchardeus, Massáude's right-hand man. Dagger does not think it's a coincidence and told us to—"

"Wait, wait. Who is Massáude?"

"Massáude. Leader of the rebel mercenaries? I'm sorry, I assumed Dagger had told you all of this."

Though I had an idea of where this conversation was going, my bewildered expression must have betrayed my ignorance.

"Never mind. Just know that the second-in-command of some very bad people is in town with a few friends, and you do not want to meet them. *I* don't want to meet them. At least not with you here."

"I wouldn't mind meeting them," Hank chimed in as he cocked a shotgun. Apparently the handgun was not enough. I let my eyes dart from window to window; I knew that I would sense them before I ever saw them, but there was something reassuring about seeing an empty landscape outside.

Zeta checked the clip in her gun, making sure it was loaded. "Let's just hope Dagger gets here soon. If Karchardeus does come around, I'll feel a whole lot better with Dagger here."

"Here, here," Hank agreed.

My thoughts zipped over to Aaram's house down the street. "What about my brother and grandfather?"

"We have already called them; they are taking precautions," Zeta said. She felt under the kitchen counter for Dagger's stashed pistol.

"What does that mean?" I asked, unsatisfied.

"It means that Aaram Gevgenis knows what to do, and he's doing it."

Before I could retort back to her, she and Hank both sighed in relief and relaxed from their tense, defensive stances, taking me off guard. I focused my senses, pushing them to feel farther. Moments later I too relaxed as I sensed Dagger pulling into the driveway; Neo and Aaram were with him. The rumble of Clementine calmed the panic in my chest. There were still mercenaries in San Diego, likely hunting for me, but with Dagger nearby, everything was under control. The two kryptes in the room seemed to feel the same way.

When he walked in, Dagger did not look any taller, bigger, wiser, or meaner. Yet somehow my perception of him had grown into outright trust and confidence. I had not seen him fight, outsmart, or outrun anyone, but he definitely looked like one no-nonsense man to have around. He began sounding off orders before Neo had even stepped through the threshold.

"Hank, you will stay with Professor Gevgenis and Neo. If anyone asks, you are here on Council business. If any human asks, you are Neo's uncle on his father's side. For as long as possible, you three will stall any other candeons from finding out that Haelo is no longer in San Diego."

I should not have been surprised, but my stomach turned anyway. *So this is it.*

"Whatever you do, do not admit that she is the Galana under any circumstances. You will continue to sell the story that she is the adopted daughter of Aaram with no noble blood heritage and any rumors otherwise are false. You will say that she is out for a dive and will be back in a day or two. That should keep them here and give us enough time to get to Panama."

Dagger squared himself in front of Aaram and Neo. "No panic, no fear, no hesitation. This will only work if you sell this as absolute truth. They need to believe that any other story genuinely surprises you. Of course Haelo is not the Galana. They must be severely misinformed. She is out diving and will be back soon."

He released his fierce visual hold on the two of them and turned to Zeta, but Aaram stepped forward. "What if it doesn't work? What if they know?"

Dagger tried to say it as gently as possible, but harsh words were hard to sugarcoat. "Let's hope they don't."

Everyone held their breath. Dagger looked to Hank before trying to reassure Aaram and Neo. "There is still a chance that none of this will be necessary. Karchardeus might not come to you when he senses Haelo is not with you; he might take off hunting for her. If not, and he refuses to believe this story... Hank will be with you. He'll do everything he can to get you out safely." Dagger allowed a brief moment for us to swallow the implications of what he had just said. "Zeta, you're coming with Haelo and me. Once we're out of southern California, you'll head directly for Pankyra. We will take a more unexpected route and meet you there. Haelo? I am very sorry, but I must break the promise I made to you. We need to leave now. You are not safe here anymore."

I couldn't stay silent any longer. "Why can't we all go together?"

Dagger had been waiting for this question. "My job is to protect *you*, and this is the best way to do that. You will not convince me otherwise. Your grandfather and Neo agree that the safest way to get you out of mercenary reach is for Karchardeus to have a reason to keep looking here in San Diego."

I shook my head. "Not okay. I'm not leaving without Neo and Grandpa."

Aaram interrupted Dagger's next command. "Haelo, dear, we will be fine. You need to get out of here; I love you too much to let you stay. We will slow you down and attract attention. This is a stealth mission—the fewer around you, the better."

Stab to the heart. Neo did not try to talk me into going; he just leapt forward and hugged me tight. I couldn't contain my sobs. Neo was my rock. What would I do without him? I noted everything about his embrace so I could recall it whenever I needed the comfort. I gripped his shirt in my fist and scrunched my face into his hair. I used to think Neo, despite being an inch shorter than me, was like a big bear, but after being around Dagger and Hank, Neo seemed just right. The perfect-sized hug. He tried not to let his voice catch, but I could hear the strain in his whispers.

"Lo, we're gonna see you soon, okay? Remember what I told you? Remember?"

I thought back to that quiet moment in the dark cave, right where my dream had ended a short half hour ago. "I remember, Neo. Of all the things I've tried to forget about that day, I could never forget that."

"I love you, Lo."

"I love you, too, Neo."

We both pulled tighter for one last moment before letting go. Aaram stepped in and gave me a hug as well, then kissed me on the forehead. "I am so proud of the young woman you have become. You've made me a better man. Thank you for bringing so much joy into my life."

His goodbye sounded way too final. "Grandpa, I'm going to see you soon! You better be in Pankyra when I get there. I need someone to walk me down the aisle, right?" I had no idea if royal candeon weddings had such a thing, but it didn't matter. He just nodded. I gave his hand a light squeeze and then looked to Neo. "Take care of him, Neo."

"I will."

"So will I," Hank said. "You have my word."

"Thank you, Hank."

"No thanks necessary, Miss Marley. Anything else, Dagger? We should get back to their house before anyone gets suspicious."

"That's all. Just be smart." He and Hank shook hands.

An idea came to me and I pulled Dagger aside. "What about the tunnel? Tell Hank about the tunnel from Aaram's house out to Mission—"

Dagger walked me farther from the group and whispered intently, "Your grandfather already knows about that; he'll disclose it if he finds it necessary. We need to take secrecy seriously. There are reasons why certain information must be guarded. Please do not speak out in front of others like that. If you want to discuss sensitive information, make sure that it is only between you and me."

"Others? They're my family. And your friends! Just the other day I asked you why I was allowed to know your secret, and you said that it just might come in handy someday and that I should know. Don't you think it would be handy for Hank, of all people, to know about a possible escape route? You're being unreasonable!"

"No. I am not." The words were final. He walked back to the group, leaving me completely at a loss for words. Rattled, I returned and gave one last hug to Aaram and Neo.

"Don't forget, Lo," Neo said as Hank escorted him out the front door. I didn't have time to ponder the separation; Dagger and Zeta marched me down the hallway into Dagger's studio before the echo of the door closing finished reverberating off the high ceilings.

I slumped in the middle of the floor, staring at the tiny gashes and scratches the brown stool had made in the wood. Zeta stood at the window with her eyes shut, searching for candeons that might be coming closer. Dagger would feel them long before she would, but she didn't know that. He leaned over the safe on the desk and ticked the dial back and forth. With a pop, the safe door swung open. Curiosity lured me out of my stupor, and I looked up to see what he pulled out.

In his hand were a handful of passports, all different colors and sizes. He tucked them into a plastic pouch, then pulled out another gun, two stacks of cash, and a worn pink envelope.

"No partridge in a pear tree?" I couldn't help it.

"Cute. Very cute," he said, though he certainly wasn't acting amused. "Zeta, you ready?"

"I just need to pack up my things."

"We need to go, now. You're going to have to pack on the run." Dagger was already out of the room before Zeta had a chance to respond.

She trailed behind him down the hallway. "With respect, sir, I can stretch my senses pretty far, and I don't feel anyone coming this way. Don't you think we should take a little time to plan this out?"

"We're leaving now. Right now. Haelo, get in the car. I'll grab your bag."

I trusted Dagger's senses a lot more than Zeta's, and the look on Dagger's face told me everything I needed to know. They were coming. I ran out to the Tahoe, praying it was unlocked. Dagger followed behind me, carrying his duffel, the plastic pouch, and my bag.

"What about my camera?"

"There's no time."

Dagger got in and started the engine. I climbed into the passenger seat, but he quickly ordered me to the back. "I need Zeta up front with me."

Zeta finally made it out, slamming the door closed behind her. She grabbed the rack bars on top of the Tahoe and, in a manner befitting a totally unrealistic Hollywood action movie, swung her legs in through the open passenger window as Dagger pulled out of the driveway.

10
GETTIN' OUT OF DODGE

We were still in sight of Dagger's house when he pulled out his phone, his thumb flying wildly over the screen.

I cleared my throat. "Texting whilst being pursued seems like a bad idea."

Dagger didn't respond. His thumb didn't stop either.

"Sealing up the house?" Zeta said, looking in the side view mirrors.

"Yes."

I squinted my eyes at his selective responses, noting to phrase my commentary in the form of a question if I wanted his participation.

"What if Hank needs to get inside?" I wondered aloud.

"Hank knows me pretty well; he won't try to get back in. If he does, he's smart enough to figure out how to do it safely."

We turned down the neighborhood street that led to the main road. Shortly thereafter, Dagger swung a u-turn and peeled out in the opposite direction.

"Dagger? That's the quickest way to the freeway!" Zeta yelled.

"It doesn't feel right. We'll go out the back way." Dagger made it a point not to look at me in the rearview mirror, as if one look would give his super sensing capabilities away.

I knew exactly why he had turned around.

"Don't question me." He peeled around another corner. "I'm your commanding officer."

"Yes, sir."

I expected Zeta to react badly to his reprimand. Surprisingly, she didn't. She pulled her gun out of the back of her pants, ready for whatever Dagger was expecting. We finally made it to a main road and raced toward the freeway.

"Dagger?" I asked, hesitant if I should continue. "How do you know they think I'm the Galana?"

"I don't, but I am not willing to take that chance. I don't believe in coincidences; Karchardeus is here for a reason, and that reason can only be you."

"What about King? He could be here for Kingston."

"He's here *with* Kingston, not *for* Kingston."

"What?" I asked, taken aback.

"Remember the other night when you went diving with your brother off of the marina docks?"

Of course Dagger had been watching. My stomach leapt at the thought. "Yes?"

"And do you remember seeing King with another candeon, leaving the marina as well?"

I did not like where this was going. "Yes."

"Those two are with Karchardeus." He was not expressing opinion.

"There is no way King is working with them willingly. He must not know who they are. Or he could be a victim. They could be forcing him!" My eyes widened as I remembered the swollen cut on King's brow. And all of those nights he claimed he had "business with Mrs. James" to discuss? What was really going on?

Dagger shook his head. "I saw them today—he is definitely not a victim."

At this, Zeta piped in. "If you were close enough to see them, then they could sense you, Dagger. And if Karchardeus knows you're here, then he knows you are protecting someone very high profile, someone like the

Galana. Aaram is the only noble in all of SoCal. Dagger . . . they know." Now Zeta was completely convinced that Karchardeus was here for me. In her eyes, this was no longer a precautionary mission.

Dagger's fingers gripped the wheel as his head twitched ever so slightly to the left. Zeta looked out her passenger window unaware, but I knew where Karchardeus and his mercenaries were coming from. I wondered how far away Dagger could sense them; he once told me that he could sense "miles and miles" away. Did that mean that we still had a good shot at making it out of San Diego without the mercenaries knowing?

"Zeta, look up behind us, to the left. I have a feeling that's them. Use your scope. Let me know if they're looking down at us."

She pulled a sniper rifle out of a long, soft case at her feet. She removed the scope, leaned out the window, and sat herself on the bottom of the window casing. The driver in the car next to us almost hit the guardrail, gawking at Zeta's insane behavior.

I looked up into the sky out the left side window. My hazy eyes struggled to focus through the city atmosphere. Then I saw it: a helicopter flying our direction.

"I don't think they can see us yet, but they are looking for something, that's for sure. They're circling low; I bet they're hoping to sense you, knowing you're with her." She caught herself mid-curse. "I wish we were in the water!" Zeta slid back inside. "We've got about four miles on them."

The catchy chorus of my ringtone trilled softly in the cab of the Tahoe. Dagger and Zeta shared a confused scowl. With the roar of Clementine and the rush of the wind through Zeta's open window, I almost missed it. I fished through my bag, grateful that I had not left my phone behind at Dagger's house.

"Do not answer your phone. Who is it?" Dagger looked at me in the rearview mirror for the first time, his tone eerily stable.

I looked at the screen and froze. Dagger reached back and took it from me.

"Kingston." He said the name like a profanity, throwing my phone to the floor of the truck, where it continued to ring unanswered. Zeta picked it up to toss it out the window, but Dagger held her arm. "Not yet."

Until that moment, I had never really known betrayal. Was it all part of a master plan? Surely it wasn't all a lie. I wanted answers. I lunged forward over the front seats, reaching for my phone, lucky that Zeta had her arms around me before I realized what I'd done.

Dagger barked, "Now's not the time. You can be angry later."

I fell back into my seat, startled. Clementine barreled under an overpass, weaving in and out of traffic, the grumbling noise in the truck so loud I couldn't hear my own thoughts. Tears splattered my jeans.

Zeta resumed calling out the location of the helicopter. When it was clear that the helicopter didn't follow us, Dagger slowed down, probably to avoid police attention. I lay down across the back bench seat and shut my eyes.

"What's the plan, sir? Phoenix? Vegas? Mexico?" Zeta asked.

Dagger didn't hesitate. "They could have access to human surveillance, including the cameras at the border. Maybe airports, too. Which is why you will be going through Tijuana: they'll see you on border surveillance and assume Haelo and I are close by. Travel down Baja and charter a flight out of La Paz. Make sure any airport cameras get you on record getting into the aircraft. Keep the plane low and bail out over the Caribbean. Get to Pankyra on the most isolated routes, take a tanker if you need to. Here's some cash and a burner phone if you get landlocked." He tossed her a plastic pouch from one of the zipper pockets of his duffel. "The first number is mine, the second is Hank's."

Lunatics. They're all lunatics.

"Got it. Baja, La Paz, parachute out over the ocean. They'll believe it." Zeta's accent was breaking free, getting more Latin by the minute. "They will think that we like the two-coast option down Baja. Bailing out of a plane is a tall order, though, even for you."

You think?

Dagger gave her a look.

"I never said it was impossible. What about the two of you?"

"We can't drive cross country—she's too young to be away from the ocean for that long."

"And probably too scared," Zeta chimed in.

"I'm sitting right here, guys!" *Did they think I was tuned out or something?*

Dagger gave Zeta a slight scolding with his raised eyebrow, but otherwise ignored my outburst. "We can't fly—again, the airport security footage. I can't risk that they will see us and track us down when we land."

"What other option do you have? Sir," she quickly added.

"We'll go north. I can't tell you any more than that."

"You're assuming that Karchardeus can catch me. And that I'll cave under torture."

My cell rang from the floor at her feet. She picked it up. "Sam? Who's Sam?"

When neither Dagger nor I answered, she tossed the phone back to the floor.

The hum of the engine changed; we were slowing down. "Get ready, Zeta. I can't drive you all the way up to the border station."

Zeta replaced the scope on her rifle and zipped it back into the case. "You keep this. I can sneak in the Browning and the Smith & Wesson, but this one is harder to conceal under my shirt."

Dagger pulled into a gravel side road and stopped. I got out to stretch as Zeta tucked two guns behind her back into her pants and slung a black cargo bag over her shoulder. Dagger walked around the truck to shake her hand.

She wiped her dusty aviators on her shirt, then tipped her head in my direction. "See you in Pankyra, Miss Marley. Good luck, sir."

He nodded. "Zeta."

She turned around and walked off into the afternoon desert.

"How far will she have to walk? We're in the middle of nowhere."

"The border town is just over that ridge. And as for how long she'll have to walk, that depends on where she borrows a car."

"Borrows a car? As in borrowing without consent?"

"Most likely." With that, he took out his phone and pulled out the battery before crushing the phone beneath his shoe. "Hopefully they'll have tracked our phones here and assume we've gone across the border. They could have almost as many resources as we do."

I looked around at the empty desert and the few bags in the truck. "Resources? We're looking pretty bare to me."

He got in the Tahoe. I was one leg shy of settling into the back seat before he stopped me. "You don't have to sit in the back anymore."

I hauled my exhausted self to the front where Zeta's rifle crowded the floor. I was too scared to move it.

"I'll get that out of your way," Dagger said, setting it down in the back.

"Thanks. I'd hate to accidentally shoot myself. Don't look at me like that, it could happen."

"Nobody wants a bleeding birthday girl." It was the first hint of a smile on Dagger's face since he'd left this morning.

Clementine roared to life. Dagger reached down by his feet, picked up my cell phone, and chucked it out the window as we turned back onto the highway.

We drove for hours without talking. I fought back tears whenever I allowed myself to think about what Neo, Aaram, and Hank might be going through. To keep myself from falling apart, I tried to think about all the photos I'd take if I had my camera: the desert landscape, the wrinkled old man driving the flashy yellow Ferrari, the crumbling fence of a distant ranch house, the sun setting behind two semi-trucks parked at a rest stop. Occasionally, we'd pass a small town and I would salivate at all of the restaurant billboards and signs, hoping Dagger was getting hungry too. Thankfully, when we finally stopped at a rare traffic light, my stomach growled loud enough for Dagger to hear.

"When did you eat last?"

"This morning. Your crêpes."

He shook his head. "I'm sorry. I should have realized . . . never mind. Let's get some dinner."

He pulled into the darkest drive-thru in the sleepy town, where we ordered at the walk-up window and then sat at an outdoor table. Crickets sang in the distance, accompanied by the calming buzz of the lone floodlight powered on the side of the fast food shack. I passed my fingers in and out of the rubberized metal grate tabletop, waiting for the greasy, tattooed attendant to bring out our order.

Dagger sighed. "I'm sorry for treating you so harshly earlier; I had to get you to safety. You deserve better than that."

I nodded in acceptance.

"You must have a lot on your mind. Is there anything you'd like to talk about?" Dagger asked. He held his breath. I could tell he wanted to be helpful, but I could also tell he didn't want to talk about uncomfortable things.

"No, I'm fine."

He exhaled, then bowed his head. Dragon-Tattoo brought out our order, glancing back and forth between the two of us.

"Lover's spat, eh?" he said. I could see his breath in the cold night air.

Dagger's aura flared momentarily, but the emotion was gone before I had a chance to figure out what it was. Dagger looked up at the teen with a perfect *Seriously?* eye-squint, which smoothly morphed into a definite, non-squinty *You need to leave*. The attendant rolled his eyes and shuffled back into the small building. Heavy metal music spilled out of the open doorway before it closed.

"Sorry about that," Dagger said. "Human tact still shocks me. Most of the time, at least." He was hoping to stimulate conversation, but I had no desire to talk. "You really should eat. We've got a long drive ahead with minimal stops."

I opened the paper bag and pulled out a pouch of onion rings while Dagger ate his burger unnaturally well—not a single corner-mouth-gloop or bun-crumb-in-the-scruff. Every time he opened his mouth for another bite, his teeth shined like he'd just come from the dentist. His chiseled jaw tensed slightly with each bite. He belonged in a commercial. Meanwhile, I slicked fried crumbs from my teeth with my tongue and hoped that I had remembered to pack floss. *Should have ordered the shake,* I thought as I dumped the uneaten onion rings onto the papered tray in the middle of our table. I'd have a go at the chicken fingers instead.

When eating no longer offered an excuse to not talk, the awkward silence peaked. I had to say something. "Hank and Zeta treat me funny." I winced as soon as the words left my mouth.

Dagger lowered his cup from his mouth. "What do you mean?"

"They bow to me, and use phrases like 'It's an honor to meet you,' even when it's pretty obvious that Zeta is annoyed."

"You are the Galana." The way Dagger said *Galana* made me feel a little sheepish.

I didn't know how to respond. I grabbed one of the few rings in the middle of the table and pushed the rest toward Dagger. "You said we were going to Panama. Where are we *really* going?"

Dagger took an onion ring. "North," he said. "And we're staying inland; there are significantly fewer candeons on land than in the water, which means we can avoid the possibility of running into spies if we can avoid candeons in general. I can't risk you turning in the water, where it is that much harder to protect you during the long transitional sleep. If Massáude knows you haven't transitioned yet, then he'll know that we'll avoid the water. The only other way to Pankyra is by plane, but the problem with flying is that airports—with their security cameras and witnesses—are out of the question."

"So how do we fly into Greece without going through an airport?" I asked.

Dagger got up to throw away our trash. He stretched, looking around naturally, not at all like a security professional scouting an area. He beckoned to the Tahoe. Once inside, he didn't start the engine. "I helped out a friend in the U.S. military awhile back. He owes me."

"We can't just stow away on a military plane."

"We won't be stowing away."

Dagger still hadn't started the car, giving me the liberty to ask another question. "Who exactly is Massáude? And Kachardus, or Karchudleus, or whatever his name is?"

"Massáude is the leader of the rebels. He is a descendant of a mutinous noble named Kryos."

I laughed. "Can you hear yourself?" I lowered my voice in imitation. "*Leader of the mutinous rebel descendants... noble rebels... Kryos... May the force be with you....*" I laughed again.

Dagger did not.

"Sorry." I cleared my throat. "Yes, Aaram told me all the scandalous details about the Basileus's brother Kryos and Galana Vespa. They had another kid after she left the Basileus, right? So Massáude is like their great great great great grandson?"

He nodded. "Massáude has no conscience. The only reason the rebels haven't done more damage is because he's smart enough to know he would lose if he challenged the monarchy. He's biding his time. He's using people. If he had his way, he'd kill anyone who disagreed with him and everyone that got in the way, but his intelligence, his *cunning*, keeps him in check.

"Karchardeus leads a team of mercenaries as Massáude's second-in-command. Though brutal and violent, he is at least smart enough to not feed Massáude's sociopathic side. He's incredibly power hungry, just doesn't have the royal lineage that Massáude has. Lineage goes a long way in our world."

I didn't need the reminder. "And you've met him?"

Dagger put both hands on the steering wheel and stared into the dashboard. He hesitated after each word as if still deciding whether or not to tell me. "Karchardeus is my uncle."

"*What?* Don't you think that qualifies as a conflict of interest?"

He turned his head away, staring out the driver's side window. "Karchardeus and four other members of the Krypteia defected to the unorganized rebels ten years ago. He saw an opportunity for power and took it. When my father tried to stop him, Karchardeus killed him—his own brother. A year later, he killed my mother at the battle you remember from your childhood. We both became orphans that day. I assure you there is no conflict of interest between Karchardeus and me."

"Dagger, I am so sorry."

"I grew up in the Krypteia world. Death is something we are trained to deal with."

"Why are you telling me all of this? Why are you telling me *any* of this?"

"I'm your bodyguard, and the most important part of that relationship is trust. It is my duty to keep our relationship open and honest. I know a great deal about you; it's your right to know about me.

Your grandfather can't keep us from talking anymore. If you ask, I will tell."

"What happens when we get to Pankyra? Why build all of this trust and then drop me off at the castle gates?"

"I will remain your bodyguard as long as Basileus Alcaeus wants me to be. Your marriage to Griffin is not the end of the rebel threat; Vespa made sure of that." I smirked just as he put up his hand. "No. No bad imitations or movie quotes."

An unexpected flood of comfort came from knowing that I would not be alone among strangers in Pankyra. Dagger was a friend. A mysterious warrior friend, but a friend nonetheless. I reached over and flung my arms around his neck. He patted me on the back twice and then leaned away. I settled back into my seat, not knowing whether to grin or feel . . . disciplined.

He amended his warning. "Though the threat is not over, there is a little more safety in your being wed. The rebels will have a harder time convincing the candeon population of an alliance between you and Massáude—no matter your defiance in the matter—if you have already committed publicly to Griffin. Alcaeus believes it might even be enough to force Massáude to give up his distorted royal ambitions."

"You don't look too convinced."

"I'm not." His fingers flexed.

"You really ought to loosen up a bit. Seriously, I haven't seen your face relax, like, ever." Not that I was feeling any sort of relaxed.

He turned the ignition, and Clementine thundered with a confident growl that helped drown out the load on my mind. Back on the highway, my curiosity again peaked.

"You'll answer any of my questions?"

"Within reason," he said.

"Does anyone call you Dag?"

He cocked his head. "Of all the questions you could ask me, your first one is if anyone calls me Dag?"

"I thought I'd start easy."

"Okay." He smiled. "Well, then, no. No one calls me Dag."

"Why not? It seems like a natural nickname. Just think of the possibilities. 'Yo, what-up, Dag?' Or what about the completely new meaning behind 'Dagnammit'?" The word brought up memories of Lauryn that I quickly brushed away. Since I was feeling so much better than I had in hours, I wouldn't let it get to me that he didn't laugh, or even grimace for that matter.

"Another question: how long have you been a kryptes?"

"My family has been a part of the official Krypteia since it was formed, over two hundred years ago. Our clan had been warriors of the sea for almost a thousand years before that. We start training as children. My first assignment was nine years ago."

"After your mom died?"

"Yes."

"You were young. Fourteen?"

"It was an unusual situation. We don't normally join until after transition, but . . . my capabilities were needed."

"Can you talk about it?"

"I'd rather not."

Even though it wasn't a definite "no," I didn't want to pressure him. "Does Zeta have special powers?"

"What makes you think that?"

"She told me that she wasn't from an original Krypteia clan. You said that you all were from the same clan in the southern African waters. I'm assuming that she got in because she has a unique talent."

"Very observant. Yes, she does." He didn't elaborate.

"How come you know about her, but she can't know about your powers?"

"Extra capabilities are carefully guarded secrets—we don't want enemies to know what we can do. But, sometimes missions require that your team know your talents. I was on assignment with Zeta in the Caribbean a few years ago, and as her commander, I had to be aware of her ability."

"But you've managed to keep your talent a secret this long?"

"I have been ordered to keep it secret from all but the Basileus, the Prince, my commander, and you, despite the disadvantages on team missions."

"Why me, again?"

"I can almost guarantee that you will need to know later; it is better that you know about it now than freak out or not trust me when the time comes."

"Oh. Right." The future didn't look especially carefree.

Out the window, the landscape was thicker than it had been previously, with snow in patches underneath the trees. It didn't look like any part of California I had ever seen. I wished that I had been paying attention to the road signs. I tried to think back, attempting to remember any landmarks or signs suggesting where we were, but I was drawing a blank.

"Dagger? You mentioned before that you came to San Diego two years ago. You also said that you came into this whole history a long time before that. What did you mean?"

He didn't answer this question right away, as he had the others, though he did not fidget, move, look around, or otherwise stall; he only stared rigidly straight ahead into the headlight's path.

I waited a very long minute. "Dagger? What did you mean?"

Clementine sped up. "Only that my talents have helped you in the past. I think it's my turn to ask questions."

It was like they say when you are on the verge of death and your life flashes before your eyes, only this time it was because I had to search for a moment in time when Dagger Stravins would have intervened in my childhood. It should have been a thought frenzy, but after the week I had been through, it felt like just another link in the crazy-chain. I came up empty. Dagger didn't expound, but I gave him a pass, not wanting to acknowledge to myself that I was the one who needed a break from this topic.

"All right, then. What is your first question?" I asked.

"You're not going to ask me about the past?"

"Not tonight. I don't think either of us is ready for that conversation."

He twitched. Not quite relief, not quite disappointment. There was something in his posture; I just couldn't put my finger on it.

Dagger interrupted my stupor with a question. "What was your favorite birthday?"

"You mean besides this one?"

He acknowledged my sarcasm with a weak eye-roll and gestured for an answer. I shut my eyes to think. There was the birthday when Dad, Neo, and I bodysurfed waves with dolphins, though thinking about that one only made me wonder how Neo and Aaram were faring back in San Diego, and I did not have the emotional strength left to deal with that again. There was another birthday after Tilly was born when Mom and I went shopping for swimsuits. It was my first human shopping trip. I bought Tilly a tiny hair clip: sparkly turquoise with a pink plastic flower on the end. I had thought it would keep her sole wayward curl—the one right in the center of her hairline—away from her face (her curl always tickled her eyes in the swaying currents of the reef). I remembered that mom bought me shave ice, which I devoured so fast that I thought my brain was dying. She told me it was called a brain freeze. It took me a few years to want to eat shave ice again. It was definitely a memorable birthday, but not quite my favorite.

"There was one birthday, my eighth birthday, when we were trying out living in a human home on an island, I don't remember which one, and my dad told me that there was a surprise in the backyard. I ran out there but didn't see anything. I looked behind every bush . . . under every rock. I even looked up into the trees. I finally gave up, turning back to the house where on the back porch stood my Mom, Dad, Neo, and Tilly, all surrounding a cake with so many candles I thought it was on fire. They sang 'Happy Birthday' four times with lyrics that they had made up to describe all the fun things we did that year. After I blew out the candles, I reached around for a big family hug and knocked over the cake. We tried to pick it up, but frosting smeared *everywhere*. The cake just crumbled away in our hands. We sat cross-legged on the porch and ate it off the floor. The neighbor behind us came out when he heard the squealing and laughter and asked why we were eating food off the dirty porch. My mom yelled across the rickety fence that he'd eat it too if he knew how good it was."

I smiled, remembering the red and purple sundress and yellow galoshes she wore that afternoon. She was a beautiful woman. I was recalling the way Tilly licked pink frosting from between her fingers when Dagger brought me back to the present.

"That sounds like a great day."

I sighed and looked out the window at the menacing mountains beyond. "It was."

He gave me a few minutes to reminisce before asking, "What is it about photography that you love so much?"

It was not a question I was expecting. I shrugged and shook my head. "I don't know. One day my friend Sam gave me a disposable camera. I've been carrying around a camera ever since. I guess it's because I don't have any pictures of my parents or my sister, Tilly."

"For what it's worth, I'm sure your parents would be very proud of the strong young woman you have grown up to be."

"Thank you. I like to think they look down on me. That I make them proud." I wished I knew how to express how grateful I was for him, but I was scared that if I tried, it would come out all mushy.

"I suspected your reasons for loving photography, but one I can't figure out is the sports thing. How is it that someone who never ever goes to any sporting events—not for lack of opportunity—can be so into sports statistics? And not only that, but be really, really good at it? I've been following your basketball and football fantasy leagues. Haelo, you're killin' it."

His sudden informality and almost awkward attempt at American lingo helped me relax for the first time in days.

I raised my brow and nodded cockily. I *was* killin' it. *Too bad Aaram made me promise not to join the money leagues.* Putting aside my pride, I answered. "Honestly, and I know you'll think I'm pretty lame for saying this, but there's a silly part of me that just wants to be part of the crowd. I'm so different—literally a different species—from everyone. To be one of thousands rooting for an outcome . . . it makes me feel like I'm a part of *something* in this world that I live in. I can't be, you know, *in* it, but by being a fan? Well, I can be part of it. And I wish I could actually go to a big game, like game seven of the NBA finals, or the FIFA World Cup championship, or even just the last few innings of the last game of the World Series. I'd even go to the Superbowl if one of the teams actually had real fans in the crowd instead of thousands of corporate light-weights. I'd love to sit in the most diehard fan section of the Oakland Raiders or the Yankees or, or, any team for that matter. Can you imagine the intensity of being in that? *With* that?

"But I don't go to games because I physically can't stand the buzz; all those human auras tingling and sparking with extreme excitement, or anxiety, or anger. I mean, I'd have to sit in a dark empty house out in the boonies for a week just to recuperate. Neo can do it, Aaram can do it. I can't. It hurts. I don't know, maybe something is wrong with me. So instead of subjecting myself to debilitating physical intensity in order to be a part of one team, I keep up with *all* the teams. The fact that I'm good at it is probably just passion combined with a good memory and a knack for statistics." I sighed. "Math is predictable. It's comforting." I had never had the need, or the inclination, to explain myself on this matter before. But there it was.

Dagger looked thoughtful. "So, when human emotions intensify, you can feel it?"

"Easily," I answered. "Aaram once told me that when I mature into an adult candeon, if I try really hard, I might be able to feel a difference in someone's aura. Being the stubborn little girl that I was, I tried and tried, thinking that if I practiced enough I'd learn how to do it before I was an adult. The more I tried, the better I got at it. Now, if I really want to, I can tell even subtle changes in human mood. I can tell when my teachers are peeved even before I walk in the door."

"Haelo, that's a big deal."

I thought for a moment. "But everyone can do it. All adults, at least. And I'm almost an adult. *And* it's not with candeons, only humans—I haven't been around enough candeons to practice on them."

"No, not everyone can do that. Hardly anyone. Your grandfather was speaking about our ability to sense big emotions, like mortal fear, something big enough to noticeably change an aura—something you'd be able to tell by body language, anyway. What you can do is very exceptional. You're very sensitive to auras."

His last few words trailed off into a mumble. Suddenly, Dagger scowled and closed his eyes.

"Dag? What's wrong? And please watch the road!"

When his eyes shot open, I saw the same controlled adrenaline from our escape out of San Diego. Panic fluttered in my chest. I couldn't tell if it was fear or a hot flash, but heat started to blur my thoughts and vaporize off of the back of my neck. I prayed that it was not a hot flash.

Dagger pulled a handgun out from underneath his seat. "Remember when I said that knowing my extra capabilities would be helpful in the future? Well, here we go."

He slowed down and searched outside of the car windows. The only light came from the headlights and the stars. I blinked a few times, trying unsuccessfully to clear a little dry haze. Dagger slowed dramatically, shut off the headlights, and turned off of the road onto a patch of large stones where we wouldn't leave obvious tracks pointing out our highway exit. He must have sensed the mercenaries behind us. Once we reached the forested bracken about fifteen yards from the road, he sped up as fast as was practical, dodging in and out of trees and boulders. We were definitely leaving a trail now, but if they'd missed our initial exit, then it didn't matter anyway. We drove for a few miles, even crossed a shallow creek. Clementine jostled on the rugged terrain, causing me to hit my head on the roof more often than I thought necessary.

We finally stopped behind a short ridge. Dagger got out and sped around to my door. "Come. We'll walk from here." We grabbed our bags and took off into the dark forest, farther and farther from the highway, deeper and deeper into the trees.

Deceptively slippery moss adorned anything it could on the uneven, rocky ground. Without warning, I slipped. Before I hit the ground, Dagger caught me around the waist. I hadn't realized how heavy I was breathing until I felt my ribcage expanding rapidly beneath his arm as he set me right.

"You okay?" he asked, looking me over. I nodded. He took my bag and flung it over his muscled shoulder with ease.

"Thanks," I breathed. He didn't respond. I looked longingly back toward the direction of Dagger's Tahoe. "Wouldn't it be best to stay with the truck? Then if the mercenaries get close we don't have to *run*?"

He still did not respond. For as nice as he usually was, he sure could be a jerk sometimes.

I could see my breath; it felt dewy on my face as we rushed forward. I once again cursed the haze in my eyes that made it cumbersome to run through rugged terrain. A mile later, a sharp ache in my side burned as I tried to catch my breath. I tripped again; this time Dagger was too far ahead to catch me. My shoulder scraped along the bark of a tree as I crashed into a fallen trunk, helplessly rolling down a short encampment and landing in the muddy bank of a small creek. Dagger was by my side before I had even realized what happened. He looked me over, making sure I was fit to stand, then pulled me up by my arms. I yelled, dropping my shoulders back into the mud as Dagger gently released his grip.

"You dislocated your shoulder. This is going to hurt."

"What?"

"Just close your eyes."

He braced my side with one hand and forced my shoulder back into place with the other. The echo of my scream ricocheted in the forest. After my teeth unclenched, I looked down at the shredded sleeve of my shirt.

"What is all the blood from?" I panted, gliding my fingers over the liquid dripping down my arm.

Dagger ripped my sleeve farther up past my shoulder and examined the wound. He cupped some water from the creek and trickled it over the gashes. "We need to clean you up, but we've got to get to that hill first. Can you make it that far?"

I nodded. Dagger helped me to my feet and watched me as I started upwards, making sure I was steady and able to make the ascension. I was light-headed and in throbbing pain; still, each foot continued to climb in front of the other, despite my inner pleas to sit down. At the last steep ridge, I held my good arm out for balance, which Dagger grabbed in order to help me as I slipped in the loose volcanic gravel. His hand was cold and strong.

When we finally made it to the top, I fell to a large rock and cradled my arm. Dagger set down the sniper rifle and both of our bags, then pulled out a clean shirt and small pouch. He drenched the shirt with a water bottle before gently wiping as much blood and mud as he could from my arm, shoulder, neck, and face. Staring at the thick veins in his forearm distracted me from any pain.

He stopped wiping. I looked around. "Why did we ditch the Tahoe?"

He ignored me and opened the pouch, retrieving a first aid kit. He ripped open an alcohol wipe and dabbed my wound. I watched his face, waiting for an answer to my question. There was a little spot of gray in his five o'clock shadow, and a lonely freckle sat in the outer crease of his eyelid. I tried once again to remember where I had seen such unique, light gray eyes.

He worked quickly, picking out pieces of bark and wiping with the alcohol until the wound looked clean.

"Why are we here?" I asked, a little softer this time.

"I can feel them a few miles back. We have to figure out how they tracked us. If they have someone with abilities like mine, they'll come up the mountain to us. If they somehow put a GPS tracker on Clementine, they'll go right to her and spread out from there. If they keep going past where we turned off of the highway, then they are following traffic cameras or eyewitness accounts. Either way, we need to know." He narrowed his eyes and stared into the empty air in front of him. "They are just about at the turn-off point."

"How far away can you sense, exactly? I mean if they are just now getting to tha—"

He pulled out a set of expensive looking binoculars from his bag and studied the shallow valley in the distance. "Here. See?"

He held the binoculars in place; I stepped on a rock to be tall enough to see into them and Dagger put a hand on my back to steady me. The contact felt more intimate than it should have.

My shoulder hurt like the dickens, but a few breaths later, I managed to steady the view. The image in the lenses was filtered in digital green—night-vision. "I can see the highway. There's a dark jeep and a bigger SUV. Which one are they?"

"Both."

"That explains why neither of them have their headlights on." I stepped away to let him look. My bag rested unopened on the ground, an embarrassing reminder that I did not pack anything that would be of value in the wilderness. *No night-vision goggles or first aid kit there.* "Can they sense us from the highway? How far away is that, anyway?"

"They shouldn't be able to. Not until they get within a half mile, mile at most. We're a little over a mile and a half from the Tahoe and about four and half from the highway." He held his gaze on the two SUVs. "They turned off exactly where we did. They've been tracking Clementine."

"What do we do?" I said, panic rising in my voice.

"We wait."

"Wait? We're sitting ducks!"

"Haelo, we wait. Once they sense that we're not with the truck, they'll fan out looking for us. We'll go back, find the GPS tracker, destroy it, and leave."

I lowered my voice. "How will we get back to your truck if they are surrounding it?" I didn't know why I was whispering.

Dagger held his breath. After lowering the binoculars, he exhaled and explained, "You already know that I can sense others at extreme distances. You also know that I can hide my aura from the senses of others. What you do not yet know is that I can also hide yours."

I instinctively looked down at myself, then back to Dagger.

"If I have enough contact with another candeon, I can extend my abilities to hide their aura as well. We can sneak past the mercenaries that way."

My eyes bugged. "You are one hella-awesome bodyguard!"

The startled smile that erupted from his face was mixed with a whole lot of confusion.

"I do what I can."

We smiled at each other. I almost laughed, but he whipped around to look through the binoculars, watching for a minute before he narrated what he was seeing. "They just got to the truck. Karchardeus looks... upset." Dagger smiled at the word, amused. He hissed. "That hurts." Now Dagger was the one upset.

"What? What hurts?" I looked him up and down, trying to decipher what sort of evil the mercenaries could possibly be doing to Dagger from such a distance.

"A short, pudgy one just wailed on Clementine's hood with a baseball bat and left a huge dent." Then, speaking to himself, he added, "So much for professional courtesy."

If I wasn't so relieved that Dagger was fine, I would have been irate that he had me so worried over a stupid dent. "Wait, did you say a pudgy one?"

"Yeah, why?"

"May I see?"

Dagger handed me the binoculars. They were insanely powerful, so it took me a moment to steady the view to find the mercenaries and cars below. I counted seven men and one woman. One faced away from us, barking orders. He turned around to fume at the empty Tahoe. My stomach clenched. The resemblance to Dagger was astounding, the only major differences being slightly darker skin, a facial scar, a solid thirty years in age, and the sneer of a James Bond villian. Karchardeus. Something about him made me want to throw up. The mercenaries behind him started to disperse into the wilderness; he took a path headed in our direction. A short, sweaty, rotund man with hairy arms and a bald spot stayed behind.

"Dagger, I've seen that one before."

"Which one?" he asked as I passed the binoculars to him.

"The one staying behind with the cars—the squidgy guy who dented Clementine."

He watched. "When and where did you see him?"

Once again a feeling of betrayal swept over me. "With Kingston at a café in San Diego. Two years ago." I slumped. Dagger put his hand on my arm.

"Haelo, this does not mean that Kingston has been siding with the rebels for that long. He could have been played. I bet he didn't realize who he was dealing with until recently." He turned back to the binoculars. "He certainly knows now. He's in the Suburban."

It was salt in my wound. He wasn't just chummy with the enemy; he was helping them track me down.

"We need to get going." Dagger zipped up the binoculars into his bag, loaded all of our gear over his shoulders, and then held out his arm toward me.

"What am I supposed to do?"

"Until a connection is established between our auras, we need to get . . . close." He sounded a little embarrassed, but not enough to take away the authority in his voice.

I walked forward. He wrapped his free arm around me, tucking my head in his warm shoulder. I fit perfectly into his side. His breath hitched as I closed my eyes.

Butterflies. My stomach rippled with millions of them.

An inaudible buzz began to emanate from every part of me, growing and building until my aura felt like it might burst out. Suddenly, it flared up. I winced, thinking my head would split open.

Right when I thought I had no other choice but to let go of Dagger and fall to the ground, my intensified aura popped. Gone. It was like turning off the hum of a fan that had been going for eighteen years. I still felt just as alive as I always had, but with a clear sensation, as if part of me were missing, allowing the other parts to focus front and center in my physical awareness. I looked up at Dagger; he looked down the mountain. He released the embrace but didn't break contact, sliding his left palm down my good arm until he could clasp my hand. Of their own accord, my fingers closed around his. His breath hitched again. Or maybe that was me.

He cleared his throat. "Whatever you do, do not let go of my hand."

"Okay."

"And Haelo, don't think I didn't notice that you called me Dag back there," he teased.

"I told you it was catchy. It was bound to come out eventually."

He shook his head and started down the mountain.

We didn't run this time. We walked carefully among the trees, never out in the open. We didn't talk, either. I watched my footing, hoping not to stumble—one damaged shoulder was bad enough. The first time Dagger had grabbed my hand, I only noticed how cold and strong it was; now his hand felt comforting, and protective, and gentle, and calloused but not rough, homey instead of scratchy. The kind of hand I would want to hold me. Cautiously, he moved his hand along my forearm to my elbow and held me steady while we crossed the narrowest part of the creek along some stones.

We were more than halfway to the car when Dagger pulled me down behind a mossy fallen log. He put his finger to his lips, using his eyes to warn me about something over his shoulder. We sat in complete silence, my breath so shallow I might as well have stopped breathing altogether. Thirty seconds later, I had to take a long drag of air to keep from passing out. A twig cracked in the distance, making my heart race. I didn't even attempt to sense the mercenaries; I was too panicked to get an accurate reading, anyway. A small voice in the back of my mind assumed that maybe I wouldn't be able to sense any aura without feeling my own.

Dagger squeezed my hand three times to get my attention. He looked firmly into my eyes and showed me how to breathe. I tried to imitate his steady breaths, but my heart would not calm down.

Two more cracks.

A group of birds fled from the safety of their nests in a tree twenty yards away. I looked up to Dagger with saucer eyes. He shook his head and caressed my hand with his thumb. I shut my eyes, racking my brain for something distracting to think about, but the best I could come up with was to think the alphabet backwards. It helped. A little.

Before I got to 'Q', Dagger squeezed my hand again. I peeked, barely, through one eye. He beckoned behind himself with a tilt of his head and mouthed, *They're gone.* He immediately stood.

It took some time before I could join him. This was all still a whirlwind for me, and cautious seemed like the way to go. He helped me over the fallen log and we continued on, though I was much more hesitant than before.

Just as I was getting the hang of the forest terrain, Dagger slowed down, pulling me back toward him as he whispered, "Soon you will sense Kingston and the short mercenary. Stay calm and quiet; they cannot sense you as long as you do not let go of me. Watch your footing. Once we get closer, I will take care of them."

My eyes widened. I couldn't ask him what he meant by that because as soon as he finished, he led me around a bend and behind a squat boulder.

Something sparked and fluttered on the fringes of my senses like a sparse shadow of my own aura. I focused and barely made out that it was Kingston ahead. I sensed another nearby. I heard the slow pull of a zipper and saw Dagger lift the sniper from its case. I shook his hand, frantically trying to get his attention.

"Haelo," he breathed, mouth barely moving, "you need to trust me." He pulled up the sleeve of his shirt. "Slide your hand up my arm. I need both hands."

I did as I was told. His muscles felt like concrete. Dagger assembled the rifle and perched the tripod on top of the boulder, making for himself an ideal scoping position. I stared at the back of the Suburban, thinking back to my first date with Kingston. I liked to think that he had actually enjoyed being with me—we had talked so comfortably that night. *Please don't kill him.*

I nearly jumped out of my own skin when Dagger fired off two shots, readjusted, then fired off one more. The rifle was extremely quiet; I knew none of the mercenaries in the surrounding area heard the shots. I trembled so badly that Dagger had to grab my hand and hold it against his arm to maintain our contact.

"Haelo, I only shot out their tires." He looked in my eyes until he was sure I understood, then went back to the scope. I took a deep breath and remembered what must have been the sound of the tires being hit.

Dagger once again narrated what he was seeing. "The short one is scrambling around trying to figure out what happened. Kingston is hiding in the back seat of the Suburban. Wait, Shorty just took off into the trees to go get the others. He's too jumpy to be a mercenary; he's probably Massáude's eyes and ears for the mission. Come on, let's go."

Dagger packed up the rifle. He walked us forward so confidently that I could not doubt he knew what he was doing. When we got to the edge of the small clearing where the three SUVs were parked, he pulled out a sleek grenade and crept forward in a crouch toward the Suburban.

"Don't hurt him," I pleaded in a quiet inhale.

Dagger looked at me incredulously. When we got to the back of the Suburban, he beckoned to his upper arm. I once again slid my hand up. In one swift motion, he lunged forward, swung open the door, and threw the grenade into the front seat. He slammed the door and we both sprinted behind the nearest tree.

The blast was not what I expected. No fire, no explosion, just a loud bang.

"What was that?"

"A modified concussion grenade. He'll wake up and be fine, maybe a broken eardrum or two. He likely won't remember what happened, which is good for us. It was either that, or kill him, because I can't let him figure out how we snuck down here undetected. We need to go—three others heard that and are on their way back."

We ran hand in hand to Clementine. Before he opened the door, Dagger ran his free hand along the undercarriage, where, near the back tire, he picked out a small, flat square with a tiny antenna and red LED light. It looked like a movie prop. He put it on a rock, picked up a larger rock, and crushed the tracking device. I flinched feeling Dagger's muscles at work.

I sat in the driver's seat while Dagger tossed his shoulder baggage into the back, then scooted over when he climbed in as well.

Of all the things Dagger had done with me stuck to his arm, starting the Tahoe seemed to be the most difficult: I had to reach over him to hold his left arm. He was visibly flustered as he fumbled with the gear shifter beneath me.

He finally got the transmission in gear and floored it out of the clearing. The path back to the highway was just as bumpy as it was the first time we blazed through. By the time we cleared the tree line and pulled out onto the highway, the sky had lightened into a beautiful, deep indigo, as if everything had been washed in egg dye.

We were at least five minutes down the road when Dagger commented nonchalantly, "You can let go of my arm now. We're miles ahead of them." He flashed a smile. "And I should probably tell you that you could have switched arms." His gaze followed my arm from where it stretched across him to my shoulder, to my neck, to my wide eyes a mere eight inches from his.

I blushed. When I released my grip, the buzz of my aura hit me like a turbine. All my life, my aura had been something that I never really noticed. It was a part of me; I never had to think about it. It took not feeling it to even recognize that it was there in the first place. Dagger's aura soon joined us, as well.

I scooted back into my seat against the passenger door. Though I managed to calm my heart rate, I still felt the warmth of my blush in my cheeks. Neither of us said anything. A few mile markers later, Dagger shifted slightly, an excuse enough for me to finally look at him. It was then I noticed three little crescents still indented in his arm. "Oh, sorry! I didn't realize I held on that tight."

He rubbed the nail marks on his biceps. "It's okay, and it's better than the alternative. Thank you for not letting go back there; that would have put us in a tough spot."

For the first time since Dagger had wrapped me in his arm at the top of the mountain, the unspoken tension between us cleared.

I relaxed against the back of the seat. "You're welcome, Dag."

He rolled his eyes very dramatically before murmuring under his breath, "Great. That's not going to get old at all."

II

OUTSTANDING CITIZENS

We pulled into an empty, dusty parking lot in the next town. I found a spigot in the back corner and tried to rinse away as much of the residual mud, blood, and dirt as I could, then quickly brushed my teeth. A wide tree on the edge of the lot proved to be a decent place to duck behind to change into fresh clothes. I emerged feeling loads better. Though a hairbrush would have been nice.

Dagger got out a tool kit and an Arizona license plate from underneath Clementine's back seat. After switching the plates, he started pulling something off the side of the car. I bent down to help. We peeled away the black paint job on the bottom strip of the Tahoe as if it was nothing more than some sort of silicon sticker, revealing the true, shiny chrome. Next, he lifted the hood to forcefully tap out the dent with a large rubber mallet. The remodel wasn't perfect, but at least it looked different than the original dent, maybe even unnoticeable to the casual passerby. Clementine looked like a new girl.

Back in our seats, Dagger mumbled something about how he finally got to show off her chrome.

We had just escaped deadly mercenaries and he worried about how his car looked. "I always thought it was cliché, but 'men and their toys' is a real thing, isn't it?" I waited for a retort, or even a glimmer of a smile. Alas, no.

Dagger was not paying attention. He sat completely still, eyes unfocused. I had seen it before: he was feeling for candeons. After his mini-trance, he relaxed and started the engine.

"Can we stop for some food?" I asked. It had been hours since the few onion rings and sole chicken strip I had managed to get down, and even longer since a real meal.

He agreed with a nod and went through the only twenty-four hour drive-thru we could find on the town's main road. In a gesture worthy of Neo, I ordered nearly the entire left side of the menu. Dagger raised his eyebrows but had the sense not to say anything. After paying and pulling out of the drive-thru, he turned back the direction we had come.

"What are you doing?" I yelped after a quick and painful swallow of milkshake.

"Haelo, you have got to learn to trust me."

"I do trust you, I just want to know." I held my perturbed eyebrows as if to say *Don't I* deserve *to know?*

"Here, watch."

Right outside of town, we pulled over alongside a hitchhiker—the grubby, hairy, toking, hippie, friendly-looking kind. It was so stereotypical it was surreal. Dagger rolled down the passenger window, calling out over me. "Hey there! Where're you headed?"

The backpacker walked right up to my window and yelled, "Making my way east! This is going to be an awesome sunrise, yeah? I can feel it in my bones, man!"

I had to shake my head to get the ringing out of my ears. He had an overgrown, blond beard and a fringed vest. His pants were held up with the biggest belt buckle I had ever seen: a glass-encased scorpion surrounded by an intricate pattern of mother of pearl and turquoise stones.

Dagger nodded and yelled back, "Climb on in, buddy!"

Dagger was off his rocker. "Jessica, dear, can you make room for our awesome new friend? Maybe let him sit up front?" He was hinting at something, to which I was oblivious. But if I was going to be Jessica, then he was going to get a new name too.

"Sure, Edgar. I'd love to."

If looks could kill, I'd be smoldering on the side of the road. I grabbed my food, climbed into the back, and casually tried to hide the rifle case underneath Dagger's duffel. Our awesome new friend hopped in with an eager smile. He smelled of wet leather, Corn Nuts, and weed. Dagger merged back onto the highway with a small cloud of dust.

"Thanks, guys! I sure do appreciate it. I'm Ed, by the way."

I couldn't help it. "Ed and Edgar! It's like it was meant to be. Cheeseburger, Ed?"

Ed nodded enthusiastically. "Cheeseburgers at six in the morning? Heck, yes! You two are my kind of people. We're like bosom buddies." He took the offering, then turned to Dagger, pity radiating from his face. "No offense, man, but your mom really named you Edgar? Did you git teased?" His concern dripped with sincerity.

Dagger looked at me in the rearview mirror and sighed. "Yes, Ed. I did."

"That's rough. Kids these days." Ed shook his head in disappointment, wiggling out of his backpack until it plopped on the floor.

"So, Ed," Dagger said, "Jessica and I are trying to make it back to our friends. They had some car trouble but managed to track down another car, and now they're just about to hit the road." This was Dagger's roundabout way of keeping me informed of Karchardeus' progress. "Jessica, honey?" He reached back and grabbed my hand again. My stomach flipped at the word "honey," even though it was an innocent charade. His gold ring felt much warmer than it should have. "Would you like to lie down back there? You look really tired."

I understood. We were going to drive in the opposite direction, hiding our auras, and use Ed as the human presence for the mercenaries to feel when we passed them.

Ed concurred, "Yeah, Jessie, you look pretty wiped."

This time, Dagger smiled. I snuck in a quick pinch before holding tightly to his hand and lying down beneath the view of the windows.

I felt my aura flare, weaker than before. It faded back to normal with a disappointed twitch in Dagger's wrist. Dagger tried again, but failed. We weren't close enough.

"Edgar, I'm getting kind of cold," I said, leaning forward into the empty space between the seats. Dagger got the hint. He wrapped his arm around me, still holding tight to my hand. Once again, my heart fluttered and my breath hitched. Acceptance, protection, care... connection. *I could get used to this. No. What is wrong with you?* My aura flared and then... pop! Once again, the strange feeling of emptiness heightened my other senses. The clarity only made the angry butterflies in my stomach feistier. The proximity to Dagger toyed with my emotions, and frankly, I wasn't sure how much longer I could handle it.

I pretended to yawn and fell back onto the seat, still holding Dagger's hand.

For the next twenty minutes, Awesome Ed and I talked about his adventures. He had started in Portland, hitchhiking the coast all the way down to San Francisco, then turned east, zigzagging across California. He wanted to see everything that the pioneers, gold rushers, ranchers, and Wild West cowboys got to see. He showed me the journal that he kept with dried leaves and wildflowers pressed into the pages, all gathered from the places he had been so far. He also showed me his collection of trinkets picked up from the side of the road. There were keys, jewelry, empty matchbooks, and coins, each with a story. *Talk about hermit-hippie-lonely-anthropologist.*

Twice, Dagger's thumb swept along the back of my hand, then froze. I prayed for Ed's conversation to distract me.

After Ed's *make your own soap out of things you can find in the dump behind a restaurant* spiel, Dagger squeezed my hand twice in a chivalrous warning before releasing it. My arm had fallen asleep, so when it hit the floor, painful shocks rippled up to my neck, making the hum of my returning aura even more sensational. I had to blink nearly thirty times to get my bearings.

Ed had begun a stimulating topic of conversation on the finer aspects of preparing road kill when Dagger cut him off, "Ed, buddy, I need to head up a little road pretty soon. I'm afraid this is where we part ways. Can I take you to the closest bus stop? There's one about a half mile up the road. I don't mind doubling back."

Dagger's phrasing and manner of speaking with Ed was informal...natural. In contrast, it made his normal way of speaking seem even more formal than it had before.

Ed shook his head, "Oh, no. Thanks, though. Do you see this landscape out here? Man, the Head Honcho upstairs certainly knows His craft. I'm gonna chill up in that tree and watch the sunrise. Did I tell you it's gonna be a good one? I can feel it in my bones!"

Dagger and I smiled at Awesome Ed. He was certainly one of the most genuine people I had ever met. We all stepped out to say goodbye.

"Ed, I'm really glad we picked you up. I just wish we had more time to hang," I admitted. "I'll never forget you."

He pulled me into a big, swaying hug. "You two are some pretty outstanding citizens. Way to be! You mind if I take another burger for the road?"

Dagger put his hands up. "Don't look at me—I already ate mine. She's the one with the appetite."

I gave Dagger the nastiest look I could muster. "Sure, Ed. Take all you'd like. Just leave me the onion rings. And the milkshake. And here...let's split the egg and sausage biscuit." I handed him the rest of the food and went in for one more hug.

Ed shook Dagger's hand vigorously. "Thanks for the ride, bruh. Take care of our Jessie," he added with a wink. Dagger fumbled a goodbye as Ed walked off into the brush, just another day in the life of Ed.

Dagger got back in Clementine; I waited a moment. If ever there was a time when I wished I had my camera, this was it. I peered through my squared fingers and "clicked" my imaginary camera.

Dagger sighed in respectful impatience.

"All right, all right, I'm coming."

The rest of the day was a blur. I slept most of it, only waking for the occasional pit stop and food break. I remembered driving through a place called Redding, but after that it all started to run together in glum forests and snow-covered mountains. Dagger looked tired. I offered to drive; he didn't even pause to consider it.

"I'll sleep when we get to the border," was all he said.

We drove slowly through the main street of a town called Centralia, a funny name for a place in the middle of nowhere. Dagger pulled over at a little café.

Finally. Something not deep fried.

"I'll have the spicy beef salad," Dagger said to the waiter.

"Yes, sir. And for you, Miss?"

"Turkey club?" I said, unsure. "With fruit, not fries."

"Absolutely. It'll be right out."

Dagger unrolled his fabric napkin and placed it on his lap. I did the same and told myself that my sore shoulder was the reason I looked so unnatural at it.

"Dagger?"

"Yes?"

"Why are we stopping? You've been flying thirty miles over the speed limit and rushing through drive-thrus all the way up here. The longest we've ever stayed in one spot is the length of time it takes to fill up your gas tank. Why the sudden need for a sit-down restaurant?"

"We're not being followed, at least not closely. I need some real food."

I nodded, still feeling like I was missing something.

"Excuse me," he said, "I'll be right back. I need to run an errand." Much to my bewilderment, the bodyguard who hadn't strayed more than five feet from me in over twenty-four hours got up and left.

I sighed, twiddling a fork on the clean tablecloth. A playful giggle between mother and daughter at the table nearby interrupted my utensil ballet, and I felt no shame in listening in on their conversation.

"He'll never go for it," the daughter said between giggles.

"Sydney, you may not know this, but your dad is quite the karaoke star—or at least he was twenty years ago. He'll love it." They both looked at each other, and then burst into another giggle fit. They looked so happy.

I missed my mom. I wanted to laugh with her in a café over an inside joke. But she was gone, and it did me no good to long for what could never be. Maybe one day I'd have a daughter of my own. I was in a busy café, and other customers might notice, but I didn't care in the least about the tears falling down my face. When Dagger came through the front entrance, I wiped them and quickly replaced the cloth in my lap.

Dagger sat back down. I could tell he was struggling to come up with something to say; he must have noticed that I'd been crying. The waiter brought us our plates, leaving just as quickly.

"Hi," Dagger said.

I looked at him without responding.

"Did something happen? Are you okay?"

I dropped my head and picked up a grape.

"Haelo, please," he sighed. "I care. Please know that I care. I don't pretend to know completely what you are going through, but I do have some idea. I just . . . don't know what to say. I don't know how to talk about feelings."

I wanted to smile—I really did—my mouth just wasn't working. "I'm fine. Just having a weak moment."

He looked unsure of my answer. "You're not weak. If you'd like to talk, I'm here."

"I'll let you know." I picked up my sandwich, wishing I had ordered something that required a fork. Hesitantly, Dagger ate as well.

"We'll stop for the night at a bed and breakfast up the road. It's quiet, right on the ocean. And you can dive when we get there. We'll call Hank and see what's going on in San Diego."

I stopped listening. Waves of heat rolled in and out with every breath I took. Beads of sweat pooled on the back of my neck and in my hairline. Looking back a week ago, the hot flashes seemed like a minor nuisance. This hot flash had overtaken my entire body. My eyes were steaming.

"Haelo? *Haelo?*" Dagger looked around and flagged the waiter. "Can I get two boxes and the check please?"

Cool, winter air caressed my clammy face as I took a deep, welcoming breath. I could smell the ocean, I could *breathe* the ocean; we were close. Behind me, I sensed Dagger with a human. I opened my eyes to a gorgeous night view of a lake so smooth—almost frozen—that I could see the reflection of the stars and the surrounding forested mountains in its glassy surface. I had never seen anything more peaceful.

I sat up from a reclined, padded patio chair on the front porch of a log cabin, twisting my spine until it cracked. Dagger was behind me on the far end of the long wrap-around porch, talking with an older red-headed man. He saw me and waved goodbye to the man, then walked over and sat in the chair next to me. In the starlight, I could see ice crystals on the tips of his eyelashes.

"Welcome back. You were out cold for quite a while. I've never met someone so prone to fainting." He hesitated, stopping the natural flow of the conversation. Finally, he shook his head and added, "I thought that maybe you were in transitional sleep, but your scales weren't forming." He trailed off on the last few words, knowing how intrusive they sounded.

By reflex, I grabbed the back of my shirt, pulling it farther down over my back. Once again, I felt violated.

"Please don't be angry with me. I had to know whether or not you were changing in order to decide where we could go. It took one second." He put a hand up. "I did not touch you."

I didn't let go of my shirt. He looked down at the floor. His next comment sounded deflated, despite the positive vocabulary.

"The good news is we still have time to get somewhere safe before you transition."

He stood and walked toward the front door of the cabin, pausing at the welcome rug. It looked as if he wanted to say something. Giving up, he beckoned me into the house. "This is my friend Jo's bed and breakfast. That was her husband, Bryce, the resident handyman. We'll stay here for the night. I don't know about you, but I'm beat."

"Where are we, exactly?" I said, looking around for some sort of sign.

"In a small town near the Canadian border."

"I can smell the ocean."

"It's right behind those rows of trees on the other side of the house. It's a great property. There are lake and ocean views, from the top floor anyway." He stepped through the door and then leaned back out to murmur, "By the way, your name is still Jessica."

A woman was inside, busily stoking the fire in a big hearth. The walls were decorated in antlers and animal skins, and the smoky smell coming from the fireplace, combined with the scent of pine, added to the cozy atmosphere. Dagger picked up our bags from the hallway and escorted me to an upstairs bedroom.

"This is your room; I'll be right across the hall. Here's your sandwich. Do you need anything else? Water, toothbrush?"

"No, thanks. I think I'm good. Where's the bathroom?"

"There's one connected to your room. It's late and you've had a rough day; we'll wait and dive in the morning. Good night, Jessica." He tipped his head down the hall, reminding me that the humans were still awake—possibly listening—at the other end of the house.

"Good night . . . Edg—?"

"Dagger."

Right. Because that makes total sense.

I shut my door louder than intended, wincing. A thought came to me before I had the chance to open my bag, and I crossed the hallway to knock on the opposing door just seconds after Dagger had shut it. He opened it before the third tap of my knock.

"You said earlier that we could call my grandfather."

"I did. Come on in." After setting his baggage down by the foot of the bed, Dagger rummaged through a paper grocery bag on the nightstand, ignoring the receipt as it floated to the floor. He pulled out a packaged cell phone and ripped the plastic open. It was that crazy-impossible plastic. I was impressed.

After fiddling with activation for a minute, he handed me the phone. "Keep it short. Don't say anything about our location, the weather, the time zone, anything like that."

I looked at the screen as it dialed an unknown number. There was a slight *click* before Hank's voice cautiously answered, "Yes?"

I put the phone to my ear, "Hi, Han—"

"No names," Dagger interrupted.

I nodded. "Hi. I'd like to speak to . . . our mutual friend."

A long pause.

To my relief, Neo answered. "Hey there, kid."

I couldn't speak as warm tears welled up in my eyes, forcing me to look to the ceiling to keep them from falling.

"How are you doing?" he asked

I swallowed, then answered in a teary laugh, "I'm fine. It's been a long two days, but I'm fine. How are you and, um—"

"Doing okay. I'm here with the big guy. We had an interesting first day, but it's been pretty quiet since."

I already knew Hank was there. *What about Aaram?* I didn't know how to ask without giving away who it was that I was talking about, so "And . . ." would have to do.

"And our other *older* mutual friend went on ahead of us, as was the plan, to meet up with you. We haven't heard from him since." The last sentence trailed off in uncertainty.

My hand started to shake. Dagger held my shoulders to comfort me. His eyes were confident, which gave me hope that Aaram was okay.

I summoned the courage to speak. "I love you."

"I love you too, kid. I'll see you soon. Promise."

I dropped the phone from my ear and stared at the glowing screen, wishing to see my brother's face. The line stayed achingly open, as if neither Neo nor I wanted to hang up, then abruptly went black. I took a deep breath, watching as Dagger tucked the phone into his duffel as if it was nothing more than a phone. *It is nothing more than a phone.* I resisted the urge to steal it away and hide it under my pillow.

I had so many questions, but the big one trumped them all. "Why did Aaram leave Hank? Now he's out on his own, vulnerable and—"

"He'll be fine. I'm sure he had his reasons for separating from Hank."

"But how will he get to Pankyra? Aaram is all but human, I doubt he even knows where Pankyra is."

Dagger's placating sigh didn't help one bit. In fact, three more seconds and my temper would have manifested in a most unladylike way. Lucky for him, he spoke first.

"Your grandfather is a member of the Global Council. He's been to Pankyra at least twice annually for the past twenty-five years. He knows how to get there, and he knows how to do it safely."

"What?" Aaram had always tried to downplay the fact that we were candeons; now I was supposed to believe he was in the middle of it all? My expression seemed to encourage Dagger to further explanation.

"Each region of the world has two candeon delegates to represent their interests. There is one appointed noble and one elected representative for the majority. Aaram is the Honored Noble Delegate for the Northern Pacific Province; he has been for twenty-five years now. He can get himself to Pankyra. He can dive, take his private plane, or even access his pola magic for a ride. Though if he flew, I doubt he would have left Hank and Neo behind."

My eyes grew wide, and not because of the mention of some private plane I had no idea existed.

Dagger smiled. "Yes. The candeon world has magic. In English it sounds like some sort of witchy juju. It's actually quite powerful. Did you think that your abilities to sense the auras around you and summon ocean currents to move you at your will were *not* rooted in magic?"

I backed up to a chair in the corner of the room, settling in for another deluge of information. What had happened to the days of pop quizzes, movie nights, and scrounging for gas money? "So you're saying that we're not just water people. We're witches, too?"

"No, not witches or warlocks or fairies. Yes, we have magical capabilities, but only because someone, or something, gave them to us, with very rigid constraints." He countered my squint with certainty. "Your grandfather is safe."

He sat down on the edge of the bed, resting his elbows on his knees with clasped hands between them. "We've had experiences the last couple of days with mercenaries, but don't let that make you think the oceans are crawling with rebels. We are avoiding ocean travel only because I don't want you to transition in the water and because of the unlikely chance that we happen to travel via a route exposed to rebels. In reality, the rebel population is well under three hundred candeons in the entirety of the Earth's oceans. The good guys out-number the bad guys a hundred-fold. The bad guys just have a dangerously unwavering passion for what they are fighting for."

I did the math. The size of the oceans, the number of candeons, the number of rebels. . . . He had a point. I pulled up my knees, folded my arms, and dropped my head. Magic, Global Council, private plane, bad guys . . . all swirling around in a never-ending carousel of confusion. I tried to rationally process it all, I really did.

"Dagger, I can't do this. I'm a normal girl, relatively speaking. I go to school, I do my homework, I have friends, I judge the popular kids, I flirt with boys. I'm as human as a non-human can get! Juju magic and, and, and mercenaries, and betrothements to candeon princes is really not my thing." *Betrothements?* "Really, I just want to go home, live my life, and wish you all the best."

"I am sorry, but that will not happen."

"And I'm sorry, but the candeon race is *not* going to like their new Galana. Trust me, you'd be doing us all a favor if you just take me back and forget I exist."

He didn't flinch; I even waited a silent minute for it. Like a coward, I fled to my room and collapsed onto the Native American throw blanket that stretched across the bed; Dagger gave me a moment alone before following me in.

He shut the door with an unexpected calm, standing with his hands on his hips. Though not mean, his bluntness was just as intimidating. "Haelo Marley. I've tried to be patient, but there is something that you need to hear. You are a strong woman. You are the Galana. It's about time you started acting like it. Pouting, crying, and wishing for a different life will do you no good. Now stand up and accept what you are!"

I flinched, speechless. Dagger didn't apologize; he stared directly at me, daring me to challenge his command. I nodded shakily and kept silent.

"No! Haelo, say something! Don't just accept me talking at you like that. Fight! Be that woman who saved the little boy. Be fearless!"

My eyes misted, my jaw clenched. "I don't have a say in where I live or who I marry. I don't get to go to college and make mistakes and 'find myself,'" I added subtle air quotes. "Being upset about it is the only thing I have left keeping me from being a mindless puppet on the monarchy's shelf. It's the last thread of control I have."

He shifted his weight. "What are you talking about? Do you really feel that way?" His question was so quiet I wasn't sure I heard it correctly. "Haelo, it's . . . it's not like that at all. I don't know how else to change your mind."

A voice in the back of my head repeated it was perfectly okay to pout about an arranged marriage. It was okay to *rage* about an arranged marriage. However, I knew that though it was understandable, the pouting really wasn't getting me anywhere. And I trusted Dagger. We didn't move for a moment, Dagger's hands still on his hips.

"I have something for you." He walked out into his room. Soon, he returned carrying a paper shopping bag and a brown package. "Here. Sorry it's not wrapped."

"What is it?" I asked, still too shaken to reach out for it.

He placed the box on the bed in front of me and sat down on the edge. "A birthday present. I know it's late, but happy birthday."

I didn't move. I wasn't even curious about what was in the box.

Dagger tried to rally my spirits with a kind face. I slowly let go of my defensive, curled position and slid the box closer. I picked at the tape on the edges unsuccessfully.

Schriiiip. Dagger sliced through the tape with a pocket switchblade and had the blade back in his pocket in seconds. I didn't move, mostly because I didn't want to get in the way of another switchblade sneak-attack. Dagger nodded a *go ahead.*

Underneath the dense packing material was a bulky, new, digital camera.

"It's waterproof," he commented. "Griffin knows how much you love photography. He wanted you to be able to photograph wherever you are. It's from him."

I nodded in appreciation. It was extremely expensive, and very practical. "You told him I liked photography?"

"Of course. He wants to know all about you."

A new feeling flickered in my chest—not excitement by any means, but at least Griffin seemed a little more like a real person. *He wants to know about me?* Before I could come up with an appropriately enthused "thank you," Dagger handed me the paper bag.

"What is this?" I asked, confused.

"I told the prince you like photography and he wanted you to have the best of the best, unlimited photographic possibilities. This," he said, pointing to the paper bag, "is the other part of your gift."

I reached inside and pulled out an old, stiff leather case with rounded corners, yellowed stitching, and a metal clasp. The clasp rattled welcomely when I opened it, in harmony with the creaking hinge. Inside, a beautiful vintage camera nestled in thinning red velvet; underneath, some old film. I couldn't help but smile. It wasn't the gift (though a stellar gift it was), but the thought that made me happy. Despite however unconventional and completely unexplored our relationship may be, the prince had really tried. He tried to understand me. He *wanted* to understand me. The fact that he might really care who I was, accommodate who I was—even in just this small way—, was a comfort I hadn't allowed myself to expect.

"I take it you like it," Dagger said hopefully.

"How did he find it?" I picked the camera up and ran my fingers along its edges.

Dagger's jaw twitched before he shrugged. He looked out the dark window.

"It's perfect."

He nodded, lips tight.

The weight of the vintage camera in my hands felt so good. If only it were daylight—the old film wouldn't work at night. Though none of my fears diminished, this small moment of cheer washed over me, bringing with it a new wave of energy and hope.

Dagger stood from the bed and reached for the door handle. "I'll leave you alone now. I'm sure you want to eat. And shower."

My gaze shifted bashfully. I *was* pretty grimy.

He stepped one foot out the door and then turned back to me. "I didn't mean to sound patronizing earlier. I just . . . I can see who you are capable of being and I, I don't know. I want you to be happy." He looked deeper into my eyes and moved like he was going to come towards me, but stopped himself. He turned back to the door as his eyes lost a little of their glimmer.

I didn't want him to leave, but I said nothing to call him back. Before the door clicked shut, I mumbled, "Thank you." I wasn't sure if he heard.

The hot shower rinsed away the grime, blood, sweat, stress, and tension. I felt clean; I felt lighter. The bed cradled me in fluffy down feathers, soothing away all anxious thoughts of Pankyra and my future. *And Dagger will be there*, I thought as I let my worries go. I fell asleep to dreams of snow falling outside the window.

12

MIRIAM

Too early for beams of light to pierce the thin curtains, a blue glow crept out from behind the trees, making the log cabin bedroom decorated in northwest Native American art feel younger, fresher. I brushed my teeth, threw on some clothes, and grabbed the old camera.

Outside, giant trees blocked the horizon. I looked around for a higher vantage point, concluding the only one reasonably accessible was the roof. I tucked the camera inside the large pocket of my hoodie jacket and climbed onto Clementine's icy hood. From there, it was a sketchy ascent to the roof of the carport, where in between grunts, I thanked my usually not-so-lucky stars that I didn't have to worry about any friends with camera phones. The snow-covered shingles were slippery under my shoes, so each step had to be carefully thought out. The far end of the cabin had two stories, and to my bewilderment, a ladder was perched and ready to help me to the top. *Thanks, Bryce,* I thought with a smile, grateful he had probably been working on his honey-do list up here recently. When I reached a chimney, I perched the camera on top to stabilize the shot and rested against it for balance.

The view was breathtaking. Dagger was right about the lake views from the back of the cabin and the distant ocean views from the front. The smell of the ocean called me to dive. I inventoried myself: the headache had reached annoying, it wouldn't be long until the haze in my eyes turned debilitating, and lotion was not doing my papery skin any favors.

I took four incredible shots just as the sun broke through a gap in the mountains. The snowy peaks were nothing like the flat beaches of San Diego, but the sunrise somehow reminded me of the sunset pictures I had taken just outside of Belmont Park with that first camera Sam had given me. Maybe it was just the spirit of the place. I felt like I could fly away into whimsical dreams built on hope and carelessness. At the same time, I felt like each breath grounded me, centering me with the steady rotation of the Earth.

It was the perfect view for both thoughtful solitude and romantic embraces. I shook off daydreams that I knew might never happen, embracing as much as I could the blessing of the three hundred and sixty degree panorama of beauty that helped fill the lonely hole in my chest. I could have stood there forever. I didn't want to think about my future; I wanted to stay in that present moment. Eventually, however, the sun would rise and fall again, just as it did every day, and I would have to be a part of that round. I had to smile and take my days as they came, one at a time, good and bad. I'd win some; I'd lose some. I'd kick butt... and cower.

Dagger's voice called out to me from below. "Jessica? I would feel a whole lot better if you came down now. You're making Bryce and me anxious."

With my moment now tainted, I packed up the camera and stowed it back in my hoodie's pocket. I froze before taking the first step onto the ladder: down was going to be a whole lot harder than up. A careful crawl across a short peak and a few slides later, I was back on top of Clementine.

Bryce fumed with impatience, slapping his hammer over and over again in his palm, his tool belt twitching with each *thump*. Dagger was behind him, fighting back a proud smile behind his furrowed brow. His grin made me grin, which made Bryce huff back into the cabin.

"What did I do?" I asked as I took Dagger's hand and hopped off of Clementine's hood.

"You were operating outside of the fine print on their insurance policy. One broken neck, and they're liable. One death, and they're out of business."

"Please. I wasn't going to kill myself."

"You and I know that. He doesn't."

"Then why were you anxious?"

"You could get seriously hurt. Griffin and Alcaeus would have my head if I brought you back in a wheelchair."

"Your head?"

"A figure of speech. But they just might." He winked.

Inside, a woman with thick, wavy hair (the same woman I'd seen at the hearth the night before) set the breakfast table for four. "Hello, there! I'm Jo. You gave us quite a scare, missy." Her scolding, raised eyebrows were offset by her naturally warm and welcoming demeanor.

"I am *very* sorry. I should have thought it through. I didn't mean to worry you." My stomach growled just as the fantastic, sinful smells of bacon and sausage wafted in through an open door.

Breakfast was a juxtaposed combination of an angry Bryce and a polite Jo. That didn't prevent me from partaking of the life-altering breakfast of smoked bacon, homemade sausage, pan-fried potatoes, and fresh-out-of-the-oven bread that if given the chance could single-handedly sway an election.

Dagger tried to keep Bryce's mind off my roof escapades by reminiscing about a time three years ago when he had stayed with them during a severe storm. Dagger laughed, Jo laughed, and even Bryce unwillingly grinned—Dagger knew how to handle people. He was like Kingston in that way, only genuine. A few jokes later, he had Bryce rolling about an incident of frozen underwear. This was a new side of Dagger. He was almost... playful.

I tried to keep up with their conversation, but it was full of inside jokes and half-told stories. It sounded like Dagger had come to stay for a few days and ended up staying for a few weeks, helping them around the house and doing something—I didn't catch what—to help with a swindling loan shark situation their neighbor had found himself in. Or maybe it was a bookie? I wasn't sure, but I didn't doubt that Dagger would have been quite useful.

At a break in the laughter, Jo sighed. "So, Jessica, Dagger tells me that you are his half-sister? He never mentioned a sister before."

Dagger spoke up before I ruined our cover. "Yes, Jo. We're on a sort of bonding road trip. Our mother died recently, and we never really connected before that."

Jo was in the middle of giving us her sympathies when a fierce heat boiled over in my chest. At first I thought it might be from anger at the way he so casually combined our mothers, even if just for a cover story. Sweat rolled down my neck and seeped into my collar as the room started to bend and dance, morph and sway. This did not feel like normal anger.

Suddenly, my chair slid back. Dagger swung me up into his arms and headed for the stairs. He called back, "Excuse us. Jessica is anemic and faints easily. I'm going to take her up to lie down."

When we got to my room, Dagger set me down on the bed and ran into the bathroom for a wet towel. The ice-cold terrycloth barely soothed my forehead. Dagger sat next to me.

"Do all candeons have hot flashes like this?" I breathed. "I'm on fire! I feel like my lungs are melting!"

"No. The Makole's tracking has stalled your transition. Your hot flashes have taken a hiatus for so long that they're coming back with a vengeance." He turned the cold hand towel around. A vein in his neck pulsed as he watched me with deep concern. "I never made it to Hawai'i, so I have no idea who is tracking you or how much they know. It could be that the tracker has guessed that your aura is fighting back against transition—yielding, if you will, because of their efforts—and they have stopped searching in order to jump-start your transition. If that is the case, then your transition will come quickly, and they'll be able to track you even faster. We need to leave. I'll have a hard time trying to protect you here, and an even harder time explaining a two- or three-day sleep to Bryce and Jo. We need to get somewhere safe where you can sleep through your transition without the prying eyes of humans."

"Can't we stay here? You can tell them I'm sick, contagious, even."

"No. I have a safe house in Alaska; we need to get *there*. I just pray that you can make it that far. First, you need to dive; it's been four days since your last one. We'll go as soon as this heat subsides."

"What do we do? It's snowing. Bryce and Jo will ask questions if we go . . . water . . . swimsu—" I couldn't finish my thought. The heat was so intense that I couldn't make sense of the room around me: the replica totem pole in the corner swayed like an inflated clown punching bag as Dagger's face swung back and forth in front of me. The lamp's glow slowly faded out.

"Stay with me, Haelo. Now is really not a great time for this. *Haelo?*"

The dark cave crumbled around us, leaving a small hole in the back. Neo held me by the shoulders, forcing me to look at him. *That's our way out. They won't be watching the back.*

It didn't feel right.

Neo, where are we going to go? We can't hide! They can sense us! Let's wait for Mom and Dad.

Neo put his arm around Tilly's waist and grabbed my wrist. He had us halfway to the back before Dad's voice stopped us.

Neo, Haelo, grab Tilly and sit in the middle of the cave, close together. Cover your heads and don't move! Help has arrived. You must listen to me. Take cover and don't move!

I looked at Neo, too scared to give him an *I told you so*. We did as we were told, putting little Tilly between us, embracing in a protective hug. The turbulent waters outside the cave entrance calmed. I pulled my head up to look outside.

The shadows, currents, and sloshing bubbles were gone. Neo grabbed my neck, pushed me back down, and covered me with his body. Everything went eerily silent. Too silent, in fact.

Neo gently squeezed the back of my neck. *Haelo, no matter what happens, we are family. Nothing can break that. Remember that. Always remember that.* Then to both Tilly and me, Neo thought, *I love you. It's going to be okay.*

I held them as tightly as I could. With every passing, quiet second, my heart beat louder and louder.

A deep *CRACK!* thundered in my ears. The ceiling of the cave ripped apart down the middle, exposing us to bright sunlight. Both sides of the walls pulled away with unnatural force. I peeked through Neo's arms at the expanse of broken coral and rock still tumbling down around us. Candeons swirled about, intertwining their currents and bashing into each other in a violent, surreal ballet. I tried to spot our parents, but everyone moved so fast I couldn't even distinguish genders.

Two sped toward us. I screamed, releasing any air still lingering in my lungs. Neo gripped us tighter. I shut my eyes just as the approaching candeons slammed into an invisible shield ten feet away. I looked up in disbelief, shocked as the shield reacted with a mesmerizing display of peculiar, red fire and vibrant veins of electric color where the candeons had hit it. The otherworldly sound of their impact vibrated my entire body.

A hoarse, angry voice whispered in my head, *Miriam. Come to me now or your family will suffer.* The man's voice made my skin crawl and my heart race. He used my given name. No one ever used it. My parents rarely mentioned it.

Dad's voice broke through my panic. *Neo, Haelo! Grab Tilly and head north toward—ggrrruhhh!—toward the island until you see a boat!* I could hear him fighting. Was he winning? Was he losing?

Miriam. Come to me now. I am not a patient man. Everyone you love will feel the pain that comes from my disappointment. The calm, sadistic voice did not echo in my head; it was too heavy to echo.

Neo, get your sisters to that boat!

The two voices wove in and out of each other, paralyzing me. Neo pushed off the bottom of the ocean floor and pulled Tilly and me with him. Other candeons tried to attack, but the shield held steady around us as we swept ourselves north, a wispy trail of that red fire flickering behind. A large candeon with black hair and a scar from his ear to his chin came at us from the front. His grin terrified me.

This time, the shield faltered with his impact, but quickly regained its strength. The scarred candeon went limp and tumbled to the ocean floor. We continued forward. Mom and Dad pulled up alongside, all five of our combined currents driving us toward the island. Mom took Tilly from Neo, wrapping her in an embrace.

The longer you make me wait, the more I will hurt your family. Give up, Miriam, sweet child. Come to me. I am only cruel when I have to be. I promise I will not hurt you, you have my word.

I looked around, searching for the source of the heavy, gravelly voice. Neither Mom and Dad nor Neo reacted to the threat; I knew I was the only one hearing it.

I warned you, Miriam.

Six candeons slammed into the shield at once, the noise of which coursed through my body in waves. Mom and Tilly spiraled out of the protection of the shield, Tilly ripped from her arms. Mom lunged forward to grab her ankle and pull her back into her protection. Dad and Neo split apart, though Neo managed to hang onto my wrist as we tossed in the violent surge.

Dad's voice screamed at the two of us, *Get to the boat!*

Three of the attackers closed in on Dad just as other candeons came to help him. Suddenly, the allies turned away from Dad, leaving him helpless. Instead, they raced to aid Neo and me. I wanted to yell out to them to go back to my father, but my mind was paralyzed with fear. Neo pulled me forward as he sped north.

I looked behind at our lifeless mother sprawled out upon a rocky crest, her swaying hair mourning in the rippling currents of the fighting around her. Tilly lay beside her, tucked beneath her limp arm. I could not feel either of their auras.

They were gone. My mother and my sister were gone.

My mind flashed through disjointed memories like a photographic strobe light. I lifted my free hand to grasp Neo's wrist, then buried my face in the tangle of our hands. I felt the brief, warm prickles of tears streak away from my eyes.

Allied candeons raced alongside us to fend off attackers. But for every one of our allies, two enemies appeared and pulled them off to fight until once again, we were alone. Neo shook me, pleading, *I need your help!*

I tried to summon more current. It was a feeble attempt. I was too heartbroken to add much to our escape.

Haelo, they're coming! Help!

I opened my eyes. The scarred candeon had caught up to us. He cautiously touched the shield over and over again, grinning with each test. The shield popped and cracked, zapping his hand with colorful veins, like a rainbow of lightning.

I felt for Dad, but I couldn't feel his aura anywhere. I told myself it was just because we were much farther than I was capable of sensing.

The nefarious whisper crawled into my head again like poisonous syrup. *My dear girl, don't fight it. Come to me. My colleague will escort you safely away from this wretched chaos.*

The scarred man tipped his head and smirked.

My grief and terror could wait. I tucked my chin, squinted my eyes in anger, and summoned the currents with every ounce of life I had left. We catapulted forward. I did not look back at the pursuing attacker for fear it might shake the uncertain courage I now clung to. Unfortunately, the farther we got from the fighting, the weaker the shield seemed to be.

Lo, I can see the boat! Neo pointed at the surface in front of us.

I shook my head. *What about Dad? We can't leave him behind!*

Neo tightened his grip. *We're dead if we go back. Dad told us to get to the boat.*

But he needs our help!

There was no use in arguing. As we approached the boat, the shield faltered, then dissolved.

Once again, the sadistic voice spoke. *Miriam. Your protection is gone. The Krypteia is occupied with my army of mercenaries. You have nowhere to go. Let go of your brother's hand and come back to me.*

Neo and I gave one last push before we blasted through the undercurrents and into the shallows that we could not control. We swam the few meters necessary to break through the surface near the back of a speedboat. My panicked breath made it almost impossible to pull myself up the back ladder. A candeon woman with flaming red hair and a charcoal, skin-tight bodysuit helped us onto the deck and then rushed back to the controls, leaving Neo and me huddled together. Before she could throttle the engine, the scarred candeon pulled himself up over the side of the boat and landed with a substantial, terrifying thud.

I stopped breathing. In the water, I hadn't noticed his clothes. Now that he was standing in front of me, I saw his dark brown bodysuit riddled with fresh holes, exposing ripped and bloodied skin. There were at least fifteen pockets of various sizes, one of which was torn open with a plastic pouch sticking out. He had tattoos on his fingers and knotted, long hair that snaked over his shoulders. The scar ran from his left ear, across his scruffy cheek, and then cut down toward his chin. I backed into the corner seat and pulled my knees up, desperately trying to pull Neo down with me, but he stood courageously beside me.

"Karch," the woman said, "don't do this. Come back to us." She maneuvered herself between him and me.

Shadows of seagulls circled the area as if we were live prey to ravenous vultures.

He scoffed. "Do you really think Alcaeus would forgive me? I'd be going back to a death sentence. Get out of my way!"

She crouched down into a defensive stance. "No. If you want her, you'll have to deal with me first."

Karch smiled. "Okay."

With unfathomable speed and agility, he pulled a knife out of a pocket and went at the woman. She blocked his first stab and kicked him in the gut. He didn't flinch; it didn't affect him like it should have. In a menacing display of contempt, he sneered his lip and flared his nostrils. The knife reflected a blinding ray of sunlight as he tried again, this time slicing across her forearm. She looked at the wound, then curled her face in fresh hatred.

"You know what, Karch? I never liked you. Sideron tried to write you off as a misunderstood, lost little boy. I didn't believe it for a second."

They both twitched in agile preparation, waiting for the other to strike.

"He tried to help you, you know. Even after you left. But it didn't matter, he wasn't your brother anymore; he was your enemy, right?"

Karch flinched and stood a little taller. "Shut up, Magari! Do me a favor and run." His slightly shaken countenance didn't match the aggression of his words. "Hunting season...."

Magari cocked her head to the side. "What's wrong, Karch? Feeling guilty for killing your own brother?" With that, she dropped to the ground and sideswiped his legs out from under him. He tried to brace himself, but his face hit the rail as he fell. She stood up, looking down at him with a disgust I had never seen.

Karch laughed as he wiped blood from his nose. "No, Magari. I don't feel guilty; he's the one that should have let me go."

Magari stepped back in shock. Karch swung his legs out and wrapped them around her ankles, pulling her to the floor. He raised the knife. Magari writhed and twisted, trying to break free from his hold. She looked toward a small door by the controls, then her eyes widened and she tipped her head down in a nod. She whipped back around and kicked the knife out of Karch's hand. Grunting, they stood and Magari sprang forward, wrapping her arms around his chest.

A seagull screeched as he tried to force her off, but she kicked off of the seat and pulled him over the edge. They both hit the water just as other candeons surfaced around the boat. I was too panicked to tell whether the newcomers were allies or enemies.

Neo went for the controls.

"Neo, what are you doing? You don't know how to drive a boat!"

He ignored me and flipped switches. When nothing happened, he tried a few more. I opened my mouth to protest, but my breath caught in fear as a large hand clenched around Neo's forearm, pulling him away from the controls.

I screamed as Neo wrestled with the new attacker. They both stumbled overboard as well.

I shivered in the corner, quietly sobbing. The water went quiet as I prayed over and over again. My family was gone; I had nowhere to go, no one to go to. In minutes, my entire life had been ripped apart. I had never known death, and now it consumed me.

Startled, I noticed an older boy squatting down inside the small door. He held his finger to his lips, beckoning me forward. I must have been hallucinating; I couldn't sense the boy—he was not candeon or human, just my imagination. I shook my head. He beckoned again, his cool, gray eyes urging me to comply. Not knowing what else to do, I crawled forward.

An ear-piercing blast slammed me against the side of the boat. I covered my throbbing ears and looked over my shoulder. The back end of the boat had been completely blown away. Black smoke billowed high into the air. Within seconds, four inches of water, swirled with smoky streaks of fresh blood, pooled around me. *Whose blood? Whose blood?* I held myself and rocked back and forth, humming my mother's lullaby as I headed down with the boat.

Then everything went black.

13
AURORA BOREALIS

It took me a panicked moment to distinguish between dream and reality. My rapid breathing was real. The cold, musty smell was real. My clenched fists were real. The boat and the water and the explosion were dreams. Terrible, remembered dreams. I could sense Dagger in the room, sitting next to me. The light hurt my eyes when I finally opened them, old mascara pulling on my eyelashes.

I looked around for something familiar, desperately needing to be grounded. I was sure that I had never seen this room before. Across from me a large, crackling fire burned in the stone fireplace with books stacked along the mantel. Two wooden chairs and a small table with a Celtic-plaid tablecloth sat in front of a backdrop of stained wood paneling. A subtle, frigid breeze tickled my back through the open window behind me, and the shadows of sheer curtains danced across the fireplace. In the far corner was a tiny, vintage kitchen, complete with an old-school fridge and a wood-burning stove. The bed was small and not so fluffy, but the sheets I clung to seemed to be clean. Despite being freezing cold, the room was friendly and inviting.

Yet I wasn't comforted. I still felt the pangs of panic from my vivid dream. "Dagger! I dreamed it! I saw everything that I've buried away. I, I watched my mother and sister die, and I watched the mercenaries rip away my father!" My words stuttered and slurred as I shook.

Dagger came closer and sat on the edge of the bed. I sat upright and immediately collapsed into his side. Through a cracking voice, I continued. "I saw you, Dagger. You were there. And your mother, and Karchardeus. How did we escape? How did Neo escape?" I pulled away and looked him in the eyes. With his serious brow, five o'clock shadow, and a newly buzzed head, he looked more like a soldier than ever.

He didn't tiptoe through the answer. "I hid our auras and pulled you into the sinking bow of the boat to wait. Because they couldn't sense you, everyone thought you died in the blast. And, since Galanas can't be killed, they assumed you weren't the Galana after all. After everyone moved on, I took you across the Pacific to your grandfather who was waiting, as per my mother's previous instructions, right off the California coast. No one knows how you actually got out of the battle except for you and me. As for Neo, a unit of the Krypteia saved him and took him to Aaram, as well. You lived with Aaram unnoticed by the candeon world." He lifted his hand to my collarbone, stopping just short of touching me. "That's where you got that scar . . . the blast on the boat. Your blood was everywhere."

My eyes never left his; I needed answers. "What about my father?"

"He was attacked by three mercenaries and never seen again."

"He could still be out there." My imagination clung to fragments of hope.

"No, Haelo. He's gone. His aura disappeared moments after being surrounded."

"Your aura disappears! Maybe he can do that, too! Or maybe someone else hid his—" He didn't have to cut me off; his pitying, sympathetic look alone stopped me mid-sentence. I dropped my head. "Why didn't you tell me?"

He lowered his arm from my back and looked out the window. "You didn't want to remember."

He was right.

"Would you have ever told me?"

"I don't know. Probably not."

I hovered somewhere between a broken dam of raging emotions and a calloused desire to permanently erase the entire memory. I knew dwelling on the battle did me no good; it would never put my family back together. But....

No. I did my best to push away the memories. I sat up a little taller, wiping away the unhelpful tears. I forced myself into the slightest of smiles.

Dagger took my hand and pulled me up from the bed. "Here, put your shoes on."

I did, and followed him out the door where he waited with a few granola bars. Because of the temperature and smell, I expected snow and mountains, but when I stepped outside, the word *mountain* just didn't quite cover it.

The tiny cabin sat against the side of a small valley in the shadow of a steep, intimidating mountain ridge twice the height of any mountain I had ever imagined, blanketed in snow and ice. On the other end of the valley was a narrow opening to the ocean where a floating seaplane rested, tethered to a spike in the ice shelf. The plane looked like it was straight out of a World War II movie. For a moment I couldn't remember why I had been so panicked, so sad. A rush of hope, maybe even delight, freed the emotional burden from my shoulders.

"It's rare to have such clear weather this time of year. We're lucky." Dagger held a small broken branch and picked away at the bark. "This is my parents' old place. They used to come here when they were on leave, before I was born. It was their getaway, I guess."

"It's beautiful. The plane as well?"

"Yes. It was in pretty shoddy condition, though. I had it restored a few years ago. It's a Grumman G-21 Goose." He smiled at my uninformed head nod. "It's one of the small amphibious flying boats."

"Flying boats?"

"It means it has a hull and can take off or land on both water and—" He acknowledged my teasing brow. "Yes. Flying boats."

I laughed. It felt very good to laugh.

He gave a sheepish chuckle, then asked, "Are you thirsty?"

I nodded. "And the bathroom?"

"Yeah, um . . . frozen pipes." Dagger scratched the back of his head and then pointed to the tree line.

"Great," I said with a half-smile, traipsing off into nature's ladies' room.

Once the short tour was over and we were back inside, I took a seat at the table. "Nice haircut."

Dagger bent over to take off his wet shoes. "This is normal. The longer hair was just so I'd look a little younger for high school—the surfer look," he said with finger quotes like he was mocking the person who told him to do it. "I hated it, couldn't wait to buzz it off. But it could have been worse, right?"

I laughed.

"Well, whatever."

Dagger went to the counter and poured two glasses of lemonade.

Lemonade? Just because candeons were not threatened by freezing temperatures didn't mean a hot drink in the dead of winter wouldn't be appreciated.

"Here," he said, handing me a glass.

"Thanks?" I wondered aloud.

"You're welcome?" He mimicked my questioning tone. "I'd offer you something warm, but you've been sweating through some pretty harsh hot flashes. I thought a cold drink would feel good."

I took a sip. It did feel good. "How long was I out this time?"

Dagger shifted in his seat. "Haelo, it's Friday morning."

I drank and tried to recall what day "yesterday" had been. I wasn't quite to the bottom of the glass when it hit me that I had been sleeping for four days. A sickening weight pulled me down from the inside, tightening my chest. My hands started to shake; I put the glass down before I did something stupid with it.

"Have I...?" I couldn't say the words out loud.

"I believe you have. Though I have not looked at your back. I learned that lesson."

So it had happened. I was now an adult. I was a Galana. Every sensation I had tuned to my lower back. "I don't feel any different." Physically speaking, it was all a little anticlimactic. I hadn't quite caught up emotionally.

"Most dry candeons don't. You will notice a difference when you get in the water."

Water? "It's been eight days since my last dive. I don't feel that weak."

Dagger picked up our glasses and took them to the sink. "You're an adult now. You don't need to dive as often." He had finished rinsing the glasses but kept his back to me. "And I dipped you in the bay out here after we landed."

My face burned with embarrassment.

He spun around and clamored, "Fully clothed! Your temperature had skyrocketed, and I worried. I thought that the icy water would help, and not just because you needed to dive—your frozen clothing kept your temperature away from dangerous."

A long ten seconds of silence passed between us. He paused, his gaze assessing me. I let him stew in uncertainty before I finally relaxed into a reluctant grin. He sighed and shook his head.

I shrugged. "You know, if I didn't like you so much I'd probably lock myself in a bathroom."

His smile was bigger this time. "Sorry about that. I thought I was being helpful."

"Thanks for looking out for me."

"You're welcome."

I straightened up. There was no point in dragging this on. I reached back and touched the back of my shirt, feeling the smooth, uniform scales—like meticulous rows of flaxseed—through the fabric. *There. It's done.* Part of me wanted to rip them from my back, knowing that the patch of smooth scales now proved who I was. A strange thrill festered in the other part of me: I was an adult who could not be treated like a child.

Dagger leaned forward, gently touching my forearm. "When you're ready, there is a mirror in the bathroom. You'd probably like a bath as well. I'll get your suitcase." He got up and placed my bag next to a narrow door by the fridge before walking outside.

I stayed at the table as vague shadows of thought—as if nothing more than ghost lace—billowed in my head, each trace leading to another, none of them substantial or whole enough to hold their own. Prince Griffin; the Loma Heights spring musical; the government project I never finished; magical fire dancing around a circling horde of witchy candeons; the orange stray cat loitering on Dagger's back fence.

I rubbed the scales through the fabric of my shirt, terrified that if my fingers touched them for real, they would somehow be more permanent. When the sun climbed just high enough to break through a mountain pass and flood the room with the bright light of late-morning, I released myself from the stupor.

The bathroom was large, considering the tiny main room. An enormous, old copper washtub took up most of the floor space, leaving just enough room for a pitcher of rinse-water, a cast-iron something that must have been a toilet, and a mirrored sink. The old toilet seemed to laugh at me, flaunting its frozen pipes and giving new meaning to the word "remote." The washtub was filled with lukewarm water—Dagger must have heated stockpots from snow all morning. My heart once again felt enveloped in gratitude.

I was not ready to see my mosaic, so I sank straight into the tub. A bath wasn't the same as a dive, but the water felt deliciously close enough. In the ocean, saltwater changed my skin into tough, durable flesh. Here in this tub of melted snow, my skin was as soft and supple as ever. I watched beads of water drip down my skin as I raised my arms from the water; I squeezed my calf which, without tough skin, yielded easily in my grip; I watched my fingers and palms wrinkle with time. I was almost human. So close.

I bathed and washed my hair before ever looking in the mirror. Each time I moved or twisted my spine, I could tell that each individual scale was stiff, yet the mosaic as a whole was flexible. The mosaic slid along the edge of the tub when I reached over for the soap. From what I could tell, the patch was a little larger than a football on my lower back.

When I finally stepped out of the tub and wrapped myself in a towel, the terry loops of the fabric didn't catch on the scales, but rather glided over them as if made of polished pearls. I pulled out a sweater and a clean pair of jeans and got dressed, still without ever touching the marker—the branding—on my back.

In the mirror, I was a stranger. It was the same me: the same dark hair with uneven volume favoring the left side, same sharp jaw line just like my mother's, same deep-set green eyes and dark eyebrows. I wore the same blue and gray rugby sweater that I had worn last week at school and my posture was just as so-so as it had always been. I rubbed the scar on my collarbone as if it were the true test of whether or not I was still me; a brief memory of bloody water swallowing the boat streaked across my mind.

Yes, nothing had really changed. My eyes just struggled to recognize myself. *There is nothing you can do to change any of it. Just look.* I pulled up my shirt a few inches and turned sideways.

Subtle, iridescent hues of cobalt, turquoise, periwinkle, and indigo wove across the small of my back, then climbed in a graceful curve halfway up my spine. No other candeon mosaics that I had ever seen curled up the spine like that. The scales were clear enough that I could see skin through them. There were two oval-shaped, intricate clusters of darker hues flanking a larger kite-shaped center pattern with scalloped edges and designs. It was nearly symmetrical, the inner patterns differing on each side, vaguely reminding me of long-forgotten images of my parents' mosaics. Some of the inner intricacies on one side also reminded me of Neo's mosaic, but the overall design was most like Aaram's, despite the difference in color and perimeter. Beautiful. And degrading. All at the same time.

I couldn't touch them; touching them directly would make them more real. For now, seeing them was enough.

A stinging mist pricked at my eyes. The impending tears cleared away some of the dry haze and made the design even more high-def. It really was breathtaking in all the right and wrong ways.

I don't know how long I stared. A minute? Ten? Maybe only seconds.

A quiet knock at the door brought me back to the present. "Haelo? Are you okay?" Dagger quietly asked.

Blinking, I dropped my shirt and opened the door.

He stood unsure of himself, just as much at a loss of what to say as I was.

I shrugged. "It's there. And blue." I waited, but he remained quiet. "It could be worse. Lauryn would tell me to demand a refund; she always thought tramp-stamps were tacky." I tried to stay composed, but failed miserably. I fell forward and hugged his chest, burying my head in his collar. He gave me a moment, then softly pushed me back by the shoulders.

I knew he was just being professional—he was my paid protector, not my comforter—but that small degree of rejection hurt more than King's treason.

He tried to say something. It never came out.

I stood there, held back by his hands, and closed my eyes. The first of the tears fell straight to the floor, not even bothering to wet my cheek.

I had spent days in self-pity. And every time, I vowed to be stronger. I thought I *was* stronger. I still had my mind; I still had my body; I still had memories, dreams, friends, and family. Sure, I now had a path (mandatory though it might be), but it didn't change who I was. *No,* I thought, *I am stronger.*

I took a deep breath, straightened my shoulders, and wiped the last tear from my lashes. "I'm okay, I get it now. I'm strong. I don't need to cry anymore. It's not even that I don't want to cry, because I do; I . . . maybe I don't have the right kind of tears."

His face softened when he sighed. I didn't know or care what it meant; I only hoped that my new conviction would last.

We spent the afternoon walking through the little valley. He showed me the seaplane at the end of the ice shelf, and then the trail to the deep woods at the back of the cabin, all the while sharing stories from his childhood. I told him about my parents, the few memories I had. I was in the middle of a story about how Dad and Neo used to catch these ugly sea cucumbers and try to get Tilly and me to eat them when I realized that I had told these stories to Kingston just a few weeks ago over dinner in a romantic restaurant. I mumbled something incomprehensible and looked around for a change of subject.

"Dag?"

He smirked. "Yes?"

I stopped walking and put my hands in my pockets. "How long do we get to stay here?"

"Not much longer. We have a flight to catch out of Kodiak Island Coast Guard base tomorrow."

"I thought you said the mercenaries might be watching airports."

"They won't find us on this flight. I know a guy. He owes me a favor." He scrunched his brow. "Did that sound as lame as I think it did?"

I nodded. Eagerly.

I didn't want to leave. The past week had been a blur. Erratic emotions, life-changing news, traveling, transition. Every day was a rush to *move*. This quiet valley cradled, with its quaint cabin in this vast wilderness, this wild corner of the Earth, was the perfect place to stop. It would be so easy; just . . . *stop. Stop!*

I caught a brief glimpse of a bird tucked into the snowy branches at the edge of the valley. I envied the bird. He was probably cold and lonely. Maybe even bored. But he was free. If he felt so inclined, he could stay right there by that tree for the rest of his life, never going much farther than a quick meal might necessitate; or, he could take off and never look back. Whatever the choice, it was his prerogative.

My stomach growled. The afternoon sky had morphed from white to purple since Dagger's last story. The white mountains silhouetted against the rich sky were enough to pull my mind from selfish thoughts. I went inside for the vintage camera that the prince had given me, but by the time I loaded the film, the sky was too dark.

"Let's get something to eat," Dagger said. He put his hand on the small of my back to lead me back into the cabin. For a split second, his fingers stroked the mosaic through my sweater. He quickly moved his hand and apologized. "I'm sorry. I wasn't thinking."

"It's okay," I said, a pleasant shiver running through me. I suppressed a scolding gasp. I was *engaged*.

Inside, Dagger lit two butane lanterns. I sat at the table, thinking carefully through my next words.

"You don't need to apologize. I shouldn't be ashamed of it, right? You can see it if you wish." I didn't want to show him, but I wanted to want to show him. I hated feeling ashamed of who I was.

"Haelo, you slept for four days. I know you transitioned and that you're the Galana. You don't need to prove it to me."

I tried not to show it in my face, but I was relieved. He already knew, so what difference should it make if he saw the evidence? He started a fire in the stove and pulled a jar of sauce and a box of pasta from the cupboard, whipping together dinner in under thirty minutes—quite a feat, considering the pot of snow he started with.

"Don't worry," he said as he put a loaded bowl in front of me, "it's not crêpes."

His consolation was unnecessary. I wouldn't have cared if it were awful. To be honest, I wouldn't have even noticed. I ate ravenously. Four days of fasting would do that to a girl. When my bowl of alfredo pasta was gone, Dagger offered me a protein bar, which I took gratefully; I was too hungry to feel self-conscious. Half way through the peanut-butter brick, I asked Dagger a question that had been pricking my mind. "Now that I've transitioned, will the tracker in Hawai'i be able to find me?"

He cleared our bowls and sat back down. "I don't know. I'm hoping that you will be able to feel her tracking you now that your senses are more acute. If you do feel it happening, then I can hide your aura. Either way, I will sense anyone coming. And," he hesitated slightly, "we'll be in Pankyra soon enough."

I ignored his last comment. I didn't want to think about it. "My senses don't feel much different. I can pinpoint your location a little better. That's about it."

"You've spent a lot of time with me, so you were already more sensitive to my aura. You will notice a difference with others, trust me. There's just no one to feel out here. Speaking of your new senses, would you like to go for a dive?" His smirk caught my attention.

I had never dived with Dagger before, at least knowingly, and the thought was a little intimidating. But the way he looked at me—an outright dare—somehow charmed me into accepting.

I went for my suitcase. He *ahem*ed and produced two thick, footed wetsuits.

"Are you serious? It's cold, I get that, but, seriously?"

He held one suit out closer to me. I didn't take it.

"It *is* cold, Lo. It's February in Alaska. You might not freeze, but I guarantee you'll at least appreciate an insulated layer. Besides, it's the steel mesh within the suit that we might need."

"Lo?" I echoed, not even acknowledging the rest of his words.

His eyes widened in sudden embarrassment, his face twisting into a grimace. "Excuse me, *Miss Marley.*"

No one but Neo and Sam ever called me Lo. I half-expected to tumble back into nostalgic thoughts of them. Nothing. I waited. Still, nothing.

I grabbed the wetsuit and headed into the bathroom.

I donned a swimsuit first, then went for the neoprene. As I tugged and pulled and twisted into the unnecessarily tight suit—*might as well have given me a straightjacket and corset*—I pondered my name. For nine years I had officially been Haelo Marley. Neo, Aaram, and I were the only ones who knew anything otherwise. Did Dagger know? My parents had always called us by our shortened middle names, Haelo and Neo, so going exclusively and legally by those names was not a huge change. Except for the recent dream, I hadn't thought about my birth name in those nine years.

Miriam Anhaela LaReym.

A strange thrill came from saying it in my head. I had associated that name with danger, and now . . . well, it was pretty dangerous to be me, anyway.

I struggled to reach the long zipper down the back of the wetsuit. I finally gave up and called for Dagger. "Can I get a little help in here? This is really tight."

He answered hesitantly from the main room. "Yes?"

I threw open the door and walked out, turning in front of a suited-up Dagger to show him my unruly zipper. "This suit is a prison."

It wasn't until that moment that I remembered my partly exposed mosaic. I froze. It very nearly felt like my scales took fire. I blushed so deep my cheeks tingled with hot, red embarrassment. My entire body stiffened to the point that even my sweat glands no longer worked. I stood still and quiet, not breathing, not sweating, not blinking. Dagger didn't move either. The air in the room thickened.

Involuntarily, I finally breathed in. "I'd do it myself but I can't reach it."

He stepped forward.

Calm down. For crying out loud, everyone has a mosaic. Mine is just different. I'm ... different. This train of thought only reminded me that the design on my back was the reason I was not in San Diego with Neo and Grandpa Aaram; it was the reason I wasn't laughing with Lauryn or chatting with Sam, and even more distressing, it was the reason I was headed to an unfamiliar, ancient city to be wed to a stranger.

Careful not to touch my skin, Dagger gently pulled the zipper up and over the tied knot of my swim top. My blush flared. Each click of the zipper rang louder and louder in my ears as it made its way up to the nape of my neck. The last *click* echoed in slow motion.

As I searched for something, *anything* to say, Dagger headed straight for the door and exited quickly. I stared at the back of the open door. *Was it my mosaic? My reaction? Was it my nearly bare back?* With a minuscule headshake, I slowly headed for the door, shaking off any insecurities before they could creep up and fuel an analytical dissection.

I was expecting a dark night; the sun had set over an hour previously. But outside, the bright white of the glacier-cloaked mountains reflected the starlight and made the valley glow with a cool, blue tinge. I followed calmly behind Dagger, who was already halfway to the water. I didn't run to catch up. With every exhale, an icy cloud of vapor fell back into my face.

Dagger sat on the edge of the ice shelf next to the green and gray seaplane, motioning for me to join him. I chose a spot two feet away and sat, hesitantly. The hull of the seaplane reflected the starlight in a thick layer of shiny, wet ice.

Before I put my legs in, I asked, "How are we supposed to dive if we're in wetsuits? We'll drown if our skin can't absorb the oxygen in the water."

"These are wetsuits, not drysuits." He looked like he wanted to smile.

It was a chide, though somehow it lightened the mood. As I lowered my feet into the bay, the water slowly made its way through the layered neoprene and then hit my skin with an icy, refreshing jolt.

The sensation was magnificent. Despite the wetsuit, my skin took it all in much more efficiently than before. No wonder adults didn't have to dive very often; when they did dive, they got much more out of it. I imagined that the discrepancy would be even greater without the suit. I shut my eyes and tilted my head back.

Dagger chuckled. "Pretty great, huh?"

I only smiled. Talking would disrupt the glory of it all.

"Before we get in, I want you to do something," he said.

I nodded contentedly.

"*Feel*. And not for humans or candeons. See if you can feel other things."

It was an odd request. I stretched my aura senses out as far as I thought I was capable of, but try as I might. . . . "I don't feel anything. Just you."

A moment later, Dagger was gone. Or at least, his aura was.

"Try again, without my aura to distract you. Really *feel*."

Not since the park in San Diego had I experienced the strange and uncomfortable sensation of knowing he was sitting next to me, yet not being able to sense him—I even peeked through squinted eyelashes to double check that he was still there. He caught me. I quickly closed them, like a child dropping the lid back onto the forbidden cookie jar, and tried again. I took a moment, then exhaled slowly and calmed every muscle in my body. I relaxed, letting my senses melt out even farther. A light breeze tickled my neck as I opened up to the possibility of really *feeling*.

My steady breath aligned with the unheard rhythm of the valley behind us. I felt incredibly grounded. Someone could have told me all the secrets of the universe, and I wouldn't have been surprised by any of them.

Something pricked at the edges of my liquidized senses. I guided my feelings around the aura, surrounding it, deciphering it. I had never felt an aura like that; it seemed large, but not as complicated as a candeon or human. It felt pure.

"What is that?" I asked, turning my head to the north.

Dagger's aura came back, fuzzing up the connection I felt to the mysterious aura in the distance. "That is a polar bear."

I smiled. "Really? No one ever told me I'd be able to sense animals."

Dagger turned toward me. "When you told me you could sense changes in human emotion, I thought you might be sensitive enough to feel animals. Most candeons are either too busy and distracted, or just incapable to sense anything that's not candeon or human. Except for maybe a large, distressed whale in a desolate area. It takes a focused, calm intent in order to pick up on the pure and uncomplicated auras of animals."

"It's amazing. I feel so . . . spiritual, almost."

"It is a very spiritual thing, being that close to a wild animal."

"How close are we?" I asked, looking desperately in the vicinity for a glimpse at an animal I'd only ever seen in pictures and movies.

"She's almost a mile up around that bend."

"That's not close," I said, only slightly deflated that I wouldn't get to see the bear: my elation at having actually felt an aura that far away had me grinning.

"I didn't mean 'close' physically."

The beauty of the mountains, glacier, ocean, and night sky captivated me as I thought about not only my connection with the polar bear, but the grounded sensation as well. I did feel close, and it had nothing to do with proximity. Again, I shut my eyes and let my senses glide toward the bear and beyond, seeping into the cracks and crevices of the jagged terrain, searching for others. Dagger hid his aura, allowing me a cleaner palate.

I had never felt so insignificant, and yet so connected. The more I relaxed, the more I sensed the tiny flickerings of a few other animal auras, though not nearly as strong as the entire aura of the polar bear. I thought about Dagger and his other clan members trolling the shark-infested waters of southern Africa, feeling for the dangerous auras. No wonder he had mastered this skill.

I could smell the snow, taste the salty air, and hear the gentle lapping of water on the ice. I tried to focus on the polar bear and deduce a specific location. After three attempts, I gave up and left the bear alone. It was much easier to pinpoint humans and candeons.

Dagger's smooth voice melted into the moment. "Shall we dive?"

"Absolutely."

We dove forward into the icy black, hitting the water at the same time. The relief was indescribable. It was as if I had found an instantaneous cure to some unrealized ailment. I wanted nothing more than to rip off the wetsuit and feel the salt water permeate my unshielded skin with the nourishing infusion of salt, oxygen, and minerals. We sank deeper into the bay, under the icy, crystallized shelf. All around us, smooth, beautiful ice formations glowed with the starlight above. Dagger swam without the aid of a current, farther into the ice.

Come on, I want to show you something.

I followed without question. The farther we went, the more protruding and sharp the ice formations became. We didn't talk; there was no need. We weaved in and out of giant crystals and through caves and tunnels. My arms and legs burned; I had never actually *swam* that hard for that long. I couldn't use the currents—there were too many dangerous outcroppings of sharp ice. Though my skin was tough, and steel mesh lined my wetsuit, I didn't trust myself to accurately navigate a current through the maze of deadly, beautiful ice.

There, Dagger thought, and came to an abrupt halt.

Faint whispers of green and purple danced above the ice shelf. Dagger kicked off of a shallow, underwater ledge and surfaced through a small opening in the ice. I joined him.

The midnight Alaskan sky glittered with innumerable stars. Even more stunning was the expanse of wandering Northern Lights waving like scarves of frayed silk.

"This is the reason I come up here," Dagger said, leaning back on his elbows atop the ice shelf. I lay out on the ice next to him.

"It's beautiful." There was nothing else to say. I felt Dagger's eyes on me.

"Yeah, beautiful," he whispered.

I was suddenly hyperaware of our proximity. Another inch more and our legs could touch. All I had to do was turn my head, and if he was still looking at me, our faces would be dangerously close—I-wonder-what-he-tastes-like kind of close.

A few more seconds, and I might have done just that. Luckily, Dagger cleared his throat.

"Can you feel the bear? She's right behind that iceberg cap." His aura once again disappeared.

I sat up straighter, willing my thoughts elsewhere, and closed my eyes, feeling for the bear.

"Yes. Wait, is that her baby with her?"

"Both mother and daughter are curled up sleeping. I'm surprised you could tell there were two auras there."

I kept my eyes closed. "It's perfect. This whole . . . night, or wilderness, I don't know. Can't time just stand still? Can't we stay like this?" I felt myself smiling, even though my gut clenched in preparation for disappointment. The ice crystals in my hair tinkled as I lay back down to stare into the dancing sky.

"It is pretty perfect out here tonight," Dagger sighed.

I was about to giggle and rein in my stretched senses when a sickening, invasive feeling crept up into the edges. "Do you feel that?" I questioned Dagger.

His voice sounded carefully skeptical. "The caribou herd eight miles to the south?"

"No, the prodding. Like something is trying to creep in—"

Dagger lunged at me. My bare hands were braced behind my neck, so he gripped my face instead. His body pressed against my side. Our auras flared up like a gas explosion and then popped. I felt naked. Though my vision, hearing, and all other senses were now on hyper-drive, the one sense I depended on the most was uncomfortably absent.

Dagger's face hovered inches above mine, distracting me into a new kind of discomfort. Too stunned to say anything, I stared wide-eyed at his calculated expression. He studied my eyes, his gaze darting back and forth between each one. His facial scruff twitched with each dart. The weight of his chest took my breath away; his heartbeat pulsed against me. My own heartbeat thudded in every cell of my body, and I was sure he felt it.

"Are you okay?" he asked, his voice loud in the silence of the ice and distant mountains.

"Yes. Why wouldn't I be?" It was a lie. Something had changed, and I was scared. His intensity and rigid muscles screamed their reminders—he was a frighteningly skilled soldier. But it wasn't him that I was scared of. His hands held the sides of my head, fingers in my icy hair—firm, yet gentle. When I finally took a breath, I smelled him. Not detergent, or cologne, or food, or anything else but *him*. It felt so right, and so severely out of place. There was something out there, something he was protecting me from, and I was consumed with *him*.

"Can I have your hand?" He released one of his own and held it out as an offering. For a split second, I interpreted his request romantically.

I scolded myself. Our reactions to this shared event were likely vastly different. I placed my hand in his, struggling against the pangs of mortification, so he could continue hiding my aura.

He carefully pulled his fingers from their place in my hair and let go of my face, making sure the connection would still hold through our hands, and then pulled me up into a sitting position.

For the second (or third, or fourth) time that night, butterflies danced in my stomach as I let my imagination run wild. I pictured him holding my hand, just because. The sounds of laughing with him over a meal flittered across my thoughts. I foolishly let my mind wander back to when, just minutes ago, I imagined what it would feel like to kiss him. Would he kiss me back? Would he wrap his arms around my waist and hold me? Would he put a hand in my hair? Would his touch wander to my mosaic?

Dagger's voice startled me. "I think that was the tracker. Can you describe what you felt?"

His words yanked me out of my fantasies. I blushed before realizing he was talking about the uncomfortable presence I had felt just a few seconds ago.

I tried to explain. The words were shaky at best, and not because of fear. "I don't know. I, I . . . there was this . . . it was like creepy, foggy vines trying to crawl in. It felt intrusive and, and—"

"Did you feel the tracker's searching get close to you?"

"I don't think so. It stayed on the edges. Is that enough for the tracker to find me?"

"I don't know. We'll hide your aura for awhile, just to be sure."

We sat there on the ice shelf for an eternity. I tried to calm my heart rate and guide my misdirected emotions into healthier avenues, but holding his hand didn't help in the least. I couldn't help but add Dagger to the list of things I'd never have, all because of this stupid mosaic. Where was that courage I had found earlier today? It smothered underneath anger, and confusion, and panic. I fought hard against my desire to rip off the wetsuit and scratch away at the scales on my back.

"Please don't cry," Dagger whispered.

"I'm not crying," I declared, forcing my unwavering eyes to his to speak the truth for me.

"I will not let anyone get to you. We'll be in Pankyra very soon, you have my word." He moved in front of me, putting his other hand protectively around my shoulder. "Haelo, please tell me what you're thinking. I can't console your fears if I don't know what they are."

He was quickly breaking down my defenses. I couldn't tell him about the butterflies in my stomach or the rapid flutter of my heart. I didn't have that option. *Dagger* wasn't an option. The numbed, slow words flowed out before I had time to think about them. "I'll never have my own life. I'm not Miriam, the future Galana anymore; I haven't been for a long time. And I don't want to be. I'm Haelo Marley."

Saying "Miriam" out loud felt like a slap to my soul. Dagger released his hand from my shoulder and returned to his spot alongside me.

With a steady, alpha voice, he responded. "I understand. Of all people, trust that *I understand* the longing to live a life free from an obligation already laid out ahead of you."

His words might as well have been aimed at my heart—I was his obligation.

"I've tried to make you see it. I don't know what else to say other than that it doesn't matter what your name is, you *are* the Galana, and many people have died trying to protect your right to that life. You could have been abducted into a horrid existence, but sacrifices were made to keep you safe from that."

The image of Magari falling from the boat in a fight with Karchardeus flashed through my mind. "Your mother? Is that where your mother died? Over the side of that boat?" I gasped, knowing that if it were true, then I was the reason Dagger's mother was dead.

He didn't answer at first. I looked down at our hands—his unflinching, mine spasming in cowardice. Just when I could take the silence no longer, he spoke softly.

"She saved us. And then, yes. She died."

I shook my head. "Dagger, I don't know what to say. It's my fault. If—"

"It is *not* your fault. Karchardeus killed her."

"But—"

"Haelo, my mother died protecting innocents. There is honor in that. She would never let a Galana or her son fall into the hands of Massáude and his mercenaries. She is an example, not someone to be pitied."

It was very apparent that he had come to terms with the murder of his mother, and there was nothing further to discuss. I suddenly understood why he was so bothered by my complaints. I had whined, even wept bitterly over who I had to be when his own mother had sacrificed herself on my behalf. *Who else? How many?* I no longer felt ordinary guilt. Now, I felt debilitating shame. I leaned away from Dagger. It made me sick to think that he was comforting the ungrateful catalyst to his mother's death. I couldn't look him in the eye; I didn't think I'd *ever* be able to look him in the eye.

"We need to get back to the cabin." He stood and pulled me up.

We slid into the water feet first and swam hand in hand through the blood-thirsty ice crystals back to the seaplane and cabin.

We packed up quickly, throwing clothes and supplies into open bags. Dagger continued to hold my hand and hide our auras, which made packing difficult. We had to dress quickly with our backs turned to each other; Dagger didn't want more than a few seconds to go by without my aura hidden. I could tell it made him uncomfortable to stand there while I changed, though he didn't say anything. As for me, I was more than uncomfortable; I was shaking.

Once dressed, we joined in a side hug while he hid our auras once more. That done, he released me, mechanically holding onto my hand to maintain contact. I could feel his ring against my fingers: hot, like it had been sitting next to an open fire. Just like every time before. Dagger zipped up the last duffel and escorted me outside.

Back out on the ice shelf, I had to jog to keep up with Dagger's pace. Before he opened the plane door, he pulled up his sleeve and tipped his head at the crook of his arm. I slid my hand up to his elbow. He bent down over the edge of the ice, forcing me to do the same, and threw his fist into the water. My eyes widened as an eerie, orange glow radiated out of the gold ring, casting Dagger's face in its warm light just as a blinding burst of flames rocketed from the glow, shooting through the water and out of the bay toward open sea. The backlash shook Dagger's arm and made me slip to my knees on the ice. Dagger quickly lifted me up to the seaplane door without any sort of explanation.

The inside of the plane had been emptied of all passenger seats. It was an empty shell except for the pilots' seats and a few boxes in the very back. Dagger relaxed slightly once in the cockpit. I tried to slide my hand down to his, but he moved it back up to his elbow. "Please, Miss Marley, could you continue to hold my arm? I need both hands to fly."

Miss Marley.

I followed his orders.

"It was a message," he stated. "A *pola* message."

I shook my head in confusion. *What was a message?*

"The ball of fire that came out of the ring was a message. I just let Basileus Alcaeus know that you have matured and that we are leaving the safe house. I also told him that you're being tracked." I should have been surprised, but I wasn't. "It's going to be a long flight. If you can sleep, I'd recommend it."

I thought he was joking. *Sleep?* As we took off out of the bay and into the aurora borealis, I looked out the window to say goodbye to the little cabin behind us. We could have stayed there. We could have said *screw it* to the candeon world and created our own. But, as much as that fantasy made me weak in the knees, Dagger would likely look upon me with pity at the suggestion. Maybe even disgust. *A confused, weak little girl*, he'd think. He was taking me to a fiancé. *My* fiancé.

The cloud cover crept over my last glimpse of Dagger's valley. A sad farewell to an almost dream.

14

THE SIXTH MAN

The mid-morning sky hung in darkness when we landed at the snowy Kodiak Island Coast Guard base, an unsettling calm before the storm. A foreboding wall of clouds approached from the south horizon. Dagger squinted his eyes, feeling for auras. Almost immediately, he shook his head in annoyed frustration, though he did not tell me why. I was too curious to let it go, so I tried and tried to sense life on the base. Without the grounding balance of my own aura, any other auras out there just danced and strobed as little whispers, nothing solid enough to be sure about.

He taxied the Goose back up the runway and onto a designated tie-down just south of two towering hangars. Carefully, he lifted my stiff hand from his arm. My aura hit me like a tidal wave, allowing the auras of nearby humans to tingle and spark from behind the walls of the warm buildings. I could feel exactly where the humans were, and even though I had never met them, I could immediately tell their gender, size, trajectory, and even subtle hints at their mood.

"Wow."

"Please ignore the humans," he said tersely. "Can you feel the tracker searching for you?"

"I don't think so." I was too scared to release my senses out far enough for a sure conclusion.

He nodded and opened his door. "I need to have a word with an old friend. We'll have to hurry if we're going to make it out before the storm, so you stay here. Don't worry, there are no other candeons within thirty miles of the base."

Thirty miles? "When you said you could sense for miles and miles, you meant...."

"Miles and miles." Dagger jumped out and headed toward a collection of buildings.

I waited in the dry seaplane. Something between a scoff and a giggle escaped my nose when I realized that the Goose and I were quite the compadres: it had recently gone through a transformation with shiny new paint, and sometimes it was wet, sometimes it was dry. I wondered what the plane would prefer if it had the ability to choose. I had always preferred the water. Until recently, at least.

I watched Dagger hesitate at a door. He looked back and paused before beckoning me to join him. I tossed my unruly hair back, pulled the hood of my jacket over my head, and climbed out of the plane into a thin layer of old snow. The wind whipped at the drawstrings on my jacket, and the icy snow crunched under my shoes, the sound muted by my hood and the hum of the approaching storm. It would have been easier without the bulky clothing, but I had to keep up appearances. To my left, three lone men stood idle in the stirring winds next to one serious-looking helicopter. I was a few feet from Dagger when I noticed the first of the whirling snowflakes. He held the door open and followed me in.

A friendly receptionist greeted us with a bowl of candy at her desk. She pointed at a table across the room with piping hot coffee machines. I didn't care much for coffee, but the hot chocolate packets got my attention.

"See, Dagger. No lemonade. *This* is the beverage of choice in Antarctica," I quipped as I poured hot water into a styrofoam cup.

"We're not in Antarctica. That's the other end."

Fail. "Close enough."

Dagger tried not to smile. The receptionist's giggle made me roll my eyes.

"Sam?" I said the name out loud before my mind had time to catch up. *Sam? Sam!* I could feel his aura in the next building over. I had leaped halfway across the room when I stopped to consider what I could possibly say to him. *Hey, Sam! So, Alaska, eh?* It was pointless. I couldn't see him. *But what was he doing here?* He was a Coast Guard rescue diver; he must have come on official business.

Dagger pulled me back by my wrist. "First, we need to make sure our flight is ready. We can deal with Sam later."

Deal with Sam. He was someone to be dealt with. Was my entire childhood just a scam to Dagger? A holding pattern before the real life began?

Dagger led me down a series of narrow hallways before arriving at a large door. A plaque on the wall read "Rear Admiral John P. Booste." I sensed two human auras inside, both men. One of them trembled with anxious nerves.

Dagger knocked.

"Come in."

Inside, a man with a robust mustache and an official uniform sat behind a desk. The other man stood in the center of the room with twitchy eyes and a sweaty forehead. *The nervous one.*

"Please excuse us, Lieutenant." Admiral Booste dismissed the standing officer.

Dagger waited until the door shut. "Admiral."

"Colonel Stravins. I expect you're here to collect on the favor owed you."

"Yes, sir."

The Admiral sighed. "I've got a confiscated Gulfstream in hangar two. She's fueled and ready to go. You won't get clearance for take-off when this storm reaches land, so you'd better get going. I hope you brought another pilot with you."

"No, I'm going to need one of your pilots. One that will mind his own business."

"I only have one here with ratings for that plane and you can't have him," the admiral said with rehearsed authority.

Dagger didn't move while he thought through his lack of options. Finally, he faked a smile, stating confidently, "I know someone. It won't be a problem, sir."

Admiral Booste tucked his chin; he was not buying Dagger's lie. "It is illegal to fly that plane without two qualified pilots."

"I understand that, sir. Though that is the least of my worries at this point."

The admiral clenched his jaw.

I wondered what Dagger could possibly have on this man. I flinched at the thought of FBI officers barging through the door and arresting all three of us.

Admiral Booste stood. "You should know, six men landed in a Blackhawk a half hour ago. One of my petty officers claimed he saw guns. We searched them and their chopper but only found two hunting rifles. How they got their hands on a titled, registered Blackhawk is beyond me. Their IDs check out as well." He paused and glanced wearily at me before turning back to Dagger. "Those men looked military-trained. Are they your kind of people?"

My eyes widened. I was more surprised that this human might know about candeons than the fact that six dangerous-looking men were on base. Dagger and I both knew that the six the Admiral spoke of were not candeon; we would have felt them. Dagger looked concerned, nonetheless.

"Where are they now?" Dagger's voice was respectful despite being mildly interrogatory.

"Three are tying down their bird. The other three are in the building next door. They said they came to hunt. I have a couple of officers keeping a distant eye on things, but I have no legal reason to hold them—so be careful."

Dagger reached out and offered his hand. The admiral shook it.

"Thank you, sir."

"You're welcome. Am I right to assume that this means we're even?"

Dagger smiled. "Almost, Admiral. Almost."

He escorted me by the elbow to the door.

"One more thing, Colonel Stravins. I need that plane back by next Thursday; it's evidence in a drug trafficking trial and I'm only holding it until then. I do not intend to explain a missing jet to the Feds."

Dagger didn't comment; he just walked me out, shutting the door behind him. He pulled me aside when we turned a corner in the maze of hallways.

"Miss Marley, I understand that you'd like to see Sam. But we need to leave as soon as possible. These men that Admiral Booste mentioned could be human recruits working for Massáude."

"Do you think the Makole tracker in Hawai'i found me?"

"I believe so." He studied my reaction, possibly waiting for me to cry or stammer or tremble.

It would have been easy to give in to my scared, vulnerable side—I probably would have if it hadn't been for Dagger's anticipation of it. I didn't want to be weak, and I didn't want Dagger to expect me to be weak. I stood up straight, raised my chin, and took an anchoring breath. "Tell me what to do."

Dagger's surprised but delighted expression fueled my conviction even more. At that very moment, I found something I had been missing for the past nine years of my life: gumption.

"Wait here while I get—"

"No. Put me to use."

I had seen my grandfather, my brother, and my parents proud of me. I knew exactly what it looked like. On Dagger's face, however, "proud" was too small a word. He was elated.

"Now that, right there, is the woman I knew you could be." His beaming smile soon faltered when he realized exactly what I was asking. "Wait . . . I can't risk you—"

"Dagger."

He smirked, tipped his head forward, and stared me in the eyes. "Are you ready for this?"

"Absolutely."

He reached behind my neck. For one blissful, anxious second, I thought he was going to kiss me. He pulled my hood up around my head and tucked my hair inside. His hand lightly grazed the sensitive spot just below my ear. My skin burned where he had touched.

"Stay with me. Don't let anyone get a good look at you," he said quietly. As he pulled his hand out of my hair, one of his fingers slid across my blushing cheek. "We'll get our things from the Goose first."

He stood back and subconsciously flexed his shoulders, arms, fists, and neck while he scanned the auras around us. I tried to feel as well, though I was too flustered to get much from it. I watched Dagger instead.

Suddenly, like Jekyll and Hyde, his countenance morphed. Though not physically drastic—a new fierceness in his eyes and hardness in his jaw—it was enough. I almost didn't recognize him. He looked unquestionably lethal. I was so taken aback by his terrifying new look that I hoped he wouldn't look me in the eyes. In one smooth motion, he pulled a handgun from the back of his belt and checked the clip. He stalked down the hallway like a shark.

Is this a get-away . . . or a hunt? I hesitated to follow. He beckoned me forward without looking back. Taking care to conceal his gun, he led me out into the escalating snowstorm.

Back at the Goose, Dagger climbed in and tossed our duffels onto the fresh snow. He was holding the sniper case out for me when his phone rang. He dropped the rifle back on the floor of the plane's cabin and pulled me inside where we both had to hunch in the low ceiling of the plane. Dagger held the phone to his ear while his other hand held a readied gun. I leaned in close to hear the conversation.

"Nice rifle you have there," said the man on the other end of the phone.

Dagger used his forearm to back me against the far side of the cramped Goose's cabin. Someone was watching us, someone who had Dagger's burner cell number. We both scanned the areas where we felt human auras. I felt five viable locations: the three men by the Blackhawk helicopter about a hundred and fifty yards away, the man and woman in the air-traffic control tower at the other end of the base, a man in the hangar directly in front of us, two men on the roof of a far building, and at least twelve people in windowed rooms of the building we had just left. All the other humans on base were deep indoors, except, of course, the admiral and the receptionist.

The man on the phone continued. "Before you go and do something stupid, know that I also have a rifle, and it's aimed at your forehead. And I'm a pretty good shot."

Dagger's eyes darted to the few possible sniper locations he could see from inside the plane. I couldn't keep my eyes from the illuminated screen of the phone.

"You have a choice. Let her go, or take a bullet to the skull. Either way, we're taking her with us."

Dagger responded in a tone so calm and menacing I almost felt nervous for whoever he was talking to. *Almost.* "You have severely underestimated my advantages." He looked from me to the open plane door. I quickly shut it.

He slid down the window coverings on the far side while I followed suit on the others. He turned the cell on speakerphone and put it on the floor. Before I had finished blocking out the rest of the windows, he had the rifle assembled.

"Dagger, Dagger, Dagger . . . what are you doing? I have heat sensors, you know. Do I need to turn them on? You can't hide from us."

Dagger lunged at the phone and pressed the mute button so he could talk freely without the listening ears of the mysterious sniper. "Haelo, take off your jacket. We've got to let our bodies cool to the outside temperature. I'm willing to bet this human doesn't know that we don't give off much of our own body heat."

I stared incredulously, thinking of the sweltering transition I just went through. He was too focused to notice. Quickly, I took off my jacket and shoes. I pressed against the icy-cold aluminum walls of the Goose and shut my eyes as I felt my body temperature steadily drop to match it, then took a moment to be grateful I was done having hot flashes. When my breath no longer warmed my throat, I opened my eyes.

Dagger had taken off his jacket and shirt. He. Was. *Beautiful.* The contours of his muscled torso looked as if cut from stone. A walking, talking, hi-def specimen of man-perfection. If ever there was a body that could distract a woman down a path of poor choices, it was his. I breathed through my gaping mouth, and hoped he didn't notice any change in my aura. Thankfully, pressed up against the frigid walls of the plane, my body was too cool to blush.

We overheard another voice with a thick Chicago accent in the background of the caller's phone. "I don't understand, sir. They were there. It's like they just—" The comment muffled.

The original caller came back with a rattled slip in his voice. "Don't forget, you're cornered. Where you gonna go, Dagger? We slit the tires on your plane."

Dagger's face furious. He raised the rifle and lay out on the floor, then shut his eyes, aiming out one of the side windows. I caught a brief glimpse of a tattoo on the side of his ribcage, beneath his right arm. It looked like some sort of symbol or hieroglyph, but I didn't know from what language. Using only his aura sensing, Dagger narrowed in on an unseen target and double-tapped the quiet rifle. The glass shattered, sending a flurry of wind and snow into the Goose. I jumped. Dagger turned around to see if I was okay.

The background voice on the phone yelled to another, "Call an ambulance! Franco's shot! Franco, look at me, man. Franco?" And then the line went dead.

"Dagger! Did you kill him?" I tried to yell the words; they sounded more like a muted catch in my throat.

He stood. "If it weren't for the window and the snowstorm, I would have."

I crouched near the cockpit. It was one thing to see spies and soldiers and police shoot villains on TV; it was an entirely different thing to watch someone you knew shoot to kill in front of you. I didn't know what to say. I shook my head in shock.

"Haelo, you heard what he said. He was going to shoot me. What I did was self-defense. I was protecting you." He stepped closer to me with his hands out. "Haelo. We don't have a lot of time. Please. I need you to trust me."

When he finally reached me at the front of the plane, I nodded in understanding and gathered my wits. He held out my jacket. I took it, careful not to touch the deadly hands I was scared to admit I admired. He sighed and went back for his phone. His forearms flexed while he dialed.

The other end picked up after one ring.

"Admiral Booste.... Yes, sir.... I know, sir.... There are two men on the roof of building C. One is shot and needs medical attention. You were right; they were here for us. I trust that you will take care of them and the other four who—no, sir. Three are running from their chopper to hangar two. I need them gone. I don't know who or where the sixth man is. I am assuming your men will recognize him." Dagger nodded his head, "Yes, sir. This means we're even." He hung up.

I stood still while Dagger disassembled the sniper rifle. He threw on his shirt and jacket, careful not to look at me. We waited in silence while two Coast Guard teams approached and collected the three men in the hangar and the two on the roof.

Dagger opened the door. Outside, the icy wind howled. Our duffel bags were covered in snow. "Let's go." He jumped down and held out his hands for me.

I fell into his arms before I could give myself a moment to change my mind. He wrapped his hands around my waist, lowering me to the tarmac. This time, I blushed. He picked up the bags and rifle, then took off into the blizzard. We darted around a row of planes, past four helicopters, and toward the far hangar.

A sliver of mild panic itched in my chest when I sensed Sam headed in our direction. There was nothing I could say to explain this. *No, Sam, we're not fleeing the scene of an attempted murder—we're just here for kicks. Oh, this? It's a sniper rifle. No big thing.*

Dagger held open a side door. Once inside, he set down the three bags and cursed. "Haelo, go hide the rifle behind the crates over there; I'll intercept Sam. Don't let him see you."

I obeyed. The crates were stacked next to the only plane in the massive hangar: a sleek corporate jet. I ducked behind just as the door opened, sending in a flurry of blizzard snow. Dagger slid into place against the wall next to the door. When Sam came in, he walked right past Dagger.

I peeked through a gap in two crates. Sam looked around carefully, keeping his hand on a gun against his right hip.

"Haelo? It's Sam," he said, slowly grapevining along the back wall. He peered behind every desk, tool chest, and box. Eventually he'd get to my crates.

"Haelo? I need to talk to you. It's about your family."

I gasped like an idiot. Sam's head snapped in my direction. Before he had the chance to approach me, Dagger stepped from the back wall and cocked his gun.

"Don't do it, Sam. Put your hand down," Dagger instructed.

Sam had pulled the gun from his hip. I couldn't stay hidden any longer; I launched myself from behind the wooden crates and ran to Dagger's side. Sam faced Dagger, his hand still gripping his lowered weapon.

Dagger shook his head. "You're the sixth man." It was not a question or even an observation—it was a disgusted truth. "Do you know what Massáude would do if he ever got to her? Do you know the kind of life she would have?"

Sam fidgeted uncomfortably and turned his chin slightly to the side, looking wearily at Dagger. "Who is Massáude?"

Dagger didn't flinch. The only thing that changed was an added anger in his eyes. "Don't try. It's embarrassing. And it's insulting to me."

Sam's wary expression only deepened.

I stood between them. "Dagger, put the gun down. This is just a big misunderstanding."

His jaw clenched. "Haelo, he sold you out to Massáude. He's not your friend."

Sam stepped forward. Dagger raised the gun to his head.

I searched Sam's body language for clues. "Is it true?"

Sam's eyes pleaded with mine. "No! I'm your friend. That's why I'm here."

I wanted to believe him. "Where are Aaram and Neo? You said something about my family."

"We're trying to find them. But for now, I can get you out of here and away from *him*."

I shook my head in a doubletake. "Dagger's here to help."

The way Sam looked at me made me wonder if I had gone crazy. "That's not even his real name. He's a fraud, Lo! He's taking you away to be the prisoner bride to some prince!"

I knew "Dagger" wasn't his real name, and I knew where he was taking me. *Had* I gone crazy?

"'Haelo is not my real name, either. And,"—I couldn't believe what I was saying—"I'd rather be the prisoner bride to a prince than the prisoner bride to a psychotic closet-dictator. I've heard his voice, Sam. Massáude is evil. He killed my parents and my little sister. I trust Dagger; if he says Prince Griffin is a good man, then I believe him."

Sam clenched his jaw. Dagger came forward and handed me the gun. I pointed it at the ground in front of Sam while Dagger tied his hands up.

"Lo, you don't have to be anyone's bride. And I have no idea who Massáude is! Just listen t—"

Dagger put a strap across Sam's mouth, muffling his words.

Something didn't sit right. *Sam is my friend.* Then again, I'd thought King had been my friend. Was everything about my life a lie?

Sam's cryptic phone call in the hospital flashed back to me. *Yeah, I know. . . . Of course I like her, I wouldn't be doing this if I didn't. It's just . . . But what if I steer her elsewh—? Are you sure this is fair to her? Then I'll do my best.*"

I looked to Dagger for some sort of comfort, but he was busy hauling Sam off to the airplane.

"We need to go now, or we'll never make it out before the snowstorm really hits," Dagger commanded as he walked Sam up the plane's stairs. I followed.

I tossed the handgun into the first seat at the plane's entrance. "If I see one more gun, I'm going to start a political action committee."

Dagger raised his eyebrows.

The jet was decked to the nines in corporate luxury. I took a rear-facing seat near the front. Dagger tied Sam down to the back seat four rows behind me, then took Sam's phone from his pocket and pulled out the battery, chucking the pieces under another chair. Sam tried to yell something over and over again through the gag in his mouth. Eventually, Dagger sighed and pulled off the strap.

Sam did his best to sound convincing, "They'll never let you leave. It's a blizzard out there! And you've only got one pilot in a Gulfstream G550."

"What do you know about a Gulfstream G550?"

"Not enough to pilot one!"

A glimmer of satisfaction flashed across Dagger's face. He walked back down the plane's ladder. I looked out the window as a uniformed Coast Guard officer entered the hangar, pulling a small suitcase behind him. After a brief conversation with Dagger, the officer walked around to inspect the jet, opened the massive hangar doors, and joined us inside. He didn't say a word; he walked right into the cockpit and sat in the left-side seat. The admiral must have changed his mind about the pilot we "couldn't have." Dagger joined the pilot up front.

The blizzard outside howled at us as we taxied to the runway. I was scared, for sure, but with that fear came courage. I sat waiting for take-off, knowing that once we were in the air, I had questions that needed real answers. And Sam and Dagger were going to give them to me.

15

RELOCATION

I didn't have a watch, but I had sense enough to know at least an hour had passed since take off, the first twenty minutes of which were vomit-inducing turbulent. I decided to count to ten before knocking on the cockpit door.

At "seven," the door clicked open. Slowly, Dagger came and sat across from me. I knew exactly what to say—I had been stewing over my questions long enough. I stared right into him, ready to fire off the first one, when his distressed eyes stopped me. At first I thought he felt regret. I quickly realized, focusing his aura, that he was *concerned* for me. He didn't feel bad about his actions at all; he looked genuinely sorry for *me*. It took me completely off-guard.

When he spoke, he did so gingerly. "Did you mean what you said about being a prisoner bride?"

It was not a question I had expected, let alone prepared for. "That I'd rather be with the prince?" I asked cautiously. *Wasn't that a no-brainer? Prince vs. rebel terrorist?*

"No." He looked back at Sam, then to the closed cockpit door before lowering his voice. "Do you think that being married to Griffin will mean a life lived as a prisoner?"

My gut reaction was to say yes, but a flood of recent conversations flooded my mind and turned my response into a question. "Yes?"

"And you are still willing to go?"

I sighed, thinking carefully. "Look at my alternatives. I'll do what needs to be done. If that means marrying the prince to keep the candeon race from—"

He leaned forward and wrapped his hands around mine, bringing me to silence. His voice was low, quiet... humble. "You will not be a prisoner. You will be the queen of our people. You will be able to do good things and help those that struggle; no one will be in a better position to make our world a greater place. Prince Griffin is not your master, he is your opportunity." He let go of my hands. "He's not going to lock you away. You will not be his prisoner, his puppet, or his trophy. I would never take you to someone like that. I am sorry that you thought such of him... and of me."

I lowered my eyes, but Dagger raised my chin with his finger. "Griffin is a very lucky man. And you... are a lucky woman." He looked away with a miniscule scowl.

I didn't know how to read his hesitancy. "You really think so?"

"I do."

"Dagger?"

"Yes?"

"I can trust you, right?"

He scowled. "Of course. You can always trust me."

I looked over his shoulder to Sam tied up in the back. "Do you think he's lying? I know Sam, Dagger. I think he really believes what he's saying."

"If that's true, then he doesn't know that he's been working for Massáude." Dagger paused; I could see his mind wading through thoughts and theories. Suddenly, he stood and marched back to Sam. I unbuckled my seatbelt and followed.

"Who are you working for?" Dagger questioned.

When Sam didn't answer, Dagger pulled the ties tighter around Sam's blanched wrists until the pain was too much to stay silent.

Sam winced and grunted. "I'll only talk to Lo."

"No. You'll talk to me."

Sam clenched his jaw, then turned his head to me, snubbing Dagger. "You don't have to go with him. I can take you away from all of this. There is a safe place for you—"

He wasn't getting to the real answers fast enough, so I cut him off. "Who sent you here?"

He grimaced. "I can't tell you that."

"How long have you known about me? About what I am?"

"I've known for about a year, but I didn't really believe it until I saw you out in the ocean during that storm. You saved that little boy, Lo. He's happy and healthy because of you." He'd been lying to me all along. He didn't even have the decency to drop his head in remorse.

"You lied to me. You let me believe that we just happened to run into each other. You pretended to rekindle an old friendship—you even *kissed* me—when all along you were spying on me. Tell me who you're working for, Sam. I overheard you talking to them on the phone in the hospital."

Dagger's chin jerked in my direction, his eyes questioning.

Sam squirmed. "Lo, that's not fair—"

"Don't call me Lo."

Dagger flexed an arm—I held my hand out to calm him. I didn't need him to fight this battle for me. I sat in the seat opposite Sam. "Who sent you, and how did you find us?"

He shifted uncomfortably.

"Answer her questions," Dagger warned.

Sam gave in, but kept his answers vague. "About a year ago I got into some trouble. This guy helped me out, even helped me graduate the academy. He talked about strange things, and before I knew it I almost believed him. He showed me what he could do; he knew about you, Haelo; he knew that we'd been friends. Then I saw you out in the middle of the ocean during that storm—I almost called you by name, but I knew he didn't want that. He wanted to wait until after you had, you know, got your...."

"Scales." I finished his sentence, making sure he understood that scales and other such candeon things were nothing to be ashamed of. *I* was not a freak.

He looked warily between Dagger and me. "Yeah. Scales. He said you deserved to live out a normal life for as long as possible."

"Who is he?" Dagger demanded.

"I don't know his real name. He told me to call him Beilstein."

I turned to Dagger for answers, but he looked just as confused as I was. From what Sam had said, Beilstein seemed to care; he wanted me to have a normal life. It didn't sound like Massáude at all.

Dagger interrupted my stupor. "How did Beilstein know where to find her?"

"I don't know. He called last night and said she was up in the boonies of Alaska and that I was to meet up with five special ops guys to go get her—to *save* her." He turned to me and amended, "To save *you*."

Dagger grabbed my arm and escorted me to the front of the plane. He whispered, "Your transition stalled for months because someone was attempting to track you. If Massáude had Sam and Kingston, then he already knew where you were. Why would he need the Makole tracker?"

"What are you saying?" Somewhere, I knew what he was getting at.

"That it wasn't Massáude using the tracker. Beilstein is not Massáude; Sam is working for someone else."

I glanced back at Sam. He was studying his restraints and tugging at various points.

"Who else would have a reason to find me?"

"Maybe someone wants to cash in on a reward for a missing Galana. Maybe a disturbed noble thinks he has enough royal blood to marry you."

I felt more and more like a piece of trophy meat. I deserved answers. In a quick, unbridled daydream, I imagined myself slapping Sam across the face, his cheek pulsing with a pink blotch the size of my hand. I shook off the unfulfilled thought just as Dagger put the strap back over Sam's mouth.

When he met me at the front of the plane's long cabin, Dagger motioned to my empty chair. "We'll sort all of this out once you're safe in Pankyra. Let's get some rest, we both need it." He tucked a stray lock of hair behind my ear. His hand hesitated in my curls for a second before he jerked back as if I'd burned him. With a mumbled apology, he stepped into the cockpit.

My heart raced. Sam's squint from the back seat felt like intrusive. I wasn't imagining the romantic tension between Dagger and me; Sam could see it to. I couldn't look at him or I'd end up doing something stupid, so I moved seats, facing forward away from Sam. Staring out the window, willing myself to think about anything but Pankyra, Dagger, or Beilstein, got harder as the minutes dragged on. I closed my eyes and pretended I was on Aaram's couch, listening to Lauryn dissect her latest read—I needed someone who wasn't in the middle of my insane life to distract me. The muted hum of the jet engines couldn't drown out my heavy thoughts, but it was acceptably soothing in a not-nearly-enough-but-I'll-take-it sort of way.

My ears popped, waking me from a sleep I hadn't realized I'd taken. A flannel blanket was draped over me and a small pillow lay under my hair. The plane was descending; I could feel it in my head. *How long had I slept?*

I whipped around. Sam was still tied down. He had drool in the corner of his sleeping, gaping mouth.

Out the window, the peaceful, blue glow of dawn broke over a sprawling city. There wasn't any snow or especially high mountains. It looked sleepy.

A ripple of turbulence woke Sam and knocked my blanket to the floor. I took a deep breath, attempting to cling to every last minute of the ending flight, knowing that when we landed, I would no longer be Haelo Marley, or even Miriam Anhaela LaReym for that matter. But a *Galana*.

I thought I had at least ten more minutes, but we landed after what felt like seconds. The jet taxied away from the terminal gates, stopping instead on the outskirts of airport property. Grasshoppers rioted in my stomach, not butterflies. The steady drone of the plane's engines powered down, sucking out any last shred of comfort until I felt naked and claustrophobic. *You can do this. You have already decided. Do not let them think you are weak.*

Dagger exited the cockpit and crouched beside my seat. He wore a charcoal suit and pressed white shirt, no tie. His eyes were gentle and patient.

I smiled to mask my apprehension. "Greece?"

"Yes. We're in Athens."

I nodded.

Dagger put his hand over my clammy wrist in a comforting gesture. "In a minute, three Krypteia guards are going to board the plane. They're not here for you; they're here for Sam. I will be with you the whole time."

I glanced back at a very nervous Sam, whose eyes pleaded with me for help.

"Where are they going to take him?" I asked.

"He will be held in a secure facility until my commander and I have a chance to interrogate him."

I didn't want to know what that meant. "Dag, I really don't think he meant any harm."

He smiled at the nickname. "We will sort that all out."

"He has a sick mother and little sister who depend on him. Please remember that."

"I will. But my priorities are to keep you safe and find the truth." The other pilot opened the cabin door, dropping the stairs to the tarmac. Dagger lifted his hand from my wrist. "Do you need anything before we leave the plane?"

"Are we going to Pankyra?"

"Eventually. First, there is someone outside who has waited a very long time to meet you."

Instinctively, I let out my senses, feeling for who might be the prince. Just outside the plane, I felt two groups of candeons. There were twelve total, including both men and women. Besides a little excitement, their auras all felt normal except for the massive size of most of them. Dagger studied my reaction.

I didn't know what emotions I was supposed to be feeling. My mind and my heart and my gut twisted in a traffic jam of anxiety, anticipation, terror, hope, and self-doubt. The only thing I was sure of was that I needed to be strong. Dagger stood and held out his hand to help pull me up.

"Can I have a moment in the restroom?"

"Of course. Here's your bag."

I fished my toiletries pouch and a set of fresh clothes from my duffel and headed to the lavatory. Before I shut the door, I watched as three kryptes (a man and two women), boarded the plane. Though not in matching uniforms, they were dressed all in black and radiated lethality.

One of the women I recognized, confirmed by her familiar aura. It looked like she winked at me, but I could not be sure through her dark aviator sunglasses. An unexpected wave of relief settled in my chest: Zeta had made it safely out of Mexico. And though I wasn't sure if we were friends, exactly, it was still comforting to see someone I knew. The other woman, at least eight inches taller than Zeta and much more solid—the kind of woman that would have been intimidating on an NFL defensive line—flicked a switchblade and sliced through Sam's ties. I jumped. Thankfully, Sam understood not to fight back. They escorted him off the plane where I sensed two others surround him, one of whom felt like the friendly giant, Hank.

I closed my eyes and unsuccessfully felt for Neo. Sam and the five kryptes sped off, presumably in a very large SUV. Dagger stood in the aisle, living up to his promise that he would stay with me.

The bathroom was surprisingly large and trimmed in shellacked, golden wood, casting my hair in a warm, almost red hue. The jeans and purple sweater I had pulled from my bag looked casual, but I didn't have anything that suited a meeting with a prince, anyway. I dressed, brushed my teeth, combed my hair, and even refreshed my lackluster make-up. In some startling way, I wanted to please Griffin. I fidgeted in disappointment for not looking the part—I wanted him to treat me like a princess, not an obligation.

Before misty tears could smudge my mascara, I twisted to the side to take one last look at my mosaic. The weaving patterns of blues shimmered in the lavatory lighting. *It really is pretty.* It suited an elegant, beautiful princess, not me.

Outside the bathroom door, Dagger stood with his arm extended, waiting to officially escort me out of the plane. I took it gratefully.

"How do I look?" I asked, desperate for some encouragement.

"As your bodyguard, it is not my place to say. But as your friend," he waited for me to look him in the eye, "you look perfect. He's a very lucky man."

I couldn't help but hug him. "You said that already—I think you're running out of material." I paused in his embrace. "You'll stay with me, right?"

"I will never be far away."

I let go. "What does that mean?"

"It means that I will always be close enough to protect you," he said, then added with a silent *but* . . . "I don't want to be a third wheel, Haelo."

The gravity of his words weighed down on my precariously proud shoulders. This was it; this was when my life restarted. I could not be with Dagger. I *wanted* to be with Dagger, and admitting that made my future seem even more daunting. But Dagger and I were never going to happen. *You're just making things worse.*

From now on, I was with the prince. The mosaic on my back felt more like a branding than ever. Instinctively, I reached behind and rubbed the scales.

"I'll have to show him, huh."

"He knows who you are, and I have vouched for your mosaic. I don't expect anyone will be impolite enough to ask you to prove it. You might not be able to hide it for long, though. Traditionally, the Galana's wedding dress shows her mosaic."

I felt like a cheap prize.

"There is something you should know," Dagger added before stepping forward toward the cabin exit. "Prince Griffin has always known that he would marry you . . . but as Miriam Anhaela LaReym. I've told him that you go by Haelo, but it might take him some getting used to."

"It's okay, Dagger. Going by Miriam seems like a fitting way to say goodbye to my old life."

Dagger stopped just short of the door. "You don't need to say goodbye to that life; that's what makes you who you are. You're still Haelo Marley. Don't let whatever happens next take that away from you."

I kissed him on the cheek. The electricity that pulsed between us didn't surprise me. Ignoring my feelings for him and trying to move on with Griffin was going to be one of the hardest things I'd ever have to do.

Dagger's smile looked pained. Had I crossed a line? Was he offended by my rash kiss? He turned to the door and stepped out ahead of me. I took a deep breath and moved into the light of the morning sunrise.

Rows and rows of farmland stretched beyond the airport fence. Three shiny black Range Rovers had parked thirty feet back from the jet. Seven people stood waiting between the SUVs and the stairs. Five of the seven were obviously members of the Krypteia, the way they stood dressed in black, ready for anything, slight bulges under their clothes where they kept concealed weapons.

Of the remaining two men, one was older, mid- to late-thirties, dressed in a smart suit. The other, much younger than the first, wore trendy gray slacks and an expensive-looking navy sweater over a plum button-down shirt. They stood side by side. I knew which one was the prince: not only was one too old to have been born the same day as me, but the younger one—the one my age—had the entitled expression and posture of a prince. Everyone except Dagger stared at me in anticipation.

Don't trip. You'll never live it down.

Dagger stood at the bottom of the stairs with his arm held out to assist me. Before I reached the last step, the young man in the sweater stepped forward to offer his own hand, rendering Dagger's assistance unnecessary. Dagger tipped his head forward and stepped back.

"Hello, Miss LaReym. I am Griffin Alexander."

16

BLIND DATE

I didn't know what to say. *Your Majesty*—with a curtsy? Maybe a nice, formal *Pleasure to meet you*. We *were* betrothed, so *Good Morning* sounded appropriately friendly. *Oh, screw it.*

"Hi." I smiled, a faint hint of a blush warming my cheeks.

The answering excitement in Prince Griffin's eyes forced my lips into a bigger smile. He had black curly hair and a freshly shaved, baby-smooth face.

I shook his extended, uncallused hand, which made him chuckle. With a patient smirk, he took my fingers and brought the back of my hand to his lips, demonstrating what he had originally intended. I blushed again.

He turned to Dagger. "And you! It's good to see you again, cousin." They embraced and slapped each other on the back.

Cousin?

Dagger grinned and answered, "You too, you too. It's been a long time."

Griffin looked back and forth between Dagger and me. "He has treated you well, no?"

"Of course." I replied.

Dagger cleared his throat.

"Ridion has always been my favorite cousin, my favorite person, for that matter. I hope you are okay with him as your bodyguard." His accent was *very* Greek.

"Ridion?" I asked, confused.

"I go by 'Dagger' when I'm on assignment. In *private*," he looked pointedly at Griffin, "my family and fellow clan members can call me by my given name, Ridion."

I froze at the flicker of pain deep in my chest. *Why had I never asked him his real name?*

Dagger was quick to offer reassurance. "You may call me by whatever you wish. You are certainly now a part of my family—*our* family."

I nodded and raised my eyebrows, hoping it hid my true, uncertain feelings.

After a brief, awkward silence, Griffin interjected, "Speaking of family, Miss LaReym, I imagine you'd like to see yours."

"Yes, please!"

His laughter was contagious, accented with adorable dimples. "Very well. You shall see them before the day is over. But first, I would like to show you something." He tucked my hand into the crook of his lean, toned arm and walked me to the middle car, where the man in the suit stood waiting. "This is my personal bodyguard, Theo. Theo, this is Miss LaReym."

"It's nice to meet you," Theo said, tipping his head down in respect.

"And you," I responded, unsure of how a Galana was supposed to behave in such situations.

"And these," Griffin said, gesturing to the five kryptes behind us, "are members of First Team: Nikolas, Rebecca, Wingo, Stevens, and Vernado. They provide security to the royal family. They have been anxious to meet you."

I shook hands with each guard, repeating their names. They were all quite professional, though Rebecca seemed unabashedly friendly.

Theo opened the rear door.

"Shall we?" Griffin asked rhetorically.

I climbed in as gracefully as I could. The prince followed. Theo referred to *Ridion* for orders and was told to drive. Dagger got in the front passenger seat.

Griffin spoke in Greek to Theo as he started the car, then turned to me. "My apologies. For a moment I forgot that you only speak English. I have a special breakfast surprise for you. Are you hungry?"

I wasn't hungry at all. "Starved."

He smiled. His voice dropped to a near whisper. "The past few weeks have been difficult for you, yes?"

I couldn't respond without crying, so I just nodded my head. My misty eyes gave me away.

He brought his hand up as if to stroke my hair but thought the better of it, letting it fall back in his lap. "I am very sorry. I wish that you could know my heart; I do not want for you to feel sorrow."

I composed myself. "It's not sorrow. It's just been a lot to handle."

He nodded and then kissed me on the forehead. He had very honest eyes. Of all the scenarios I had prepared for, this version of Griffin was not one I had expected. Hoped for, maybe, but not expected.

I glanced at Dagger. He stared out the car window at the city passing by, looking distant, deep in thought. Our car pulled into a side street and parked, followed by the other two SUVs which parked on opposing sides of the main road. Dagger opened my door.

The surrounding high, stone walls were covered in vines. It smelled of crisp gardens and sweet pastries. The smell reminded me of a morning not so long ago when Dagger had attempted strawberry crêpes.

Griffin escorted me with his hand on my back as Theo led the way through a small back door, Dagger behind us. I stole another glance at him, but he wouldn't meet my eyes.

We ate waffles, fruit, pastries, and eggs in a private room of a gorgeous restaurant. It hadn't yet opened for the day, which kept the atmosphere quiet and surreal. Griffin commented that he knew I loved waffles and had the chef prepare them especially for me. I gave a grateful nod to Dagger, who sat with Theo at another table nearby.

Griffin asked me questions about my life in San Diego; he wanted to know about my friends, my home, my favorite things to read, and my photography. He even brought up sports and math, though admitted he didn't follow sports. For those few minutes, I felt a connection between my past and my future.

"I'm sorry I didn't get you a gift," I mumbled. "But thank you so much for the cameras. They're beautiful."

He looked confused for a split second. "Cameras?"

Dagger coughed from the other table.

Griffin smiled and shook his head. "No, no, do not apologize for that. I have everything I could ever want now that you are finally here. And though I am late, happy birthday. I'd love to see the photographs you have taken now that you can shoot in the water."

I couldn't tell if my smile looked as genuine as I was striving for. My wide eyes probably hinted at my embarrassment. I hadn't used the expensive camera at all. It was still in its packaging. He didn't mention the vintage camera. I nearly brought it up so he'd know just how lovely a thought the old camera was, but Griffin had stood, his hand extended toward me.

From the restaurant we drove to a grand hotel.

"Do you know how to skate?" Griffin asked.

"Skate? Like roller-skate?"

He laughed again. We stepped out of the elevator onto a rooftop lobby. Just outside the large glass windows stretched an empty outdoor ice-skating rink overlooking the city. My reverie was interrupted by the attendant that brought us skates.

I held the blades of death by two fingers. "I've never done this before," I warned Griffin, but he didn't take the warning seriously. You would have thought I was gearing up for a tightrope walk across the Grand

Canyon the way I painstakingly laced up my skates, trying to stall as much as possible. My ankles shook as I stood and ebbed slowly toward Griffin, leaving Dagger and Theo to wait inconspicuously in the lobby.

The prince held my hand as I stepped onto the ice. With one arm around my waist, he supported me while I swayed and faltered. Though not entirely uncomfortable, I did feel more obligated to his embrace than excited by it.

Slowly, we glided around the empty rink. The wind didn't help my agility—as a matter of fact, I think Griffin preferred the task of bracing me closer every time I stumbled. After a few laps I started to—*thank goodness*—get the hang of it. Eventually we circled around to the far edge, where he pointed to a set of ancient white columns among the panoramic view of Athens.

"That is the Acropolis and the Parthenon."

"It's beautiful," I muttered, gliding in toward the railing for a closer look. Big mistake. A second later we were both on our backs. Griffin laughed, his head cocked back to expose all of his teeth. I fought for a breath but couldn't catch one, the impact having knocked the wind out of me.

"Miss LaReym, are you all right?" he said through dwindling chuckles.

Behind him, I saw Dagger running across the ice toward us.

I finally caught my breath. "Yes, I'm okay. I tried to warn you," I said with a hint of *told-you-so*.

Griffin sighed in amused relief. Dagger stopped a few feet from us, his countenance oozing with overprotectiveness. The prince stood and helped me to my feet as I brushed the melted ice dust from my backside.

"I am very sorry," he apologized. "I wanted to do something, ehh—small-key? Low-key?—so we could talk and get to know each other. Maybe we should take this date elsewhere."

"That's probably a good idea." So I was on a date. A date. With the future ruler of the candeon world. My *fiancé*.

Theo called from the lobby entrance. "Your Highness, Basileus Alcaeus is on the phone. He wants to speak with you."

"Excuse me, Miss LaReym. I need to take this." Griffin kissed my hand and skated to the lobby.

Dagger came up behind me. "Are you hurt? That looked like a nasty fall."

I carefully spun around. "No, I'm fine. A little winded, but fine. If I find out that you blabbed about this to the whole Krypteia, you're dead."

His brow shot up in playful offense. "I would never!"

I rolled my eyes. This was a new kind of banter between Dagger and me: forced and awkward, like we were both trying to prove that we were friends. I fidgeted with the cuff of my sweater.

"How come you never told me he was your cousin?"

He turned his body ever so slightly so that we were directly in front of each other. Even through his tailored charcoal suit, I could see the muscles of Dagger's broad shoulders and biceps. "Technically, we're second cousins. Our mothers were cousins. And, I don't know. I guess it never came up."

"His mother . . . the Galana?"

"Yes. Her name is Cora." He studied me. "She is the kindest woman I know; Alcaeus calls her his angel. She is a patroness of the arts. It was she who encouraged me to sketch and paint—she thought I needed an outlet that wasn't viole—" He caught himself and tried again. "Tactical."

"She sounds lovely."

"She is. She's like a second mother to me."

The way he spoke of her brought out an innocent, childlike side of him that I hadn't seen before. For all his polished, efficient mannerisms, this new side was quite captivating. The corners of his eyes wrinkled with his smile. *Stop staring at his lips.*

Griffin joined us right as I was about to ask Dagger more about his youth. "So sorry, that was my father. He sends his welcoming love." He took my hand and led me back into the lobby.

"Thank you," I said. "I've never skated before. And the view of your city is incredible."

Griffin nodded. "You're welcome. I like to think of Athens as my city. Pankyra is wonderful, but it is not like Athens."

My curiosity raged. I waited until we were back in the car before I asked any questions. "You mentioned Pankyra. What is it like? I mean, I don't know anything about it."

His thick accent made his description even more resplendent. "It is beautiful. And clean. It has libraries, galleries, monuments, everything every cultured city claims to have. But there is no—how you say?—progression. Dynamic. It doesn't have the people, the . . ." he stewed over an unexplainable idea. "The *vibe* that human cities have. In Pankyra, every weekend is filled with theater engagements, concerts, discourses, and grand dances. Everyone attends, like you are not a part of anything unless you are a part of everything. Individuality is hard to come by. It is a city of great wealth, yet everyone has the same boring, well, wealth." Griffin seemed genuine in his judgments of Pankyra, though his expensive watch and shiny black calfskin shoes left a tinge of hypocrisy. I didn't know what to think of him. Though not impressed with "boring" wealth, I doubted he knew how to live without it.

I tucked away my evolving impression of the prince and came back to the conversation. My previous conceptions of Pankyra were now completely dashed. Concerts and dances meant music. Libraries meant books. None of it made sense in an underwater world. "I thought Pankyra was underwater? Like a glowing Atlantis of pearls and gold deep in the Mediterranean. Are you saying it's dry?"

"Mostly," he mused. "And Atlantis is not as elegant as you have described."

"Atlantis is *real?*"

"Atlantis is a crumbled ruin full of sharks, beggars, and thieves. It is much more exciting than Pankyra, but no place for a lady."

For some reckless reason, his description only made me feel adventurous. If he was trying to discourage me from visiting Atlantis, he was doing a poor job.

"Do not worry, Miss LaReym. You will see Pankyra soon enough."

I glanced at Dagger who stared out the window, pretending not to listen. I knew he would hear my next request, and I hoped he would understand.

"Your Highness? If you'd like, you can call me Miriam. 'Miss LaReym' is. . . ." I didn't know how to finish. A pile of awkward gibberish fuddled about in the back of my brain.

"You don't need to explain, I think I understand. I was only trying to be respectful. As for me, please call me Griffin."

He smiled at me. Though I certainly did not love him, he *was* charming. And kind. And attractive in that skinny, classy, preppy-hipster clash sort of way.

The car stopped in a secluded courtyard. Theo opened my door, gesturing to the far corner archway where two gleaming Vespa scooters stood parked at the ready.

"I want to keep things simple today, nothing intimidating. Would you like to see Athens?" Griffin asked, a twinkle in his eye.

"Remember the ice skates? Are you sure you want to put me behind the wheel of that thing?"

"No wheel," he smirked, "handlebars."

With carefree abandon, we zipped around the city, followed closely by both security SUVs. Even though the weather was cold and overcast, Athens bustled with an excited energy. Griffin pointed out some of his favorite restaurants, shops, and gardens. For some touristy reason, I expected stark white buildings with blue doors and roofs. Instead, every street hosted an array of different architectures: classical, boxy, renaissance, modern, Spanish, and everything in between. One recurring theme was the earthy red rooftops. The gardens were pretty, though I could tell that the barren flora would be gorgeous in the spring.

My hair billowed in the wind. Normally I'd pull it back and out of my way, but it felt rather freeing and appropriate as we scooted around the dense city.

Eventually, we stopped at a used bookstore in a quaint—if slightly claustrophobic—old neighborhood. Griffin introduced me to the owners, a wrinkly pair of siblings who squabbled over what book I would enjoy most. Griffin's sure smile and charismatic banter helped them decide on a 1930s adventure novel.

"But I can't read it. It's written in Greek," I giggled.

Griffin thanked the crotchety old siblings and took the paper-bagged book. "Then I will just have to read it to you." Outside, he tossed the book to Theo, who stood waiting next to the first Range Rover.

"One last stop on our tour of Athens," he said, chivalrously gesturing to the open door of the car.

"What about the scooters?"

"Already taken care of."

I climbed in. Once again, Theo drove, Dagger sat shotgun.

I pretended to sightsee through the heavily tinted window while I thought about the prince. He was more alluring than I expected. A little spoiled maybe, but thoughtful, sweet, and engaging. Confident without being overtly cocky—which suited the title of prince, I guess. The only thing missing was a delicate, enamored damsel draped in his arms.

The city passed by in a blur. Outside of a museum, effortlessly floating on a pedestal, posed an ancient statue of an elegant goddess. She looked noble, beautiful, and feminine, like a fantasy.

"I'm not what you were expecting, am I?" I slipped.

Griffin watched me, a grin playing gently on his lips. "Miriam, my entire life, I have known of you, *waited* for you. And in that wait, I've done my best to learn as much about you as possible. Ridion has told me much. And you look just as lovely as you did last autumn. Why would you not be what I was expecting?"

My face froze in a polite smile. *Last autumn?*

Dagger didn't even cough, feigning oblivion to the conversation.

"Do not worry." Griffin leaned closer. Too close.

Get used to it.

How long did I have before a wedding? Days? Weeks? Years? There was no obvious way to tactfully bring up the subject, so I went for the kill.

"Griffin, I know why I'm here. I know who I am. What I don't know is what comes next."

Though he pulled back slightly and needlessly adjusted his watch, he didn't seem surprised by my question; he had to have known it was coming. Our caravan of shiny Range Rovers pulled over next to a sleek, modern building. Theo and Dagger got out, leaving Prince Griffin and me alone in the shaded car.

Griffin took a deep breath and reached for my hand. "We talk. We get to know each other. This is an unusual courtship, yes? I know that you do not love me, but someday we will care for each other, maybe even love." He lightly squeezed my hand.

"Do your parents love each other?"

"Yes, they do. I have never seen a couple as devoted and loving as my parents, and they met on their wedding day. They have been happily married for thirty years now."

It gave me hope. In almost a whisper, I asked the burning question. "When is our wedding day?"

He sighed and looked at our hands, hesitant to give an answer. I feared the worst. *Tomorrow? Today? Had we just arrived at the ceremony?* Maybe getting it over with would be the best thing for me—less time to dwell on the unknown. *Focus on the good. This is an opportunity, remember.*

"For your own safety and to assure our people, my parents wanted us to wed immediately." He paused. "And heaven knows I have looked forward to our marriage for many years now. But, I understand that you need some time. I have convinced my parents to let us have a longer engagement." He waited, assessing my reaction, then said, "The Council gathers every spring and autumn, and the next Council gathering is as far as my parents are willing to wait. We will wed in late March, seven weeks from today."

I sat back into the fine leather seats. *At least I know.*

There was a moment of quiet between us, though surprisingly not uncomfortable.

"This stop is now a little, eh . . ." he fished for the English translation. "Anti-climate?"

It was just funny enough to half-laugh, lifting the serious conversation. "I think you mean anti-climactic."

"Yes, that is what I mean. Come, I have something to show you." He left the car enthusiastically.

I took a moment to myself. *Women get married all the time. Griffin is great. And I have seven weeks to get to know him.*

Dagger stood just outside, his back to the car. I desperately wanted to know how he really felt about all this.

Just as I stepped onto the sidewalk, the first droplets of rain spattered perfect dark polka dots on the concrete. I looked up, relishing the wet freckles on my face. Before I could really enjoy the midday shower, Griffin and Dagger rushed me inside.

I gasped at the glittering excess before me.

"Every bride needs a ring," Griffin said softly.

The luxury jeweler had been cleared of customers, leaving nothing but black velvet and glistening stones. I didn't feel like a kid in a candy store, I felt like a moron wandering into a back-room mafia poker game. My eyes darted around the room, looking for the first sign of *Excuse me, Miss, but why don't you wait outside.*

Griffin took my hand, leading me to the first counter. Hundreds of diamonds sparkled beneath the spotless glass. I stared bug-eyed at only a small fraction of them before he convinced me with that twinkle in his eye to move to a back counter.

"*These* are more suited for a princess."

He stood back a little while I glazed over at the sight of the enormous diamond rings in front of me. "I really don't think I can wear any of these."

"Good! Because I have already picked yours out."

An attendant emerged from behind a red velvet curtain carrying a richly finished wooden box big enough to hold a small tiara. I really hoped it *wasn't* a tiara.

"Your design is ready, as promised." She set the box gently on the glass counter and left.

Griffin waited until she was gone, then reached for the lid. "I know this is late and out of order—"

In a panic, I lowered a firm hand onto the box to keep him from opening it. My eyes fixed on my naked ring finger, refusing to look Griffin in the eye. "Please." *Shut up, Haelo.* "I'm not ready for this. Can we wait? Can you ask me later?"

I finally looked up to see Griffin fighting back a soft smile, like a patient father trying not to laugh at the irrational insecurities of his child. "You are prepared to marry me, yes?"

"Yes, Griffin, I am. I'm just not prepared for a proposal." *Oh, of all things.*

He closed his eyes and nodded in understanding as his smile finally broke. "As you wish, my dear. Though I cannot promise to wait much longer. Traditionally, the proposal comes before the wedding." He offered his arm and escorted me to the door. Theo went back to collect the ring.

Outside, the rain had picked up. Dagger shielded us to the car with an umbrella. I held out my hand to catch what few raindrops I could. As I stepped into the back seat, Dagger glanced at my bare hand—he had been outside the jeweler during the non-proposal. I snuck back an unsteady gaze and slid into my seat.

The rain echoed on the ceiling inside the car, modulating into a smooth drone when we accelerated.

Two minutes into the drive, Dagger pointed to a side road. "Theo, pull over here."

Theo parked the car in the refuge of a large tree.

"I'll drive," Dagger instructed.

Theo got out of the car, shut the door, and walked around the back. While he was still outside the car, Dagger turned to Griffin and me. "Your Highness, I will feel better once you both are safely in Pankyra. I feel too many unfamiliar candeons here in Athens."

"Yes, Ridion," the prince agreed just as Theo reached Dagger's door.

Before Dagger peeled back onto the main road, he picked up a handheld radio and sounded off orders. It was all in Greek, but there was no mistaking the authority in his voice. A quarter mile down the road, the two other Range Rovers and two more Escalades had us flanked on all sides, falling into line as both escorts and backup. There were at least four candeons in each SUV. I had never been around so many in my entire life. The buzz was electric.

Griffin gave my hand another squeeze. "Don't worry, Miriam. This is just precautionary."

Twenty minutes later, we stopped at the familiar far end of the airport. The jet had gone. In its place were two sleek helicopters. Dagger opened my door and held my hand for balance as I stepped from the car. His hand felt warmer than the prince's, though it had nothing to do with temperature. I almost didn't let go.

The rain had subsided, leaving a fresh, nostalgic smell behind. The tarmac puddles reflected the overcast clouds and gave the area a dreamlike sense of symmetry.

Dagger helped me into the luxe helicopter. Griffin sat beside me, with Dagger and Theo sitting rear facing behind the two pilot seats. It was both unnerving and relieving to sit face to face with Dagger.

The helicopter soared over the coastline and into open water. New sets of islands appeared on the horizon every time I looked out a window. Though I knew how inappropriate it was, I couldn't keep myself from frequent, curious glances at Dagger. *What was he thinking?*

Every so often, his glances would meet mine, and he'd look away just as quickly as I did.

I wasn't sure how long we'd been in the air when Griffin leaned over and said with a sort of rehearsed, obligatory pride, "Just over there. *That* is Pankyra. Or at least her outer shell."

I looked out the deeply tinted windows at an island three or four miles wide with no beaches or shallows. The entire shoreline rose from the sea in steep, harsh cliffs, at least three hundred feet up, as if the original shoreline had fallen off into the deep ocean. The terrain was mostly cragged rock, with a few staggered patches of low brush, not enough to hide the one enormous white mansion on the eastern end, unexpectedly modern with large windows and box architecture. The oddest part was the cluster of twelve concrete helicopter pads about seventy-five meters from the mansion. Only three of them were vacant.

My stomach flipped when we touched down. The men climbed out first; Griffin helped me down, then took my hand. I told myself to calm down before I worked up a nervous sweat.

First Team emptied the other helicopter and assembled in a half-circle around the front perimeter of the house. Dagger nodded his head in friendly respect to the five kryptes and then paused in front of Rebecca, the only female in the unit. She sighed and grinned. I couldn't hear their words, but there seemed to be some history behind their short exchange of pleasantries, noted by Dagger's sheepish eye contact and fidgeting stance.

A half dozen guards in sharp suits came out of the large art deco door and lined the front steps of the entrance. Standing in the open door frame, just in front of the indoor shade, were two older yet exquisite candeons, a man and a woman. The woman wore an elegantly pleated mint chiffon dress and a glistening tiara in her pale red hair, pulled back into a voluminous high bun. The man had a ruler-straight part through the side of his salt and pepper hair, a very square jaw, a starched white shirt, and a surprisingly regal bright blue suit.

The woman greeted me first with a voice so welcoming I could have hugged her. "Hello, dear Miriam. We are delighted to meet you." She offered her fragile-looking hand.

"It's lovely to meet you as well." My nervous voice caught.

She smiled encouragingly. I expected pomp and circumstance, but she seemed completely genuine. "I am Cora, and this is Alcaeus."

The kingly Basileus shook my hand. Despite the many fine wrinkles, he looked healthy. And rich. And very royal. I wanted to burn my sweater and jeans.

Alcaeus grasped Dagger by the shoulder, the way a father shows manly affection toward a son. Speaking to me, he said, "Ridion has told us much about you; I hope you don't mind." Then, turning to Dagger, he practically sang, "It's great to see you. It's been a long two years."

"Come, let us show you our home," Cora beckoned. She took my hand and led me inside. Something told me I was really going to like her.

The house was beautiful: crisp white furniture with gold upholstery tacks and legs sat atop gray, blue, green, and peach patterned carpets; the grand front entrance had high ceilings, clean architectural stonework, and enough seating for at least thirty people; antiquated Greek, Roman, and Egyptian statues stood between each window, one of which seemed oddly familiar. Griffin noticed my quizzical staring and said, pointing to the nearly naked statue, "Picture her without the jewelry . . . and with no arms."

"Is that a complete Venus de Milo?" I gasped, impressed with myself that I remembered the name.

"That is *the* Aphrodite de Milo. The Romans often tried to take credit for Greek accomplishments. Our family has always had the original." He spoke like an obligated tour guide, then winked at me. I remembered the way he described his feelings for Pankyra while we were in Athens and nodded at his good-sportsmanship.

We walked through the front room, past a high marble desk flanked with two more suited guards, and down a long hallway with at least five elevators on one side and floor to ceiling windows on the other side that allowed views to a meticulously manicured inner courtyard. Stepping through a heavy, ancient looking archway, I noticed a steep set of stairs spiraling wide into the deep bedrock of the island. The steps, walls and ceiling were all granite. Two kryptes led the way down the stairwell, followed by Theo, Alcaeus and Cora, then Griffin and me. Dagger took up the rear.

The seemingly endless stairs were lined with sconces, casting arcing shadows as we descended lower and lower into the island, my spine shivering in anxious anticipation. Griffin put his hand on my back. I smiled at the gesture.

We must have descended at least four stories before a shimmering, warm glow began to emanate from farther below. We came around the last bend to where the stairs ended in a lavish room stuffed with silk pillows, rich tapestries, and gold-leafed antique furniture. It was a large room with high ceilings and a handful of small chandeliers, a strange, beautiful mix of Victorian architecture and textiles straight out of an Arabian dream.

Guards dressed in formal military uniform appeared from each side of the base of the stairs, standing at attention. They bowed to Alcaeus, Cora, and Griffin (who all dipped their chins in acknowledgment), stared at me for a few very uncomfortable seconds before bowing, and then shook hands with Theo and Dagger. They stood pin-straight, speaking quietly in Greek to Dagger, who spoke back with calm authority. They nodded once in tandem and resumed their posts.

How high up in command is he? I wondered, staring at Dagger. The prince's bodyguard took orders from Dagger; the Pankyra guards took orders from Dagger; I half expected Griffin to take orders from Dagger. I snorted when I realized that he already had. The royals all turned to me with raised eyebrows, though Griffin wore an enormous grin.

"Miss LaReym," Alcaeus announced, gesturing to the palace sitting room we stood in, "welcome to your home."

17

DINNER PARTY

Dagger took a deep breath. I hadn't known him very long, but I had picked up on his mannerisms enough to see that beneath his calm was a diluted sort of agitation. Either something was bothering him, or he was getting antsy with boredom. Or both.

Cora left the Basileus' side and stood in front of Dagger. "Oh, Ridion. Seeing you standing here brings back such wonderful memories. It's good to have you home," she chimed, beaming.

"It's nice to be here," he answered. I noticed that he didn't say "home"—and his smile seemed only half as big as Cora's.

"And now that you are Miss LaReym's personal guard, I should hope we will see more of you than we have the past six years." She glided back to her husband. Alcaeus put an arm around his wife—they really did seem happy together.

She grinned at Dagger and turned her attention to me. "Let's get a tour over with so you can lie down. I'm sure it has been a very long day."

Griffin stepped forward and took my hand. "This way, my dear."

Theo stayed in the Arabian sitting room; Dagger tried to stay with Theo, but Alcaeus insisted he join us. They showed me guest rooms, a library, and a—no joke—*spa* on the same floor. I noted the spa's location for a planned return. We descended a grand staircase (much to the angst of my now burning quadriceps) and entered an enormous ballroom with two identical chandeliers—the biggest I'd ever seen. Prince Griffin had spoke of galleries, concerts, and dances; I now understood what he meant. Past the ballroom was another series of rooms: parlors, another library, a music room, and a very long dining room.

In each room, Alcaeus would say something serious, like pointing out the portrait of a long-dead ancestor and remarking how noble, or brave, or wise they had been. Cora would wink at me. Griffin would mumble something saucy under his breath like how one particular *noble* ancestor once stabbed his own stubby finger during a State dinner because he mistook it for a rather large gnocchi. I giggled; Alcaeus didn't seem to notice, Griffin outright beamed. And though I expected Dagger's restrained smile, he only looked away.

Try as I might, a yawn escaped my throat. Cora pivoted at just the wrong moment and saw it.

"Miriam, you must be exhausted."

"A little," I admitted, then quickly regretted it. *Don't be* that *daughter-in-law. Suck it up.*

"Let me show you to your room. You can unpack, settle in, and rest before dinner."

Despite my self-reproach, my gratitude showed; I needed a break from standing amongst royals.

Cora led the way into the hallway. Griffin bowed to me, releasing me from the room. It felt like a chivalrous act, not a royal etiquette obligation, so I didn't bow back, but I left the room uncertain, hoping and praying I had interpreted it correctly.

I was so consumed with second guessing my behavior that I didn't at all pay attention to where we were going. There were stairs involved, and more than a few hallways. Cora finally stopped in front of a very tall, very intricate gold door.

"This is your suite. I took the liberty of stocking your closets. I hope you don't mind." She paused and looked me over, placing one delicate hand on my arm. "I am glad you're here. Griffin has been so lonely.

You can show him what life is really about." She kissed me on the forehead. "And I believe there are two people in there who have waited very patiently to give you a hug." She smiled at my wide-eyed excitement when I felt the familiar auras. "I'll leave you now."

As soon as she disappeared down the hallway, I swung the door open with every ounce of impatient joy I had.

"Neo? Grandpa?"

Neo's bear hug was the best feeling in the world. When Aaram joined in, the tear dams burst.

"I've been so worried about you two."

Neo chuckled. "About us? It took me two and a half days to get here and Grandpa beat me by eighteen hours. We've been worried about *you*. It's been over a week! What happened?"

Aaram stepped back to get a good look at me. I couldn't read his face; it was some sort of unsettling pride/pity mishmash.

"Well," I said, "we fled north from San Diego and . . . traveled. A lot. There were a couple of cabins, a bloody fall on a mountain, a stoned hitchhiker, a flying boat—true story—an icy dive under the Northern Lights, an attempted murder, and some sort of Hawai'ian, witchy, voodoo tracker. We drove, ran, flew and probably a bunch of other things while I slept."

Neo and Aaram gawked. Finally, Neo spoke up. "So, it was a big week, then?"

"You could say that." I almost laughed.

Aaram zeroed in on my last comment. "While you slept? Honey, have you . . . ?"

"Yes, Grandpa. I've transitioned." I didn't want to talk about it; there was nothing to say. "I've missed you both," I breathed, and went in for another hug.

"Love you, Lo. I'm glad you're safe," Neo said. For a slow-motion second, I was eight years old and back in San Diego, holding onto Neo and thanking God that I still had him. We were both entering a new stage then, with an unfamiliar grandfather and a human way of life. Today did not feel much different.

Aaram put his hand on Neo's shoulder. "Come on, let her rest. We'll see her at dinner." They both gave me one last hug before heading for the door.

"Lo?" Neo said. "Sweet digs, though, right? Maybe this whole Galana thing isn't all that bad. Just don't expect me to bow or call you 'Your Highness.' I've seen what you look like when you wake up in the morning—there's nothing 'Your Highness' about it."

I punched him in the arm. He beamed.

I followed them to the door. "I don't know what I'd do without you both here."

Aaram gave me a wink. Neo looked up and down the hallway, careful not to appear too impressed. "See you at dinner, kid," he said, then put his hands in his pockets. I watched them until they turned a corner in the long hallway.

I expected the huge, antique door to squeak when I shut it, but it glided to an elegant close. The furniture was exquisite; the marble floors were cushioned with thick, white, fur carpets; every flat surface was covered with gorgeous displays of fresh flowers; and the enormous bed looked fluffy enough to get lost in. But something was off. I leaned against the door and tried to figure it out. It was on the tip of my tongue when a thunderous knock startled me, causing me to slip and knock over a delicate crystal vase filled with roses.

"Haelo? Are you okay?" Dagger asked, barging in and hitting me with the door. I caught my balance on the side table booby-trapped with shattered crystal and thorny rose stems.

"I was. Until you came in," I remarked, staring at the blood pooling in my palm.

"Let me get that." He picked up the vase's wide satin ribbon off the floor and carefully wrapped it around the deep cut. He held my hand close to his chest, examining it for any broken bones. "I'm sorry. I shouldn't have—"

"It's okay. It was bound to happen. You're talking to the girl who cracked her elbow on her own trash can, remember?"

"How *do* you make it through the day?" he asked, walking us over to a chaise.

I watched the pattern of the lace curtains sway in shadows on the floor. Suddenly, it dawned on me exactly what was so strange about the room. *Sunlight!* Loads of it streaming through the many windows! We must have been in a room cut out of the side of the island cliffs. I moved to a window for a view of the ocean.

"What in the world?" I gasped, looking out the window at a glistening, old world city, compacted into a massive cave. I saw buildings, towers, columns, stairs, walkways, bridges, gazebos, and rooftop courtyards all intermixed with a scattering of narrow waterways, almost like the back neighborhoods of Venice. There were plants and gardens everywhere, with vines growing on many of the walls. All this . . . in a *cave.*

The strangest thing was the bright light. It shone almost indistinguishable from sunlight except that it didn't come from a single source; it came from a pattern all interconnected, like a maze, in the distant center of the high, marbleized ceiling of the cave. It reminded me of a luminescent deep-sea fish I'd seen on National Geographic (though had yet to see in person). It was eerily similar to sunlight despite a very light, cool tinge, like dawn on a stormy day.

I looked closer at the city below. People walked the miniature bridges between buildings and sat down for meals on their rooftop gardens. I even saw a young girl playing fetch with a puppy. It looked perfect. Like a dream.

"Welcome to Pankyra," Dagger huffed.

"It's unbelievable. A whole city tucked inside an island?"

"Sort of. The water channels are accesses to the majority of the city, which is underwater. The wealthy live up here, but the working class—the real lifeblood of the city—live below."

"You seem more proud of the working class than the wealthy."

"I am."

I studied the picturesque city beneath my windows. Maybe it was too good to be true.

"Will I ever know them? The people, I mean. Here I am, a Galana. A future queen. Some sort of *mother* symbol. But I don't know them at all. What kind of mother is that?"

My eyes grew wide with horror. Who were these people? I honestly had no idea. What exactly did it mean to be a *real* candeon?

I was about to become the world's most disappointing poser.

"Give it time. Someday, they will be *your* people. There is no one—at all—better for our people than you."

I scoffed. Like a child. A particularly immature child.

"Fate wouldn't have chosen you otherwise, Haelo. You'll see."

My chest tightened. Time didn't just freeze, but disappeared. And for a moment, I felt it. Fate. Destiny. *Purpose.* My aura, my *soul*, recognized Dagger's words, and it terrified me.

Far in my mental periphery, Dagger got on his phone and ordered a first-aid kit. When the words *to Miss LaReym's private suite* left his lips, metaphorical ice-water doused the fire his conversation had kindled.

Here and now, I chanted, shaking my thoughts free. Emotional survival mode. *Here. And now.*

A servant brought the kit to the door two minutes later.

"Here, let me fix your hand properly." Dagger unwound the bloodied satin ribbon, tossing it onto a writing desk. The alcohol wipe stung in my palm, just like my bloody shoulder had on the mountain in California. The real burn, however, came from Dagger's touch.

I stared at the stained ribbon, desperate for benign conversation. "Should I rinse it in the sink first?" I asked, pointing to a large copper basin filled with water on one of the sideboards.

"That is not a sink," Dagger informed me as he inspected my cut. "That is a *pola* basin. Remember that message I sent to Alcaeus? With my ring in the cove in Alaska? Pola basins are how a dry candeon receives those messages. But we'll have time for that later."

"Thanks," I whispered, "for everything."

"You're welcome." He finished securing the gauze and then put the first-aid kit back together. "Dare I ask how you left the jewelry shop without your engagement ring?"

"I got scared."

"Scared?"

"Yeah, I got scared. I know we're getting married; I just froze. I don't know. The proposal is supposed to be this exciting, amazing declaration of love. It's one of those life events girls look forward to. I couldn't. . . ." I didn't bother finishing my thought.

Dagger sat still, not knowing what to say.

I put aside the unsettling conversation and asked something that had been on my mind all day. "Dagger? Or is it Ridion? I don't know what to call you."

He sat up straighter. His tone took on a trained, rehearsed quality. "You can call me whatever you wish, though please do not call me 'Ridion' in public." He stood. "I should go. My commander requested to see me."

"So far, everyone has answered to you. It's hard to imagine someone else being your commander."

He barely grinned, momentarily breaking his cold professionalism. "I am the ranking kryptes. I answer to my commander, the General, for all things mission related, and the royal family for all things pertaining to my duties here. It is true, I outrank other members of the Krypteia."

"They respect you."

"I have earned their respect."

"How did I get so lucky?"

"My particular set of skills was required."

I didn't want to pursue the conversation any further; it reminded me that I was just his responsibility. "Dag, before you leave this room, I need some answers."

He folded his arms and waited. Clearly, he took orders from me, as well.

"Griffin said something about seeing me months ago. What did he mean? Why didn't you tell me?"

Without even the slightest gathering pause, Dagger explained, rushing through the words. "He wanted to see this bright, funny, strong young woman that I had been telling him about. He came, I hid his aura, and we walked into the auditorium pretending he was blind and I was his escort. We watched your choir concert from the back row, and he went home."

"That's it?"

"That's it. He wanted to see more of you, but I convinced him that you deserved your privacy."

"Thank you."

He dropped his head in acknowledgment.

My questions weren't over with. "Neo said he got here days ago. Not that I'm complaining—why did it take us so long? I mean, they both got here before I transitioned. We could've made it that fast, right?"

"It wasn't safe to go an obvious way." He took a deep breath. "But mostly, I thought it best you got used to the idea of being the Galana before getting thrown into it. I hope you had enough time to think things through, and figure out who you are."

"Alcaeus and Griffin have a lot of trust in you."

"I have earned that as well. They've been good to me."

I stared at him, rallying my courage for the next question. "Why didn't you tell me your real name?"

"I wanted to," he started and then paused. "I have to be 'Dagger' whenever I'm working. I *am* Dagger. The royal family and my clan back home in the Indian Ocean are the only ones who call me by my given name. To be honest, I was just as surprised to hear it today as you were—too many people were around. I need to protect the identity of my family and my clan, and I keep my name private in order to do that." He saw the hurt on my face. "But I hope you know that in private, you are, without hesitation, among those I trust with that name. I will tactfully speak with Alcaeus, Cora, and Griffin about being more careful. They should not use 'Ridion' in the presence of others."

"I still don't know what to call you."

He sighed. "I'm not sure what to call myself."

I thought about it, then asked with a careful smirk, "Dag?"

He looked up with a new light in his eye. "Dag works."

We shared a smile. Griffin was great; but he was not Dagger. I dropped my gaze and went in for my last question. "What about Sam? Will you interrogate him today?"

"No. We'll let him sweat for a day or two. I will let you know what he says when it's over."

"I want to be there, Dag—I deserve to be there."

"I'll see what I can do." He took a short bow and opened the door. "By the way, dinner is a formal affair. You'll want to go through the closet. Cora has impeccable taste; I'm sure you will find something to wear."

I slumped. "I wore a thirty dollar dress to prom last year. I have no idea how to get . . ." An embarrassing attempt at posing failed, but I still needed to prove my point, so I waved my hands in an outline of a sensuous silhouette. " . . . formal. And there is no way I'm going to that spa where the other women can corner me with questions that I don't know how to answer."

Dag smiled. "I think I know someone who can help. I'll send her in." He closed the door softly behind him.

I turned around to face the elegant suite, breathing in the thick, but not overwhelming, smell of fresh flowers. I flopped on the bed and shut my eyes despite the fact that a nap was an impossible pursuit. A restless half hour later, I decided to investigate the room. In one corner of the suite was an open entryway into a glamorous sitting room, and then a bathroom, complete with a tub big enough for a horse. Double doors marked the way into a closet—if you could even call it a closet; it was bigger than Aaram's family room. One end was lined with drawers and shelves of shoes, the other end rivaled a trendy boutique. One particular section oozed with an intimidating amount of floor-length silk, lace, and chiffon—the formal section. I didn't dare touch it.

A light knock on the door saved me from further investigation.

I opened it up to a pleasing sight. Rebecca, the female member of First Team, stood at the ready. "Hello, Miss LaReym. Dagger said you might need some help."

"Sweet heavens, yes!"

She ventured into the bathroom, asking, "Salt or fresh water?"

"Um . . . fresh?" I responded, thinking I was saving someone the arduous task of hauling in salt water.

She turned on one of two bath faucets and poured a lovely smelling oil into the already bubbling tub. She dismissed herself into the closet to peruse dress options while I slipped into a much-needed bath. I glanced at the gilded, etched labels underneath each faucet and blushed. *Salt water, spring water. I should have surmised as much.* Between the warm water, soft glow through the windows, ergonomic recline, silky bubbles, and relaxing aroma, I didn't stand a chance; Rebecca had to wake me forty minutes later with an "ahem." A plush robe cradled me in incredible softness—I had no desire to get dressed.

Rebecca had originally picked out an azure blue sleeveless gown, but I quickly put the kibosh on that particular color—no one needed reminding that I was the Galana. Instead, she found me a lovely blush pink short-sleeved dress that did wonders for my very non-voluptuous chest. I congratulated myself on not looking like a surfboard.

I always thought I did an okay job with make-up; then Rebecca showed me the magic of an eyelash curler, cream eyeliner, bronzer, and blended shadow. So much better than my usual blush-and-mascara routine. After she secured the last curl in my romantic up-do, she opened a cabinet in the bathroom filled with jewelry.

"Here, something simple," she said, and handed me obscenely large diamond stud earrings. My chest tightened at the reminder of Griffin's wooden ring box.

By the time two hours had passed, I'd been washed, polished, made-up, dressed, primped, bling-ed, and shoed. "Rebecca, you're amazing. Thank you."

"You look sublime, if I do say so myself."

Sublime? Maybe English wasn't her first language. But.... *I'll take it.*

She tested my nail polish, making sure it was dry. "I'm glad Dagger thought of me."

The way she said Dagger made my stomach knot. "How long have you known him?"

She adjusted the swoop in my hair. "We grew up together in neighboring clans; he taught me how to feel for shark auras—I guess you could say it was our thing. Did you know you could do that? Feel animals? Anyway, he left for Krypteia duties when we were thirteen. He must have some secret special ability because they don't usually enlist warriors that young."

She double-checked my dress to make sure it hadn't wrinkled. "I missed him. My whole family missed him. Luckily, I joined the Krypteia a few years later and we sort of rekindled. He mentored me, helped me climb through the ranks, even prepared me for First Team, the royal protection unit which I was *completely* intimidated by, but his guidance helped me focus my intimidation into precision. He was the captain of the Alpha Agema—the highest special ops unit—until a couple of years ago when Hank took over."

I chanted to myself to prepare to be happy for them. "So, are you two...?"

She blushed. "Not any more. We were engaged at one time—I thought he was the love of my life. But that was a long time ago."

A sharp pain quivered in my chest. I felt as if my banished hopes of Dagger were slowly evaporating from my ears, evidence for all to see. "What happened? If you don't mind my asking."

She sighed. "I never really knew what he was thinking; he always kept his emotions to himself." She cleaned up the stray blush powder, carefully putting away the rest of the make-up and hair products. Her distant eyes looked to the past. "I will always care for him, but I couldn't give him my all if he wasn't willing to show me he could do the same. He had feelings for me, but try as I might, I could never get him to talk about it."

"You called it off." I meant to say it to myself.

"Yes. I did. Sometimes I wonder if it was the right thing to do. When I saw him face to face this morning for the first time in over two years, it brought back a lot of great memories. He still makes me feel special."

She stood next to me in the floor length mirror and studied her work. "Beautiful! It's not very often I get to do this girly stuff. Mostly I just train, provide security, and listen to a bunch of egos bet each other on who can do what the best. This was fun. Thank you."

I smiled, trying to mask my thoughts.

"Now, before you sit down, smooth out the back of your dress. And make sure you talk, sit, or stand *after* Galana Cora has. If you don't understand something, just ask Prince Griffin or Dagger, they'll explain everything." She suddenly sounded like a super type-A personal assistant.

"Dagger will be there?"

"He always is when he's in Pankyra—he's Alcaeus and Cora's favorite. They treat him like a son."

I nodded in understanding.

"I'll be there, too. Working, of course. Oh, if you can avoid it, don't sit by Alcaeus' sister, Helen. You'll thank me later."

The room went quiet after she left, reminding me how alone I really was. I sat by a window and studied the city below. The glow above had grown darker, much more violet than before. For the first time, I noticed the ceiling. A few glimpses of the interior walls of the cave showed that they glistened with mineral deposits like a trillion tiny stars. The waterways below twinkled with the reflections of the glittering cave above. I should have unpacked my camera, but something about its surreal splendor kept me from exposing such a city to a camera lens.

I searched for a distraction, eventually succumbing to thoughts of Dagger and Rebecca. They were probably perfect for each other, and I wanted to hate her for it. *Why should I care? I'm getting married in a few weeks.*

A proud knock sounded from the door.

I stood. "Come in."

Griffin entered, his hand still on the door handle. In just the right light, his black tux vacillated between deep green and midnight sheens with his movements. I had never seen anything like it before. He looked incredibly handsome. His eyes dilated as he looked me up and down, murmuring something in Greek.

"Excuse me, my dear. You are—" *Please don't say sublime.* "—stunning."

Right then and there, I made a choice. I didn't want to hang on to Dagger; I didn't want to quietly wish he stood here in place of the prince.

Whether I wanted it or not, I held a queenly title in my hands, and the candeon people deserved a loyal queen. "Your Highness?" I took a breath, lengthening my spine. "I mean, Griffin." My voice calmed to a regal steadiness. "If and when you are ready to ask me, I am ready to hear it."

He let go of the door. As he approached, I prepped myself for his proposal, expecting him to get down on one knee. Instead, he cradled my jaw in his palm.

"May I?" he asked. After my slight nod, he kissed me softly. And with noble acceptance, I kissed him back.

His baby smooth face smelled of aftershave. I could sense the restraint in his sigh as he slowly pulled away. "You have made me very happy." His smile was contagious, which lead to another kiss.

"Come. Before this dinner begins, it would be my honor to ask you something."

I took another breath and let him lead me down the hallway to a different wing of the palace where a solemn kryptes guarded a small, inconspicuous set of spiraling stairs. We went up, eventually emerging onto a small rooftop deck lined with hundreds of low candles. The cave above us gleamed in the warm glow. The pattern of light in the far center of the cave ceiling had almost faded completely, allowing the city below to twinkle with only the light from windows, globe strand lights strung across bridges, and torches burning along the waterways.

"It's breathtaking," I gasped.

He took my hand. "You are breathtaking."

For the first time, I noticed the fine wooden box resting atop a pedestal.

His face was close enough to kiss. "Miriam Anhaela LaReym, I promise to work for your love every day for the rest of my life. Be mine? Not just my wife, but my friend, my companion, and my partner. Give me your trust, that someday I might earn your heart."

He lifted the lid of the box. In a tufted pillow of dark velvet rested a massive emerald-cut white diamond surrounded by vibrant blue sapphires. The sapphires continued around the band. The flames of a hundred candles danced through the facets of the diamond, making the ring look like it was on fire. I didn't know what to say.

"The sapphires come from my great-grandmother's tiara. She was a Basilessa."

Griffin lifted the ring from its pillow. He smoothed my shaking fingers with his hand and slid the heavy jewel onto my left ring finger. "Marry me?"

My nightmares of a cold, callused husband disintegrated. Griffin was a kind man. He was thoughtful and happy. He was a princess's dream. *I could be a princess,* I thought. *I could learn to love him.* I already liked him a surprising lot.

"Yes," I whispered.

He kissed me again, more heated, more hungry than before, though careful not to overstep royal propriety.

We took one last look at the flickering glow of the city below.

"We will be good together, Miriam. You and I."

Griffin escorted me from the rooftop deck back into the elegant palace hallway. We walked arm in arm down another flight of stairs and across a foyer before entering the grand dining room.

The bustling room went completely silent. Fifty people stood around like clustered statues, staring at us. Griffin patted my newly affianced hand resting in the crook of his arm and whispered, "Do not worry about them; they are just amazed by your beauty. And they are probably just realizing you are the new Galana. It is always one of my sisters on my arm."

"I didn't know you have sisters."

"That is because the younger is a pest and the older thinks she has better things to do than to be a part of this family."

I didn't know whether or not to take him seriously. He escorted me forward to the first clique, reanimating the frozen room.

"My dear Miss LaReym, this is Delegate Nkosi Stuart of the Caribbean, and his wife, Tessa; General Stratos of the Krypteia; Cousin Hagne, my father's first cousin; her husband, Talos Tolomeo, Pankyra's city manager; and their son, Isander." He gestured proudly to me, "This is Miss Miriam LaReym, my future wife."

It stabbed like an ice pick to my kidney to hear Griffin say "wife" in front of other people, making things even more real. I gathered my wits and said hello, desperately trying to be proper as they all stared and bowed. Something about the way General Stratos bowed gave me more respect than I deserved. Everyone else behaved like they were meeting a celebrity; the General seemed genuinely humbled. Griffin escorted me away to the next cluster of people before Hagne or the delegate had time to pull us into conversation, which was clearly their eager intention.

"Miss LaReym, this is my father's sister, Aunt Helen; her daughter, Cousin Iris; and Delegate Cecilia Kostopolis of the Mediterranean. Ladies, my fiancée, Miss LaReym."

Each one took a quick glance at the rock on my ring finger. *It's not an engagement ring,* I thought, *it's a beacon.* Old Aunt Helen looked me up and down with squinty, judgy eyes, then burped. I tried my best not to smile. We left a flurry of excited whispering behind us as we moved on to the next greeting.

Griffin continued to escort me around the room. In the midst of introducing me to another delegate, I noticed Dagger over the shoulder of a local noble. He wore a black suit and skinny black tie, one of the few men in the room not in a tux. He smiled at me and raised his champagne glass. I smiled back.

A pause in the present conversation interrupted my distant, silent exchange with Dagger.

"Oh, yes, it's lovely to meet you, Delegate LaFleur," I said, hoping I offered what the pause needed.

We circled the entire room, greeting everyone, including Aaram, Neo, and Penelope, Griffin's twelve-year-old sister. She didn't seem like a pest; she was actually quite sweet, even gave me a hug. Dagger avoided our rounds, standing alone by the hearth. I couldn't help but watch him whenever he happened to be in my field of vision, though I tried to be subtle about it. Periodically, one of the younger women in the room, most notably Griffin's cousin Iris, would attempt to flirt with him, to which he would graciously fend off their advances.

I recognized a lone man in a dark corner. It wasn't until I noticed Rebecca in the opposing corner that I realized who the man was—First Team was here, camouflaged in the dim perimeter of the room. I looked from Dagger to Rebecca. He was looking at her; she stood erect, professionally observing the room.

Griffin was in the middle of telling me the latest gossip of the noble families when the room went immediately quiet. I turned to see Basileus Alcaeus and Galana Cora enter: Alcaeus in a burgundy three-piece suit (which almost distracted from his pointed, uber-shiny dress shoes), and Cora looking perfect in a cream silk A-line, smooth up-do, bright red lipstick, and pearl drop earrings. A mini tiara rested in the upper fold of her bun. They smiled and waited while everyone bowed, then took their seats at the head of the long table, followed by Griffin and me. Everyone else sat after we had. I looked around for Dagger and found him seated near the other end of the table.

Alcaeus stood. He spoke in halting English, pausing frequently mid-sentence. "Thank you all for coming this evening. I am sure you have realized why we are having this dinner. If you don't mind, I'll speak in English as Miss Miriam LaReym has not yet learned Greek."

Yet?

"Tonight marks the beginning of a wonderful future." He hesitated often between words, leaving poignant breaths of expectation. I fought back a smirk. *But give the man credit*; he certainly knew how to keep his audience on their toes.

He raised his glass to a toast. "To Griffin and Miriam. May your love be every bit as wonderful as ours has been." He kissed Cora's slender hand. I couldn't help but picture him as a judge in a modeling competition: a deliciously endearing mix between a classy fashion executive and a tired mayor of Whoville.

Dinner went off without a hitch, unless you count a partially deaf Aunt Helen shouting at the servers. I didn't eat much: for one, the dress was awfully tight while seated, and two, I just wasn't very hungry. Griffin chatted merrily with our table neighbors. Every few minutes, I glanced down the table to Neo for a silent laugh—he was most definitely out of his element. When dessert came looking like a piece of modern art, he mouthed the words, "You've got to be kidding me" into his tower of chocolate spirals.

After dinner, everyone except Princess Penelope followed the Basileus and Galana Cora into a large parlor where a band played mellow American jazz standards straight out of a 1940's Hollywood night club.

I left Griffin's arm on the pretense of mingling. A handful of short pleasantries with some nobles (and more than a few dreamy stares at my engagement ring) later, I finally found Aaram in an amiable debate over voting rights with a delegate from a province in the South American Atlantic. After an introduction to the delegate and a request to listen to their thoughts, I stood patient and quiet, awestruck at how connected and immersed in the candeon world Grandpa Aaram had been all this time. Regretfully, as I had nothing to contribute to the discussion, I was easy bait to Cousin Iris when she pulled me away.

"Congratulations, Miss LaReym. You must be thrilled," she said in a shallow, giddy coo. My natural instinct to combat her counterfeit enthusiasm started with a sarcastic quip, but I was going to be a princess, so I had better start acting like one.

"The rumor is that Dagger Stravins has been your personal bodyguard, correct?" Her English was British perfect, including the refined accent.

"Yes...." I acknowledged warily.

"And you have spent time with him?"

I didn't like where this conversation was going. I snipped out an appropriate response to what I thought a catty question. "You could say that."

"Just between us girls, you wouldn't happen to have any advice for an interested woman, would you?"

"No, I wouldn't. Excuse me." I bolted from her fishing and headed for any sort of excuse that I could find. I ended up alone in a back corner, searching the room for Neo.

"You look beautiful," Dagger's voice comforted me from behind.

I turned around to the patio.

The band went silent between sets, then picked up with a catchy rendition of *Beyond the Sea*. "You, too. I mean . . . you know what I mean. Nice suit. You clean up well." I couldn't be sure my eyes weren't ogling. *Stop staring!* "Oh, thanks for sending in Rebecca; I'd have come out a disappointment if it weren't for her."

"Not possible." He coughed and amended, "At least, I'm sure Griffin thinks so." His gaze drifted to my ring. "He proposed, I see."

I raised my brow at his glass. "You drink?" It was a stretch for conversation and I knew it. Dagger smirked. Apparently he knew it as well.

"I don't—it's water."

We stood together in awkward silence as I stared out into the glimmering city.

"Haelo, are you okay?" he asked.

"Close enough, I think. A month ago I was an American high school senior and today I'm in an underground palace meeting world dignitaries at an engagement dinner party—*my* engagement dinner party. Oh, and my fiancé happens to be the future Emperor of the candeon race." I sighed. "I'd say I'm doing okay, considering."

He stood still, unwavering. "And you will be the Empress. If you ever need to talk to someone—" He paused and thought through what he was saying. "Griffin is a good, understanding man. Don't be scared to open up to him." He took the last drink of his water and placed it on the patio guardrail. I was surprised the glass didn't shatter with his force.

An hour ago, I'd been almost happy—Prince Griffin was surprisingly charming. Seeing Dagger again skewed that near-happiness into disappointment. Who I should love and who I wanted to love were two different people. They were cousins. They were friends. A prince and a soldier. My fiancé and my bodyguard. They were both going to be a daily, integral part of my life.

A footman approached us carrying a folded note on a silver tray.

"Excuse me," Dagger said, opening the stiff paper. His neck flexed in frustration.

"What's wrong?" I asked.

"Sam is being difficult. I need to go. It's probably time he started talking anyway."

"Dagger, I want to be there."

He glowered at me. Finally, after a few stealthy glances around the candlelit room, he spoke softly. "I can stall for an hour at most. If you can find a way to excuse yourself by then, I will pick you up at your room and take you to Sam's holding cell."

"Thank you."

"Don't thank me yet. You might not like what he has to say." He looked past my shoulder and then mumbled quickly, "One hour," just as the band cut for a break.

A light hand on my back made me jump. "Miriam, dear. I overheard Aunt Helen asking your whereabouts; I think she is on the prowl. I've come to both warn and save you." Griffin kissed me on my cheek. "Isn't she beautiful, Ridion?"

I could tell the name made Dagger uncomfortable. He politely resisted looking around at the many people in the room who might have heard it. "Yes, Griffin, she is. Pardon me." He gave a short bow and left the room.

"He used to be charming." Griffin shook his head in mock pity. "We should play cupid and find him a girlfriend. What do you say?"

"He's probably just tired. It's been a long week." I took Griffin's arm, letting him lead me back into the room.

I made it through another half hour of superficial conversation with proper guests before I admitted to Griffin that my shoes were killing me. He suavely excused me from the party and walked me back to my door.

"Thank you," I said. "Today was nice. Not many girls can say they went ice-skating and rode scooters through Athens with a prince."

He kissed my hand. "Of all the things that have happened to you these past few weeks, I am flattered that our date was even mentionable."

"It was a memorable date." I giggled at the thought.

Griffin leaned in closer. "And not many girls can say they are to become a princess, married to a prince."

He hesitated in front of my lips and veered to my cheek. My fingers twisted together. Something in his touch felt hungrier than before, and I wasn't so sure I wanted it.

When he pulled away from his kiss, his eyes never left my mouth. "Miriam," he breathed. "I have been waiting and preparing for you my whole life. And now you're here. Tell me to leave before I lose myself completely and kiss you senseless." He took me in his arms, pressing me against the door. His kiss was hard, possessive. I tried to writhe out of his tightening grasp, but it only ground the bones in my wrist against the molding of the door. I couldn't breathe.

I finally pushed him back enough to speak through gasping breaths. "Tonight was wonderful, but you need to go." I didn't want to offend him, but I certainly wasn't going to let him take advantage of me. My lips already felt swollen. I wasn't sure if he heard me, he had redirected his passion to my neck. "Griffin, please! You're hurting me!"

He stilled. His arms released me, and he pressed his hands against the door on both sides of my shoulders, looking down at the floor. "Yes, I should go." When he raised his head, he didn't look me in the eyes; he watched himself trace a finger along my collarbone. "I should . . ." he whispered to himself as his lips once again moved toward the base of my neck.

Then I remembered the week of self-defense in tenth grade P.E.

Just before my knee made contact with his nethers, he pulled away of his own accord. He shook his head in shock and regret. I stayed still, scared to move and angry as ever.

Griffin put his hand to his forehead. "Miriam, I am so sorry! I do not know what came over me." He stared for a moment at the marble tile. "There is no excuse for it."

He extended a hand to lead me away from the door. I didn't take it.

The carved details of the door scraped along my back as I slid to the floor. I kept my hands to myself, tucked behind me.

He stepped back in shame, the guilt manifested in his eyes.

A black suit appeared in the hall. "Griffin?" Dagger questioned, confused. He looked at me on the floor, lips swollen and hair mussed, and then to the pacing Prince. "What happened?" he growled. His jaw clenched in the same anger I felt.

Griffin exhaled. "Please forgive me, Miriam. I will *never* treat you like that again. You are my queen . . . I will always give you that respect." He buttoned his tuxedo coat and left, avoiding Dagger's glare.

Dagger dropped to one knee. "Haelo?" he asked softly, waiting for a response.

I peeled my eyes away from Griffin's retreating back and looked at him. "I'm okay." I tucked a stray curl behind my ear. My neck tingled like a fresh carpet burn.

"No, this is not okay. You don't have to be *okay* right now. What happened?"

I didn't answer, only pleaded with my eyes that he not make me talk about it.

"Haelo, tell me."

"Not you. Please." I exhaled, then swallowed back the quiver in my bottom lip. "I'll talk to Aaram."

He dropped his face into his hands and sighed. "Here," he said, offering an arm.

I took it, stood up, and quickly let go. "Let me get changed. I'll meet you outside."

"I don't think—"

"Don't make me go to bed thinking about *this*. Please take me to see Sam."

He nodded and stepped outside the room.

I stared at myself in the bathroom mirror. A red, flustered splotch pulsed across my collarbones, leaving my scar a stark, pearly white. My wrist ached and my fingers shook as I tried to take out my earrings, the facets of the diamond and sapphires on my hand casting unwelcome, quivering glimmers under the vanity lights.

"No," I fumed aloud, slamming one earring onto the marble countertop. *I am a strong woman. I deserve to be respected.* A calming sort of power surged through my veins. I held my chin high and took a deep breath.

I met Dagger just outside my door. Though I was in jeans and flats, I felt taller, more empowered, than I had in the dress and heels. I left the engagement ring behind. "Let's go."

"Are you sure about this?" he asked, eyeing me, trying hard to convince me to stay. He still seethed about what Griffin had done—I could tell.

"Absolutely."

He led me down a steep back staircase and through a nondescript door into a dark, bricked tunnel. It was a long, quiet walk until we reached some sort of locker room.

"These are the palace kryptes' quarters. Follow me."

I felt for nearby auras. The closest ones seemed too calm and unmoving to be awake. However, because it had been difficult to feel any individuals in Pankyra with so many auras humming in the background, I didn't fully trust my feelings. "Is it okay that I'm down here?"

"You are the next Galana and I am second-in-command of the entire Krypteia—I don't think you need to worry. Everyone down here is asleep, anyway."

I stopped walking. "No, Dagger. I am betrothed to the prince and running around in the dark with my bodyguard. Are you *sure* this is okay?" I wasn't nervous; I was being honest.

His slight falter would have gone unnoticed to most. "Yes. General Stratos knows you're coming."

We walked past what might have been dormitories, a kitchen, a dark stone pool (possibly an outlet to the ocean below us), and an intimidating gym. Eventually, we came to an iron door. The guard outside the door stood when he saw us and saluted Dagger.

"This is Miss Miriam LaReym," Dagger informed the guard. "She is the new Galana, Prince Griffin's fiancée."

The shocked kryptes took a deep bow and apologized for not doing so earlier.

"The General is expecting us."

"Of course," said the guard, opening the door and standing aside.

We stepped through to a large, narrow, concrete room, two stories tall, lit with harsh fluorescent bulbs. General Stratos stood near the door, still in his tux. "Miss LaReym. Colonel Stravins."

"General," Dagger responded.

"The prisoner refuses to eat, drink, or speak. He somehow managed to slam the night guard's head against the wall."

I stepped forward. "I'd like to see him."

"Respectfully, Miss, I cannot let you. He's not stable, and I don't trust him."

"He's my friend—*I* trust him. And I can get him to talk."

General Stratos exhaled authority through his nose. "Colonel Stravins must stay between you and the prisoner. He will escort you out at the first sign of danger."

"Thank you, sir."

"Miss LaReym, you are the future mother of our people. Though I appreciate your respect, I do not expect you to call me sir."

"With all due respect to your traditions, General, I will always give you the reverence your title deserves." I added a subtle nod when his eyes widened in surprise. He nodded back. "Dagger, please lead the way."

A monitor glowed at the far end of the room, displaying the feed from a video camera on the other side of another iron door. On the screen, Sam stood in front of a steel table, feet apart, hands folded.

Dagger stopped me from opening the door. "Let me restrain him first."

"No. We need to find out what's going on. He won't talk to me if he feels threatened."

Dagger stepped in front of me, cutting off my access to the room.

"What's he going to do? He can't kill me, remember?"

He slowly maneuvered out of the way. Griffin's indiscretion had changed me, and Dagger knew it.

The heavy door creaked when I opened it, but not loud enough to overpower Sam's sigh of relief at the sight of me.

"Sam?" I stepped closer; again, Dagger intervened. "Sam, please sit down. You look exhausted,"

He shook his head.

"Here, I'll sit down too. Please, Sam—for me."

He thought through my request, and then sat down in a chair opposite the table from me. An untouched sandwich lay drying on a plate.

He very well could have been working for Massáude, but until I knew that for sure, Sam was still my friend. I kept my voice calm and friendly, a difficult feat considering the empowerment I now felt. "Tell me why you went to Alaska."

"Beilstein told me you'd be there."

"Why did you wait until I was there? Why not tell me about Beilstein before, in San Diego?"

"He didn't think you'd be taken so soon. He wanted you to graduate high school. He's just trying to protect you." Sam's responses seemed automatic, like he'd been playing them over and over in his mind for hours.

"Protect me from what?"

"He wants you to have your own life. He doesn't trust this future they have planned for you. When he told me that you'd be taken away and forced to marry, I agreed to help save you."

The word "forced" had taken on new meaning tonight. I stared at the sandwich, unable to think of another question. Dagger took over.

"How did you communicate with Beilstein?" he asked.

Sam's stare never left me. "Haelo, I know this sounds creepy, but you've got to believe me—I'm your friend. I couldn't just let them rip you from your life and haul you away. Beilstein is looking out for you. He... loves you."

Dagger grabbed him by the back of the neck.

"Dag! Stop!" I yelled.

He released Sam and stepped back.

I remembered Sam's awkward kiss on my cheek and the rushed kiss in the park. "Is that why you kissed me, Sam? To put doubt in my mind about marrying a stranger?"

He sat a little straighter. "Beilstein said that if you knew what you were missing—" He quickly turned to Dagger. "And by missing, I mean *choice* and *options*—that you'd jump at the opportunity to run. I'm sorry, Lo. It wasn't my idea."

"So, Beilstein wanted me to fall for someone besides the prince. To give me a reason to flee." That had already happened *without* his interference, and judging by the looks he gave whenever he saw Dagger and me together, I'd bet Sam knew that.

He nodded.

I moved my chair closer. "What could Beilstein have possibly said to make you leave your mother and Norah? They need you, Sam."

Though my voice had grown quiet with my last statement, the intensity in my tone broke Sam's focused disillusionment. Tears slid down his face; he didn't try to stop them. "My mom died. The day after you saw me in the park. Norah's with my sister in Idaho."

"I am so sorry. I had no idea."

"I came over to tell you, but Aaram said you couldn't talk. You ignored my calls and texts. That's when I suspected you were changing. I told Beilstein; he said that you hadn't, that he would know. He was so confident." His lip quivered. "Then on the day of my mother's funeral, Beilstein called and said we had to get you out of San Diego as soon as possible. He said we'd have to be careful because you were guarded even more closely. I showed up at your house with his special ops team later that day, but everyone had gone." He folded his hands into his lap. "A few nights later, he called and said you had transitioned into an adult; we were told to rush to Alaska. The team and I left immediately."

"Sam, he took advantage of your grief. I don't need to be saved."

He stared through my eyes right into my soul. "Then you're just as manipulated as he said you'd be."

18

BLURRED

I lay in bed the next morning thinking about Sam, Prince Griffin, Beilstein, and (despite my pathetic insistence that it was a bad idea) Dagger. My life was a mess. I wasn't regal enough to be a princess, I wasn't normal enough to be average. I had nothing to fall back on. Over the past month, things that I might have considered absurd had become a part of life.

A ladies' maid brought in breakfast on a gold tray, a note from Griffin wedged between the plate and a teacup brimming with more flowers.

Dear Miriam,
I cannot begin to express my shame. Please know I absolutely meant you no harm. I will understand if you choose not to see me today.
Your humbled servant,
Griffin

It was a start.

I finished breakfast and was putting the tray on an end table when another ladies' maid entered, this time struggling with a heavy statue. It was a deep, marbleized, polished green and stood two feet wide and about a foot tall. Something about its elongated medallion shape looked familiar, like a horizontal stretched football with two holes in the middle.

"The first wedding gift arrived for you this morning, Miss LaReym. Would you like me to put it on the table?"

"Yes, please. Who is it from?"

"I don't know. I can find out for you if you wish."

"Yes, thank you."

She dismissed herself and left. I was drawn to the statue. Where had I seen that shape before? A knock at the door snapped me from my reverie.

"Coming," I called.

I opened the door to a puffy-eyed Dagger. "Couldn't sleep, either?" I asked. His relaxed posture and the wrinkled corners in his familiar gray eyes and lazy smile made me weak in the knees. He looked like *home*.

"Good morning, Lo." He noticed his slip and shook his head. "Excuse me, *Miss LaReym*."

I smiled; the nickname had actually sounded quite perfect. "Don't apologize; screw the hoity."

He tried not to smirk. "I've come to fetch you."

"Oh."

"Don't worry, it's for a casual meeting."

Oh, that smile! Could my heart be any more in trouble? "Let me get dressed."

He stood in the suite's sitting area while I rummaged the enormous closet for my own clothes, which I found in a bottom drawer tucked sneakily away in the bowels of the closet—probably to help guide me toward princess-worthy clothing instead of my American high-schooler garb. *It's a garb kind of day.*

I met him back in the sitting area a few minutes later, wearing comfy pants and a cotton tee.

Dagger escorted me to a small but elegant sitting room where a wrinkled woman with a dark umber complexion and silver hair, wearing a red shift trimmed in delicate, white shells and embroidery, eased from her chair. Though short, she held herself with a noble posture I didn't expect from someone her age. She approached me with shaking hands, speaking in a language—neither English nor Greek—I couldn't recognize.

Dagger translated. "She says hello, that she's been waiting to meet you."

"Please tell her hello! Who is she?" I asked.

"She is my great-grandmother, on my father's side. Fayanza."

"Oh!" I gasped. She came forward. Gently grasping my head in her hands, she studied my countenance as her thumbs memorized the contours of my face.

"Please excuse her; this is how she meets people. Her eyesight isn't what it used to be. She knows that I've been watching over you. She . . . she came to wish you well on your wedding."

She winked at me, then moved her attention to Dagger. "Encheridion, Encheridion," she started before speaking mischievously under her breath to her great-grandson.

"Is that your name? Encheridion?"

He huffed at his matriarch and spoke to her with mild, loving sternness before answering me. "Technically, yes. But she's the only one who has ever called me that mouthful. I went by Ridion my entire childhood—even my official military record is under Ridion."

"What does it mean?"

"It's an old Greek word for a knife, or dagger. My parents knew from the beginning that I would be a member of the Krypteia, so they gave me a Greek name, just like their parents gave them." He seemed disappointed, as if—to him, at least—a Greek name was not something to be all that proud of. Not like intended, anyway.

Fayanza took both of my hands in hers and spoke to me, almost in song.

"She's giving you a blessing—it is tradition among my people."

When her blessing was over, she wiped a tear from the corner of my eye and nodded, pleased with herself.

Dagger promised to be back soon and, arm in arm, lovingly escorted his great-grandmother out. It was then I noticed her bare feet.

I waited on a velvet-tufted chair when the ladies' maid from earlier padded softly into the room.

"Excuse me, Miss. I found the note that came with the statue. My apologies, I didn't see it earlier." She brought it to me on a small silver tray and left in a hurry.

Dagger came back just as the note dropped from my frozen hands to the floor. "Haelo?"

"Dagger! He sent a gift!"

"Who? What are you talking about?" He picked up the note and read it aloud. "*A talisman of the finest beilstein jade. May it remind you of happy days to come.*" His eyes shot to my hands. "What talisman?"

"It's not a talisman; it's a statue in my room."

"Show me," he commanded, his bodyguard instinct overtaking civility.

Back upstairs, Dagger looked the jade statue over, searching for a clue. I sat on the bed. Staring. Waiting.

Dagger's temples pulsed as he thought. He finally gave up and pulled out a cell phone. He spoke in Greek; I couldn't hear the speaker. Slowly, my anxiety cooled behind curious anticipation. He stopped talking and paced the room, waiting for some sort of answer. He nodded once and abruptly hung up. "Beilstein is a kind of jade mined in Germany. Does that mean anything to you?"

"I don't think so. But I've seen that shape before. I just can't remember where."

"I should go talk to Sam," he said. He looked to the open door and waited, probably sensing someone approaching; I was not yet used to the buzz of hundreds, if not thousands of nearby candeons to be able to focus on one aura very well. Seconds later, Neo appeared.

"Hey, Lo. Aaram is at some sort of Council meeting. You want to hang out, maybe go explore the city?" He noticed the smooth, green statue. "Hey! I haven't seen that in years!"

Dagger immediately perked up. "You know what that is?"

"Sort of. Dad used to carve those out of koa wood when we were kids, but they were a lot smaller. He made us necklaces out of the carvings. He said they were a talisman against bad dreams or something."

I stood. *Sam said Beilstein loved me. Beilstein Jade.* "Dagger, your name is another translation of your birth name. Maybe *Beilstein* is, too. It's a talisman." I realized, pointing to the statue. "My father, Jade LaReym, is Beilstein."

Dagger's brow wrinkled in sympathy. "Haelo, I was there. Your father was surrounded by rebel mercenaries and killed. His aura faded out."

"So can yours!"

"*Haelo.* We are not alone." Dagger didn't have to look at Neo; I knew exactly what he was scolding me for.

Neo interjected. "What's going on? Lo, Dad died. He's gone."

"No, Neo. He's not gone. He's been trying to save me!"

Neo's twisted stare didn't sway my belief. He held my wrists and spoke with a nurturing, no, *condescending* tone. "Let him go. Don't live through that again."

I ripped myself from his grasp. "I need to see Sam!" I ran out of the room, leaving Dagger and Neo racing to catch up. I turned a hallway corner and slammed into Griffin. We both tumbled to the floor.

"Miriam? Are you all right? What is—"

"Griffin," Dagger started, not nearly as winded as I was. "We've just come across some information that may be a clue to who is behind your fiancée's attempted kidnapping—we are on our way to confirm that information with a prisoner."

Theo, Griffin's friend and bodyguard, stood a few steps behind, squinting, analyzing.

Griffin looked from Dagger, to Neo, to me. "I'm coming with you. Theo, stay here." I bit my tongue and didn't argue. Theo nodded his head in compliance.

Down in the dark holding area, Neo and Griffin monitored the camera feed while Dagger and I went into Sam's enclosed cell. I paced back and forth anxiously as Dagger started the questions.

"Where did you first meet Beilstein?"

Sam didn't answer.

"When did he tell you that he was Haelo's father?"

This time, Sam winced.

I fell into the chair in front of him. "Please, Sam. Tell me what's going on. Where is my dad?"

Sam dropped his head to the steel table. "Beilstein sent us to save you. He said there were mercenaries out hunting for you and that if you ever got to the palace, they'd steal you away. I was supposed to keep you from getting here." He lifted his head and stared fiercely into Dagger's eyes. "There is a traitor in this island. She is not safe here. She deserves a life free from this constant fear of being abducted. Beilstein can give her that. You seem like you care about her—how could you bring her to this life?"

I bolted from the room before Dagger and Sam could see me tremble; I had forgotten that Neo and Griffin stood just outside. Courage boiled in my chest at the sight of the prince. I was not the vulnerable girl I had been. I had him to thank for that.

Dagger emerged from the cell and looked to Griffin for orders.

Prince Griffin squared his shoulders. "I think I understand what needs to be done. I have lost your trust, Miriam, and I intend to strive every day for the rest of my life to earn it back. I will not put you in danger. You are not safe *here* until the traitor is discovered." His jaw twitched. "Ridion, or . . . or *Dagger*, I am holding you responsible for her safety. Get her out of here and away from Massáude's reach. I'm sure she wants to see her father—I know I would if I thought mine had been dead for nearly ten years. General Stratos and I will vet out the traitor."

He stepped closer to me and dropped his voice to an intimate quiet. "I only ask, Miriam, for one thing. Tell me that you will return? Tell me... that we will one day wed?"

I didn't know what to say. My *father* was out risking everything to keep me from all of this. *My father!* I couldn't commit to Griffin now! I ignored the reminder that I had already made a choice and accepted my fate. There were too many questions, too many sides to too many stories. After the longest two and a half weeks of my life, I had finally, *barely* prepared myself to marry this stranger, and now every inkling of that acceptance had been tossed to the curb. I certainly didn't love him. After last night, I hardly respected him. It was time to bolt.

"I know that I don't deserve it," he continued. "I know that it will take time to earn back your trust. But I—" Griffin took my hand, staring at my ringless finger. "We do not have to make an announcement. No press, no pictures, no interviews. Just between us. I want to know that one day we will be a team. That you will be my wife, and I will be your husband. Can you do that for me?"

I studied his eyes with guarded curiosity. He was giving me a choice. Did I even really have a choice? What could I do? Say no? *Run?*

Despite tradition, despite my genetic markings, despite the power of the monarchy and the resources at their disposal to make sure I *couldn't* run, an idea was emerging from the center of my newly found courage. I couldn't tell Griffin *no* right now. But, I could stall. I could give myself time to figure out how to give Griffin and the centuries-old candeon royal traditions the proverbial middle finger. A "yes" now was not an "I do" at the altar. After all, I had loads of practice evading and telling half truths to humans, so why wouldn't I be able to mislead my fiancé? And no matter what, I was leaving on that fiancé's orders to go find my father.

"I need to go. I need to do this. But. . . ." I looked to Dagger. He looked to the far wall, between Griffin and I, his face like stone, completely emotionless. "I'll come back." I purposely left out the part about coming back to be his wife.

Griffin kissed my hand and then my cheek. He lingered by my ear and added, "Thank you, Miriam." He stepped back. "You have my word that I will do everything in my power to find this traitor. You will not live your life in fear."

My guilt was minor and short-lived.

I looked from Griffin to Neo and finally to Dagger. A long road lay ahead of me. I had no idea what my future held, not in a few hours or twenty years from now. I didn't know where to begin to ferret out the truth about my past or even my present. Everything was blurred, as if someone had steamed the watercolor story of my life, ink now running down the page, but what I did know: I was the Galana and Griffin was the prince—and though I wasn't quite sure what I could do about that, I had just enough self-respect to figure it out.

"Go find your father. And please, keep me updated; let me know you are safe." Griffin left the room with one last glance at Dagger, reminding him aloud, "She is my one and only. Whatever it takes to keep her safe."

The door slam echoed in the high ceilings of the bare, concrete room. Neo and Dagger both stood silent, Neo looking utterly confused. Dagger's stone face couldn't hide the fight in his eyes and the shallow, rapid breathing in his chest. He was warring with himself.

In five weeks, my life had completely about-faced. I couldn't go back to my friends, my high school; frankly, I no longer wanted to. I had thought that coming to Pankyra was the beginning of the last, long chapter of my life. It wasn't.

With a sudden, icy catch in my breath, I remembered Dagger's words from the day before. *Someday, they will be your people. Fate wouldn't have chosen you otherwise.* And I knew. Deep in my soul, my sober heart knew I wouldn't escape that fate. Was I grasping onto this sudden adventure knowing full well it would lead me right back to this palace?

My life dangled at a precipice. It would splinter. It would blossom. It would free fall into a series of choices and paths that would mean something. I didn't know what, but I felt it nonetheless.

I was the Galana. I was a future mother. I was also a daughter, a sister, a friend, and a target.

I clenched my fists. "We should pack. Sam and Neo are coming with us."

Definitely *not* the end.

PRONUNCIATIONS

Wondering about some of the odd names in this series? Here's where they came from. Pronunciations are sometimes Greek, sometimes twisted from the original Greek into something we'll call a Candeon dialect.

Basileus: (Bah-SILL-ee-us), from an ancient Greek word for a king or emperor.

Basileus Agothos: (Bah-SILL-ee-us A-go-THOHs) from the Greek word *agathe/a,* which means "good."

Beilstein: (Bile-stine) German word for nephrite jade, which is a play on words for Haelo's father Jade.

Galana: (Gah-LAH-nah) from the Greek word *galanos,* which means "blue."

Gevgenis: (Gev-JEN-iss) Americanized from the Greek word *Evgenis,* which means "noble."

Griffin: mythical creature

Karchardeus: (Kar-KAR-dee-us) from the Greek word *Karcharias,* which means "shark."

Keakahana: (Kay-ah-ka-hahn-ah) from the Hawai'ian words *keaka* and *hahana,* which mean "shadow/essence" and "hot"

PRONUNCIATIONS

Kryos: (KREE-ohs) from the Greek word *Krýos*, for "cold."

Magari: (Mah-GAR-ee) from the Greek word *Margaritari*, which means "pearl."

Makole: (Mah-COH-lay) from the ancient Hawai'ian word *Mākole*, which means "red-eyed."

Pankyra: (Pan-KAI-rah) from the Greek words *ankyra* and *polis*, which mean "anchor" and "city."

Ridion: (RID-ee-un) from the ancient Greek word *Encheiridion*, which is a special kind of war dagger.

Sideron: (SID-er-on) from the Greek word *sidero*, which means "iron/anchor."

And lastly, **Haelo:** (Hay-loh) From the Latin name "Halo," which means having a blessed aura. Though if I'm being honest, was serendipitous. Because when I started this story, I made it up.

THANK YOU

Thank you, Dear Readers, for enjoying this part of Haelo's story with me! *Haelo Hunted,* book two in the Candeon Heirs series, is up next. There's mystery, and fighting, and magic, and a deeper dive into our villain, and *kissing*. You can find it wherever you buy books.

As always, book reviews can do wonderful things for an indie author. I happen to know for a fact that bright sunbursts of rainbows and chocolate rain from the heavens every time an author gets a nice review. Feel free to leave one wherever you found Hiding Haelo. And if you enjoyed this book, tell your friends! You can all get together and draw wild conclusions about where this story is going.

Be sure to check out tmholladay.com for updates and extras (including character photos, maps, a soundtrack playlist, and a Candeon family tree)! And as always, I *love* to hear from readers, so send me a line at tara@tmholladay.com. We'll chat.

There are some very special people who I'd like to thank for their influence on this book.

To Lauren Bullock, the best girlfriend out there. Thank you for your encouragement, ideas, and those thinker suggestions that keep my story on its toes. Mahalo nui loa.

To Lauren Dickerson, a dear friend, and my biggest fan and cheerleader. Thank you for making me believe that others would love this story as much as you and me. The next Olive Garden brainstorming round is on me.

To Mekeli, Hailey, and Brooke. A girl needs her sisters. Thank you for being such awesome ones. You're always there when I need a Haelo-sized kick in the creative pants. I horde your love, support, input, and jokes.

To Aunt Reita. Thank you for being my first beta editor. And a special thanks for being the wonderful force to be reckoned with that you are. Everybody needs an Aunt Reita.

To my parents. For being such solid examples and inspiring me to be better.

To my editor, Tamara Heiner. This book would still be gathering metaphorical dust in a file on my laptop if it wasn't for you.

To my cover artist, James T. Egan, for the stunning covers you've done! And your absolute professionalism and creativity. You are a joy to work with.

And lastly, to my incredible husband & best friend, Nick. Thank you for our forever. And thank you for handling things like a boss during those long writing Saturdays. Our children would be weekend mongrels without you.

About the Author

In a letter to Ms. Pat Broyles, my third grade teacher, my eight-year-old-self vowed that I would be a writer. That desire was shadowed by other dreams and goals, and by college was forgotten. In my last few semesters, while in an elective creative writing course, I started writing *Haelo*, a pretty terrible rough draft that still makes me blush.

I graduated with a Bachelors from BYU-Hawai'i in World Music Studies, studying composition (the surprisingly useful hippie degree), and then a MPA in Public Policy from Grand Canyon University (the practical degree).

Though writing novels is my go-to creative outlet, life stays pretty busy with motherhood, music, church service, and home renovating. I live in my home state of Arizona with my husband and three kids, and only sometimes wish we were back in Hawai'i.

My dream job, *(besides writing novels from a hammock in the forest)* would be movie score composing. I'm a total fan girl for Hans Zimmer and Martin Phipps.

I'm also a sucker for watermelon, chips & salsa, and sunglasses.

You can find me on Instagram (@tmholladay) and TikTok (@tm.holladay). Or send me a line at tara@tmholladay.com.

ONE LAST THANKS

I spent a summer after my high school graduation doing humanitarian work in Beria, Moçambique. There, I fell in love with a people I wish I could call my own. I still think about several of the mothers, families, villages, and—most especially—the children that I had the honor of interacting with. It is a beautiful land, home to beautiful people.

Thank you, Dear Readers. Thank you, so much, for helping me contribute to the cause of others less fortunate. A portion of the sales of all of my books go to the wonderful, efficient, and effective causes of: Care For Life, which works to alleviate suffering, promote self-reliance, and instill hope to the poverty-stricken villages of Moçambique, Guatemala, and the Sudan; and LDS Humanitarian Services, which prepares humanitarian supplies for use worldwide and trains those desiring to develop employable skills to become self-reliant. I also contribute to both local and worldwide efforts in the aid of refugees. Because we need to make the world a better, welcoming place.

Made in the USA
Middletown, DE
23 August 2023

37261495R00198